Praise for Ingeborg Lauterstein

"The Water Castle has an exotic assemblage of characters and a youthful narrator whose voice mimics grotesqueries and illusion so faithfully that a terrible reality emerges...It's language is, by turn, as lurid and somber as its event. it is faithful to human tenacity and betrayal."
—Boston Globe

"She transcends pedestrian historical fiction and eschews simplification about the holocaust and its prelude. This is an engrossing story of people in radical transition, and, specifically, about a girl tough enough to thrive in the confusion, like a brilliant amoral animal, with all her senses intact."
—New York Times Book Review

"With dauntless parician vigor, Lauterstein embraces both the 'reality of the fantastic' and the reality of monstrous human delusions...a splendidly mesmerizing, startlingly fresh treatment of a familiar nightmare."
—Kirkus Reviews

"In this sequel (*Vienna Girl*), the adolescent, at war's end in Vienna, is beleaguered by enigmas of the past trailing clues into the present. and she attempts—afire with her own untried passions—to find her way through mirror mazes of deceit and masquerades, as nazi era dragons, witches and princes turn ordinary...a fully fleshed, stinging probe of humanity's propensity to 'remember to forget' the crimes and the fateful, doomed seductions of the past."
—Kirkus Reviews

Also by Ingeborg Lauterstein

The Water Castle
Vienna Girl

Visit www.ingeborglauterstein.com
for more information about books and articles by Ingeborg Lauterstein,
her upcoming appearances, and reviews of her work.

ISBN 0-9770640-0-X

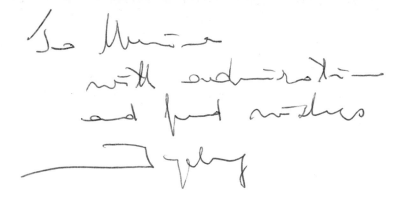

Shoreland

INGEBORG LAUTERSTEIN

To my great editor Professor William B. Hunter.
Heartfelt thanks to my son Adrian who designed the book
and to Peg who sustained me. Many thanks to Peter Anastas and Jane
Mayhall, Ray Franceur, Cliff, Ina Hahn, Cynthia Fisk, Jonathan, Jim,
Margaret, all my wonderful friends—especially Jeanne and Bobby, my
immortal teacher Charles Olson, and Caroline Gordon

All the good blood in the world, all the Germanic blood that is not on the German side, may one day be our ruin. Hence every child of the best Germanic blood whom we bring to Germany and turn into a Teutonic-minded man means one more combatant on our side and one less on the other. I really intend to take German blood from wherever it is to be found in the world, to rob and steal it wherever I can.

Heinrich Himmler 8, November 1938

Chapter One
Yugoslavia '41
LOVE CHILD

She should have known about those who come from nowhere: giants with white smiles, women who lure young children with sweets and sweet words from old fairy tales, but Mother liked only happy make believe.

They were leaning out of the window, "Goodbye red moon," the child said, as they watched the sun come up behind the barn. "Goodbye yesterday", said her mother. "I'll never be seventeen again. I'm in my nineteenth year now. Everything has changed." But geraniums blooming in their window boxes looked the same, so did swallows darting in and out of their nests. Cows kept grazing in the field below, and fighting men in the dark distant woods kept dying.

"For my birthday even the wind has dropped." Mother opened her arms wide "The world holding its breath!" But you could see her wide sleeves flapping in the wind. The child, wearing an embroidered nightgown just like Mother's, opened her arms and puffed up her cheeks to practice holding her breath, while the rising sun flamed up as never before and never again, turning their pale ringlets the color of newly spilled blood. "What's the world?"

"You ask too many questions," Mother said and turned around to question the dresser mirror, because she had to make sure several times a day that this love child, who had ruined her life, had not ruined her angelic face.

By noon Auntie's farm kitchen was full of women sitting around the long reapers table eating fried chicken with their hands, licking their fingers, drinking wine and talking about men because there weren't any. They passed the love child around the table with greasy hands and greasy kisses.

"Put me down! I'm not a baby."

"So advanced. Talked before she even walked," said the midwife who dressed like a nun in order to get around safely.

"Adorable!" said the doctor's new wife, who was considered adorable.

"Too pretty. Just like her mother. Too pretty for her own good," skinny Auntie said from the head of the table. "Untrained and forward. Children shouldn't have children."

The hunchback, who had come to play the accordion for Mother's birthday, crouched down beside the little one to let her press keys made from elephant's teeth. Her blouse, green as a wet frog, matched her eyes. If you admired the scar below her right eye, she'd say a tiger scratched her. When she stood up you could see that her long legs in black pants and glossy high boots did not go with her short body.

"Are your boots German?" the child asked.

"Who knows?" she started to play.

"From a dead German?"

"Who knows?" she kept saying, when Mother came over with chicken, wine, and questions about Him. "So you never even gave Him my letter?"

"German officers are beginning to pull out. Passing letters to them is dangerous. They no longer look at me or talk to me, when I make music for them." She strolled away playing something sad with a fixed smile the child tried out at once.

"Don't make those faces. They'll stick," Mother said and followed the musician, taking small steps in high-heeled shoes she had borrowed from cousin Bibi. The child followed behind her walking on her toes.

The woman started to play a German song about red poppies the child knew from dancing and singing with Mother to the radio. But now Mother refused to dance and kept pestering the musician about Him.

"Remember, I was the one who asked Auntie to hire you for my birthday!"

Twin girls who often came to help out milking the cows got up from the table and twirled together, holding each other by the waist, poppy-red skirts flying up from lace trimmed underpants and fat legs. So the child showed off tango steps in her new dress and twirled to show off her new lace.

"Look at the little angel!"

"Born actress," said the doctor's wife, who never wore any underwear and took singing lessons.

"What would you like to be?" the musician asked in a loud voice.

"Invisible," the child said. The musician laughed too much. "Not a bad idea these days." Then she played the song some more while women at the table swayed, singing about red poppies glowing like hearts. The doctor's wife stood up, shrilling the German words, and Frica, the white mongrel, howled along in the garden under the kitchen window.

"No German songs!" Auntie shouted.

Mother snatched up her embroidery basket from the stove bench. Her face flushed pink as her pink dress. "Don't always follow me!" she said to the child and stormed out into the rose garden.

Women clattering dishes at the sink beside the window talked about young women in the woods fighting alongside their partisan men. Not likely they'd come away from the woods for the harvest. Cousin Bibi, with her little pink lips and dark bird-eyes, wondered whether Mother's school-friend, the lawyer's son, would ever come back.

"How about the child?"

"Maybe she can tell him it's his," Bibi said.

"Come on, now!"

"He doesn't have to know. Auntie can keep her."

The child kept on practicing the tango step around the table, a chicken leg in each hand.

"Sit when you eat," auntie called to her.

"Children make Auntie nervous," said the musician and changed to a sleepy tune, while the little one nibbled the crust off the legs and threw the rest out the window to her dog, Frica. Then she skipped across the room to the side-board, where the crystal flask full of rose-water he once brought for Mother from Bulgaria sparkled in the sun. Mother said that a Fifinella invisible as fragrance inside the bottle was under a spell to make your wish come true. But you must not open the bottle until the time came.

"Don't touch!" Auntie called across the room.
Firefly lights from the flask sparkled on sideboard pictures of Auntie's dead saints, dead sons, dead husbands, and the child's outstretched hand. The music stopped. "Put that bottle back!"

"Now—at once!"

"Bad girl!" The women shouted.

"You'll drop it!"

The bottle shattered on the tile floor, with the fragrance of thousands of crushed roses, screams of anguish. A chair fell over. "Now look what you've done!"

"You devil!"

Would a Fifinella become visible outside the bottle? The child turned around and around, looking up to the ceiling.

"Where is your mother? Wait till she finds out!"

She felt dizzy, stumbled and fell. Splinters pierced her knees. She screamed and ran out the back door.

"Serves you right."

"Let her go."

"Better out of the house."

The perfume of dead roses and glitter-glass would be the child's last memory of home and their last memory of her.

War was only a word she heard when she began to say Mother. Germans and Partisans were whispers among mirror-gazing women. When she learned to walk she learned to wait, preen with them, and listen for men to come back from something terrible. Now she was running away from something terrible.

No one called, "Come back," when she went out the gate. White Frica stayed under the kitchen window with her black ears pricked up, waiting for more chicken legs to come flying out. The cows grazing in the meadow never raised their heads when she climbed over the gate, ran uphill, and vanished in tickle grass where butterflies flickering among poppies, corn flowers, and buttercups made no sound at all. Everything was in a big hurry to bloom this year.

When she reached the road, she put spit on her finger and rubbed it on her scratched knees. She picked two dusty wild strawberries. Ate one and saved the bigger one to lure the invisible Fifinella, on the flat palm of her hand, the way you feed a horse or a cow. "I want to wave to a car. Bring me one, Fifinella!"

Cars, like birthdays, Christmas, Easter, came along like magic and vanished—puff—in a cloud of dust. The one the Genie sent made less noise than the bees in the rose garden, where Mother would be sitting, embroidering a table cloth with cross-stitch roses. The frills on the new dress Mother had embroidered bounced when you jumped up and down at the side of the road, waving to the car until it came closer. Slowed down. Stopped.

Giants got out, brushing dust off their black coats, with accordion-player smiles, saying words she could not understand. Then a princess appeared from the back seat and her smile was gold. She was dressed all in lilac. "How sweet. You have a strawberry for me? You smell of rose-water. So pretty," she said in a sing-song voice. "They like golden curls."

Many gold bangles jingled when that princess opened a box full of hats decorated with flowers and feathers. "Come, sit with me, precious! Let's try one of my magic hats on for size!"

She smelled too sweet. You had to sneeze when she opened a compact to powder first her nose, then yours. The mirror caught the glitter of her big ring.

"If you drop your ring, will it break?" the child asked.

"Never!" She stuck a chocolate into the little mouth. "A diamond will even cut glass. He gave it to me." She pointed at the man sitting beside the driver. "His name is Vogel. Bird." The man turned his beak nose and said something harsh. "He looks like a chicken hawk, don't you think?" Her nose was small, but her mouth big when she laughed. You could admire golden teeth. The child laughed with her and bit into the candy. The raspberry filling inside the chocolate left a sharp taste.

"Now, the hats. Let's see the white panama—stylish, but tight." A line appeared between the thin line of her eyebrows. "All those sweet curls." Her long, light hair brushing the child's cheek smelled of violets. "You like red, of course, but this bonnet's too big, isn't it?" Such a game could have gone on for a day, a week, a year.

"Now, isn't this little brown felt with silk flowers adorable? A perfect fit." The box clicked shut. A veil, sparkling like a spider's web after rain, tickled the child's nose. She clapped her hands and they both laughed. The woman's laugh turned into a cough." In such a pretty hat, such a pretty angel child should get to ride in this big, beautiful car."

"That's Frica barking!"

The car door banged shut. She bounced against the woman as they drove away fast and faster on the bumpy road. She had to hold onto her magic hat, while she looked out the back window to watch Frica, eyes frantic, chasing the car, barking and howling as she fell behind.

"My Frica!" The child reached for the door, but those fragrant arms held her down firmly while the car splashed through a brook, leaving Frica far behind. Stones hit the fender bang, bang, bang, like a hunter's gun, while startled rabbits criss-crossed in front. The car went bump, as though it had hit one.

When she cried out for Mother, the older man turned his head barking strange words. The driver slowed down as though to stop and turn the car around. The men kept interrupting each other, shouting in anger until the woman leaned forward between them, her hair whipping the cheek of one, then the other as she turned her head to coax them both with sing-song words that calmed them down. They drove on in silence after that."Men," the woman said and dried the child's tears with a sweet-smelling handkerchief."Listen to the church bells. Maybe a jolly wedding in that village up on that hill."

Two petals fell down from a pink rose in a little crystal vase above the side window. "A funeral," the child said."For Partisans."

"Hush. Don't ever mention them!" the woman said. "Men always find a good reason or a bad reason to murder each other." She put her arm around the child. "What's your name?"

The child shook her head.

"You don't want to tell. I didn't tell him my real name. Doesn't matter. He'll call you Hilde anyway. I'm Hilde. All the girls he takes along are Hilde. You don't think it's funny? I do. That candy makes you sleepy. How about a little nap?"

But they caught up just then with three peasant women on three mules, who blocked the road riding side by side. Dressed up in white Sunday finery embroidered with bright flowers and red patterned kerchiefs, they went on knitting and chatting as they swayed in the saddles. The mules flicked their tails.

Vogel and the driver whipped off their uniform caps. Their short cropped hair was dark. Vogel had a round bald spot, which flushed when he reached over and honked the horn three times.

The child jumped up and waved: "Baker's wife! Baker's wife!"

A perfumed hand clamped over her mouth. "Please stop that!" the woman spoke softly, while she pulled the child down so hard that she shrieked and wailed. "Be quiet. Or else—*oder sonst*. That's what he always says."

"Or else," the child echoed.

"One has to play along!"

But the biggest mule, who didn't know about playing along, kicked up its hindlegs at the car. The rider dropped her knitting. She shook her fist as the car drove over it and left them behind in a cloud of dust. "We mustn't cry," the hat-lady whispered. "They won't stand for it. Here—another sweet. Give you sweet dreams of high mountains sugared with snow."

"Tastes funny," the child said.

"High, high mountains. Lots of children to play with."

"I want my mother to come along. "

"There'll be others." The woman quickly handed her the mirrored compact to admire herself in the soft brown felt hat decorated with poppies and cornflowers made of silk, and that glittery web of a veil. Perhaps the little angel would want to powder her pretty nose? She went on in a bedtime story voice. Would she like to keep the pretty hat forever?

"Smile!" The woman frowned. "You better listen—or else. What did I say just now?"

The child's eyes wanted to close. "Pretty, pretty," she answered with the accordion-player's smile. "Or else."

"So I did. Always smile. Remember! And everyone will be good to you."

Chapter Two

New England '86

WHO ARE YOU?

She wakes up from a fever dream of reaching for a hand she cannot see, calling Mutter, Mother in German, a language she had been forced to learn when she became Liese and then promised to forget when she turned into Lizbeth and Liz. Shutters are closed, the room is half dark.

Doves in the garden go on and on with their "Who, who, who are you—who who?" Morning doves or mourning doves she wonders while all she doesn't know and can't do, must not do and must do, scatters out of sequence like the pages of *Stolen Child* on the dark heirloom quilt.

The old house by the sea is too quiet. Chris often keeps both television and radio on. He even stopped winding up the old calendar clock. Only the doves keep time with their mournful nagging call and a sluggish sea sloshes over rocks below the terrace, on and on, back and forth, endlessly agitating and pestering like unwanted love.

A door bangs downstairs and Chris starts opening and closing kitchen drawers. Something clatters into the sink. Never before has she allowed herself to be sick for days and stay in her own room. He hates sleeping alone. He also hates open doors and installed self-closing devices, but today he propped hers open with a cast-iron toad.

"Liz. You awake? I have to hurry," he calls up from the kitchen stairs. "Braggert gave me an early appointment. Don't worry about my breakfast. I'll just have to grab a muffin at the Beach Cafe again."

Desertion and neglect were forcing Chris to drive to Boston and seek help. A cupboard door slams and the tinny tick of the kitchen timer starts hacking away seconds like a time bomb, while he rehearses fitting all his problems into one session to get his money's worth from one of his three psychiatrists.

So far, each doctor thinks he is the only one. Chris gives Dr. Haupter, Dr. Bigfield, and Dr. Braggert turns. He would repeat to each doctor the terror of the boat explosion, which killed his parents and his twin Sis when he was just over four years old. Narrating in the manner of an introduction to a new episode of a T.V. series, the melodrama of his near drowning and burns; travels with Gramp, plastic surgery, followed by the story of Liz, the adopted replacement Sis he had married after Grandfather died. How unfair it had been that the old man had left her the family house by the sea, which should have been his. And the farm to Dora, a mere protege. Chris, of course, had inherited almost all the money, but he would never mention that because the doctors might increase their fees.

From the canopy bed she has outgrown, Liz discerns—as never before her virus—the happy lilt in his voice while he rakes back forth over resentments past, present and still to come. Isolated words —my wife, her house, darned kid—the refrain of old anger turning into rage about lost tuition money. Mike bouncing out of Marshfield Academy. His son! Liz taking him to Shakerville, another expensive Berkshire school. Now at Grove Academy. The most expensive.

He raises his voice as he goes on with his rehearsal, talking faster and more urgently about waiting for her to come home and make dinner while she was playing in the snow and catching a deadly germ, unable to tear herself away from Mike and other juvenile delinquents, who he says keep third-rate boarding schools going. He lowers his voice when he talks about dinner with neighbor Ellen, but sounds off like a lawyer when he gets to Liz, under contract with the publisher Thomson & Perkins, wearing herself out and making herself ill writing *Stolen Child*.

"How can she write a memoir? She was only five years old when my grandfather brought her here. She wasn't supposed to talk about any of it. Now she's trying to make herself into another Orphan Annie. Writing a book about herself, when she doesn't even need the money. Trying to find her mother! She's already Mike's mother—God help us. Married and happy. A lucky woman. Very lucky. She has good times with me. Always did. Why rock the boat?" The timer shrills and rattles before Chris has quite finished complaining about paying for her expensive digital computer, another health hazard. A door bangs shut.

The new Dec Mate II dedicated word processor on her desk has been waiting like a horse in the stable while she remained in a stupor without thoughts, without fears, until a dream of drowning woke her up. Could reaching for an invisible hand be a portent? She has been waiting for the contract from Thomson & Perkins. The memo from her editor is still on her night table. She turns on the reading light.

Dear Lizbeth:

I received a note from a Mike Plant with his idea for enhancing your memoir of a stolen child by including details of Himmler's special furniture made from the bones of concentration camp victims. I thanked your young son, and told him that my authors always have the final say. The Heinrich Himmler letter you wish to use works well. We return the first chapters to you for corrections and changes.

Best, Robbie

What if they consider her unhealthy and unworthy since she allowed herself to get pneumonia? She must write: "Please, Mike, do not send suggestions to improve *Stolen Child* to my editor behind my back." Maybe her writing is not good enough. Few of their writers have switched to computers. But Mike typing this letter with one finger makes her smile. which deletes a reprimand once too often as she postpones it.

"Who, who, who who are you?" The mourning-morning doves keep hooting and never worry whether they are good enough. She gathers up the manuscript in a frenzy. Nothing is missing.

Germany '44

Something inside a pump house went smack-smack-whak,oeeeee,eee,geeeee, like a pig being hammered and slaughtered. There was a padlock on the door. Later, when she would secretly peer through a nut hole, it was pitch black. But the "or else" of having to smile, be blond, be healthy; the "or else" of having to change into a German lowered there in the dark.

The magic hat was still on her head when she woke up alone in the car. She was covered with a shawl the color and fragrance of wood violets. High, sugar-capped mountains the woman had promised towered over the world. "Hilde, where are you?" No answer. "You invisible like Fifinella? Mother, Mother!" But no one heard it; the noise went on. A cold draft blew through the car window, shedding the last dry petals from the dead rose in a crystal vase. She remembered the shattered crystal bottle, that no good Fifinella who had fulfilled her wish but brought her the wrong kind of car, and stuck a thumb into her mouth. This gives you snaggle teeth, but there was no Auntie around to stop her; no one to tell her not to be scared. She sucked furiously until that smack-whack Oeeee gave up.

In a field below Vogel and the driver were talking to a stout woman buttoned up in a dark cape, who was supervising big boys and girls shoveling manure onto a wagon. When then the pump stopped you could hear voices of children from gray houses that looked like railroad carriages alongside a paved square. In its center a flag on a tall pole furled and unfurled the German crooked-cross in the breeze. The farmhouse down below was made of dark logs, not white like Auntie's. The geraniums spilling over window boxes were red, Auntie's were pink. Only one brown horse and two sheep grazed in the field. There were no cows on this farm, but piglets frolicking around their mother in a large pen were pink like the ones at home.

But where was the rose garden? Where was the dog? When she got out of the car in her creased, frilly dress and flower-trimmed woman's hat calling for Mother, children put down their shovels and

laughed. So she straightened her hat, stuck the
thumb back into her mouth, and turned toward the
piglets.

"Just look at that litter of pigs. All perfect.
Animal breeders never take chances," Vogel was saying to Hitler School director Grete Faser. "Are
children less important than pigs?" Vogel took a
step closer to her. "We've travelled through dangerous territory with this valuable child. Remember
the beautiful Hilde, my interpreter? Gone. Deserted
when we stayed overnight. After all I did to make
something of her!"

A rooster crowed. Hens cackled. Squash in full
bloom grew outside the windowless small house and
rambled on around the pig pen. "You've done wonders.
The children are thriving." Vogel turned to the
work troop, which had lined up facing him: boys in
white shirts and shorts, girls shirts and skirts;
hair the color of cornfields, light skin that
turned the correct light gold in the sun. In
"Ordnung!"

His beady eyes darted from school and dormitory
barracks that needed new roofs, to the foot of the
garden to the camp director cottage. "You were able
to have your little nest painted yellow since my
last visit. You're doing well up here. And you,
liebe Frau Faser, are blooming!" She was fat like a
huge infant dressed up as a woman. On the washing
line behind her yellow cottage danced oversized
black underpants and brassieres trimmed lavishly
with lace. Vogel could not suppress a smile, but
covered his mouth as though he had burped. "The
peace here!"

"Heavenly peace," echoed the young adjutant.

Vogel patted a tall boy on the shoulder with his
cane.

"Can that really be Jan?" The boy had a narrow,
manly face and wore a swastika arm band.

"Look at those long arms and legs. You see, Frau
Faser, I bring you only the finest. I was a first
rate stage director, but casting is my real talent." Vogel affected a wounded hero limp, back and
forth between the matron and Jan. "Ready for uniform!"

Frau Faser flushed. "You're joking. His voice has-
n't even changed. Besides, he's in charge of my

work troop. We've got to farm or we'll starve." Jan
blew his silver whistle to order his troop back to
work, and helped push the wagon loaded with manure
past Vogel.

"But you're lucky to be able to farm," the adjutant spoke up.

Beautiful boys like that one made Frau Faser
feel ugly. She turned her back on him. "Food trucks
have almost stopped. We can't possibly grow enough
to survive up here."

The adjutant, who had been a promising young
actor, delivered a recitation about the bombing
raids, which he wasn't supposed to talk about.
German families losing everything they owned.
Starving. German children dying. Vogel raised his
hand to cut him off. "All the more reason to save a
fine specimen like this." He pointed at the child
standing beside the pigpen. "Perfect head size.
Established with that hat. Using hats my idea.
Correct pelvis, arms, legs, measured while she was
sedated."

Frau Faser observed how the adjutant crouched
down and put his arm around the thumb-sucking toddler dressed up in foreign frills and a woman's
hat. "Another valuable child saved from going to
waste in a Slav hovel," he said with a grin.

But this was no joke. The truth hit her like a
stray snowball: Himmler experts had declared Slavs
in their hovels less than human, but tens of thousands of their light-haired slavic children had
been rounded up and declared Nordic! She now looked
Vogel straight in the eye and said, "I'm not
responsible." While she made it clear that it was
the official inspector who regularly checked the
doctor's report and sorted children out. "Hair has
to stay light, legs and arms the right length—or
else."

"Oder sonst," the child repeated and ran back to
the car.

Vogel, pacing back and forth, quite forgot to
limp. "The way she picks up German—imagine." But he
was thinking of how even fat Faser had already
picked up the peculiar "or else" from his interpreter.

"We had a waiting list for adoption. We had
orders to Germanize as fast as Wehrmacht trucks

delivered foreign children," the matron went
on. "That's over. Nowadays no one wants to adopt.
There isn't enough food."

"A big boy eats more food then this little one.
I can take Jan off your hands," Vogel said.

She flushed and trampled a wild daisy. "The oldest one, our leadership boy. Never!"

"We need valuable girls to replenish," he said.

"Girls, not infants. A year ago she would not
have dared to behave that way, but German troops
suffering unimaginable losses had withdrawn from
Russia and were leaving the Balkans. Vogel's mission in occupied countries had come to an end.

"One has to plan ahead. Your doctor has the
injections to get girls ready for early mother-
hood."

"You can't be serious. This one is barely out of
diapers and belongs in Lebensborn."

Major Vogel retreated a few steps when she
brought up Lebensborn, where fanatical young German
girls used to come and mate with any assigned S.S.
officer and left infants behind for Fuhrer and
Fatherland.

"At Lebensborn Sonnen-heim they still have plenty
of provisions stored away for maternity. Still
plenty of nurses for infants and toddlers," Frau
Faser went on. "Only thirty kilometer from here—
or," she eyed Vogel, his adjutant, and the child
brazenly, "is that where you got her?"

The adjutant laughed and the little one laughed
with him. Vogel's tone of voice remained mild and
confidential: he had not fathered this one or any
other Lebensborn child.

Frau Faser watched the way the child pulled the
boy adjutant towards the sheep. "I didn't say you
were the father, Major!"

"She waved to us on a God-forsaken dirt road.
Wanted to come along. Just look at the smile, the
large blue eyes set far apart."

The matron, who had dark-brown protruding eyes,
flushed. "They might not stay blue!"

"She needs a warm sweater," the adjutant said.
"Her hands are ice cold. And if you don't want her
here…"

"Children have to be old enough for school and
farm work. New children are simply out of the ques-

tion and-"

"Food shortage. I know. I'll see what I can do."
A theatrical hand signal from Vogel sent the adjutant to fetch boxes of provisions from the trunk of
the car. The child walked beside him and was
allowed to carry a package.

"Liebe Frau Faser," Vogel limped towards her. "You
know of my position with the National Socialist
Welfare Association—"

"They gave me a citation," Frau Faser said. "My
records are impeccable."

"No paperwork," Vogel said, "No records in this
case. But you must report on her progress to me
personally. I'll give orders for regular supplies.
And here comes little Hilde with coffee! Rarer than
gold."

"Hilde, Hilde. That was your interpreter. And you
already delivered us two girls named Hilde!"

"The first one I brought you was adopted.
Richtig?"

Jan and his troop stopped shoveling and turned
around. Questions hung in the air, while hens
clucked in their coop, children recited in the
school barracks, bombers droned in the distance
accompanied by smack-smack-oeee of the pump house
starting up again.

"We lost Hilde the second. A fever." The matron
turned to the little one and whipped off the hat to
check for head lice. Her coarse hand parting the
pale ringlets began to tremble, and the tremor
passed onto the child. "Not another Hilde. You're
going to be Liese."

"Leeese." The child liked new words. The beauty
in lilac, called Hilde, had promised her a lot of
other children and another mother. Another mother
had sounded like another candy, better than the
first one. She picked up the magic hat, smiled so
that everyone would be good to her, and took Frau
Faser's hand.

Slow footsteps of Chris carrying something up the creaky stairs remind Liz
that it made no difference whether her book was published as a memoir, a
fable, or a novel, she has broken the vow of silence that had been imposed
on her as long as she can remember. All for her own good. Shoreland is a

town where nothing much happens and everyone knows about it. When Liz beccame ill, Chris had called first the doctor and then neighbor Bonnie, who would pass the word. There are get-well cards, a basket of flowers. The room is fragrant from spicy cookies Bonnie had brought, with herbs from her garden and soups, preserved cherries and wisdom that you can't expect much attention from a doctor when you're never sick. "It's not survival of the fittest, but the survival of the weakest that makes a doctor big." The Hitler School doctor saw to it that the weak did not last.

The fragrance in her room blends with the unforgettable disaster in Auntie's kitchen: spilled perfume from thousands of crushed roses, the sting of splintered glitter-glass. Imagined memory is an opiate holding her spellbound as a Fifinella under the dictate of this new day. She quickly puts her manuscript into the envelope and sticks it under her pillows.

Chris enters and puts a glass of orange juice on her night table among get-well cards, unloads a pile of mail at the foot of her bed in one fast motion, and finishes buttoning the vest of the gray English suit he wears for doctors and concerts.

They could still pass for brother and sister. Nino, the barber, gives Liz and Chris identical Amish haircuts—not too short—just right. Perfect match. Nino laughs at his own jokes. Their thick, wheat-colored wavy hair, good even teeth, long limbs would have passed inspection of Nazi race experts. Growing up in this small-town family house, they were a team. Even now much of the old complicity remains, when it comes to keeping the well-being of Christopher Plant a secret from both sympathetic Shoreland women and Boston doctors.

"I didn't think you should be bothered with that just now," he says when she reaches for the letter from her publishers, which has already been opened. Her signed contract. "I called and told them that you made your-self quite ill with all that writing."

"It's not true. You had no right to say anything! What if they'd decided not to give me the contract? " She fumbles for the note from her editor. "You are doing well. Keep going!" which would have worked better than antibiotics.

"You can always talk to a psychiatrist instead of all this writing."

"Too expensive!"

"Because I have three of them." This makes him laugh, and she laughs with him as she always did when they were children. He sits down on the bed, ready for the hugs and kisses he always needs from his wife after he has behaved like a mean brother.

"You might catch my bug."

"The writing bug?" He laughs at his own quick answer, but she doesn't. "Don't worry about lunch. I'll just have to eat out." He forgives her with this little reproach. Then opens the shutters to let the sun in. "Bye, beautiful."

The sun blinds her. Not ten days, but years of her life seem to have passed her by. There are still patches of snow Chris avoids on his way to the garage. Dressed up in this suit, he looks tall walking in bouncy step as usual when he is about to take all his problems to a doctor. The wind plays with hair he brushes forward over a slightly receding hairline.

Liz always knows how he feels. Gramp had acquired her to comfort his orphaned grandson and left to her the old family house by the sea as a final reward for her German obedience training. Hitler School children had been trained to forget who they had been and speak German. Gramp had asked her to forget German when she learned to speak English and turned into Liz. Chris came as an irresistible obligation. Hitler School children were trained to adapt and be adopted. She wants to run out there and throw her arms around him. At the same time she is glad he is taking his resentments of her flu and her writing out of the house.

In Nazification School sickly children were sorted out by the doctor as a genetic danger to the Master Race and taken away by the inspector. Did she make this clear? Foreign children had to adapt and Germanize fast—or else. For each word that was not German, Frau Faser would hand out a smack in the face with her big left hand. "Will you smack me if I say a German word?" Liz would ask American Gramp in halting English again and again, just to see him throw back his shaggy head, laugh loud, pick her up, and kiss her cheek with a smack. "No, but I'll give you a presents if you speak English. How about a new hat?"

Liz does not remember getting that old brown felt hat out of the closet and placing it on a tall bottle of rose water on the dressing table. One ragged silk poppy and a faded cornflower remain. The veil was lost in the German woods the year the war ended.

That hat, rose water, and the desk with the Dec Mate II computer and the printer, on the right side of her bed, are her choice in this house, almost everything else, had always been here, or else it had been chosen for her. Well chosen, all of it. This room, had been furnished by English granny, during her one visit. There had been a discussion behind closed doors with Gramp about separating the seven year old boy and girl, when he had declared, they were meant for each other.

Through the open door drifts the faint smell of garbage that has not been taken out. Piles of dirty dishes waiting in the kitchen. Bait, all of it to get her to put her manuscript aside. The grand old house on the bluff has always been a lure for women to work their lives away. Up and down the stairs, back and forth between sink and stove in the big kitchen. Keeping everything up, dusting the banisters, washing windows, shining brass, starching little white frilly curtains, repetitious and predictable as the mourning-morning doves, generation after generation, always the same. But nothing can ever be quite the same since she allowed herself to become deadly ill and stay in her own room. Yet, giving up and giving in was a luxury, as getting old one day could be, even dying here in the girlish canopy bed, in her own room in this old New England hometown.

She picks up bills Chris left on the bed and takes it all to her desk. A pharmacy bill. From the Shakerville School a bill for books that were left behind when Mike bounced. A bill for Mike's new clothes that have already been stolen at Grove Academy. Telephone bills torn open by Chris to expose all the long distance calls Mike made to friends while he was in between schools. If she tries to question Mike, he simply talks her down with a final, "I hate boarding school. I'll just take off for Cal." A bill from Dr.Haupter, Chris's Freudian psychiatrist; a newsletter from the Riverbay Church with a picture of the well-fed minister, an exorcist, able to get the devil out of kids. But doesn't that mean that he himself fears the devil within, in the same way as a hard Faser smack betrayed fear in her own heart. Finally, one of those picture cards with the smiling face of a missing child:

HAVE YOU SEEN ME? 1-800-843-5678. National Center for Missing and Exploited Children. Name Laurie Clark. 3 years old. Height two feet, ten inches, eyes blue, hair blond.

On the other side of the Laurie Clark picture card is a photograph of ugly jewelry:

DYNAMITE PENDANT ONLY $9. ORIGINAL VERSION SOLD FOR OVER $300. Austrian crystals atop the dynamite sticks look more like real diamonds. A beautiful ruby crystal is the lit wick. For the dynamite young lady you are!

How many Dynamite Pendants would be sold? Thousands? A million? While the smiling picture of blond Laurie —a stolen, or abused child— would advertise to millions the multitude of seductive little ones that are up for grabs. Liz takes the card to the cedar closet and sticks it into her hidden file box. When she pushes the box back into its dark recess, her old leopard skin jacket falls off the hanger.

A trophy from New York in the sixties. No one wears anything that stylish here on the North Shore. She drapes the soft black and yellow fur over her flannel nightgown. The stale fragrance of a precious perfume—a whiff of Chris and Liz as twins during their Manhattan masquerade at loft parties, happenings, art openings; the Russian artist Catulle, whose cartoon-like image of her as a seductive girl-child had made brother and sister fashionable guests at day and night penthouse celebrations. A masked ball at the Plaza, the ultimate in bravado and timidity of the fashionable, who lived in terror of not being seen in the right place in the right costume. Before the peace, integration and animal rights movement, the right fur had been an essential uniform. A girl dressed and talked like her mother, especially if you didn't have one. Now mothers dress like teens to be accepted by them.

Her neighbor Ellen, her friend the school psychologist and happily divorced mother of two wild grade school boys, gave her LOVE AND LEARN, by the best-selling Beatrice Strout, the 'femininist.' The ultimate get-well present. The blurb on the dust jacket says, "CELEBRATE YOUR LIFE TODAY. STAND EVERYONE UP. HAVE A DATE WITH YOURSELF. STEP OUT AND STAND OUT. LET THE WORLD KNOW YOU EXIST!"

Why not leave the doubts and obsession of a writer behind with the flu, dirty floors, unmade beds, dusty everything? Make a getaway to Boston. Lunch in the sun at Marion's, her favorite outdoor café—something she hasn't done once this year?

She dresses up in black trousers and the leopard skin fur coat with matching earmuffs, and hurries away as though someone were waiting for her. For once she drives her station wagon within the speed limit. A red Corvette cuts in on her. She slows down, polite as usual, even to the impolite on the highway. Then the Corvette slows down suddenly too, forcing her to change to the fast lane. It follows her, tailgating. She sees aviator glasses, bare shoulders. It is chilly, but driving around half naked like this makes a man a man on the North Shore, where a boy's right to strip to the waist might well outlast the right to bear arms.

He ends up driving side by side with her, grinning at the blond in the leopard skin get-up. Liz floors the gas pedal. He is ready for a race, but two trucks burst across the intersection and the red car recedes into a lollipop. She feels as though she were not driving but driven south like the clouds in the high wind.

Chapter 3
ENDANGERED SPECIES

In the parking garage a man opens his car door: "Hey, leopard, over here!" Falsetto voice, white face, red ball for a nose, fuzzy purple wig, painted smile. The fellow is costumed as a clown and acting like one. She doesn't give it a thought until she gets to Mario's and recognizes that clown with the painted smile in the picture on an artist's easel. A bit of a clown himself, the artist costumed in a blue smock and straw hat, is dashing off his quick, slick impression of Newbury Street, while she stands behind the privet hedge at Mario's outdoor café waiting for a table. His brush flicks all over the canvas, but keeps returning to a small girl in party dress, running to that clown in the purple wig and reaching up for his animal-shaped balloons. Slapdash all of it, yet precise as Liz's memory of running away.

She watches the artist brazenly dot winter grass with daffodils and tulips, which wouldn't come into bloom for another two months. How about those pink apple blossoms on young maples? Crowd pleasing, a sunny picture, symbolic of President Reagan's never-never land Spring 1986, which is still to come. The clown in the purple wig had already moved on from selling animal-shaped balloons to accosting a woman in the parking garage. The artist combined the future with the past. Am I not doing the same thing in my writing? Liz can feel herself sink into doubt, fatigue, and the guilt of having allowed herself to be weak and ill.

Young children out for a walk with mothers, grandmothers, or baby sitters, or unemployed fathers, are still holding onto the string of an alligator or tiger "Save the predators" balloon. Someone is always trying to save something these days and sell something for a charity of their own invention. A small boy with a tiger balloon stops and points at Liz, who is standing behind the privet hedge. "Did you shoot det tiga?"

A boyish young woman jerks him away. He lets go of the string, and howls while the balloon rises. "Your own fault. Shut up! " When he is silenced by a slap, Liz ducks and takes cover behind a Gypsy-type woman selling daffodils, roses, and pussy willows. Reggae music drifts out of an open gallery window, while the balloon drifts up and up over the rooftops.

A group of men come crowding in behind Liz. "Was kein Tischerl! No little table!"

Austrians always use diminutives. They look like students, laughing, competing to impress their leader. The moment the waitress waves to Liz, they're ready to pounce on her table. Their leader, a much older and more distinguished-looking man, makes them stand aside and bows.

"*Gefaehrdete Gattung,* endangered species," she hears him say behind her back." And I don't mean the leopard pelt."

"Right. Such a woman is an endangered species these days," a young know-it-all speaks up, in nasal German.

"Anything delightful is endangered all the time, Karl. You are too young to believe that."

One word of German now, and they would apologize, invite her to join them, ask questions she would hate to answer. She shivers in the sun; orders seafood chowder in an unnatural, high-pitched girlish voice. Then she has to cough and her eyes begin to stream.

"You have a cold," says the young waitress. "How about some nice hot tea?"

"I don't get colds!" Liz sees the menu tremble in her own hand.

"I understand," the girl beams. "My aunt is a Christian Scientist."

Liz has to laugh.

"Hot tea all right then—lemon or cream?"

Lemon is too European. "Milk."

Two tables empty. The Austrians pounce and push them together, scraping the tile floor. Their leader sits down at the head, facing Liz.

"Waitress," he calls. Dark hair, white at the temple with one thick white strand, sets off his winter tan. He is wearing a turtleneck sweater under a safari jacket. His face is pleasantly lined when he smiles, teasing the young waitress, flirting with her a little. The young men are architecture students from Vienna, he tells her. He is having fun showing them the renovation of old buildings. Then he asks them, "How about hamburgers and beer for everyone, to give this lovely girl a break?"

He does not give Liz a break. *"Wie alt?* How old can the leopard be?" he asks.

"About thirty-two," says the youngest looking Austrian. "The best age for love."

The older man studies her as though planning a renovation. "That would be nice. She is over forty, I would say."

He is right, but Liz passes for under thirty when she feels less tired. Older men often look for signs of aging in younger women, she tells herself. Trying to appear indifferent under the assault of his knowing eyes. While one of the young men admires in German her long neck, another one her short cat face and light hair. Listening in is shameful in every way.

"There was a girl, with that hair and smiling lips, in Zagreb, Yugoslavia." He lights a cigarette and inhales deeply, "I was a boy in uniform. An aspiring actor. So they trained me as an observer. I loved observing women."

"That hasn't changed!" interrupts the upstart.

"We were sitting around just like this. And we spoke in the Berlin or Hamburg dialects. So no one would understand."

"Discussing women," says the upstart.

"The hair on the legs, the ankles—oh, my God! Then this schoolgirl comes along. We all shut up and gape. You couldn't take your eyes off that lovely face. A Slav, and the ideal German blond."

"What happened?" asks a stout fellow who was not likely to have romantic adventures.

"She knew we were watching her and deliberately stopped at a store window to fiddle with her school bag. Girls that young are impossible. I wish to God she had stayed home that day." He gives them time to laugh. "No joke," he says in English. "I took a rose out of the vase on our table. She became shy. Nervous about being seen with a German officer. Clutched the stem so hard she pricked herself. A drop of blood formed.

She looked at me, smiled. I was lost."

It sounds rehearsed, and also familiar, as though she had heard this story before. But where? From the moment he saw Liz, he seemed to talk and move with the deliberation of an actor following a script while the young men look embarrassed like parents of a child that prattles, bored with the sentimental twaddle about thorns, roses, of the good-old, bad-old Hitler days, the war that everyone was supposed to forget.

Liz once asked her editor, a former OSS investigating officer—somewhat like Vogel—whether he or some of his Army friends had fallen in love in Europe. He said, "we couldn't help it." American Army men often became obsessed with European girls they had deserted. Especially when there was a child. He always tried to tell those fighting men—and himself—that making love as though it were the last time was unique—the girl was not. This was not always true.

"Sex?" asked a student.

"She was an amazingly sensuous, child. We laughed a lot and hid away together in a requisitioned villa. Then she vanished I searched for her everywhere. Searched for her after the war, but couldn't find her. Looked for her in other women. I even collected paintings of a little blond girl that look like her," the older man persists. "They are worth a lot of money now. The artist, Catulle, became quite famous. "

Liz gets the whiff of exhaust from a stalled Volkswagen Beetle, while she is accosted by the insulting memory of the Catulle, the Russian artist getting drunk on champagne the last time she sat for him, and telling her a similar story about his own long lost love, a little girl, who looked so much like Liz.

"There is something Walt Disney about the way he went on to paint so many versions of the same face. A seductive child. Quite photographic. A fine technique of glazing in oil—rather like of Salvador Dali. "

Liz drops her gloves and dips under the table hiding, as quite often in New York when she was spotted as the model for one of those wide eyed Catulle paintings of child-women that became fashionable with Audrey Hepburn and the shocking novel Lolita. A blond Easter-bunny sweet student declares obsessions with little blondes definitely retro. "Mulatto girls are far more beautiful. Just look at them. Sensuous walk. Flashing eyes. Such white teeth! Genetic diversity is invigorating. Agricultural breeders know all about that." As though compelled to reenact that scene at the café in a foreign town they all start to discuss black, blond, redheads on the sidewalk arguing in loud German for and against planned breeding. These men mean no harm, Liz tells herself. No one who evaluated her and singled her out, like an animal for its pelt had meant any harm. Major Vogel pointing at thoroughbred piglets to justify his idea of finding valuable children for the procreation of the Master Race, is as true to life as darling Gramp or this group of strangers, because male theories are essential for appropriations in business, war or lust. Facts get in the way.

When the waitress brings hamburgers and beer, the leader of the group, carefully cuts the hamburger into small sections, bringing each bite to his mouth without bending forward as though someone were observing this trained observer. The young men forget about women and gobble their food. Typical students, too young to ever learn the shameful secret of Hitler schools, where young children had to endure the scrutiny of deranged men. No reward for perfection, but dread of punishment, even death, if you did not measure up.

Only the collector of Catulle paintings, the man with those prying eyes, was old enough to have known of this truly endangered species. How much did Catulle tell the collector about his model? When Liz began to pose for him, Catulle drank champagne, painted and told her that a young aunt had been able to smuggle him out of Russia as her own baby, after his aristocratic parents had been killed by the Bolsheviks. So Liz had accepted a glass of champagne and told her own secret story of a stolen child for the first time.

Catulle, who had painted Liz with the body of a seductive little child, drank in the story of German injections that turned little girls into women. On the sidewalk, a boy, like Liz's son Mike with long, light-brown, wavy hair is holding forth to three girls. If someone invented shots that would keep them all young forever, they would certainly go for it. Whether following the old American dreams of youth, personal success and wealth, or the old Hitler dream of Nazification and procreation and appropriation for the power and the glory of the Thousand Year Reich, kids who have to be perfect will always feel imperfect.

The waitress brings chowder and tea for Liz. "Nice and hot. I'm leaving you extra milk." And on the milk carton a missing child, Laurie Clark, is smiling. Have you seen me?

Her own smiling photograph had been posted in Europe after the war.

Long pale hair, eyes set far apart like Laurie Clark and millions of stolen, missing children of the past, present, and still to come. She eats like a starving child and burns her mouth.

"What would your father and mother say if you married a Negro girl?" asks the upstart.

The Easter bunny shows his protruding front teeth. "At least they couldn't say a black girl is a fake. I brought a beautiful blond girl home and they said she was a fake; her hair was bleached. I was supposed to look for real blondes! And how would I know?"

"The complexion. They flush easily. The leopard is real," the upstart says with authority. "Could be an actress. They don't wear make-up during the day."

"Not so loud," warns the leader. "She might understand German."

To look busy, Liz takes her diary and a pen out of her purse. She doodles a hook-cross, then blackens it into the big cross of the German Red Cross Search Service posters.

WER KANN SAGEN, WHO CAN TELL MY NAME—WHERE I COME FROM—WHERE I WAS BORN? FOR EVEN THE SMALLEST INFORMATION AM I GRATEFUL.

Forgotten words. Young children forget. Nazi race experts had given orders to select the youngest. Thousands of fair-haired children in occupied countries had been stolen, like silks, diamonds, fur coats, perfume, art treasures, and food, to make up for shortages in the Reich.

Liz flips the pages she filled in her diary, takes up her pen and writes: I was told I was lucky to be made into a German, lucky to become a Catholic in Vienna. Lucky to turn into a proper nice little English girl in Norfolk with Granny. And then very, very lucky to become an American, Chris's sister and his wife. Mother of Mike. WHO AM I, WHO?

"Actress, no. *Niemals!* A writer. "

The leader of the group makes it sound like a verdict. Woman and writer. A truly endangered species. She would get up at dawn to write and rewrite, scrutinizing each word and sentence. Now, trapped at her table and scrutinized in German, the past is catching up with her—or is it the future, like the blossoms in the painting? She writes fast on pages she left blank while she was sick, onto spring pages of her 1986 diary and summer days that are still to come; overwriting the future with the explorations of a half remembered, half evoked story of her past.

FASER'S PET

Frau Faser led Liese to the yellow cottage, put her
own huge gray sweater over the thin dress, and made
up the cot for her at the foot of the big feather
bed. Frau Faser, like the child's mother, talked a
lot and had a bad temper, and told stories about
Adolf Hilter in a sing-song tone like Mother's
make-believe. Liese got the meaning before she
learned the new words, especially when she had to
pray, "Fold my hands, bow my head, thank Fuhrer for
my daily bread." Frau Faser made the child pray not
only to Adolf Hitler, but also for him, and for the
secret, all-powerful miracle weapon he promised
would destroy the enemy and bring victory.

From Frau Faser you learned German words that
growled when she worried out loud about things
going wrong; the enemy landings and going hungry."
I hope this useless child won't forget how good
I've been to her, sharing my own food."

The other children in the school barracks ate in
a narrow room which divided the boys' dormitory
from the girls' and had a kitchen at one end. In
German class some of the big children secretly
pinched or punched Liese, the new Faser pet, saying
bad words in Polish or Czech until a teacher, named
'Goose' because of her long neck, pounced on them,
calling them dirty Slavs and smacked them hard.
Everyone had to speak German here.

Children would whisper: "Wait till the Hitler
doctor finds out Faser's got you in her house!"

When they were first unloaded at Waldruh, they
often thought they had been taken to Adolf Hitler
himself, because the doctor did his best to both
look and shout like the Fuhrer. They all remained
terrified of his branding iron, needles and knives,
but most of all of the reports he wrote sorting
them out for the Herr Inspector, who'd arrive unannounced to declare them racially worthless when
their bodies changed.

"The inspector took the last Hilde away with
him,when Faser got tired of her," they'd say to
scare Liese, because they were scared.

"I'm not Hilde, I'm Liese," she told them.

She had known how to keep a secret and be a
secret as long as she could remember. Either hidden

away as a little disgrace, or dressed up to be
shown off among country women. In secret Mother had
taught her German words and German songs and dance
steps,to prepare her for a time when "He" would
come and take them to Berlin with him.

So Liese learned German fast in Hitler School.
No one spoke her language. Frau Faser ordered Liese
to forget even her old name, but her mind—like the
Faser cottage—remained cluttered with mementoes.
Like doctor Faser's old dentist's chair she often
bumped into when performing cartwheels. How could
she forget Mother when she had to dance for the
matron to music from the radio, sing Lily Marlene
and keep telling Mother's "happy forever after"
stories to Frau Faser?

At the end of the day the matron took hairpins
out, let her braids hang down on each side of her
big face, and settled down into her, padded sofa
with a glass of wine to feast on thick slices of
dark bread and drippings sprinkled with pork crackling and salt, while her hungry eyes feasted on her
collection of sunny paintings of castles by lakes,
Venetian palaces and their reflections, and orange
groves. "Land where the orange trees bloom!"

The child had never seen an orange. "But where
are the people?" she asked.

Frau Faser did not say anything.

"How about animals?"

Since she had received a slap for asking questions, she concluded that the animals had all been
eaten, and people who ate them had all been sorted
out, listed as unworthy and imperfect by the doctor, and taken away by the inspector.

So Liese put Mother's "happy forever after" into
the empty palaces, orange groves, and the castle-
by-the-lake scenes, where a little devil no one
wants turns into a valuable girl everyone wants.
After several glasses of wine, Frau Faser would
sometimes interrupt a story to correct Lise's
German, gazing at the paintings with less longing,
and with more regret about the tub of lard, thirty
eggs, and two kilo of cheese that she had paid for
them to a man who had the key to a secret mountain
cave full of hidden museum and Arianized art treasures. Her own treasure of food and wine locked into
the pantry was no secret. You could smell the

smoked meats and sauerkraut.

When Frau Faser was pleased with the stories
Liese told her, she would treat her to both bread
and drippings, and that special "unhappy forever
after" story of her baby sister, Liese Faser.

A photograph of pug-nosed Liese Faser stood on
the dresser: her potato face, frilly dress, and a
big bow on top of her head tinted pink and the
tight corkscrew curls egg yolk yellow. She had
dark, impudent eyes. Everyone had loved little
blond Liese, especially their father, the dentist.
He'd hurt people all day long pulling or filling
teeth, and in the evening he'd be tired. Little
Liese Faser, the mischief, would hide his slippers
or his pipe, or put a rock into the cushion of his
favorite chair. But he always blamed Grete and beat
the big sister until it really hurt. It was the
only time he ever paid attention to her. After he
had beaten Grete he would hold her on his lap and
hug her hard. She had hated that more than the
beating.

Now Grete Faser, Hitler School Director, beat
children as she had been beaten to make her good,
and hugged Liese as she had been hugged after she
was beaten. "I tried to hold Liese back, I didn't
push her. She was pulling my hand so hard, I had to
let go so she stumbled back. Fell to her death."

"Why?" The child asked.

Frau Faser gave her a good smack for asking such
dumb questions. When in doubt, her answer was
always lashing out with a good kick or a smack,
which stifled her own secret questions and worries.

Before Herr Doctor Finkel arrived, Frau Faser would
push Liese's cot into the pantry and give her a
slice of dark bread and an apple for supper with
the warning not to touch any of the stored food.
The key turned in the lock twice, but the board
wall left gaps for bars of light, warmth and fragrance of the roasting hen. Liese was dunking some
of her bread in the tub of hot chicken fat that
stood on a shelf to cool, when she heard the thud
of his boots, and the hysteria of his 'Heil
Hitler!'

The door banged. "So you have another Hilde."

"Liese," Frau Faser said in her false baby

voice. "I have to report to Vogel personally. He wants her safe."

"Safe, with you!" He guffawed "You better put her into the barracks."

"She's too young."

"She's got to be branded. Even if she's still in diapers."

Frau Faser opened the oven and you could hear the hiss-sizzle of basting. The branding iron hissed, the children said.

"Let's have a look!"

"She's asleep."

"Why the secrecy? Is she deformed, or a Jew?"

"You know about Vogel. She's perfect. I think his adjutant is the father."

"What? Waldruh might be a youth ware-house, but it's not a nursery for officer's bastards. She has to be evaluated!"

"They have already examined her," Frau Faser went on and flaunted her connection with the powerful officers who could sort out even doctors–even Generals–as worthy or unworthy.

"I have my orders," the doctor said.

"It never suits you when I have a child."

"A child? How about Hilde one and Hilde two? Questions could be asked." He suddenly lowered his voice. "After the war."

"You better not talk about that." Frau Faser said in her matron-voice.

"We're alone here."

But Liese was listening and the pantry mouse had come out of her hole and sat with her ears pricked up.

"I'll say she is my own child! You could be the father!"

"What!" He snarled. "How about your other men."

"There aren't any up here."

"And Wassbacher?"

Frau Faser's harsh laughter sent the mouse scampering into her hole at once. A piece of furniture was pushed. Glasses clinked. Something fell with the ping and rolled on the floor.

"Not now," Frau Faser said in a baby voice. "Dumplings will spoil."

Later, during the kitchen feast, the pantry mouse ate Lise's crumbs, and sat up to groom herself all

over. Her tawny fur was touched with russet, chest
and paws were white as snow. She finished off by
trailing her tail through her mouth three times.
Last time Liese was locked up, she had found the
nest of her babies-pink as tiny piglets-behind the
onion box. Now the fragrance of baking lured the
mother-mouse into the kitchen and haunted the child
with dreams of birthday feasts.

Liese woke up with a start. A monster on a rampage was thrashing about in the kitchen. "*Zum
Teufel*-to the devil, filthy vermin! I'll show you."

The child trembled for Frau Faser. Something hit
the wall and shattered. A jar fell from the pantry
shelf onto Lise's cot, hitting her leg. She pressed
her lips together and was holding onto her hat with
both hands for magic protection from stomping and
smashing, when the smashed mother mouse dragged
herself back under the door, leaving a dark trail,
fell over in a bar of light, twitched, gasped,
stopped moving.

Frau Faser had turned her radio on to calm the
doctor. A woman singing the tango-song about poppies in bloom was interrupted by the announcer. The
Allies had invaded the coast of France.

"Filthy vermin," the doctor called
out again.

Liz feels cold. When she looks up from writing, the men have gone. The
waitress is collecting dishes, her long braid swinging from side to side. Liz
can't believe that that man has simply walked away. He must be waiting for
her somewhere. Then, as the waitress warms her tea, the flower vendor
comes over. "He wanted to buy you lots of roses, but I only had three left."

"That's cool!" the waitress says. "Guys always give you roses at the
Grateful Dead concerts. But they never last."

"It's the thought that counts," says the vendor.

The waitress giggles. "A twenty dollar tip! They were really different!"

The artist has folded his easel and a police car is standing by. A short,
stout officer with a big ruddy face loads the painting into the trunk. Then
he comes over to ask Liz whether she has seen a clown or was molested in
her fur coat by anyone. This clown had been selling balloons. "Seems to
hate fur coats. You saw a man in the parking garage? Face made up white?
Did he try to get you into his car? Lady, you got out of there just in time.

Ten minutes later, who knows?" The clown had cornered an off-duty nurse and slashed her fur. A fake fur, as it turned out. Dumb clown didn't know the difference.

They were taking the artist to headquarters with the painting. So that he'd be able to draw the face under the clown make-up with the help of the nurse and computers. The policeman escorts Liz to her car in the parking garage. On the third level she spots a red, round clown nose. The officer gives her a phone number, just in case she remembers something. "You take care now! Call anytime. Always lock the car."

Chapter 4

SCRUTINY

The fur coat goes back into the cedar closet. Better not get dressed up again like that in town, Chris says. Too many creeps around.

"Do you think someone could still recognize me as the Catulle model?" Lis asks after dinner. She is lying back in the chaise in his music room. He keeps tilting his head toward the right speaker, since it is impossible to judge the sound of his new recording of the Berliotz Symphonia Fantastique against rasping and gushing sounds of waves at low tide. She has to repeat the question. "After all those years? No way. Crafty Catulle. You made him disgustingly rich. You look tired. Take a rest. Help you to get over it all."

But how could she get over the picture of a small girl running away from Mother towards a clown, when she is trying to depict a bright world where sinister clowns lure children? Upstairs on her bed, she turns on the reading lamp, and reaches for her notebook, because writing transcends the humiliation of helplessness Liese had endured and Liz relived at the cafe.

Liese reported to Jan, the troop leader, that the vermin had landed in France and how the vermin mother mouse had come to a bad end last night. Her vermin babies had come to a bad end too.

Some of the children had been told their mothers

were bad women who came to a bad end. Jan said Frau
Faser and the teachers lied. Liese told him that
her mother had not come to a bad end. She was too
pretty for her own good, sitting in the rose garden
on the Auntie farm, embroidering a tablecloth with
roses. He wanted to know where the farm was. She
told him that it was at the bottom of the field,
below the road, where the black car had picked her
up. Jan had been forced into the car by Vogel in
Norway. His hair was almost white, eyebrows and
lashes gold, eyes ice blue. He was clever and
worked hard for the women. Frau Faser relied on him
as the head of his leadership troop. And he relied
on Liese. Who else could let him know what the
women were saying?

In the meantime Frau Faser was pleased with herself, declaring she was losing weight, since she
shared food with the child and Doctor Finkle. She
washed her own and the child's hair in rainwater,
which she collected in a wooden barrel. Rinsing her
own long brown hair with ammonia, she let it bleach
in the sun. The local dressmaker used the last of
her fabric and thread to make matching pink dresses
with little pink bows for Frau Faser and Liese.
Matron was turning the clock back, the little woman
said. Frau Faser's fleshy face widened into a complacent smile.

One dark morning Frau Faser took some of her
precious coffee to Dr.Finkel's windowless office.
Liese was allowed to carry a dish with biscuits.
They wore the new pink dresses and ribbons in their
hair. It was warm, logs were supposed to be con-
served, but smoke rose from Dr. Finke's chimney on
this sunny day. Inside they met blazing heat; Frau
Faser stood dumbfounded. The doctor was stuffing
children's files into the stove and ordered her to
keep her mouth shut. All that remained of his
Hitler mustache was a white triangle below his
nose. "We don't want anything to fall into the
wrong hands," he said.

Frau Faser sidled up to him. Pink as her pink
ribbon from the heat, she assured him that the
English and Americans would soon be chased back
into the water and the Fuhrer was sending all those
flying bombs to England. Dr. Finkel glared at the
child, his green eyes bulging and bloodshot."I must

remind you that my latest orders are to keep only the pure Aryan-type children and the most reliable staff up here."

Liese had learned that non-Aryans were useless vermin like mice, while other non-Germans could be useful like farm animals. Her dish tilted and a biscuit dropped. Frau Faser snatched the dish away, while the child picked up the biscuit from the floor and offered it to the doctor on her flat palm the way you feed a horse that might bite.

He ignored this and asked the matron to hand him the color chart, which he held up against the child's cheek. "Hold still! Not that pure *Himmelblau*, heaven-blue. Don't move!" But when he came at her with a pair of scissors to get rid of that wrong color, she closed them tight and ducked. Her hand crushed the biscuit. She forgot to smile.

"Not your eyes, Dummkopf!" Frau Faser took her by the shoulder. "Only a hair sample." The curl he cut off was category one. No sign of dark roots. But he was still holding the scissors when Frau Faser picked Liese up and put her on the surgery table. "Don't cut me. Don't cut me! Don't stick me with the needle." Frau Faser slapped her. The doctor put the scissors on the table and took a tape measure out of the drawer, which he wrapped around Lise's head as though he had to measure before he cut. "Good!"he said."*Sehr gut.*"

Frau Faser did not release her grip. Tears ran down Lise's cheeks when the doctor lifted her skirt and exposed the big lace trimmed underpants that had belonged to the last Hilde. Children's records were still burning. The room was hot. "I'm cold." She shivered."So cold!"

Early the next morning, a squadron of bombers droned over the mountains. Minutes later they unloaded left-over bombs on the Sleeping Princess mountain chain and blew up the face. The doctor came in through the back door, surprising Frau Faser in a huge lace trimmed nightgown that had yellow egg stains on the front.

"I didn't ever believe it would come to this. It's only a matter of time. I had my orders just like you. But we medical men could end up getting the blame. I have to think of my wife and two daughters."

Frau Faser jumped up, bursting into tears, but
cheered up at once when he reached into his pocket
for a gold bracelet with a glittering star and took
her into his arms. Frau Faser kissed him on the
mouth. "How did you get that, you evil man? It's
not from some dead Jew, is it?"

"*Wer weiss*, who knows. This star might be a good
protection for you one day. When they talked in
undertones about the American Jew army invading
Italy, Liese quite forgot to be invisible and asked
whether the Jew Americans would eat up all the
oranges. Frau Faser grabbed a big broom from the
corner ready to sweep her out of the cottage, but
changed her mind. "Here, here. Take it. Make yourself useful. Sweep the steps!"

Puddles gleamed in the sun, reflecting the red
of Jan's crooked cross banner, as he and his leadership troop drilled the school on the parade
ground. Liese shouldered the broom, marching back
and forth at the top of the steps, but left the
door open behind her.

The doctor's motorcycle was already sputtering
down into the valley when Frau Faser, who had
blocked ears from a cold, turned her radio on so
loud that the enemy news broadcast about the German
army retreating blared across the parade ground,
there was a crackling sound and *"Achtung, Achtung!"*
followed by the report of a bomb attack on Adolf
Hitler at Wolfsschanze Headquarters in East
Prussia.

Frau Faser came rushing out. "A lie. Enemy
lies!" She pounced on Liese, pushed her into the
house."What do you mean? Leaving the door wide
open!" Slapped her face, beating her all over as
never before." You're just as useless as my sister.
If I weren't so soft-hearted I'd...Lieber Himmel."
An ambulance decorated with Red Crosses and flying
red-cross flags drove through the parade ground
"Inspector Wassbacher! He got rid of the hook-
cross. I don't know what he'll have to say about
you!"

Was it a coincidence that Frau Faser handed
Liese the Wilhelm Busch German picture book with
stories of bad children being punished? "Sit down
and keep your mouth shut. Or else!" She dropped her
nightgown and wiggled her fat body into tight,

lace-trimmed underwear and slipped into her new,
pink dress. Buttoning it in a hurry, as she went
out to meet the ambulance.

When she brought the Inspector into the cottage,
Liese kept her eyes on the book. Her cheek still
smarted from Frau Faser's beating and her bottom
was sore in the big, hard chair.

"What do we have here?" the inspector asked.

The clock kept ticking. While the inspector
stared at her she stared at the pictures of shaggy
Strubel-Peter, having his long fingernails and fingertips chopped off and Max and Moritz, the bad
boys, ground up into chicken feed and eaten by
hens.

His soft voice came as a shock when he chatted
about the weather, his vegetable garden. Liese
became entranced by his lisp and stared at him over
the rim of the book.

"What large blue eyes she has. Where did you
find her?"

Frau Faser whispered something to him. "*Ach ja,*"
he cried out. "You're sure? What a surprise. It's
about right. Over three years."

Could this really be the Inspector who had children done away with? Children called him Spider
because of his round body, long thin legs sticking
out of short lederhosen, and long arms encased in
hairy loden. But Liese quite forgot to be scared
when she saw his happy, ugly face straw-mat hair, a
knockwurst nose, a frog mouth.

He had decided to give up his uniform, but a
pistol stuck out of one pocket and a big hunting
knife from another. For safety reasons he now had
to transport children in a Red Cross ambulance.

"How could I forget getting so jolly with you
here, Faser? The fresh trout I brought. *Wunderbar.*
Plenty of wine. We got jolly, *jawohl*, we did get
ever so jolly that one time." His murky eyes, rov-
ing around the room full of old furniture,
including the old dentist's chair, the paintings,
stag antlers, came to rest on Liese. He gently
examined her ears and found them washed and clean.
He looked at her fingernails, which he declared
echt Wassbacher. "Who hit you? Tell Papa. If anyone
ever hurts you."

Liese noted how he lathered his big hands,

rinsed them, lathered them again. At least four times, as though they had been terribly soiled and he couldn't get them clean.

Frau Faser gave Liese warning looks from the stove, where she was conjuring up a mountain of scrambled eggs for the Inspector. While he shovelled them into his big mouth to keep up his strength, the matron seemed to lose strength and became unusually silent.

"Where did she hide you?" he asked Liese.

"On Auntie's farm. At the bottom of the field," she answered, trying to lisp just like him.

"Very wise and discreet."

When Frau Faser handed him a glass of Schnapps, he held it in his left hand with the pinky sticking out to show off the gold ring, decorated with a crown and a stag, while he poured the drink down his throat. Then he went out to inspect the school barracks, dormitories and behind children's ears. Frau Faser looked red and flustered. "Don't say one word!" she warned.

The Inspector wasn't interested in words when he returned from his inspection. He wanted the children's records, which were missing. He could not reach the doctor on the telephone. Several children had to be watched. One girl, Mimi, looked frail; the big girl on hormones was growing unevenly. So he had more than one good reason to come back to Waldruh. "You have to get me records, and if they are missing, write a full report." He turned and snapped one of Liese's ringlets. "I hope you have documented the birth of this child correctly."

As Frau Faser smiled and refilled his glass with more schnapps, he started to ramble on about Schloss Wassbacher, the castle he owned. About his invalid wife, who never had a child, and behaved like one. "Tired blood." He drank a toast to good healthy women and children. "I promise you." But it wasn't clear what he promised as he stretched out on the sofa below a sunny painting and snored while the matron polished his glossy shoes.

Liese liked the way he clicked his heels when he was ready to leave, praising the famous Faser hospitality in a hoarse whisper. He went out to his ambulance and came back with a small metal box. His smile lifted the folds under his chin as he turned

to Liese. "You have Wassbacher blue blood. I expect
you to remember that our ancestors were knights and
rode to the Holy Land during the crusades."

Frau Faser was in a bad mood that evening
because the Inspector had eaten all her eggs and
she had heard bad news on the English radio station. She didn't want to talk about blue blood or
knights and the crusades, but the teacher with the
big Adam's apple, named Frau Herring, had a picture
of Adolf Hitler as a knight in armor. When Liese
asked whether this war was the crusade, Frau
Herring praised Lise's wisdom in class. The fatherland, she said, is holy to the Fuhrer. He has made
it his sacred duty to make the world part of the
new order of the Thousand Year Reich. "Lucky children, you're trained to serve a higher cause."
Liese didn't want the higher cause, she wanted
to get back to play with Mother on Auntie's farm. In
class she learned that German flying bombs were
raining down on the British while German scientists
were getting ready with their secret, all-powerful
miracle weapons.
Horst, second in troop command, asked whether it
was poison gas, a super rocket, or what. Frau
Rimpel the teacher, slapped his face. "You have
ears. I said secret! Or how could we take the enemy
by surprise?"

The editorial note on a pale-blue stick-on says:
This is going along well. But I would make it
clear that it was treason under Hitler to ask questions.
Best, Robie.

Why would the German people have asked questions while victory
after victory ripped wealth away from the unworthy enemy and brought it
to the Fatherland as booty? Liese was booty in Germany; Liz in America.
As a writer, she has become her own booty, frozen in time with her school-
girl mother, on Auntie's white farm, where the icon Frica sits waiting under
the kitchen window for chicken legs.

Liese was supposed to be asleep on her cot in
the cold pantry, while women talked about a bomb

that hadn't killed the Fuhrer. The beginning of the end. "We're a school. I had to follow orders" Frau Faser kept saying. They all agreed–children had been delivered here. No one could blame the staff. One of them started to cry because she had to follow orders in a camp in Poland where young ones that wet their beds had been moved into an unheated stable where they froze to death. The soil, in that deep ditch they ended up in, had stirred.

"At least dead children can't talk," Frau Faser said.

Chapter 5

NOCTURNE

Chris always relaxes with a nightcap on the old parlor sofa and watches the
Johnny Carson show before he goes to bed. He likes Johnny, because no
matter what goes on with the latest Mrs. Carson, or the latest world disaster, the show remains the same. Once in a while you get an unexpected
guest like Beatrice Strout, the 'femininist' author. Her cunning cat face and
the crimson superwoman outfit —not her writing—got her the show. She
uses a lot of body language and laughs at everything Johnny says.

Just as well Liz followed his advice and went to bed. Beatrice Strout,
author of Ellen's bible LOVE AND LEARN, produces the subliminal persuasion tapes Ellen uses. THE SECRETS OF JOY tape Beatrice plays on
the show makes Johnny think of parrots, monkeys swinging. The band
plays along and so does Johnny, making faces to the jungle music while
three shirtless body-builder - male-stripper types march onto the set carrying Beatrice Strout art: tall heavy windows she rescued from the
demolition of a demolished Bowery tenement and decorated with big
blotches of color, accented with genuine gold leaf.

Johnny does his little golf routine in front of one. Beatrice cautions
him, because her artwork has supernatural power, is inspired by extrasen-
sory perceptions, sells for fifteen thousand dollars and up, and brings inner

peace. An overweight young woman in the audience faints. Chris is quite certain she was hired by the author of LOVE AND LEARN.

Bea, as Johnny calls this irrepressible loudmouth, goes on and on about a woman's choice. Women have the right to put a stop to guns and killing . They give birth, raise children; why should they put up with having them killed or killing other women's children?

Johnny wants to know whether her art could stop violence worldwide. Bea stands up and faces the camera. Art can inspire, but it can't get rid of guns. She produces a handgun from her pocket, turns it sideways.

"What does it look like? No, I must not say the word on this show." Her full, pink lips form letters P E N I S. "The bullets entering flesh, bleeding wounds. Need I say more about this perverted male sexuality? What if women all over the world took guns away from men? A good beginning."

To shut her up, Johnny quickly asks whether this is in her new book. Then he wants to know how she is able to both write and paint big pictures. Bea ignores his question and talks about women artists being suppressed by men. Female writers who often had to hide their sex and publish under assumed male names. There is Liz in her own insulated room and Chris even bought her that monster computer. 'Her System.' But who knows, she might end up writing like Bea. Ellen is a big influence too. From the days when they used to jog early in the morning and talk, or rather shout to each other, because Ellen's dog Red invariably came along with them howling and barking, waking up the town.

Now Liz writes every morning and hasn't been seeing much of Ellen. Serves at least one jolly good purpose. Liz, of course, has no idea how close he is to Ellen. He started seeing her when Liz spent so much time in Boston and Mike was in trouble at Shakerville School. Chris goes into the kitchen to refresh his drink. When he refills the ice tray, he can see from the window above the sink that Ellen's bedroom lights are on. He has never been allowed upstairs. She keeps him in her office corner of the living room, where he sits upright, because she wants the patient to concentrate, while she is the one who stretches out on the couch—which is really a trundle bed. Usually she plays one of those Beatrice Strout subliminal per-suasion tapes FREEDOM OF THE SPIRIT: "You are on top of your roof. You are not afraid of falling. You raise up one foot. Now the other. You rise up! Come down again. You rise high. Now come down. Now you rise, and you are floating through the air. You are opening your soul to the universe. You speak the truth." A flute plays the same twittery tune on and on, while Chris talks about his English war-bride mother, who left the twins with a nanny and spent the war years with horses. His father, the American pilot, who brought them all to Shoreland after the war. The boat explosion which killed his parents and twin sister and left Chris scorched, clinging to a board in the icy water. He has remained stunned, because the worst happened to him at such an early age (a quote from Dr. Bigfield). While Ellen listens to his reasons for leading the life of a retired invalid, she changes the tape to SECRETS OF JOY, tin-drums and perky whistling and wild chirping. She pulls out the couch trundle bed to treat him to a massage, which reminds him of the night nurse he lived with in New York City—spoiling him, making him lazy and guilty.

A woman taking charge like that is like sex in the school infirmary. And that only happened once, when they had the measles. Chris thought he was having one of those dreams; then he woke up and discovered Jonathan doing it to him as a favor just in case measles at the age of fifteen, like mumps later in life, would end up making them impotent. They were both covered with red spots, that's all they'd ever had in common. Chris felt like a clown and couldn't get himself to return this favor. They avoided each other afterward.

Chris told Dr. Haupter, the Freudian, that gymnastics with Ellen on that trundle bed gave him psychosexual red spots. Once or twice Chris did feel those stinging guilt bites when he was coming, an odd, perverse thrill. Ellen says a man must feel proud after sex. Then she makes him feel ashamed, trying to teach him how to touch her and where and when. But Chris doesn't like to be told. She declares that she learned how to get the most out of sex from Beatrice Strout's LOVE AND LEARN. Liz is supposed to benefit from his experience. But after Liz became ill, she slept in her old room with the computer, the health hazard.

Tonight, he heard her go back to the big bed they share, in his big room. She would certainly guess he had been with someone else if he got one of those tapes and started oriental positions to music. No man can expect that kind of circus with his wife, especially when she's his sister.

With Dr. Haupter, Chris arrived at the obvious conclusion that LOVE AND LEARN ideas, counting and accounting of how to get the most out of sex, would put Liz off. Just as cookbooks can ruin your appetite. Then a good session with Braggerd got him to understand that Dr. Ellen Burns isn't just being helpful. She needs an injured man to make her feel strong and healthy. She wants Chris, and Beatrice Strout is the go-between.

Ellen doesn't know about Dr. Bigfield, Dr. Braggert, or Dr. Haupter. She won't accept a fee, but he will have to do something for her. Gramp always made a woman feel she was important even when she was not. Chris puts on the recording of Brahms's violin concerto.

The kitchen sink drip-drip-drips and needs fixing. He gets hypnotized watching snow flurries swirl in the beam of the spotlight on Bonnie's barn, then drift over Ellen's cottage. Her bedroom light on the second floor is still on. Maybe she is up there looking out of her window and listening to the waves. She enjoys swimming in rough water. Doesn't understand how he and Liz live in the house by the sea but don't enjoy the ocean because of that boat accident. Car accidents don't keep one from driving, she says. You have to rise above mishaps.

To rise above mishaps, Chris takes off his shoes and goes up the creaky stairs to the Liz room, which is lit by the computer monitor she sometimes leaves on day and night. The moment he opens the door he is overcome by the faint but putrid bestial odor and the hum of her Dec Mate II: her accomplice.

Day after day Liz would dress up in a British tweed suit and go into Boston, even when Chris told her he had a cold and was not well. He couldn't believe she was seeing computers. Had to be another man. With all this going on, how could anyone blame him for getting involved with Ellen? Chris loosens his Exeter tie. Only Dr. Braggert knew that he had Liz shadowed by Convey Protective Patrol Detective Agency. They had followed her from one computer retail store to the next. Chris paid out close to a thousand dollars. Made him quite ill, of course. There should be a way of deducting the detective from income tax just like his shrinks.

As for Liz, she'd come home from Boston, cheeks glowing, all excited like some darned debutante. First she was in love with the IBM. Then the Kaypro, because it was so nice and small and cheap. Then it just had to be the Wang, which was very big and expensive. She tried them all. Talked computers to anyone she met. Each monster system she tried was better than the last. Back and forth, day after day, she tried them one by one, until she found the most "dedicated," the most "user friendly." When strangers called her, Chris picked up the extension phone and heard them talk about soft disk, display, insert mode, software. It all sounded faintly obscene. The detective got one photograph of Liz having lunch with a 'software' engineer who must have weighed about three hundred pounds. Paul. Hardly a lover. He once called while Liz was gardening and told Chris that there was a computer sidewalk sale in New Hampshire at Computer Barn. They were selling digital equipment cheap. The best for a writer. The fat man went on and on. Most dedicated, user friendly. Dr. Bigfield got Chris to understand that Liz, as a young war child, never had any toys. So Chris told her to go to the Barn in Salem, New Hampshire, and get it over with.

No one to fix dinner. Mike, thrown out of *Shakerville School* for some prank with fuses and stage lights, was at home and ordered a pizza. She returned at midnight. Mike, his usual self, tore open the boxes. Hardly looked at the instructions and put the system together in her old room. She started writing that very night. Was up at four the next morning. Then the system "crashed," wiped out all that she had written. Chris had to laugh. As it turned out it wasn't Mike's fault at all.

"Her system" kept crashing and trashing what she wrote. All these nice young shirt-and-tie men in digital vans showed up, once even during a blizzard. They replaced parts. Software problem, hardware problem. Liz kept calling the eight-hundred number in Atlanta. No one could figure it out. Everything was replaced bit by bit. Even the brain. No wonder computer companies were going out of business. And wouldn't you know it, Mike was the one who finally figured out that the electric wiring in the room could be at fault. It was.

Ever since, Liz has been happy. She says "Her System" is always waiting for her like a horse in the stable. Monster in the stable! Now it has its own line and it behaves. And it stinks! Liz says he imagines the smell; wants him to learn accounting on the computer and get his income tax out of the way, but the moment Chris sets foot in this room, he is drained by the magnetic field.

Chapters are arranged in stacks on her large desk. He picks up Chapter 5, LITTLE PROCURER. Moves a few feet away from the magnetic field. He never wanted her to read to him. Refused her offer to read her manuscript, because he didn't trust himself to comment on her writing *Stolen Child*. He needs privacy to get enraged. "Good God! How could she!? Invention. Insults! Lies. Lies." But the bedraggled hat she used to wear when she was little sits on a Chianti bottle as evidence.

Chris dials Ellen's family number. "This is your unfriendly night tape. Do not leave a message at this hour. At the sound of the tone bug off, shit-face!" A duet performance by her two boys, who say anything they want to say and do as they please; just like Mike. There is a bang, muffled by the padding in this room, as one of the four kitchen doors he secured with strong self-closing devices in time for Mike's return, slams shut. Why does he hate those open doors so much? He dials Ellen's number, letting the phone ring twice, hanging up and dialing again, which is his signal. "Hi, beautiful!"

"It's only you, Chris! That's good." Ellen sounds sleepy. "I've had some sick phone calls."

"Are you alone?"

"Except for the boys and Red. They're all asleep. Made the most of the beautiful snow. We really should too."

"Never mind. Listen. I want to read something to you." No response. "Are you awake?"

"Almost."

"Listen to this: LITTLE PROCURER..."

"I am not a little procurer. And I resent that." Her voice squeaks; she's wide awake now and really mad.

"Not you. Want to hear it or not?" He doesn't wait for an answer: "'I'm Chris,' the small boy said to the stewardess, 'and I'm from Massachusetts.' He took off his cowboy hat and eyed her from behind the bandages with the bravado of a masked bandit. 'My father was one of the first American pilots in England. Mother was English, a war bride. Now they're both dead. My twin sister is dead too. A boat explosion. And I almost drowned and I was burned....'"

"You're writing your memoirs, Chris!" Ellen sounds professional and alert. "You're making it very real!"

"Rubbish! Can't you tell it's from her book? All about me. I used to rattle off something like that as a little kid. Kind of answering questions before anyone had a chance to ask what happened to my face and hands."

"Answering questions before they were asked. That's really good."

"It's not what I said just now. You've already changed it, and that's what she does." He gulps his drink.

"Why don't you write down exactly what you said to me about answering questions? Liz could fit that in. It's good. You could help her a lot. Why don't you tell her how you feel?"

He had always told his real twin how he felt.

"You can't stop her, Chris. It's her choice. Beatrice Strout was on the Carson show. Did you see it? She was great and she talked about a woman's choice. "

"I have a choice too. And I don't like the way she concocts and distorts in that book. I don't like female writers. They make me sick! I hate it all!"

"It was so generous of you to pay for the computer, Chris."

"Idiotic masochistic. It's noxious, just like her writing! She has no right to go public with my hurt." (Dr. Braggart would consider his outburst part of self-assertion therapy.)

"You believe in censorship, Chris?"

"You bet. "

"Chris. Wait a minute! She is writing a memoir, isn't she? Her own story. You are part of it. I haven't seen her writing, but she once said that she wants to find out who she really is. "

"At my expense!" Chris adds up the Convey Protective Patrol Detective Agency, to the three thousand for the computer, the insulation of her room. "My expense."

"She doesn't make fun of that wounded boy. Does she?"

"It's unfair to me and my grandfather. But I shouldn't involve you. Sorry to bother you. Good night!" He takes a deep therapeutic breath. "Sleep well, beautiful!"

How could Liz or Ellen ever understand that Chris and Gramp were stuck with each other and used certain lines to get along from day to day with all their hurt and worries? Everyone believed that Chris survived the boat explosion through a miracle. Actually, the zipper getting caught on his new American pants had saved Chris. His American dad, who had read about dominant twins, noticed how Sis took over talking for Chris in her loud English voice, never giving his son a chance to show off. So he took him to the captain's deck during the ocean crossing, taught him big things like navigation. Never bothered to teach Chris little things, because he considered him to be so advanced and grown up for a four-year-old. The moment they got to Shoreland, he dressed Chris like a man in those long American pants and made him first mate on his sailboat.

That morning, Chris made it his duty to fill the boat-stove. He was at the head when Mother, Father, and Sis came down to the cabin for lunch. "Chris is allowed to light the stove. I want to have a turn!" Sis was saying. Chris yelled: "No, that's my job!" English trousers he was used to, buttoned; the zipper on his new American pants got stuck halfway up. That was the last thing he remembered. There was no time to be scared. But he is scared now, gasping for air. He sticks the pages back into the envelope. Liz does not know. His doctors know only half truth.

"It was not my fault. I didn't mean to." He leaves the room like a thief and flees to the wind-swept terrace; high above the dark water he gulps icy air, and gulps the last of his drink. He turns on the spotlight to shine on the memorial cross Gramp had put up on the highest rock facing the sea. With the rush of each dangerous wave, Chris leans into the wind, allowing the freezing salt spray to whip his face. "It was not my fault! Not my fault!" he shouts and pitches the glass down into the water. Then he runs to take a hot shower. The bashing, churning water resounding in his mind, he sings the Brahms violin concerto, which glorifies the secret joy of misery.

Liz wakes up to whiskey kisses in the big bed. Mustache perfume and the threat of howling winds and pounding waves always tell her that Chris will help himself to her body. He takes off her embroidered Indian nightgown, folding it with the same care he always took in unwrapping a present.

The bedroom they now share overlooks the water. Storms excite Chris; drinking slows him down—sometimes too much—but she is used to this. She feels him follow the rhythm of the waves, submitting to pleasure easily when she is still half asleep and doesn't worry about how he feels.

Chris clings to her as though the Plant house were a sinking vessel and this night, any stormy night, his last. Waves pounding against the rocks, retreating, then gushing into the cove below and foaming the terrace. "Sis! Sis!" he calls out to his drowned twin. And every second there must be a man somewhere helping himself to a woman as though she were the last one on earth and calling out to one he lost.

I replace Sis best of all in bed with Chris during a storm when she takes my place. And he gives me more pleasure when I don't exist, Liz had written in her diary.

"Did you sleep with any of your New York fiancés?" Chris asks.

"What's the sudden interest?"

"I'd just like to know."

"You do know! You handpicked those dates for me. They were all your friends, too."

"How about old Catulle? Russian aristocrat and all that."

Above the dresser, a night light dimly shines on the Catulle "brat" the artist gave to Liz, the model. Huge, eyes, a Liz-smile, the body of a ten-year-old, a pink chemise slipping off one shoulder. An early one of the many versions of the seductive urchin he painted in oil glazes like an old master.

"A joke. His paintings turned me into a cartoon character." The stranger at Mario's had called it "Walt Disney."

"And a popular model!"

"You were all for that."

"He was wild about you. He didn't?"

She laughs. "Are you trying to give me a wicked past? What have you been up to?"

"Did you sleep with him?"

"You were suspicious of monkey-face? I thought you came along to the Hotel Pierre because Catulle fed you all that good Champagne."

"I wasn't there all the time. If there was nothing going on, why did you talk to him about your adoption?"

"Because he talked about Russia. His parents being killed during the revolution. I didn't even think he was that interested in me. "

"Not true. He was fixated."

"It all got to be impossible."

The hotel room, late afternoon. Catulle in front of his easel, already dressed in a tuxedo for a gala at the opera made her think of a circus chimpanzee. "Catulle's in love with the brat." So she tried to divert him with the stories of Liese, while he danced back and forth to her words from his folding easel. "Come away from your silly brother, boring incest, and all those nothing people. We'll sail to Greece. Good food, good Russian love. Come away." He saw in her what he wanted to see. When she said, "Chris is not my real brother," Catulle heard only the excitement in her voice that he wanted to hear. He dropped his brushes onto the palette. Love talk poured over the innocently corrupt brat he had created. His face flushed, he shed his dinner jacket. His brass-colored eyes transmitting the pathos he withheld from his calculated creation of 'the brat,' he grabbed and pawed her. Implanted a kiss all tongue and teeth. She pushed, bit, which made him tear at her clothes. Then she laughed out loud. Her best defense and a mortal offense.

"You deserted me. Running off to Europe with some old pilot," Chris now says and hugs her tight.

"I didn't run away with anyone. I ran away from having to pose all the time—not just as a model in New York, Catulle's brat, Gramp's Liz, your Sis. Everyone's fantasy. I was always everything anyone wanted me to be. From way back. In Hitler School. So I went to Europe trying to find my mother. No luck. I missed you and Gramp. I met little Roger and his father Ken. I told you all about him years and years ago."

"I don't remember."

"You never wanted to hear about him. Are you running out of material for your psychiatrists? You can always talk about your New York live-in night nurse Geraldine."

"That was after you left."

"Not true. She was already living with you for almost a year."

"Is that why you ran off?"

"You're not listening. I just told you, I had to get away from the Manhattan scene."

"Quite typical. Trying to find yourself in Europe like all the New York neurotics."

"It's not neurotic to try and find out who you really are. But as you know I didn't have much luck in Vienna. The German and Austrian authorities were trying to wipe the slates clean. No one wanted to talk about stolen children. I felt lonely and disheartened at Christmas. So I decided to go skiing on the Adelberg. I met Ken's adopted little boy, Roger, on the slopes. He had wandered away from his ski class and had such a good time with me, he pretended he didn't know where he was staying. No mother, he told me. I left messages at every hotel. Ken came looking for the kid and found me. He was divorced. A pilot. The boy was four years old. Had been adopted as a baby and didn't know where he came from either. He was used to travelling around and made himself at home any-where, with anyone he met. The way you did when you were in Europe with Gramp."

"So you found yourself another Gramp!"

"Younger. Forty-seven. Good looking."

"Old enough to be your father. What did he look like?"

"Jack Kennedy. He had thick gray hair. A pilot, so he had to keep fit. Went in for skiing, rock-climbing, swimming, "

"Sex with young girls."

"We'd get together when he had a few days between flights. Mostly in Italy. It was all so new to me. A ready-made family. You know how you never allowed us to swim? Well, Ken got me to snorkel and swim under water. I loved it. Remember how you traced me to Portofino the day Gramp died? It was our last morning. Ken bought the same blue pants and striped jerseys for Roger and me, like brother and sister. We had never been closer. Ken had to make some phone calls. I stayed on the beach with little Roger and he started to tell me about all the other girls he and his dad played with. The stewardesses, an Austrian in her big house in the mountains. The way you used to talk when you were little, about girls you and Gramp played with."

Chris burrows down under the quilt. "I don't remember."

"All the pills you get all those doctors to prescribe are wiping out your memory. They don't know about each other, do they?"

Chris is in no mood to answer questions. "You're laughing at me." He nuzzles, and kisses the familiar hollow of her neck. "How do I know that you weren't already pregnant when you moved in with me?" He puts his arm around her at once. "Not fair. Anyway. What does it matter?"

Liz pushes him away. "Mike Plant matters." She sighs and rolls over on her back. " If I had been pregnant I would have married Ken. He was a good father to little Roger. I loved him for that."

"You loved the kid. Not the man."

"Roger was adopted like me. Sometimes he made believe I was his sister, or his brother. Then again he'd call me Mama. I was Ken's first virgin. He was amazed and he loved that. He did ask me to marry him."

"That must have been after he found out that you had inherited this house. Anyway, he was too old. By now he's dead or senile."

"Why should he be? Gramp was not senile when he died."

"Yes, he was. Kept changing his will and installed a pay phone in his own house."

His anger is as familiar as the sound of the storm and the waves.

"Anyway, I told Ken I had to see you before I could make up my mind. Well, I did come to see you. Remember? And I did marry you. Ken retired and moved in with this wealthy Austrian, an older woman, who loved his child as I did. A happy ending, don't you think?" There is no response. Chris wouldn't want to know how remembering little Roger and Ken, helps her to give a true picture of his travels with Gramp.

He settles his perfumed head on her shoulder. She strokes his soft, wavy hair while window panes rattle and a branch of the birch raps three times. Stops and knocks again. Snow would sit on Ken's coarse gray crew cut like a cap when they skied during a storm. She'd stay behind him. Always afraid of not measuring up. She remembers Ken's strong, compact body surrounded by sea foam and bubbles, when she overcame Chris's fear of the sea and followed him through heavy surf. Ken had liked to run along the beach holding hands with her and Roger, then making Roger take a nap with his bunny, and taking Liz to bed. Simple as swimming or running or mountain climbing. An activity. He took her along. And when he reached out to her a second time, he had declared he was not like that with anyone else. He always tried to hide his pleasure.

Liz, sister-wife, has learned that pleasure is surprisingly complete when you expect nothing. She shifts Chris onto his pillow and covers him.

After Gramp's funeral Liz had returned to her tiny apartment in New York City. Chris never called, and she stayed away from Pete's Tavern and the friends they had shared. She felt lonely until she enrolled in a writing class at the New School for Social Research and started writing and rewriting the story of a stolen child. For the first time she was doing something she really wanted to do. Her instructor, Caroline Gordon, a well-known writer, had praised her impressionistic style.

She had not heard from Ken for two months when the phone woke her. Little Roger was on the line and asked when she was going to come to play with him. When he chatted on about a stewardess named Susan and a ski trip, Ken cut him off. "We both love you a lot. Letter writing, telephone calls are no good. How about getting married next month?" And Roger said. "Let's get married. I love you best of all."

"There is something you should know," she said to Ken.

"Well, well. I was so careful. You don't mean?"

"Not that." She'd never spoken German while they were together in Austria. Somehow never felt free to talk about her adoption. "I'll send a letter. It's a long story." She sent him the first chapter of *Stolen Child*.

Several weeks went by before Kenneth called her again. There had been a change. He had been flying out of Frankfurt, where he had to look for an apartment and a housekeeper to take care of the boy. "You mean you really don't know who you are?" He had changed into a distrustful stranger, annoyed and uneasy.

"If I lived in Germany I could get the German Red Cross to do another search for my mother."

"Hell, no! After the adoption my ex suddenly wanted to find out where Roger came from. She spent a fortune. Quite a shock...It had been her idea to adopt a foundling." Ken said he never wanted a "pig in a poke" in the first place. He liked to know what he was getting.

So Liz was just another pig in the poke. Fair hair and good looks, her smile, the right physical characteristics, *"der gute Eindruck*—the good impression—had satisfied the Nazification experts, but not Ken. She was rejected, like a fine-looking pup without a pedigree.

Her editor had once asked Liz whether she could bring out the sexual aspect of cruelty. How about the cruel aspect of love? It hurt when she broke off with Ken and Roger. A few weeks later she met Chris in the Boston lawyer's office. "You're not my real sister," he said.

Sorted out, rejected, she signed papers that were handed to her without reading them, turned and ran out of the office. When Chris telephoned she hung up. One night she came home in a cab and saw him waiting on her stoop. So she told the driver to drive on to her friend Jane's apartment. He didn't call or write after that and stayed away for almost two months. Friends asked all kinds of questions and invited her to parties, where she would have met "brother Chris." She stayed away. Until that night when rain woke her from a happy dream of a childhood sleigh ride with Chris, Gramp, and Bonnie, and being apart from him seemed no more than a bad dream. What would Gramp say?

It was past midnight with heavy rain tapping on her windows. Friends had mentioned that Geraldine, the night nurse, was out of town. She threw a raincoat Ken had bought for her in London over her nightgown. If a neighbor had not come home in a cab, she might not have been able to get one.

❁❁❁

The lights in Chris's top floor apartment were on. But as his sister Liz could take a chance, run upstairs, and ring the bell. She could hear Mozart, the Magic Flute, and wondered whether he had gone to sleep listening to the music. She rang again.

Finally he came to the door, scolding Geraldine for not using her key. "I thought you'd stay for a week. Did you have a fight with your cousin?" The safety chain rattled, the key turned in the lock. Chris tore the door open, belting his long white terry cloth robe in a fury, "You!"

When he kept changing from one bare foot to the other on the cold tile floor, she thought he might slam the door and took a step back, saying she was sorry she came. But he silenced her by throwing both arms around her. His moist greedy mouth traveled across her cheek to her lips. "Not my real sister," he told himself. This time Liz got his meaning.

Geraldine had dusted Chris's apartment and taken drapes to be cleaned. The sun lamp was her idea too. Overzealous, Chris said, to even polish the mirror another tenant had put up on the ceiling,

An overzealous Liz is now shining the dusty mirror of the past as she writes. Stirring up dust, stirring up doubts—nothing but trouble. Leave well enough alone. Look forward, not back. Did Gramp really say that, or could he have said it? Liz often hears words before she writes them, and remembers what she has written like a melody that invades the mind with both pleasure and doubt.

That rainy night, Chris put on a recording of Vivaldi's The Four Seasons, turned on the sunlamp to make it summer for Liz, and found sunglasses large as masks. They gulped brandy and she was half asleep when he kissed her and took off her gown. She would not have resisted. It didn't mean that much. Just a new game he wanted to play; the best game.

When they rested side by side and she looked up into the mirror, they appeared fastened together head to head, arm to arm. Her hair had grown long and cowled around both their heads and shoulders. More sister and brother then ever, as naked lovers she saw herself as the inseparable twin Gramp always wanted her to be.

The ceiling mirror reflected an old Plant patchwork quilt curled around their feet and the flickering log Chris had lit in the fireplace. An antique desk with the Parke Benet auction ticket still tied to the drawer, a litter of papers. As soon as Chris inherited money he became careless about paying bills.

A dog yelped and a woman laughed in the apartment below. Through the curtainless, tall windows you saw the gardens of a row of brownstones that would soon make way for a luxury apartment building. A single lighted window outlined the dark figure of a man, who wore a hat as he leaned out in the rain peering into their room through field glasses.

"There is a man watching us. "Liz said.

Neither of them moved. "What does it matter? He doesn't know who we are."

"You are my Liz," he said. Liz was sitting up. Her hair covering only her right breast: selected by Gramp for Chris, and now by Chris—helpless, a stolen child deprived of will, on display, offered up, smiling to survive. While the stranger peered over the sea of houses, glasses trained on the raft of the white bed—that drifting mirage of youth—setting him adrift in vicarious desires.

"You're going to stay with me. I'll call Geraldine first thing in the morning."

Chris had been living with Geraldine for many months, well taken care of; perhaps too well. They had met when he was having "symptoms" and a doctor put him into New York Hospital for a two-day checkup, X-rays, etc, that produced anxiety symptoms. Geraldine, the night nurse had stayed on to comfort him all day after she was off duty; and she was, in a sense, never off duty again until she went to her sister's wedding. "We're going to burn. Turn off the sun-lamp, Liz!"

Liz turned off the sun-lamp for him, obliging as any nurse. Never really free to love anyone else. She felt excited about belonging with him and ashamed of giving herself up to her consummate pleasure of pleasing.

Chapter 6
WRITING

Liz greets her digital Dec Mate II with "endlich, finally," in German, the perfect language for an assignation—with herself. A conspiracy at dawn to steal time and write, while her Chris sleeps. Stormy weather has been forecast. What if the electric power should fail? Chris refused to have a backup generator installed, but he did have her old room insulated, keeping the hazardous computer and Liz, the hazardous writer, secluded within closed padded doors and padded walls, which now muffle the waves to an endless shush—hush-hush—shush shush.

She lets herself sink down to kneel in the "back-chair" Chris gave her. A new invention to prevent back pain, but after an hour her knees will start to ache. The monitor sits on the brain box shining onto the envelope with the beginning of the memoir she was not supposed to write. Her Dec Mate II, that adamant confessor, receives the disk like a priest taking the wafer: growl, mumble growl, mumble growl, mum, mum.

The wind shakes the big hull of a house while the computer 'self tests.' TYPE THE NAME OF THE DOCUMENT YOU WANT TO EDIT AND PRESS RETURN: Creaking and grinding of a hundred prayer stools, rasping murmur; searching: DRIVE 1 DOES NOT HAVE A DOCUMENT NAMED SELECTION.

It never said that before. Did she press 'selection' by mistake— or what?

The chapter has vanished. Mother's little mistake was expected to make mistakes. The sense of loss and infantile misery comes over her each time the computer message appears on the monitor with slogans of warning or reprimand, heartless lies that echo beyond reason.

   She humbly, obediently accepts the ordeal. Same creaking and grinding, search. Peep. Peep. Chapter six. She got it back! Nothing is lost. Restarting, re-booting, you often feel you've rebooted yourself. Ready to correct, revise, dig deeper. Nothing ever seems to be finished. *Stolen Child*—her archeological dig—is risky as that tunnel dug by children, which could cave in.

I will always remain that child on the side of a
lonely road waving to strangers. I changed hands
but remained the same-that is the truth-I was given
new names and remained nameless, a stolen child.

Memo: This is explaining. Do you want this?

Best, Robbie

The furled viper of her editor's red question mark gyrates before her eye as doubt like venom darts from belly to throat to throbbing temples. Am I writing the way my school-girl mother talked? Sounding off like my kid Mike, as an authority on any subject. Caroline Gordon, her teacher at the New School had believed that certainty always comes out of uncertainty.

When Frau Faser had to give the foreign children
German names, in preparation for adoption by
National Socialist families, she had simply put
down April 20, the Fuhrer's birthday, on all their
records to make them all equally desirable. This
year, Berlin was in ruins when the Waldruh children
for the first and last time celebrated their birthdays and Adolf Hitler's with songs, yodeling,
potato pancakes, and renewed hope for the secret
miracle weapon.
   But hope vanished, suddenly like the snow in
April. Brooks turned into streams during the thaw.

The women's tears flowed at Waldruh. Spring this
year was not a beginning, it was the end. Even the
carpet of wild flowers that emerged from under snow
in the warm south wind seemed funereal: God knows
where we'll all be when they bloom again!

God was mentioned as never before while the
women gathered around Frau Faser's radio, Adolf
Hitler only in whispers. Jan was on the parade
ground drilling the entire school as usual. The
loudspeaker boomed a march; Frau Faser and her
helpers started to sob, hugging each other. Since
they weren't watching, Liese, Jan's courier, put on
her old dress with the frills under the Faser
sweater which fitted like a long coat. With it the
usual woolen knee socks that had belonged to
another Faser's pet. At the backdoor she quickly
turned around to put on the old hat she had arrived
in.

She waylaid Jan in the parade ground, threw her
arm up in her best Heil Hitler salute with tears in
her eyes. "I have the honor to report," she said in
a radio voice. "Our Fuhrer dead." correcting herself with, "is dead. In Berlin on April 30." Jan
squinted at her. "He did have his birthday and so
did we."

"He's not dead. It's not true," Jan called out
like most anyone in the hinterland of German
defeat—oppressors or the oppressed. "A lie. It's a
trick!"

Enemy trick or German trick to deceive the
enemy? "God's trick," the child said firmly, just
like Auntie looking at smiling photographs of her
dead husbands and sons.

"Treason!" Jan raised the hook-cross banner high,
marching at the head of his troop in the blinding
alpine sun. The perfect Hitler School leader. Too
perfect. Hair the color of sun on ice, chiseled
chin, sharp, straight nose, throwing his long legs
up in goose step, followed by two sway-backed drummers and a division of thirty-eight children.

The leadership-troop wore jackets and rucksacks.
They had done this before. Endurance training, Jan
would tell the women. Liese, his scout, marched
behind him now. Part of the troop. That was only
the beginning. No one to stop her. She kicked up
her legs with the heavy boots as high as she could.

There was no one around to watch Jan turn that
final drill into a parade, except for the three
crows on the roof of Frau Faser's cottage, where
the female staff listened to the forbidden enemy
radio station and wept. Berlin in ruins and in
Russian hands. The Fuhrer, their chaste hero dead—
with a woman! Lies or forbidden truth? The three
crows on the roof flapped their black wings with
their caw—ca caw—ca in response to the crah—crah
broadcast from the scout bird sitting on top of a
dead mountain pine. Jan signaled with his whistle,
ordering the divisions to continue marching behind
the drummers, while he now led his troop in goose
step up to the outhouse. Liese had to take running
steps now and then to keep up with him in the steep
farmyard. It reeked of dung. All of Waldruh, even
the dung heap and the outhouse beside it, were now
enclosed with barbed wire; but stench could not be
fenced in or out. The forbidden radio voice had
called the Thousand Year Reich a dung-pile-waste-
land reeking up to high heaven. Now, as never
before and never again, Liese breathed in the
mighty stench of rotting waste as she lined up with
the troop at the outhouse. A lengthy routine Jan
had started lately during drills which made voiding
ceremonious enough to deceive.

A big brass cowbell on the cracked door jingled
as usual when Siegfried went in and Werner followed. The others followed politely one by one in
perfect order. No one came out. Swallows flew back
and forth from cup-nests under the eaves of the
'stink-hut' circling over the barbed wire they
shrilled and swooped over the troop, free to dart
about in the cloudless morning sky.

"The Faser-baby will give us away," said Horst.

"Leave her alone," Jan said. "With her around it
all looks like a stupid game."

So she scooted ahead, before he could change his
mind. The door jingled shut. "Uhhhh!" she went and
quickly covered her mouth with both hands.The sun
shone in through two narrow boards that stood open
like shutters on the back wall, where shovels,
buckets, and a few chamber pots were stored.

No time to use the throne. Hurriedly she tiptoed
over and saw the two boys crouching outside between
the back of the outhouse and the barbed-wire fence

among empty food crates. She slipped through the
shuttered opening easily, but when she jumped, the
turf below gave way. She found herself in a trench.
"Uhhh!" she went at the opening to a short tunnel.

Jan, followed by Horst and Mimi, squeezed through
the narrow shuttered opening. Big Magda, who had
received hormone shots to become a German mother,
got stuck for a moment before she tumbled out. When
they all lined up in formation behind Jan, Liese
fell in.

"Listen!" Scrawny Mimi rolled her protruding
eyes. "I hear a car!" The others heard only drums
and marching feet, but Mimi had been recruited by
Jan for her uncanny gift to both see and hear
ahead. He rolled up the sacred hook-cross flag in a
hurry, lifted it over the fence and let it drop
into the field. *"Mach schnell!* Hurry, Mimmi. You're
first. Magda, you stay and close the boards. You're
last."

Liese raised her hand. "How about me. Me?"

"Shut up!" Magda said.

The troop stood solemnly, while Mimi crawled
through the tunnel. She emerged in the field,
brushed off dirt, and turned her head from side to
side like an anxious look-out crow. Jan followed in
one fast movement pushing his rucksack ahead.

"A car is going to come up the hill." Scrawny
Mimi was never wrong. She could both hear and see
ahead.

Jan picked up the rolled flag. The troop scrambled through the tunnel one by one, and brushed off
the soil. They had all practiced, you could tell.
Jan clamped the flag under his arm, his light hair
and shirt still covered with soil, he trotted his
troop downhill from behind one huge rock to the
next.

"Listen!" Liese said to Magda in a piping Mimi
voice. "I can hear that car too. Come on. Let's
go!"

Big Magda slowly reached up to push the two
boards back, but they wouldn't stay shut. A car
horn honked at the gate, while the troop scurried
alongside the hedge. Never out of step, never missing a drum-beat from the parade-ground drums, which
echoed from the ice covered mountains like the
throb of giant hearts.

A car grinding slowly up the steep road sent the lonely sheep in the meadow scampering down after the children and toward the woods, bleating as though it wanted to escape from being slaughtered and eaten.

"That must be Vogel in the big black car," Liese said. "They're coming to take me back to my mother."

"Then go to them. Go!" Magda pushed her rucksack into the tunnel. "Go on, then. Around the dung heap. Hurry! Scat. Get lost. And don't you fink!"

Rimpel's voice was heard with a resounding, "Liese, Liese!"

"Komm, come Liebling. Where are you? "

"Not Vogel. That's the Inspector," Liese said.

"The black ghosts in the woods are more scary," Magda said.

"The doctor told Frau Faser they're mud-people, taking the cure."

"Ghosts. Giant ghosts. I'll send to bite you dead if you fink!" Magda got down into the tunnel, thrashing her way out to the other side of the fence. It looked easy.

When the cowbell on the outhouse door jingled, Liese buttoned the big Faser-sweater, took the brim of the hat into her mouth and got down into the tunnel, pushing through clods of damp dirt. Rocks scratched both knees.

"I told you the little one isn't in here," the goose clamored.

"Consequences, Frau Rimpel!" The Inspector lisped. "I regret to say, there will be consequences! This child mussst be delivered to me without delay."

His mussst hissed like butter on the hot stove, where Frau Faser would be cooking a mountain of eggs for him. A root caught Liese's sweater by the sleeve and wouldn't let go.

"Liese, *liebes Lieschen!"* Goose kept coaxing, wandering around in her search, while sod fell down to bury Lieschen like the labor camp children who had frozen in their wet beds.

"This is unbelievable, Frau Rimpel. There will be consequences. Someone must be hiding her from me. She must be found!"

Inspector hissing his 'muss,' would be sure to

sort out a child whose fingernails and hair and
even ears were dark with dirt. The pump house
started up with the smack-smack-whak, then
oeeeeeee, eee, geeeeee. If you were caught trying
to run away you'd be tied up and locked in there
for two days and two nights without food or water. A
stag-beetle marched over Liese's arm. She moved,
because it tickled. The beetle rolled over and
played dead. So she played dead too, listening to
the obedient feet of the children Jan had left
behind to keep on marching in the parade ground.
Good soldiers stomp-stamp-strutting on and on, like
something that happened once upon the time, long
ago, but never far away.

Liz has read and reread these pages, when the phone rings. Who would call before dawn? She feels cold. Her elbow touches the keyboard. FAILURE TO VERIFY WILL LEAD TO CORRUPTED MATERIAL appears on the monitor screen. She ignores the harsh warning, reaches for the phone, and knocks down a box of paper clips. They scatter on the hardwood floor.

"Did Mike call you during the night?" The raspy voice of coach, Mike's dorm master.

"No. Why? What's happened?"

"That boy has it coming to him. They all deserve to be punched out and put into a brig."

A pump house door clanking shut. Key turning on a dank cell. "What has Mike done?" She tries to remind herself that Grove Academy is lenient. Coach, the ex-Marine, likes to scare mothers. She can hear him yelling at someone. A dog barks and keeps barking, like the doctor's blood-hounds on the trail of fugitive Hitler School children. "Has he... has he... run away?" she chokes on those words.

The answer is loud barking. "Shut up, Midnight!" the coach thunders at his dog.

Liz shivers, pressing the phone against her ear too hard. At the sounds of shattered glass, a sudden crash, it drops from her hand and clatters onto the desk. When she picks it up, she can hear boys laughing and shrieking. She has to remind herself that dogs are not chasing Mike. Midnight, the coach's fat Lab, is no attack dog. Mr. Goodley, the headmaster, always tries to reason with Mike. He hates punishment. Kids say he suffers from stomach ulcers and hasn't long to live.

Midnight seems to be barking right into the phone. A boy is coughing or throwing up. There is crazy laughter.

"Sorry, Mrs. Plant?" The coach sounds out of breath.

"How about Mike?"

"He's back."

"Is he hurt?"

"Not Mike. The window."

She asks to speak to the headmaster."Too early. We'll call you after the hearing."

"What hearing? I want to speak to Mike." There is a click. Coach, cutting an incompetent parent off to keep her guessing and worried until morning, has the reverse effect. Mike is safe. Her shoulders relax.

An editor's note on the clip board says: "Be sure to watch for transitions and logic." How about Mike, who rebels against restrictions that hardly exist, stays out half the night, and smashes a dorm window to get in, creating chaos? While Jan and the troop—in the midst of the chaos of war—would follow the harsh Hitler School order they'd come away from.

Grove Academy could suspend Mike. They could even throw him out for breaking the rules. If Mike cut himself when he came in through the window, she'll insist that he come home. "The first hundred pages must be in the mail by tomorrow, or the next day." She worries out loud in front of Dec Mate II, hissing her S like the inspector. The publication date must be no later than August, to get ahead of the Christmas books by well-known writers, who get so much publicity. Her editor warned her that a first book by a new author has to be very well written to be reviewed, and has to be very well received by reviewers to be published in Europe, which matters to her most of all. No one has any idea that she desperately wants her book to be translated and read all over the world, so that her mother or relatives would get in touch with her.

Her editor, Robie, likes the way she writes, but scratched out "cross stitches" on the first page and left embroidery. Liz, who has been writing tonight while Mike ran away, feels the despair of having failed to show her editor the significance of a mother carefully following the blue pattern of crosses with colored thread, losing herself in filling in the tracing of each flower of the design, and losing her child. Could that young mother have run out of thread and turned the cloth over to unconnected stitches and knotted threads before she looked up and missed her child and playmate? And are memories not the reverse side of the pattern of dreams and ideas in this story?

Her school-girl mother had drawn her into a conspiracy against the grown-up world. The stupid war, which took away all the young men. Women called her a selfish, spoiled girl who got into trouble in the worst way and never tried to please anyone. Liese knew how to please, the way a puppy knows how to swim.

Chapter 7

VOICE OF A STRANGER

Did she leave FAILURE TO VERIFY on the monitor to admonish herself
for her failure as Mike's mother? She now gives the VERIFY command and
the computer self-tests, tick-tick-ticking from document to document to
NO ERRORS FOUND. But has she not failed to verify her story?
Groping around like a thief in the dark, to find the pattern connecting
everything that is going on now with what she believes had happened in
the past.

The headmaster's line is busy. Liz sits at her desk in a daze. Her throat
feels dry. She should have breakfast, but must speak to the school. What if
Mike runs away to California? The back of her neck hurts. She dials once
more. Still busy. The moment she hangs up, the phone rings. She jumps.
The chair topples.

"Hi, Mom!" Mike's deep, manly voice. "Coach says he called you. He
has no right to call parents before the hearing. That's against the rules."

"It's against the rules to go out into the woods at night."

"I bet Coach didn't tell you that Havelock the terrible is back. When
he started the school, he'd shave heads as punishment. He's like Hitler. It's
a takeover. That's what you should be writing about, Mom. Fiendish
takeovers going on all over the place. Look at the Russians in Afghanistan

and Reagan and the Contras." Mike always talks about world troubles when he gets himself into trouble. She hears angry voices in the background punctuated with a resounding, "Out, Plant!"

The phone is picked up, dropped, and picked up again. "Mike walked into Mr. Goodley's office and made this long distance call from the headmaster's desk!" The irate voice could be either male or female.

"An emergency!" Mike makes himself heard.

"Out, Plant. Out!" This does sound like a man.

"Is Mr.Goodley all right?" Liz asks.

"Mr. Goodley is just fine." He introduces himself as Havelock Grimes, founder of the school.

"How about Mike? The hearing?"

"Your boy was out during the night and smashed a window to get back in. There will be disciplinary procedures."

She has a vision of Mike being overpowered, held down, and shorn like a Waldruh sheep before slaughter.

"I took a leave of absence to introduce the Concept to public schools. In the meantime it's been sabotaged here at Grove by a certain element..."

Liz humbly asks about the Concept, and slogans pour over her. Leadership Boys. Brother's Keeper. Achieving the unique potential, parental commitment. Family Education. A MUST! She foresees a turmoil of conflict among parents and among teachers. "And Mike? The disciplinary procedure?"

"Work-program duties for the day. Teach him that there is a common cause! The students who were out in the woods half the night are suspended. We'll put Mike on the early bus."

Liz feels so relieved she only half listens to the meaning of Outreach Week. Grove will be closing for ten days and Mike will be home for two weeks. Havelock Grimes promises to let her have details for the Regional Parents' Association meeting—A MUST. Retreats that will re-introduce the Concept of the unique potential MUST—"Plant has to follow orders and be a good soldier. A MUST!" No niceties. The conversation ends with that final, hissing MUST.

But Mike will not be a good soldier. There is no escape from the guilt she feels whenever Mike gets himself into trouble. The moment Liz hangs up, her mind spins whirligig visions of Mike's curls shaved, bald as a TV alien's, on the run in danger zones and the Hitler School troop in war zones. *Verschwind,* disappear, stands out in black letters on the monitor. Sometimes one German word will say it all: she was supposed to be invisible at Auntie's farm, at times in Frau Faser's cottage, and again, when she crawled out of the tunnel and followed Jan and the troop into the woods.

The child must have known from the beginning that Partisans had to remain invisible in the woods, just like Gypsies as well as English pilots sent by Churchill, and especially any leftover Jews. You understood from way back that no matter who was killing who in the war, more and more people were trying to escape from each other and be invisible.

A gray-green toad gave itself away for a second as it jumped down into a slimy pool. Frogs and toads never even know their mother and father, teacher said. The smart and strong ones survived on their own because their protective coloring makes them invisible.

Without protective coloring one had to keep out of sight under overhanging branches of pine trees. Soon she heard the troop twitter like migrant birds. She put on her hat and ran. "Wait. Wait for me!" Tripping over a root she stumbled into their midst. "I lost the veil from my hat. The tunnel fell down. I lost the beautiful veil with the jewels."

Werner said:"Go back and look for it. *Verschwind* vanish."

"I'll make myself invisible."

"You will, if you sink into quicksand," Magda said.

"Watch out for snakes," Werner warned.

"Leaches, they're worse. They'll suck out your blood," Siegfried said.

Jan said: "Enough. Leave her be! She'll come in handy."

Liese stood at attention to come in handy and report. "The Inspector's back!"

"We better move on. Fall in!" Jan said.

She stayed behind him while they ran single file along the path. Dogs started to yap and howl in the distance. "The doctor with his hounds," Jan said. "We'll go through the swamp and they'll lose our scent." They had to take off their boots and carry them wading. Liese sank down to her knees at each step with a plop. Midges swarmed around their heads, green flies stung like the doctor's needle. "Are there leaches. Are there really ghosts that bite you dead?" Liese asked.

"There are mud people," Mimi said.

One dog came bounding and panting along the path sniffing, lifted a leg to leave his mark, then howled as he went after squirrels or water-rats or the swamp flicker-lights of lost souls—*Irrlichter*, will-o'-the-wisp—which would lead you into quick-sand, to be swallowed down, slime covering your nose and mouth until you vanish. Or would you float like corpses of Partisans? The voice of an old man shouted: "Halt! Stop. Stop it at once. Poachers will be shot." Mud under a willow bulged and stirred. Magda shrieked. Two huge heads and shoulders emerged, black slime oozing from heads covered with black bathing caps. One of them was pointing a pistol. "Get out of here with your dogs. You're trespassing on the Moor-bath Institute land."

Jan raised his right arm. "Heil Hitler! We're on maneuver. Going to fight in the war."

The mud-people raised lazy fat right arms, exposing naked fat bellies. One with big wabbling bosoms clamored: "Franzl, put the pistol away—You're from Waldruh—*nicht wahr?*"

Jan didn't answer. The troop stood still. "We're from Waldruh!" Liese said.

"No wonder. Dear hearts. Pretty little dolly! Look at the costume—sweet! They're not going to send you to the front? Waldruh. Don't you remember Franzl? That man in the art-cave told us. Only beautiful children. She smiled and mud oozed off her fat face. "Very, very special."

Jan, stood at attention, holding the flag high, but said nothing. The troop remained silent.

"What an experience to actually get to see them!"

Dogs were barking again at the edge of the swamp. "Enough now. You've seen them. They're attracting the verdammten hounds. *Verschind!* Get lost. All of you!" Later, when the troop stopped at a broken bench to wipe mud off their feet and legs with wads of moss, they saw a weathered sign:

NUDIST CULTURE
MOOR-BATH CURE INSTITUTE

STRICTLY PRIVATE!
ADMITTANCE FORBIDDEN.

The lost souls in the woods had materialized as fat rich old people—the doctor had mentioned them to Frau Faser—hiding out, wallowing in mud, walking naked through the woods to get young again, while the young kept on dying for Fuhrer and Fatherland.

The troop trudged on behind Jan, carrying backpacks stuffed full of clothing. Liese, who followed behind Jan, tripped over her shoelace, fell forward, and scraped her knees. She didn't cry out. It was big Magda who whimpered. "She's holding us up. Send her back." Werner went over to stand beside her. "They'll all get bread and potato soup. We could still go back and say that Liese got lost in the woods, had a fall, and we had to go find her."

Liese put spit on her knee. "I'm not going back. The Inspector is there. I'm going to my mother!"

"Must be far away." Mimi said.

"No, not far away. At Auntie's farm at the bottom of the hill," Liese said.

But there was no farm in the valley. The path ended under an old stone bridge. What next? Which way? Even Jan became uneasy. How can you know where to go, when you don't know where you are? They stopped as though the open country road were a barrier.

At moments of uncertainty, at Hitler School, there was always an inspection. So Jan made them comb their hair, wipe their boots, dust off their uniforms, and line up for his roll call. They hadn't been allowed to cry and didn't know how to laugh, while Jan invented forbidden flaws. Siegfried, bendy legs, arms too long. Horst Albino spook. Werner, the curly with the dark roots. Magda the griper. Sad and sorry Mimi. Liese Faser's dwarf.

Liese stood tall as a valuable child with them, in her frilly dress and hat. They remained stern as statues, never more perfect. How could they give up who they had become in Hitler School, when they didn't remember or didn't like who they'd once been?

"Listen!" Mimi took Magda's hand.

"You always hear things!" Siegfried said.

Now they all heard the rumbling. Jan ordered
everyone to get down into the ditch. Liese, his
scout, ran to the edge of the road at once: A car
had taken her away, now she needed one to take her
back. So she jumped up and down and kept waving to
the covered truck. It slowed down. Stopped. The
driver did not get out. She smiled, standing proud
and tall in her big sweater, frilly dress, and
woman's hat, "Heil Hitler! You a food truck?"

The young soldier smiled. Some of his front
teeth were missing. His face was dusty and freckled. "No such luck, shorty."

"Will you take me home to Mother?"

"Where is she?"

"At the bottom of the field in the big white
farm."

"Get in, then. I'm from a farm too. Just tell me
when to stop."

"Will you take all of us?"

The children popping up from the ditch were the
most cheerful sight he had seen for a long time.
Six of them, in black and white uniforms. One of
the girls in her teens and a man-sized young boy
wearing a hook-cross armband carried the flag.
Clean, blond children.

"All brothers and sisters?"

They tittered and the big boy ordered them to
shut up. "From the same school," he said. "It was
destroyed by the enemy, and..."

"We are going to my mother," the little one
interrupted.

The soldier told Jan to hide the flag in the
back, and told the troop to be careful with the
crates as they piled into the back of the truck.
Liese in front with Jan lost in admiration of his
black fingernails, the long unshaven chin, the gap
from the missing front tooth which made a whistling
sound while he talked and talked about bombed
cities, the stench, millions of homeless on the
march to nowhere. A camp where he had seen mountains of naked bodies. The American army advancing
fast, blowing everything up. He had heard of the
Russians, worse than animals. His red-rimmed,
bloodshot eyes staring ahead on the empty road
while he drank Schnapps out of a white bottle and
gave some to Jan. Cheered up and shared his

sausage, bread and hard cheese, and stopped to give
some to the children in the back.

Liese said, "Halt!" each time she saw a farm at
the bottom of a field.

"Poor little one," said the soldier. "Wish I
could stop at a farm myself." His name was Peter.
He talked about his mother and father, their large
family, young brothers and sisters. A comrade like
a brother, killed by dive bombers.

When they drove through a village, he said,
mothers would all be waiting for sons who'd been
sent off to kill other women's sons in foreign
countries. Nothing but a blood bath. "A shame. What
a shame!"

Jan wanted to know what he carried at the back
of his truck. He didn't know. It was all sealed up
in metal boxes. "Dangerous shit!" He laughed.
"Doesn't make you laugh. Poor children. So serious.
Eine Schande. A shame!"

"Driving toward Hamburg?" Jan asked.

"Who knows where I'll end up?" Farms where mothers must be waiting flitted by. He stopped at one
to get water, some more bread and cheese. He carried fuel and water to feed the truck. Then they
rattled on, for two hours, two days, or three?
Lise's eyes got tired from looking hard for
Auntie's farm and closed. Distant thunder of guns
woke her up. They had reached a military checkpoint
not far from the front. The soldier had no idea
they were so close. You could see guards at a road-
block in the distance, a hut and two trucks. "Not a
single flag," he said. "They must be ready to
quit." He gave the children hunks of his bread,
sausage, and money. "Stay behind the truck, when
you jump down. Don't let them see you. *Verschwind*,
go, disappear."

"Wait, wait!" Jan blew his whistle. "You've got
our flag!"

But the soldier drove on to the checkpoint.
"You're supposed to die for your flag," Werner
said.

"Are we going to die without it?" Magda asked,
as they faced scorched fields with burned-out
shacks, collapsed barns, and dry cow dung. Not a
mountain. Not even a hillock. Her eyes filled with
forbidden tears.

When Jan blew his whistle, Liese lined up behind him. The troop grumbled, but fell in as he trotted them toward a charred orchard where they ate unripe rotten apples and relieved themselves politely behind the remains of a stone wall. Girls first, as they had been taught.

"They sitting down by now at Waldruh to have their soup and bread for supper." That was Mimi.

"Shut your trap, stupid girl," Jan said.

"We're not supposed to talk like that," Magda told him.

At that very moment came an unearthly roaring and clanking. The troop fell back in horror and stood aghast as the first tanks came rattling and grinding around the curve of the road. Liese ran to Jan and stood on her toes to make herself heard. "See what you've done!" As though his gruff talk had brought on the thrill and the terror of the division of tanks.

"Down on the ground!" Jan shouted.

When the first tank stopped at the road-block, a droning above the clouds came closer, grew into blasting roar of giant birds from hell, blackening the sky as they swooped, relieving themselves of black droppings. The small house, trucks, and soldiers at the checkpoint exploded.

"Don't move. Stay down!"

"Our Truck. "What happened? Peter soldier. What happened to him?" Liese called out.

"Died with my flag," Jan said. A tree by the road burst into flames that spread hissing along the stubble field as fast as the troop could run. Mimi's sock caught fire. She jumped into a puddle and ran faster. A tank on the road went poof, on fire, like Mimi's sock, but no one put it out.

"I hurt. I'm burned!" Frau Faser would have smacked Mimi for crying, and treated the wound afterward. They'd run away to be free. Free to be burned? Flames sizzled as more roaring monsters darkened the sky.

Tanks burned, three barns were on fire. The troop gathered around a dead owl beside the hedge, its wings outspread, huge eyes. No blood. Did the bird die of fright? A dead mouse lay on the ground beside it.

"Wohin? Where to?" Magda clamored.

Mimi grabbed Jan's arm and pointed. "I see a house. A house. Water. A river." She walked ahead of Jan, but the little houses seemed to recede into the far distance as the explosions came closer. No river was in sight. Bombs made deep craters in the field you wanted to hide in, but Jan signaled with his whistle. Legs tired, mouth dry, you had to keep going!

The sun broke through the cloud, shining finally on a small, burned-out village on a dusty road. The river was a gray ribbon in the distance. They found the crushed remains of trucks. Two stained helmets. One huge boot. By the time they reached the first house it was getting dark. "No lights. No lights." Jan sent Liese down empty lanes calling: "Anyone there? Please come out!"

One of the houses had only three walls, half the roof, and a kitchen stove. They found a box of matches in a tin box. Three big candles. Half a sack of potatoes in the cellar and a pile of empty sacks to keep them warm. Two rain barrels full of water. Magda found turnips which they threw to each other and then devoured. They saw people staggering across distant fields. Jan made the troop go down the ladder into the cellar. Liese slipped into an old potato sack with Mimi. Something woke her up. What if the farmers were coming back here to their house? She groped for the ladder. "Jan! Jan. You there?" No answer.

She climbed up on a shelf, where a window used to be, let her legs dangle, and sucked her thumb, while an endless thousand-legger of people in the distance trudged darkly under a glowing sky. And then it started up again. The bashing and banging tanks, the rat-tat-tatrattrrr. Lightning, bursts of thunder and the thousand-legger vanished. Liese ran out into the field. "Jan, Jan. Where are you? Come back!" Then she prayed,

> "Fold my hands, bow my head,
> Thank Fuhrer for my daily bread.
> Fuhrer, please keep them away.
> Make Jan come back."

Chapter 8

SHORELAND

Well done! It might be faster for you to reread for changes and cuts you yourself want to make along with my notes. We don't have much time. Let me know if you have any problem.

Her editor must never know of her problems. She feels feverish, hunted, and haunted. Cheeks glow, the printer pounds, so does her heart. The system ping-peeps now and again. Printout completed, she quickly tears pages apart, trims the edges, and crams the manuscript into the mailing envelope. The world as it was and as it is now remains in a mess, just like this house, this room. In her frenzy she sticks old letters and old folders with clippings she had saved for years into a carton full of old magazines from her days as a model, when she had smiled on command. Even the German letters she had received, after her Munich Presse interview "BEAUTIFUL AMERICAN MODEL IN SEARCH OF LOST MOTHER." Instead of hearing from Mother or relatives, she had letters from men of varied nationalities, looking for money, marriage, American passports, and much sex. The response from three women who claimed to have lost children was equally opportunistic. By throwing all of this out, clearing away her old disappointment, she was sweeping away the evidence of an obsession with her own childhood.

She does hesitate when she comes across clippings and articles from the demonstrations against the Vietnam War. Make love, not war! Riots on campus. Marches on Washington for integration. But also the segregation of the the young from their parents, during gigantic celebrations the new beat of tribal tunes, celebrating life or death in change-partner games during the roller-coaster high and low of drugs. Communes had formed and failed.

No need to turn away from jolly old Gramp, who merely reminded them that Liz had already been through all kinds of hell. So had Chris. He always admired anything they did, ignored whatever they didn't do and let them have their way. He pointed out to her that her abductions had been to her advantage. "All's well that ends well." She hoists the old carton to the back door, ready for the recycle van. Takes a shower and dresses in jeans Mike has outgrown and the great dark-blue sweater Bonnie knitted for him a couple of years ago. She wakes up Chris. "They're sending Mike home tomorrow morning. The founder of Grove Academy called. His voice gives me the jitters."

"Mike's voice gives me the jitters!" Chris punches a pillow in a rage. "Are they mad? They specialize in character development. Sending him home to those misfits in Harbor Square is not going to develop a thing ."

"He'd be home for Outreach next week anyway."

"Outreach! What next? I don't even want to know what he's been up to. In between being thrown out of schools he's suspended or on vacation and you're always so bloody pleased to have him home, damn you! Always on the side of the kids."

"Well, kids had been my only family when Gramp found me for you."

"That's history. You behaved yourself. Mike is a menace. The damned school is punishing me, not him. They're not doing their job at Grove. What are we paying for? I'm going to put a stop to the check I mailed to them for their building fund! We'll be lucky if he doesn't end up in jail while he's here." He thrusts a pillow that reeks of his "Moustache" cologne at Liz.

She throws it back. An early habit of turning arguments into a game.

"You know Mike's roommate, Caleb Fairfield. Last time they suspended him he got off the bus in Boston and vanished for two days. I think I'll drive into Boston tomorrow and pick Mike up at the bus station."

"No, you don't. There's a storm warning for tomorrow and the next day. God knows when you'd get back. I feel bloody awful. Must be coming down with something." Chris pulls the quilt up over his head.

When Mike is suspended or expelled from boarding school, Chris usually says he is sick and stays in bed, while Liz always goes and buys too much health food at the Coop. She loads trash and also the box full of old papers into the station wagon to drop off at the dump. Nothing is ever ordinary anymore. Rushing dark water, the bright sky, the shrieking birds. She emerges from her writing like a commorant from the deep. Trying to remember and also imagine Frau Faser, the children and the Inspector, what really happened to her long ago she is ready to marvel at a hometown teeming with eccentrics, each considering everyone else 'different,' which makes for good gossip in front of Dan's Coffee Shop among the usual cluster of mostly rotund ladies in mannish clothes, high on coffee and sweet morning glory muffins as she is on one banana and a head full of ideas.

She drives past the town beach, swerving around the white mongrel Jezebel, who always lies in the middle of Main Street. Waves thunder over the gravel, bashing the rocks of the big stone house at South Cove, which is lit up like a cruise ship. Totally renovated. New owners must have moved in. Wealthy strangers have been both welcome and unwelcome here in Shoreland from way back. Bringing change, danger, and loot, as pirates did in their days.

At Emmet Gray's hundred-year-old house, the tricolor French flag flaps in the wind. One of the most popular bachelors in town when he was president of the Shoreland bank, he used to tell Liz he was going to take a long trip to Europe after he retired. But then—with all those trigger-happy crooks, lose women, dope fiends, hijackers around—he decided to stay put and became a unique stationary bike travel buff. Riding his stationary bike at the bay window every day now except Sunday, he listens to language and history tapes and checks his own slow progress on the road map of France with an odometer; at the same time he checks for cars speeding past his house and reports them to the police on his portable phone without getting off his bike. Last year after he did Hungary, he lectured about it at the public library, and brought nine speed devils to justice. No matter how busy an old New England bachelor may be with himself, he usually has his missions. Liz has more than one reason to slow down.

Emmet waves urgently from his bike and taps on the window. The moment she pulls over to stop he comes rushing out in a scarlet sweat suit, his plump face flushed under the black biker's helmet. He's always eager to talk about Grove Academy, where Caleb, the nephew he loves, is repeating his second year for the second time. "The boy was coming to stay with me next week for Outreach. Now that Grimes fellow's on the war path. Yessircc! Had the boy locked up in jail last night. Parents in St. Kits. So I put a call in to my lawyer to get him out. But what if he runs away? Just had to get on my bike, or I'd worry myself sick."

When Liz tells him that Mike got into trouble too, he feels better, but she feels worse as she speeds off to the dump and makes a sharp turn at the gate with the big Sanitary Landfill sign, but comes to a full stop at the "Weather-house." She feels like a tourist in her own life marveling at the house Anka and Bruno Wronovska built when Liz and Chris were in first grade. The Poles had been "displaced persons" and Gramp talked to them behind closed doors before he hired them. Anka worked as the cook-housekeeper and Bruno as gardener-handyman. The only piece of America the Poles could afford to buy was the patch near the dump, and they made their down payment with pieces of gold Anka had brought with her sewn into her kerchief. Emmet, history buff, president of the Shoreland bank at that time, had helped the refugees get a building permit.

Anka had fished the little "Weather-house" out of Chris's wastepaper basket, to show Bruno the kind of house she wanted to live in. This morning Liz suddenly remembers that the Alpine "Weather-house" had really been a present Gramp gave to Liz, but Chris had thrown it away, after he had yanked out both the bad-weather-man with the umbrella and the fair-weather-woman with the basket for his train station. Liz came to think of Anka as the fair- weather-woman and Bruno as the bad-weather-guy.

Liz might well have forgotten Mother in the house at the bottom of the field, the black car, Frau Faser, the escape, the shelter, everything Gramp wanted her to forget, if she hadn't talked German with Anka and Bruno. Their little secret. Since several Shoreland sons had been killed in the war, Anka was careful never to speak a word of enemy German at the Plant house, or anywhere in town. Europe was never mentioned. After

Bruno vanished, kids scared each other silly with his ghost, because some-one whispered that Anka had buried dead Bruno under trash to save funeral expenses. Liz and Chris were already in college when Anka passed away. It was sad to see the magic house boarded up. Now Walter, known as the major of the dump, has moved in, got rid of the underbrush, and repaired the roof, and the porch. He admires the way Anka and Bruno had built and furnished their solid little house with recycled material long before anyone ever thought of such. His magisterial tiger cat sits on the stoop. Anka had adopted a one-eyed cat someone had dumped, a goat no one wanted, and a noisy bantam cock. Now a husky is drinking out of Anka's trough. Walter pets animals and talks to them and everyone else— Anka never did. She had secrets. Easy to understand for a young child who had been a secret and learned to keep secrets from the beginning.

Liz is thinking of how everything has reversed. Adults now frequently become victims of teen-age secrets and obsessions. After she unloads the bag of trash onto the pile she starts worrying out loud like Frau Faser— what will I do if Mike doesn't show up? What if he runs away and we can't find him? By the time she gets to the Food Coop, she doesn't even remem-ber putting the box of old papers into the recycle trailer. Could be lack of sleep, but the moment Liz enters the wooden shack she comes around and luxuriates in the fragrance of whole-grain, sourdough breads, freshly ground coffee. Young couples got together and started the Coop. There is raw milk, cheese, granola, and other fiber cereals, organic almonds and raisins, sprouts, herbs, pasta, organic fruit and vegetables, rotten fertile eggs, tofu burgers, and a carnival of shoppers.

Everyone stocks up on food when there is a storm warning. Even the official witch of Salem in a long black cloak with a sharp-eyed young male escort is out shopping. Middle-aged mothers, determinedly into macrobi-otics and fitness, dress as flower children and carry pale 'soy-milk babies' on their backs, while bearded boy-fathers mother rosy infants. Liz leans on her shopping cart thinking of how trends—good or bad—turn into obses-sions when neighbor Ellen comes through the door in her formal dark-brown business suit, glossy waist-long brown hair flying around her in the draft. Ellen, has a doctorate in psychology. "You look great again, Liz." School psychologist, happily divorced mother of two wild grade-school boys, Ellen is never tired and always looks great. "Single parent pot-luck dinner coming up. I'm making fish stew with a lot of herbs and vegetables. French bread, hot-spiced wine. Hope we get enough snow. Some of them like to come on cross-country skis. They'll bring the ice cream!" When Ellen started the single parents' association, she introduced everyone to Beatrice Strout dance therapy. You can hear potluck music and laughter from her cottage when they meet to dance their problems away.

"How do you feel?" Ellen asks while she bends over the organic fruit baskets. Her professional tone of voice triggers anxiety. "I'm not too sure." Did she or didn't she put that box full of old papers in the recycle van? "I feel disoriented. Worried too. They're sending Mike home. He's suspended again."

"You always worry so much about him, Liz. Remember when he started school and you went with him as a volunteer? The games you used to play with kids and dogs during recess? A riot."

Other volunteer mothers had been drawn into fascination with the then new "'open classroom." The turmoil and intrusion of each one of twenty-five children doing or not doing any activity they chose, while team-leader teachers took the team of teachers out of class to talk about education. Liz, who preferred kids to school policies and politics, would side with the children and even defend dogs when they joined into games during recess in the play ground.

Ellen is squeezing organic peaches, and picking rosy ripe ones. "I always get a kick out of Mike," she says. "Last time he was suspended, he gave me a lecture on the lack of male role models in my house." She has a wonderfully wicked smile. "And listen to this: my hyperactive dog has become the male role model for my boys since their father moved out. This makes them hyper like him and bite teachers." Ellen shrugs back her long dark hair with a squeaky laugh. "By the way, the guy who spent all that money fixing up South Cove has a girl at Grove Academy. Not his child. He's a guardian or something like that. Arthur Eckert. Bonnie introduced us. A lot has happened while you were sick. Wait till you hear about Bonnie. Born again. I'm not supposed to tell. She wants to surprise you. What would we all do without Bonnie?" She clamps her hand over her mouth laughing herself towards the pasta shelf. "You'll like Eckert. He's slightly European. An older man. Quite amazing."

This is high praise, because Ellen likes to be both amazed and amazing, but she always plays it safe. She had asked Liz to let Mike go to grade school by himself. Chris was glad Liz stopped going to school with him.

After the fourth grade Mike was sent to private country day school like any other Plant and then on to prep school, where his career as trouble-making trouble-shooter began.

"You're well again and you're writing," Ellen says as Liz heads for the checkout counter. "Don't worry so much. You're looking just great."

Excessive reassurance from Ellen, the psychologist, indicates that she thinks you're a bit off. "Spaced out," Mike and his friends always say when they forget whether they have or have not done what they set out to do. So Liz drives back to the dump to check on her box, but the gate is already closed. She takes Hawthorn Street on her way home, which is always well plowed because the head of public works lives there. Houses here remain white, shutters black—none of that new canary yellow or Disneyland pink. Christmas wreaths stay on the front door well into summer. Anglophilia— genetic, or transmitted by Channel 2 *Masterpiece Theater*, perhaps both—is endearingly odd in this part of the country which celebrates its proud history of having been the first to throw the British out.

Two boys are shoveling old Mrs. Libby's steps while she watches them and waves her cane at squirrels on her bird feeder. Mr. Wittier is shoveling snow off his sidewalk. A few snow flakes drift over rippled water in Harbor Square. Kids sitting and perching on the two benches have the light hair, strong bodies, good features of "valuable children", but do their best to appear worthless and shabby in ragged, bleached-out unisex denim.

"Hi, Liz!" Del, a teen-age Madonna, spends much time at the benches, since she stopped going to school. Hands folded over a big, big belly she likes to show off, to hide how scared she is, which must be far more lonely than hiding away among women on an auntie's farm. A disgrace was not an outcast. Svenson—a determined outcast since he dropped out of school several years ago—is now the old man at the benches. Legally of drinking age, he is homeless and gets arrested quite regularly for drinking in public. Complexion like raw steak from sleeping in a hammock or shacks in the woods. The weather is cool, no more than fifty-five degrees in the sun, but his tattered sweater is tied around the middle. Do-good women still baby the orphan-boy along. Someone must have knitted that sweater for him. This morning his baby blue eyes look dazed. He defies charity from women but craves it as he craves drugs and alcohol.

"What's up with Mike?" asks puny Tom, perching on the back of a bench, braces glinting in his permanent grin. Known as the Tick, since he is ever ready to fasten onto you with questions for new gossip.

"He's coming home tomorrow," Liz says.

"For good?" Elgar, Mike's best friend, likes to lean against the lamp-post, to support his elongated upper body. He has grown unevenly and there is something painfully uneven between the way Elgar's composes tunes on the piano that you can't forget, and his drunken sprees.

"For ten days or so."

Svenson bends over to take a swig from a flask he keeps in the top of his combat boots. Mike gave him that idea, to keep him from being arrested for drinking in public. Mike educates them on how to get protection from the law before they break it. He's great at police brutality, which infuriates little Officer Dutch, who likes to catch them. Having a Liz on the bench is protection while Mike is away.

In gradeschool, kids used to tease Mike with "Na-nana-na- you've an adopted Mom." So Mike established Liz with: "Na-nana-na. My mom's a 'Naturized Alien'; Yours isn't!" Liz has somehow maintained this undefined distinction.

While Tick holds forth to Del in his girlish voice about natural child-birth, which he watched on TV, Del lets Liz feel the baby move inside her belly. Tick tries to put his hand on the belly too, but Elgar swats him away.

Del says she can't stay on with her Mom. She is going to build an adobe house in New Mexico for her baby. But first she's got to find Jiggers in San Francisco. Her voice rises and falls as she embellishes her dreams and hopes with the profanities, which misunderstood fathers and mothers now use in an attempt to make themselves at least heard.

When the Cragley twins drive up at the benches to show off yet another new rusty old Corvette, they doff leather hats to Liz in unison. The kids all get up to admire the bumper stickers: PEACE STARTS IN THE HOME. LOCAL CULTURE—YOGURT FROM SHADY BROOK FARM. Del asks them about a ride to "Frisco."

The Cragleys promise they'll ask around. They have identical blank expressions, big bovine eyes, and talk like the good guys in old Westerns. Since you can't tell the Cragleys apart, they're able to share a job and take turns working in the fish-processing plant, frying fish. Better than frying your brains out, they'll tell Liz. They are good at telling you what you want to hear. On weekends they sell beer and pot to kids—just to be helpful and keep the Mafia and hard drugs out of their grandmother's home town.

They never deal when Liz is around.

The kids are leaning against the car. Del is worried, because she doesn't have an address for Jigger. Maybe he doesn't have one. She's passing around the dog-eared picture of a California Jigger in harem attire. "Long braids. He's grown awesome braids." No one is watching when Officer Dutch pops out from behind the ivy-covered exhaust pipe of the new sewer system. The Cragley car takes off. Kids scatter in all directions, and Liz puts her arm around Del, mother-to-be, and they shelter behind the paper store.

"Not to worry. " Del says. "Dutchy wouldn't stick me into lock-up and have me go into labor. He even gave me a ride in his own car, when I didn't want to go home."

"Don't run away!"

"I'm scared of the midwife Mom got. She prays too much. I'll be OK with Jiggers." Just have to make it to Frisco before the baby comes."

"You can come to my house, or go to Bonnie anytime. Then there is Ellen Burns, too."

When Liz gets back to Harbor Square with Del, the others are already at the benches. Tick grinning from his perch, points at her car. Dutch has stuck a parking ticket under her windshield wiper.

Running away has never been an escape, Liz tells herself. Too young for Jan's troop, Liese the little one had come in handy as his scout. Too old for Mike's troop, Liz the mother comes in handy as protection. She speeds home and flees to her desk. The need to be needed never changes, she writes.

Chapter 9
GETTING THE CALL

The Children's Crusade might be of interest.

Harriman

During the era when crusading knights plundered and
murdered their way to Jerusalem and back, children
in central Europe trying to get away from godless
wars took each other by the hand and walked towards
the sea, to reach the Holy Land. Most of them
starved and perished. Those who did reach the sea
were sold as white slaves.

Liz flops down on her unmade bed in a muddle between Jan's troop and
Mike's troop at Harbor Square. This entire day feels like an unmade lumpy
bed. Does Harriman, assistant editor, recent Yale graduate, expect a Hansel
and Gretel-type bestseller with children's crusade overtones? Children aban-
doned by parents, or children, born again, abandoning parents?

How many of the Hitler School children had walked away from
Mother when the German cars picked them up? Vogel never went looking
for children, he spotted them. Jan, the Norwegian, was already nine or ten
years old when Vogel took him away. The youngest son of a busy country

doctor, outsmarting his four big brothers must have been fine preparation for the leadership boy in Hitler School. He was a schemer. Little Liese fitted his strategies. He let her cuddle up against him at night. His skin had the natural fragrance of sweet milk. Sometimes when she had a bad dream she'd cling to him and call him Mother.

Lise's prayer had worked. The smell of fried bacon woke her up. Jan had returned. It was still dark. The troop had gathered around the rekindled fire behind him. He was browning a mountain of bacon in a real frying pan, dressed up in a man's belted black leather coat, which hung down to the ground.

"German refugees. Dead by now. Most of them," he told the troop. "They don't need anything anymore."

"The damned Americans shot them!" Magda shouted in a Faser voice.

"Panzer S.S.," Jan said.

"Why?" Liese asked.

"Because they were refugees."

You could be shot either for what you were or what you were not. "Why is it so quiet now?" she asked. Flames flickered and bacon sizzled. "What happened to the war?"

In response, Jan took his hook-cross armband out of his pocket and threw it into the fire. Flames shot up from it like dancing demons. The children backed away and gaped, then they started to leap about as though the demons had entered them, pouncing on the bacon, the hunks of bread. Lots of loot. Schnapps Magda took away from the boys prancing around Jan. Ready to go back with him to get more. Mimi and Liese stayed behind as they came and went. Blood on their hands dragging possessions wrestled from stiff clinging hands. They grabbed more food, gulped liquor and they threw up, as the greed of Hitler's war passed onto them the degradation of foraging among the murdered. Then they began to fight over the treasures. Big girls bedecked with pearls and gold. Lise's prize, a big woman's jacket with a gold swastika pin, hung down to her boots. The big girls tried to tear it away. She hid behind Jan clutching inside the left pocket the clean handkerchief embroidered with a red rose.

Boys relieved themselves among the trees squirting around.When Werner picked up Horst's sack,

Siegfried got between them and delivered punches at random. Boys at war, fighting, kicking, pulling each other's hair, with the crude violence the master race used to become masters.

Liese ran to Jan. "Why don't you stop them?"

He shook his head, went behind a tree to vomit. The fire was dying down when he finally collapsed on a thick blanket holding onto the backpack which held his pickings. Liese fitted herself against him inside the big coat he took from a dead man. He reeked of bacon and stale smoke and Schnapps. "Ah. Hilde. Here you are!"

"Liese. The scout."

"She was a great scout. The best looking one, but she'd fall down and have fits when she got scared. Faser handed her over to the Inspector." Jan heaved like old auntie as he sighed himself to sleep. His knee felt like stone.

The next day, the troop, wearing gold watches that didn't tick dragged their backpacks and suitcases along the dusty road. The sun was going down by the time they reached the river. Horst broke rank and ran ahead, lowering himself down to the water and lapping like a horse or a cow. Jan and the others scooped water up in the palms of their hands. Boys started to splash. Jan, who had learned to swim in Norway, warned them that they'd drown if they fell in.

Liese wandered off by herself alongside the river, and found a bridge hidden by weeping willows. They crossed, clambered up a steep path and came to a brick wall, where Jan made a stirrup of his hands and hoisted her up. She saw a brick house and a fountain with the statue of a child, red and yellow roses.

Liese knocked on the carved door and called, "Heil Hitler!" Then she stood on her toes and reached up and pressed down the ornate doorhandle. "Unlocked." It creaked open and she called "Heil--"

Jan pounced on her. "No more Hitler! If anyone comes to the door, tell them you're looking for Mutter."

She opened the heavy door and called. *"Guten Morgen!* I'm looking for Mutter."

"Guten Morgen" the troop chanted.

"Gruess Gott." That was Mimi.

A brown felt hat and a green one with a feather hung on the coat stand. A note glued to the mirror said: TAKE CARE OF THIS DEAR HOUSE. GOD BLESS YOU.

In the house, blessed by God, they again followed Hitler School rules, walking quietly from room to room, touching bright flowers on the wallpaper and the bedspreads. So many soft beds, quilts, and pillows. Mimi kneeled down beside a pink feather bed and burst into tears. She stared up to the picture of a kneeling girl looking up to a sky full of angels. "How can there be angels, when there are bombers in the sky?"

"Stop that. The bombers have gone," Jan said. "Get up at once!"

No one had ever talked about heaven or hell at Waldruh. Why bring up such foreign notions now. No need for Mimi to look ahead in this dear house. She seemed frightened and was ignored, because she coughed when you weren't supposed to have colds. They may have stayed on for just a week, or perhaps a month. No one counted the days. A game they played in the garden, holding hands and going around and around, faster and faster until they fell down with laughter, would go on as long as they lived–in the circle-dance of memory.

Now and again aircraft passed through the heavens as mere specks. No one gave Mimi's question a thought, until the flock of monster birds again roared over them, followed by rumbling and thunderbolt explosions. Bombs fell. The earth shook. They hid at the edge of the river until the noise moved into the distance. You could hear insects humming among wildflowers left in the torn field. Birds chirped. Liese found two lady bugs and wanted to show them to Mimi. "Where are you, Mimi. Mimi?"

❋❋❋

The phone rings. Stops. Rings again. "Mike!"

"It's only me," Bonnie says.

Liz again tries to thank Bonnie for soups and fruit she brought while she was sick, but Bonnie never likes to be thanked.

"So much has happened. Well, you just won't believe it." A giggle and a pause. "Since day before yesterday I have a career too. I'm no longer the same. Am I bothering you, Liz?"

"It's OK But—"

"How did it all happen? I got 'the call.' "

Did children get 'the call' when they walked toward the Holy Land and came to a bad end? How about the toddler led on by a Fifinella? Did Jan get the call? How about kids who run away to California?

"God's will. Imagine. In Baby Land. You know, the Linden Tree Mall. Jeff doesn't want me to talk about any of it! I was buying a set for Del's baby shower. Poor child. Boyfriend vanished in California." A phone rings. "One of my lines. Arthur Eckert. You won't believe it. I have started a help and answering service. You mind holding?"

She loves helping strangers and had looked out for Liz —that little transplant—from the moment Gramp returned to Shoreland with the two children. But then the Codgets used to work for Plants from way back when—as Bonnie puts it. The old cottage and the barn, which had been deeded to them by the Plants, had come down to Bonnie. After she married Jeff Moonbin, they converted the barn and kept ten acres of land. Ellen's husband, the surgeon, bought the cottage and left it to Ellen after he moved out.

"Booked flight 201 to New York for you, Arthur. Don't worry. Everything all set." She gives him her blessing and hangs up. "Imagine, he says I take the place of a secretary. Here, I just started my own answering and help service. You'll get it free, Liz! So you can write your book. Jeff doesn't want me to talk about any of it. The way Chris acts about your book."

Bonnie takes another call. Liz can hear her give enthusiastic advice on how to make soup with a pressure cooker. "Here I am, Liz. Where was I? Well, I was buying this gift in Baby Land. It was Saturday around three thirty. Sometimes when I stay around, mothers lets me hold a baby. You know about me and babies! I always make them smile. This dumpy little mother carried hers on her back. I couldn't take my eyes off that child. Those knowing deep eyes and curls like a halo. Something came over me. I didn't even try to make him smile. When that baby stared at me, I had to hold onto the counter. Jesus, and all the goodness in the world was shining out of that face."

Bonnie is fifty years old and giggles like a schoolgirl when she feels she is out of her depth or yours. "I knew I'd never feel ashamed of being so tall, and lonely for little babies anymore. I was on cloud nine. Can't even remember whether the mother left before I did. It was just meant to be, Liz. You know my old V.W. van. Why should it start breaking down at the Whale's Jaw Motel? I rolled to a stop. There were all those cars. You know that big blinking Water Bed sign on that long pole? Well, it was covered over with "Deliverance service and baked-bean supper, six dollars." The blinking Bar and Grill sign turned off. New owners trying to change their image, with this out-of-town prophet from Tennessee.

"Anyway, I pussyfoot around looking for a phone to call Triple A. No pool tables! Slot machines covered over with white sheets. You should have seen it. Place was packed. Christians even standing against the wall. Having the best time. Belting out hymns, or just making some up, playing along on guitars and tambourines, and jigging, clapping hands. Babies they'd brought along crying to the music. You won't believe the way sick people went up to be healed. The moment that young prophet touched their foreheads they fell over and were caught by a big man from Newton. This born-again owner of a liquor store. Everyone praying for the Second Coming, and me praying up a storm for Jeff, because he has been mail ordering more and more shoes. Anyway, I couldn't keep my mind on Jeff or the prophet, because a phone kept ringing at the desk near the door and this woman kept asking: 'Can I help you?' A lovely voice. 'I'll be glad to pass on the message.'

"I got the message, Liz. Can I help you? That's what I wanted to say from now on. Guess what. I went out and tried the van after the deliverance service. It started. Got me back to the mall. No problem. So I could buy myself a how to book, two phones, a file cabinet, and steel shelves. And you know what? That van has been running perfect since I started Bonnie's Message and Help Service." She sighs. "But Jeff's none too pleased."

Bonnie had used most of the money she got from the sale of the cottage to buy Jeff the hardware store he always wanted, while Jeff refused to adopt the baby Bonnie always wanted.

Liz says, "Mike's coming home tomorrow."

Bonnie lets out a "Glory be!" she must have picked up from the prophet and promises to bake some pies. One of her phones is ringing.

For years Bonnie did Jeff's bookkeeping, filled the orders, and attracted customers by giving advice to gardeners. Now, all of a sudden, she has branched out. Liz is reminded that Chris has branched out too when she goes down to put the slow-cooking roast beef into the oven. From the kitchen window she sees his beloved yellow Audi standing at Ellen's door, fog lights on, door ajar. Sad, like a neglected dog. This has not happened before. He usually fusses over the Audi as he fusses over himself, looking for ailments.

Long ago, when Liz's career as a popular model and her writing courses at the New School had given her brother Chris symptoms, he had found Geraldine, the night nurse. Now, after all those years, Liz's writing *Stolen Child* has made him turn to Ellen. Liz keeps herself busy, furiously chopping onions and celery, but her heart isn't in it. Impersonating the person she used to be, she stuffs the washing machine with too many sheets and towels. Finally, when she can't stand it anymore, she throws one of Mike's old parkas over her shoulders, picks up a snow shovel, and runs out the back door and down the lane to turn the Audi lights off.

At that moment a car turns into Ellen's driveway. A man gets out in the dim light. He stops at the Audi, turns the headlights off, and closes the door without a sound. Deliberate as a robot. Mission fulfilled, he goes back into his own car, turns his foglights on, drives away, and is swallowed by dense fog.

The reluctance to intrude on Ellen marks him as an outsider. Her patients, as well as old and new friends—both male and female including her ever-expanding divorced parents' support group—drop in on her, as Chris did just now, unless her shutters are closed. Tonight her windows are all brightly lit. Liz has just shut the kitchen door when Chris emerges and gets into the Audi.

Ellen often quotes LOVE AND LEARN: "You can't own anyone." But Beatrice Strout also has a chapter on owning yourself. Liz pushes snow aside as she runs back to the kitchen, her mind in a fog, about the self-ownership of writing *Stolen Child*, which has been sending Chris to Ellen and might set Liz up for grabs once more—this time by readers. Do writers get "the call" and have faith to feel safe like Bonnie? Uncertainty washes over her in ceaseless waves, where anything strange seems to be familiar, and everything familiar seems strange.

Chapter 10
OUTREACH

Soft flute music on the kitchen radio is interrupted by another storm warning: eight to twenty inches, but you never know about the weather in New England, and Shoreland sits at the tip of a tongue of land well out into the Atlantic. Waves pound the rocks below the house, where clusters of mussels must be clinging to their home-rock; gulls cry out, and the calm voice on the kitchen radio speaks of a kidnaping in Lebanon, an accident on Route 128, a boy missing in Waltham. Cheerful, matter of fact, a young man reporting everyday awful things that have happened, are going on, will happen—to someone else.

When she looks up from washing carrots, the window above the sink shines like a TV set with the picture of Mike wading through a snowbank. Turn on the light, and this Waldruh vision of a boy in deep snow would vanish.

He ignores the path she dug. He always prefers shortcuts, even when they take longer. He dips under the arch of snow-laden forsythia branches at the south corner of the garden, where William Plant is said to have found the buried pirate treasure that paid for the point of land and the big house by the sea. Several of the grand old Shoreland homes are said to have been built from pirates' gold.

In his prime William Plant had commissioned his own portraits. One of them as his own grave stone angel—just to make sure. Everyone says Mike is his spit'n image, but after a few generations Will's tight-lipped determination—to make his way on earth as in heaven—has been muted in Mike, who makes you laugh, and is determined to just have his way.

Shoreland Plants, Mike brags, came from Staffordshire, just like the Led Zepelin rockstar Robert Plant. So Mike hung an old ancestral portrait in oil of a young William Plant (determined angel) in his room, beside a poster of (determined devil) Robert Plant of eight or nine years ago—a gaunt boy with a mane of curls. A Mike look-alike and alter ego.

Liz feels safe in her warm kitchen, plenty of food in the house. Mike at the backdoor. Chris in the music room reading a controversial article Ellen gave him, about terror at an early age giving you immunity. A young woman on the radio is talking of the effect of environment on behavior. A moose that fell in love with a cow named Jessica in Vermont.

The moment Mike stomps snow off his boots in the entrance, his shaggy guinea pig whistles from the old aquarium that serves as a cage, but there is none of the usual enthusiasm from Mom—"Shut up, Ringo!" He lets the new self-closing door slam shut, and sheds his backpack and guitar case and wet leather jacket onto the floor. There is no reaction. Mom stays at the sink watching the snow. When he turns on the light her snow-picture disappears. She veers around, grabs him tight. "You worry too much. I'm O.K., Mom."

She lets go, her body taut with fear. Why? Bonnie declares he's "full of it"—the big blue eyes girls admire, the laughing mouth and firm chin. Why does his happy face make her tremble? She picks up the forced forsythia blossoms from the asparagus pot to change the water; almost drops it. "They never last in the warm kitchen."

"You always want everything to last, Mom. Just look at you in my old nerdy sneakers and jeans."

He is wearing an unbuttoned leather vest over a ragged thermal under-shirt, new tattered jeans, a trade, he'll say. Boarding school kids swap clothes in their need for something new, to be cool, like someone else and everyone else.

"And that pathetic radio you got from the dump. Dad can afford a decent one. What's that insane racket?"

"Mating call of a moose in love with a cow named Jessica."

He shakes his hair, sprinkling snow. "Cow, moose. No future in that."

Liz had followed this news story with interest last fall. Mike is right, she does want everything to last, even this strange love. A pot lid on the wall mirrors a mother with the lost smile of a toddler snatched away from home.

"I heard about you, Mom. Almost busted. How come you hang out with kids at Harbor Square when I'm away?"

"You wouldn't understand." Exactly what he would say.

"Dutch says you got in his way of a drug bust."

"There were no drugs."

"I told him that he was smart to lay off you. Or you might put him into your book as an S.S.-type cop."

"You don't know what I'm writing. You shouldn't talk about it."

"Why not? It's promotion. You used to give him cookies and extra money when he was our paperboy. Dutch will definitely run out and buy your book. Is it finished?"

"Not yet." She turns to the refrigerator and gets an onion.

"You're too slow. I can get you shrooms that really blow your mind. And it's even organic."

"Why blow your mind?" she starts beating eggs for Yorkshire pudding. Compulsively busy when Mike holds forth in the kitchen.

"Why not if it gives you great ideas?" Mike takes out his guitar, puts his foot on the rung of an old ladder chair, throws back his curls, and strums. "There is that girl, nibbling shrooms with that smile on her face showing her pointy little teeth. Then there is a cute, white, fluffy cat grinning down from a pine tree. Then there's no cat and just a grin. Didn't Alice in Wonderland eat shrooms and see grinning cats in trees? And who knows what they were drinking at that tea party? And the Mad Hatter sticking the mouse into the teapot wasn't so mad. He was generous. And then there was that caterpillar with a hubble bubble pipe."

Liz takes the roast beef out of the refrigerator. "You climbed in and smashed a window and got into an argument with the dorm master just after you saw the cat?"

"I go climbing, someone catches me by the leg. I let out a roar. There is all that broken glass, the coach, and his dog. I thought I was seeing things again." He strums a few cords and laughs. "So I tell him I was out in the woods getting ideas for my paper. He wants to know about the ideas, so I tell him about the cat and Alice. He says, a stupid idea. I tell him he has no intellect, which is true. Head for the john with my notebook and write this awesome paper about Alice tripping right there and then."

"Why didn't you leave drugs out of your assignments?"

"Because it's brilliant. My vocabulary is fantastic."

She is inclined to overspice the meat when Mike is in the kitchen. "You know they won't accept it." Nazis had come into power by defying reasonable laws, and then invented laws and rules to make outrage legal. "Grove isn't strict or unfair. So little has been expected of you."

"They expect me to put up with the return of Havelock and that's a lot. He keeps calling me boy. I'm a man! He's picking out 'leadership-boys he'll train as Gestapo informers."

How can she confront the pot-smoking, beer-guzzling poetry of Mike the outlaw, when her own queazy stomach rumbles with mistrust of Havelock Grimes, who invents his own laws?

"The screw crew, they were cool, although I said the coach had no intellect. Later he and I had another argument. He threatens to punch me out. That's against the law; I'd have him arrested for child abuse."

"You just said you are a man."

"Intellectually, Mom. But the coach used to wrestle. He's huge. So Goody-Goodley made them suspend me for my own protection. No big deal. I'd be home next week for outreach anyway. More time to reach out and help out. Where's Dad?"

"Not feeling well."

"Because I'm home again. I'd do better going to school right here. The best education is a self-education. But Dad doesn't want me around. You don't want me around either. You want to write your book." The string pings like a bullet hitting one of those metal "No trespassing" signs at the quarry. "Why are you in the kitchen? Go write. I can eat a TV dinner." At the parlor door he turns to pick up Ringo. "I think I'll write my outreach assignment on how a kid has to reach out and be a parent."

He lets go of the door and it slams shut on Liz, the parent who reaches out to be one of the kids. A secret insider of Mike's shenanigans, who tags along in her heart with the troop in Harbor Square where they hang around like pirates who have lost their boat and booty. She takes empty soda bottles into the washroom which overlooks the old Codget barn that

Bonnie and Jeff Martin converted and Codget Cottage, Ellen's house deep in snow, which takes her back to Waldruh. The Faser cottage deep in snow. Windows darkened in case bombers spotted a light. The pump out of order. Even the door sealed. Logs of wood crackling in the stove. Hoarded food in the larder. Frau Faser drinking something hot and potent, contemplating her sunny pictures by candlelight. Liese telling her the story of sun on ice, the crystal palace, where a stolen child is secluded and enshrined with the lonely Snow Queen. Didn't Frau Faser say *schrecklich schoen,* which translates into British, frightfully beautiful? Just too much—ominous—because perfection never lasts.

The flood lights come on at the backdoor of Ellen's cottage; her kids Billy and Jonathan and their crazy setter Red burst out the back door with shrieks and barking. Ellen, who is against old-fashioned make-believe or children's stories for her two boys, doesn't encourage them to visit Bonnie, or for that matter Liz. They play war games, pelting each other with snow balls, which Red likes to catch and chew up, leaping around them as they play, knocking each other down, rolling around until they are covered with snow. Hedges, fences, stone walls—boundaries they like to defy—are now all covered over and white; even the road has vanished.

Last week Ellen brought all the single mothers to see the cheerful Liz Plant kitchen as an example of the kind of 'sensuous and inviting' environment the best-selling book LOVE AND LEARN talks about. Pink geraniums trailing down over the liquor cabinet. Sweet basil, rosemary, and parsley at the window by the sink. Years before Liz went back to writing her own story, she had painted poppies, cornflowers, sunflowers, and butterflies on the white kitchen cabinets. Is it sensuous to decorate your kitchen with the memory of a summer that came early? The field flowers, the rose garden where her mother must have waited for her.

A man on the radio speaks about legislation to help victims of violent crimes. No one is immune to victimization, he says. It can happen to anyone, any time. In the home where you least expect it. Defensive living makes sense just like defensive driving. Is writing not defensive living?

She puts the small rib roast into the oven, and lies back on the wicker chaise. The author of LOVE AND LEARN, Beatrice Strout, writes about the comforts of home. According to Beatrice every room in a woman's house should have plants and herbs and a bed or sofa, especially the bathroom and kitchen. Ellen wanted her single mothers to see Liz Plant's kitchen as an illustration for chapter six, Love and Alchemy, subtitled: The Sensuous Kitchen As A Man Trap. How about woman trap?

Beatrice Strout calls herself a "femininist" to distinguish herself from feminists who compete with males for mere equality. "Femininists" know they are superior and need not compete. Beatrice warns that women will lose their psychic power by trying to be like men. In the past only the fittest women had survived yearly pregnancies. They were stronger than men. Beatrice believes in a female collective subconscious, like a host computer: secret knowledge you can link up with. It must have been Ellen who persuaded Chris that he must pay for the DEC II, even though he considers the computer unhealthy and is afraid of its magnetic field. Could it be magnetism that draws Liz back to her computer with a sudden surge of urgency?

Chapter 11
THE GUARD

Police Notices:
Officer Dutch and the chief discovered that a house
on Pirates Beach had been entered by some small
animals yesterday. There was no sign of forced
entry into the home. He said, but a hole had been
chewed through one wall and there were raccoon or
squirrel droppings on the floor. The owner told
officer Dutch the only item that appeared to be
missing was a bottle of Jack Daniels whiskey.

Mike left on Liz's desk this notice from the Shoreland Eagle to keep her in
touch with daily events, while an embossed red and gold monster grins at
her from a paperback book cover as a reminder that most people read to
get scared and sexy. He wants Mom to get real and make money with her
book. Nazis, he says, are boring now. How about the perverted ghost of
Hitler and his possessed gang turned into sex-driven vampires? Action.
Battalions of invisible S.S. chasing naked Alien women in outer space trying to have sex. Something new. Do a little research. Weightlessness and
orgasm— awesome, unreal.

Did she not come to possess those who tried to own her? Is this not
the far-out unreal truth—a confessional horror story? How about Jan? Liz

sits down at Great-Grandmother Celia's dressing table, staring at the reflection of the desklight rotund as the moon on a slow river. Country roads torn up not only by bombs, but by land mines. She closes her eyes for a moment, until she sees the house with the white furniture and garden seats. The mirage of the statue of a naked child, flowers. Outside the garden wall, a moon-scape of scarred fields. The dead or wounded must have been removed. A helmet here, a boot there. The house standing in the midst of devastation could have been mined, a trap, when Jan sent Liese, his scout ahead to the door, the way Hitler's armies had sent dogs or prisoners ahead of troops. It was clever of him to put her on guard duty after they had found Mimi half submerged at the edge of the river.

Mimi was still wearing a long white kitchen apron when the boys carried her back to the house. During the night her cheeks glowed. She had forgotten her language; now she forgot that you weren't supposed to remember Mother, Father, Grandmother. She kept calling them night and day—to the end—when her voice became weak and she shivered herself to death.

Jan ordered Liese to stand guard outside the garden wall, "If anyone comes along, you're looking for Mother. *Verstanden?*" But she could hear the clang, clang sound of the shovel when they buried Mimi in the bomb crater.

It was warm, but Liese wore the leather coat to keep herself from shivering, while she marched back and forth guarding the dear home. The empty pistol weighed heavy. Jan had said, just point at anyone who comes along and shout, "Hands up!" They would drink the remaining wine and Schnapps. Soon they'd be out of food. They had already run out of candles and had to hide in the dark cellar curling up together like a litter of mice.

The air did not stir. It was too still. She had orders to take a stand all by herself as a good German. Ready to die for the Fuhrer and the troop. She had never been left alone like this before. Her sob started like a hiccup she had to stifle on Auntie's farm when she had to be invisible and quiet as the Fifinella in the crystal flask. She leaned against the garden wall, let herself slide down, and sat worrying out loud. "No crying. No crying," until she cried herself to sleep. At day-

break she woke up with a start to the distant
squeals of a pig being slaughtered.

Mother had taught her to cover her ears with her
hands and hide under the bed with her when an animal was killed. She remembered the scent of
rose-water they had shared when they hid in a
closet. Mother had to shut out anything she didn't
like in order to live happily ever after.

Mike bursts into the room wearing a black turtleneck Liz had bought
for his father. Doors he left open behind him allow blasts of rock music to
thunder out of his room. "How did you like the break-in? You don't even
know what's going on in Shoreland, do you? This makes a great story. You
aren't even listening, Mom. You never listen."

"I hear you." Thinking of her school-girl mother tilting her head, as he
does now. She doesn't remember the language, but she can hear the tone of
a young voice reciting opinions and complaints no one had ever listened to
over and over again.

"Elgar is on curfew after dark. I'm going to see him."

"In all that snow?"

"Snow turns me on. Can you make dinner early?"

"Dad doesn't like to eat before seven-thirty. You're wearing his new
turtleneck."

"So what? You're wearing my jeans."

"Old ones. You're drenched in Dad's cologne. "

"So we share. How about early dinner?"

"After I finish this. Roast beef's in the oven."

"Cool!" He walks out and props the door open with the toad.
This reminds her that her mother—who was around Mike's age—would
leave doors open to hear what the women were saying about her. Mike
leaves her door propped open because his father wants them closed. He
can't accept restriction. " I can never accept freedom," she says to herself.
She had been proud to follow Jan's command when he had sent her ahead
as his scout, proud and scared to be on guard duty after Mimi's death.

When Liese took her hands off her ears, it was so
quiet she heard fruit fall from a tree on the other
side of the garden wall. On Auntie's farm an old
apple tree stood beside the hay barn where she hid
the big car with the yellow spokes so that soldiers

couldn't steal it. Auntie did not like losing anything or anyone. Now Auntie and Mother were coming.
She could hear the car. "Mama! Mama!"

She jumped up and a bird flew out of the thicket
over the garden wall. She heard a thump and ducked.
A moth or bat touched her cheek. She squealed like
the pig. Two smiling soldiers confronted her with
guns. She remembered to smile and they lowered them
at once.

"Gruess Dich," the fat one said in a high-
pitched voice. The other one was thin with a long
chin and wore glasses.

She remembered to keep smiling, while she followed Jan's orders and snatched up her gun. "Hands
up!"

"If you put yours up too," the stout soldier
said in funny German.

She was glad to drop her pistol down with
theirs. "You know how to shoot?" asked the fat one.

"Press the trigger."

The thin soldier bent down to check her pistol.
Said something and they both laughed. "No bullets.
You're a hero," said the speaker.

She stood at attention. "I'm a scout."

"We are scouts too."

They looked so clean and new, she felt dirty and
started to brush off her jacket, straightened her
hat. The fat one said something, reached into his
pocket. "Gum. chocolate. A sweet. It's a sweet."
Then he talked about coming all the way from
America, in lousy German Frau Faser would not put
up with.

She kept the beautiful silver paper in her hand.
Sweets had taken her away from her home. She felt
quite certain now that sweets would take her back
to her mother. So she devoured gum while they
laughed showing their white teeth.

"You're wearing mother's jacket? We want to talk
to her." The fat one spoke slowly searching for
German words. "Is she in the house?"

The child shook her head. "At aunties white
farm."

"Well, get in. Let's find her."

"Would you take Jan and the other children?
They're in the house."

Children were dangerous. Nazis used them as

spies. This could be an enemy trap. The soldiers conferred and picked up their guns and she took back her pistol. They made her walk ahead of them the way Jan did. When they came within range of the house, they crouched and approached pointing their guns. She took the fat one by the sleeve. "Don't shoot the children," she said. "Don't shoot my Jan!"

"Get them all to come *raus mit den* hands up!"

Jan marched his troop up from the basement and out of the house, where he lined them up with a snappy salute. In halting school English he told the Americans that he was Norwegian. The Germans had stolen him and stuck him into a Hitler School to make him into a Nazi. He had escaped with this troop of stolen children.

But the American scouts had been briefed about lies in Germany and did not believe the story. Why would a German army truck travel for two days and dump children in the war zone? The Americans asked Jan to take them back and show them the Hitler School camp. He gazed up at the clouds, squinted, and said he didn't know where it was.

In any case, the children had to be cared for. The Americans took them along in a convoy as mascots and prisoners, spoiling the troop with sweets. Children would say anything just to get chocolate and chewing gum. The interrogation team questioned them again and again, but remained unconvinced about Nazification of stolen blond children in Hitler Schools. No one ever wanted to know about German doctors sorting out imperfect children for slave labor. Nor did they want to believe there had been genetic experiments to perpetuate a master race with the S.S. performing as studs for young volunteers in Lebensborn, not even the judges at Nuremberg.

Chris appears in the doorway wearing his red Maxi-robe. "Have you been exposed to the computer all this time?"

He, of course, knows that she'd been in the kitchen preparing dinner when he came back from Ellen's house. Pretending he doesn't know what she has been up to, where she is or where she has been, or what she is thinking is all part of the old deserted-brother game.

His hair is slicked down after a shower, and he exudes fragrant well-being in his favorite role as the elegant half invalid. "Aren't you going to change for dinner?"

When Mike is sent home in disgrace, Chris makes a point of dressing for dinner, like his English great-grandfather among savages in the colonies. Liz enjoys playing along with him in a cosy vintage gown in the evening. She gets up and passes her fingertips over his bib of light curls—that sham hairy chest—and he shudders like a tom cat. "Don't do that to me now! We 're invaded. You simply unplug your phone up here. Juvenile delinquents have been calling Mike nonstop. A pregnant girl. For a moment I was worried. I was glad to hear that she has a boyfriend in California."

"You shouldn't listen in."

"Someone has to know what's going on. The moment Mike comes home kids arrive, snow or no snow. You better go down and guard my liquor while I'm getting dressed."

"Later." Liz remembers Gramp saying, "Go on, give little Chris a kiss." She now kisses him on the tip of his nose, and turns him around and out the open door. If Chris had not interrupted her she would not have realized that Liese had forgotten all about little kisses, as she forgot her first language. In Nazification school children were slapped as punishment, and also mild affection. Catholic nuns in the children's shelter in Vienna, she now remembers, gave blessings and touched their rosary with their lips.

Chris leaves the padded door ajar, to let kids disrupt her too. But the moment Sergeant Pepper, her favorite Beetle music drifts up through the house, her mind turns into a whirligig. The black square of the cursor twinkles, Dec Mate II grumbles and grinds, while her fingers start playing with words.

Engerl, little angel, nuns called her in the children's shelter in Vienna after the war, where naked cherubs swarmed motherless around the altar of the bomb-damaged chapel. What could a little angel have done in hell, but make a little bit of heaven? "Little Bit of Heaven" an old wine-garden song Liese had learned from Frau Faser's radio and sang for the troop of children. Drifting from Hitler yesterday into tomorrow's never-never land with spaced-out Beetles dream-sing "LUCY IN THE SKY," the girl with the kaleidoscope eyes, rocking horse

people eating marshmallow pie. Little Bit of
Heaven: iridescent mothering bubbles floating you
off to lullaby land.

Chapter 12

SHELTER

Jan and his troop of valuable children marched to the bathroom wearing warm blue trousers and match- ing sweaters donated by an American manufacturer specifically for war children. Sister had followed with the eighteen Viennese orphans, which Jan had sorted out as worthless since, since they either couldn't or wouldn't be drilled.

The nun stopped to genuflect at the painted wooden Madonna facing the carved portal of the hos- pital shelter. Her hands had come off when godless soldiers wrenched away Baby Jesus. Leaving her as a monument to abused mothers who had lost children, and children who had been torn away from Mother.

From the dark corner behind this Mother of Heaven jumped a man in a slouch cap. The nun and the children cried out. An orphan boy bawled and she picked him up. But Jan and his troop stood at attention while the man unrolled a somewhat tat- tered search placard with pictures of war children that had been posted in public buildings and even on church walls of occupied Vienna.

NOTICE
WHO CAN TELL OUR NAME?
WHERE WE COME FROM—WHEN WE WERE BORN?
FOR EVEN THE SMALLEST INFORMATION ARE WE GRATEFUL!
GERMAN + RED CROSS
SEARCH SERVICE HAMBURG
2 HAMBURG 53 BLUMKAMP 51

The man's fur mitten-paw pointed at Liese's picture among all the others. Then at the child. "This is the one!"

LIESE. BORN APPROXIMATELY 1941-42.
NOT BRANDED. NAME UNKNOWN.
EYES BLUE-GREEN. HAIR LIGHT BLOND.
FOUND AMONG WAR CHILDREN.

The cap hid the man's face, while a loden cape hiding a backpack identified him at once as one of those hunch-backed black marketeers children saw lurking among ruins of bombed-out buildings.

In foreign German, which would have earned him a good smack from Frau Faser, he talked about a young girl in his British displaced-person camp who had seen this poster with the picture of her little girl but was scared of being detained and possibly abducted by the Russians at the demarcation line to Vienna. He had a pass and so she had sent him to fetch the child for her. "I give you bacon, butter, and a big veal shank, even a bottle of whipping cream for this one small girl."

Irresistible logic and an irresistible offer. Liese took cover behind Jan, while Sister smiled and spoke softly, pointing out that many parents had lost children and so far three fathers and nine mothers had personally claimed this pretty child. The man produced a baby picture. Sister shook her head. Several of the other people who wanted this child had brought baby pictures too. The foreigner pulled the cap down to his nose, snarled like a dog, cursed in English, and pulled a fistful of English and American bills from his pocket.

Sister shook her head and said, "God forbid." With this, she reached into a folder she carried under her left arm and handed the foreigner an entire booklet of official Austrian forms that had

to be filled out by anyone claiming a child.
    He didn't even bother to close the carved por-
tal. The south wind flung it wide open and banged
it against the wall; the children cowered until
Sister closed it. "The poor man will get wet in this
downpour." She knelt in front of the wooden Mother
of Heaven, praying out loud for all those who
bartered their souls away. And quietly for those
who had nothing to barter with.

Liz gets up for a moment thinking of the nuns in the children's shelter in
Vienna, who had holy images like the wooden Mother of Heaven
bestowed on them; power and glory gleaming from baroque gilded altars.
Hitler or no Hilter, the image of Father, the bureaucrat in Heaven, had
presided from his throne of cloud. His invisible hierarchy of angels
omnipresent, like the aura of the bygone Kaiser-Reich, while in heaven as
on earth, bureaucracy went on century after century with old regulations
from the Popes and the Imperial Habsburgs, to the Thousand Year Reich,
to frustrate furtive peddlers like the man in the slouch cap, who came to
the shelter and bartered for a child.
    The Russians had invaded and punished Nazi Austria before the
French, British, and Americans arrived to declare noble old Austria a victim of Hitler's aggression. But then Austria and Vienna had been divided
into four occupation zones and remained boxed in by the Soviet army.
Food was rationed. Stores remained empty, but the children's shelter in the
safe American zone must have received supplies far more regularly than
had Hitler School. American soldiers continued to give children chewing
gum and candy. They also provided plenty of soap.

    Rain was coming down hard while Liese stood in
line for her turn in the tub. Sister had to close
the double windows so fast that a yellow butterfly
was caught in between the panes. She said it was
better off in there during the rain storm, but the
butterfly didn't know this and kept beating its
wings against the glass.
    The old hospital had wrought-iron window grills.
At this one, a big spider's web shimmered with
raindrops and insect wings. You could even see the
black legs of the spider moving at the edge where
it waited and watched the butterfly, but as long as
the butterfly stayed locked in between the double

windows zone, it was safe.

When Jan blew his whistle, Liese came away from
the window and fell in to wait in line with the
troop, while orphans, who could never wait for
their turn, kept pushing each other around, vying
for attention from the nuns. Some of them had lost
their parents during the allied bombing of Vienna,
others during the Russian invasion. Orphans suffered from colds, pimples, fevers. "You better
shape up, or you'll be sorted out," Horst would
secretly warn them. The troop had not been allowed
to cry; all but Liese had stopped smiling.

Orphans didn't smile so that everyone would be
good to them. They bawled and sniffled while the
nuns carried them in their arms, held them on their
knees, and taught them to pray. No one smacked them
when they kept asking for Mother, grandmother,
brothers, or sisters. The sturdy little nun and the
tall, thin novice Ursula always had to comfort them
one by one, to wash and dress them like babies,
assuring them that their family was in heaven. If
any of them wondered about the Fuhrer, the sisters
changed the subject and told the story of kind
Saint Francis.

In Hitler School the troop had been told that
their mothers had been bad women who came to a bad
end. Now the radio as well as the nuns announced
that Adolf Hitler had been a bad man and came to a
bad end. The German in American uniform who fed
Liese chewing gum had promised the troop that
everything would be done to find their families,
while he warned them against telling wild stories
about Nazification and the Hitler school. Jan had
overheard him warn the nuns about the well-trained
little troop, that might have been trained for sab-
otage. Not their fault, of course.

Jan and the troop talked in secret about their
escape, but never about Mimi's death or Siegfried,
who had been identified by a birthmark on his neck
and returned to his family in Poland by the Red
Cross. Siegfried didn't remember his family, didn't
speak Polish anymore, and didn't want to leave the
troop. Had he not been drilled like the S.S. to be
tough and believe in his superiority? Now he had
been torn away from his troop and sent away to be a
child in a foreign family.

Eleven-year-old Jan remembered his home address in Norway, and had spoken to his parents on the telephone. It was only a matter of days before he would be going home. "What are we going to do without Jan?" the nuns kept saying, because just like Frau Faser they had come to rely on him.

And what would a troop leader do without his troop? Could Jan go back to being the youngest of five sons? He was in and out of the tub in less than the four minutes Frau Faser had allowed. The others followed, always two boys or two girls. He blew his whistle when their time was up as though Frau Faser were standing by ready to haul out and whack a loiterer. He ignored the orphans as useless, since they either wouldn't or couldn't be drilled. "You're sickly. Your hair is too dark. The Inspector will come and take you away," Martha whispered to a big orphan named Helga, who had a runny nose. The troop remained obliging, solemn, secretive, drying themselves and dressing very fast. An American was flying in on this day to see whether he wanted to adopt one of the unclaimed children. So they all had to take a bath.

Liese enjoyed herself, splashing and singing Lily Marlene long after Jan gave his signal. Sister swung her playfully out of the tub. Liese ran the comb through her wet hair in three fast strokes. As soon she was dressed, she put on her old hat, because one day it would take her back to the edge of the road, through the field full of flowers and butterflies to Auntie's farm and Mother. "How about the butterfly?" she asked.

"It can wait," Sister Veronica said.

"But it doesn't want to wait!"

Sister gave her a hug and took the hat off her head. "You and your old hat. I'll keep it safe. But we do have to look proper today for the American."

Sister Angelica, the thin, tall, teaching nun, came gliding in on felt slippers and took Sister aside. "You shouldn't talk about it." She spoke in a low voice. "The doctor has no right to even consider letting an American have a child while relatives keep responding to the Red Cross search posters."

Sister Veronica smiled and dimpled, keeping her voice low too, while she told the Sister about the

unpleasant foreigner who had simply burst into the
shelter and frightened the children.

"Not much chance that any of these beautiful
children are going to continue their Catholic education in some Bolshevik hovel," the postulant
spoke up.

"If nobody in Poland wants me, why can't I get
adopted by rich Americans?" Horst asked.

"Because you certainly need a Catholic education," Sister Angelica said."Most important..."

"So that I can be turned into a priest or a
monk?"

"You mustn't interrupt!" Sister Angelica took
off the Russian wire-rimmed glasses she had inherited from a martyred old nun, who got them from one
of the eight Russians she prayed for after they had
raped her.

"I don't want to be a postulant," said Magda,
who had been prepared to become a German mother. An
orphan boy spoke up and said he didn't want to be a
postulant either. "I do," Liese said, because she
wanted to minister to the butterfly. But if she
opened the window, it might fly out and get caught
in the web or be drenched in the streaming rain,
shivering itself to death. Liese thought of Mimi
and shivered.

"How about becoming priests and nuns in America,
where there is plenty of food and everyone has a
car?" Horst asked.

Liese did not want to go to America. Nor would
big strong Americans want to adopt her if they
could have big, strong Magda, who had those injections to make her into a grown woman fast.
Long-legged Horst, on the other hand, had not grown
up too fast, but he had a manly voice and grew
whiskers. The Hitler School doctor had to perform a
little trick, as he called it. Horst never talked
about the operation, but learned to speak English
fast and befriended GI's. Any American would want
Horst.

When the rain stopped.Sister Veronica smiled and
said the angels had stopped weeping. "Peeing," said
Horst. Sister Angelica put her arm around him and
took him along to her office.

"How about the butterfly?" Liese asked.

"It can wait," Sister Veronica said again.

Jan whistled to line the children up, but Liese raised her hand. "Sister, Sister, I've got to go!" Then she ran back to the window, stood on a chair, opened the double panes and with her hand directed the butterfly away from the spider: If the yellow butterfly got away, then she would get away to her mother. She watched it flicker in the light as it escaped high up over the trees. The aircraft circling in the sky no bigger than the butterfly, might even be the one flying the wealthy American to Vienna.

Chapter 13
MIKE

After a good old roast beef and Yorkshire pudding dinner Mike slips a bog-green trash bag with peep-holes over his head and walks through the storm Grove Academy style. An awesome attire he had invented for staying warm and dry, as well as invisible with his six pack. The Grove Screw Crew had tried to put a stop to trash bags because of their sinister image, something like the Klan. Wrong, Mike told them. A trash bag is not only beneficial protection in a shitty climate, it's a cocoon, giving a kid essential privacy like a larva forming itself as it passes through the pupa stage.

He got this from his Collegiate Dictionary, a fourteenth birthday present from Dad, who likes to quote from Webster's to show off and win arguments. Plant men are wordy and try to have the last word. Mom has the imagination, writing stories about herself in Nazi Germany. But Mike won a writing contest in third grade with a history of Shoreland, describing this town as a favorite stopover for migrant waterfowl and seals, and migrant aliens from outer space. He put the names of birds in a footnote, which made a deep impression on his teacher, Miss Blanchfont. The name of the Alien he met at Jimmy's hot dog shack near the beach was hard to spell and sounded like a sneeze. Her face was red, her eyes red, she wore a silver hat and ate Jimmy's homemade rhubarb ice cream, a favorite with women from outer space that brings them here like wild geese.

While women from outer space could pass for migrant tourists, Shoreland women can suddenly become spaced out and turn alien without warning. Way back, when they got mad at drunks, they went after rum barrels with hatchets. (No one can stop them once they get going with their supernatural power). Rum was flowing in the gutter, and men in the gutter were lapping it up. Taverns closed down then for good, and Shoreland has remained a dry town where men get drunk at home or on boats, where no one can throw them out. Inns are losing money. Kids have keg parties in the woods and at the quarries.

This makes Shoreland a quiet town, you'd think. Well, think again. On a night like this when the sea boils, the storm might sink ships, uproot trees and throw cars into the bay, you just know that someone's doing something crazy in Shoreland. Mike Plant the third takes a shortcut through snow drifts, trudging across Plant land as the future landowner. From this spot above the inlet, you get the best view of town. Even now, in the storm, you can see cruiser lights moving out of the police station. A perfect spot for developing thirty lots with really cool maintenance-free, low-cost housing for friends, after he makes his first million with the Suicide Four rock band. Someone has to do something for Shoreland kids that are raised by nonfunctional parents but won't be able to afford to either rent or buy any kind of home in this tourist trap.

Huge foaming breakers surge and smash against the harbor wall, can-nonballing the shore with rocks, while neighbor Jeff Moonbin is blasting snow in front of the converted barn with his new blower. Everyone else waits until it stops snowing, but Jeff, a compulsive nut, is out there and has all his floodlights on. A natural disturber of the peace and disturber of the good times, Bonnie, who has no kids, always had with Mike and his best friend, Elgar.

Bonnie bought Jeff the hardware store in Riverbay. He likes to sail. Bonnie, a land person, gets seasick, and her light skin and eyes turn red from the sun and wind. Mike awarded her his most favored Alien status, way back, when he and Elgar used to arrive at Bonnie's gate shouting HO, HO, HO! at her because of her height and the Green Giant overalls she wore all the time after she had bought a dozen of them at a factory outlet sale in Maine.

In her garden beans, roses, chard, daisies, mint, sunflowers, tomatoes all grow like mad in one big patch. She would sit in the shade of her wild apple tree, feeding Mike and Elgar cookies, pies, and fresh strawberries or raspberries, and telling them old stories about the witch women on the old common who were fortunetellers and the ghosts of pirates who haunt Pig Island.

The storm has torn a slat out of a shutter at Bonnie's house, and Mike picks it up, wades out of the drift, and sticks it into the Moonbin mailbox on the porch, when Jeff blasts around the front with his blower and stops. Another automatic floodlight comes on. "You! What do you think you're doing? Sticking dirty letters in my mailbox? Phone calls not enough?" Small, stocky Jeff advances wearing a bright yellow slicker, ready to spray Mace he carries wherever he goes on Mike's trashbag. Then tall Bonnie comes running out the side door with a huge snow shovel to protect Jeff, who doesn't need protection.

"Take it easy. It's only me. Under cover. Get it!" Mike lifts the trash bag to show his face. "Just passing by."

When Jeff is around Bonnie overdoes her schoolgirl titter. "Not without having a little visit with me and some pie. Was I ever busy with my answering service! Everybody gets on the phone when there is a storm." She pulls him into the mud room with the old cast-iron stove which also heats her adjoining kitchen. Jeff's at it again with his blower. Bonnie clatters around getting the pie, which gives Mike a chance to hide the beer behind the birdseed barrel, take off his trash bag, and hang it on the wooden hook on the back door. He takes a deep breath and gets spaced out from the smell of of dried rosemary and basil, and lemon balm and lavender that hang from the rafters. Nothing has changed: logs stacked in the corner, the usual flower show of psychedelic red and pink geraniums in the bay window, always the same.

But Bonnie is no longer the same. When she comes back from the adjoining kitchen she takes off her slicker, gum boots and the old Green Giant overalls. Not even that extra big glob of homemade ice cream she serves him on the brown crust of a quarter of her deep-dish apple pie lessens the shock of her secretarial dark skirt, jacket, and white blouse. "Why are you dressed up like this? Trying to look like Ellen Burns?"

She shakes her head and smiles, showing her bunny front teeth. "I have to look professional when new customers come by to sign up." She sits down beside Mike and hands him a steaming cup of hot chocolate with marshmallows and whipped cream. "Used to be Gramp's treat when he took me along on a sleigh rides to Riverbay Variety. There was lots more snow in those days. Your parents cute as can be, dressed like twins in English tweeds. I was already in junior high, taller than the boys, miserably shy. He always said I should be one of the Rockettes in Radio City Hall. Made me feel like a million!" She scoops up a marshmallow, pops it into her mouth with the old switched-on gleam in her green, alien eyes. "He wanted me to make something of myself. Took me a long time."

"Everyone says you're born again."

"At the Whale's Jaw Motel. You've listened to my stories from way back when. This happened to be for real. The will of God. Why should my van break down at that Motel on the very evening that prophet from Tennessee was preaching? The Prophet made me think of those short, smart boys in junior high. His granny glasses getting all steamed up. Place was packed. They even came from the Cape. There was so much jumping up and singing going on, I didn't really get all the meaning of his deep Bible talk about the Devil getting into the body of animals."

"You were bitten last year," Mike says.

"Makes you wonder. Never known a dog that didn't like me. Then this out-of-town husky jumps down from a pickup truck ready to chew me up." She consoles herself with hot chocolate which leaves her with a whipped-cream moustache. "Jeff thinks everyone should carry Mace, but the prophet believes in prayer."

Mike doesn't like the faraway look in her eyes. "Why not try both to be on the safe side? You're already wicked good trying to help everyone."

"The voice on the phone in the hall kept answering phones, saying. 'God bless. Can I help you?' The Lord telling me what to do. I walk out of the service and the van starts right up. Takes me back to Linden Tree Mall. So that I could get the 'how-to' book, phones and file cabinet, and steel shelves. Even the old V.W. van has been running perfect ever since. Honest." Bonnie downs her chocolate and emerges licking whipped cream off her lips. "Some of my customers tell me my answering service is more like a ministry than a business. I get a chance to help out as much as I can and I do make it my job to put unfriendly loners in touch with each other and pass around local news."

She knows exactly when to stop. No one who has heard Mike sounding off nonstop would guess that he became a great talker by being a great listener to Bonnie stories as long as he can remember. There is the usual intermission and she serves more pie, refills the cups, boosting you up with too much sugar, too much good will. "How about Jeff. Is he born again too?"

She laughs and laughs, like Ellen's kids when they stay up too late. "No way!" Then she and Mike are quiet together listening to the new snow blower. "He gets mad when I give free advice. But Mike, I know I can help. Old people and invalids get my service free."

Bonnie had tried to heal injured animals before she ever got the Call, especially birds. This is the kind of night when a bird might get trapped in her old chimney.

"Sometimes when a sick person leaves a message for Dr. Fox, I pray with them, or if they are non-believers, I speak to Jesus for them after they hang up. By the time the doctor gets back to them, they are often healed." She eats her last marshmallow. "I did get 'that man' on the line a couple times. He makes sexy phone calls. You hang up, he tries again. When I get Jeff to take the call, he changes his voice to sound like a woman. Imagine! He does have a nasty cough, poor fellow. "

"What does he say?"

"He's vulgar."

"Why don't you report it?"

"I reported to God and am praying for his healing."

"Aren't you taking on too much trouble?" But, then, who is he to talk when he is about to tackle Ellen Burns? Goodwill must be catching. He slips the trash bag over his head and picks up the beer when Bonnie's back is turned. She walks him out the door. When Mike adjusts his peepholes he can see her standing in the doorway, her face tilted up watching the snow coming down, her green eyes shining in one of Jeff's spotlights. "Don't you just love it?" she shouts to make herself heard over the racket of her husband doing his good work with a vengeance.

Ellen's clapboard tenant cottage has turned into an igloo under snow-covered, untrimmed hedges, which is an improvement to the flaking orange paint slapped on by Al, who dates back about five years to the time when several Shoreland women had California burn-out live-in houseboys.

It is just as well the windows are hidden, because her creative boys have decorated blinds on the first floor with huge, fuzzy, prancing monsters that glow in garish tints when the lights in the house are on, making it look like year-round Halloween. Ellen follows the old Shoreland custom of keeping a year-round Christmas wreath up on the front door. The "Dr. Ellen Burns, Psychologist" brass plate on the door is framed by a Christmas wreath her creative Billy and Jonathan made out of twigs and Coca-Cola bottle caps. You can hear the twisty, whining nighttime sublim-inal relaxation tape and the door is unlocked. That means she is alone.

Mike has come to set Ellen straight. This makes the five bucks he took out of Mom's purse to pay the Cragley twins for weed, a well-earned salary. He announces himself by ringing the bell and makes his entrance shout-ing: "Me! Mike!"

Only a few of the rich strangers who freak out over old Shoreland and buy an overpriced house, join the hysterical Historical Society and turn their homes into museums for Spring Open House fund-raising tours. Mostly the new owners, like Ellen, fall in love with old houses and then gut them and call it "opening up."

"Come on in!"

Mike takes off his trash bag, drops it over his six-pack and walks right into her huge, wild, everything room. The hippie house-boy, Al, who used to live here, had been in a California jail. That gave him this special need to open up, tear down walls and doors, do away with rooms and privacy. Ellen has her office in the far left corner with file cabinets, desk, and a spinning wheel too close to the wood stove, which dates back to the old Codget kitchen. There used to be a big microwave in that corner, but Ellen caught Jonathan, the older of the monster boys, trying to play Belsen Camp with Benny the hamster and six grasshoppers. She gave Benny away, made the boys give the grasshoppers their freedom and stored the microwave. This made room for the office couch, which faces a window decorated with monsters.

"Hi, there," she says from the ironing board in the kitchen corner, where she is going through the contortion of ironing her newly washed, long brown hair. The room is pleasantly messy, and its pink walls—tested out to have a calming influence in California jail cells—also date back to Al.

Mike watches Ellen twist around over the ironing board. "Were you ever a groupie?"

She laughs. "I was invited to a loft party once. Led Zeppelin were there. I liked some of their music. Not the guys. Groupies had them surrounded. Poor teenage girls. They looked after them in a way. Let themselves be abused. So pathetic. I doubt many of them survived." Ellen shakes out her hair and puts away the ironing board. "Wild night..." Since she doesn't go in for statements of the obvious, it sounds ominous. More like a warning or prediction. "Don't just stand around. Make yourself comfortable. Sit on the couch."

Something to avoid. Especially with Red, her insane setter, lying there on his back, legs sticking up. Subliminal persuasion with the hidden message did a job on him, but not on fleas. There is lively traffic on his belly even in the winter. Mike plunks himself down on a beat rattan chair.

"You smell just like your father," Ellen says.

From Wednesday to Sunday, the psychiatrist couch, which is really a trundle bed and a flea condo, and Ellen herself reek of Dad's indelible Mustache perfume; so does Red. His fleas must be perfumed too. What if Mom walked in here? Mike has to cover for Dad. Guys at Grove Academy use Polo Cologne, but Mike drenched himself with Dad's Mustache this evening. Elgar will want to know about that new cologne. Soon every kid in town will get turned onto Mustache which Dad pours all over himself when he is going to have sex, and Dad will be safe.

Mike says, "Ellen, your dog has fleas."

"Can't be helped. He likes to run around with all kinds of dogs. The boys and I take vitamin B and they don't touch us. Doesn't work for Red."

"Who knows, maybe flea bites work like acupuncture. Make your patients disgustingly healthy and insanely switched on like Red." He always makes her laugh. Her face is not bad. She has wicked dark eyes, dresses like an office worker, in skirts, blouses and even ties. If you look at her washing line you can admire her fascinating hooker-type see-through underwear.

Dad got involved with her after Mike bounced out of Shakerville and Mom was away driving around looking for schools. Dad lost thousands in tuition money. It was disgustingly unfair. He should have taken the school to court to defend his son's honor. But he said he didn't have time or money for a lawyer. A joke. Dad had time and money to see all kinds of doctors and shrinks. He had time to sneak over to Ellen's house. He still sees her on Wednesdays when her two boys are out having karate lessons and Mom goes to the Boston Public Library to research Nazi history.

Red is snoring and twitching. The squealing and monotone Subliminal Persuasion is getting to Mike, also the swigs of whiskey he took from Dad's bottle. How can shrinks ever be of any use if they don't know what their patients are really up to? No way is Dad going to stretch out on the couch and tell Ellen that he stays in bed half the day, takes all kinds of medication, sees all kinds of shrinks and other quacks, and drinks too much. Before Ellen gets any ideas she should be told that Dad is crazy about Mom and doesn't really hate Mike all the time.

Ellen unplugs the iron. Looks into a dirty mirror, and smiles, smoothing her smooth hair. "There is something on your mind. Want to talk about it?"

Direct questions always put Mike off. "Glad you didn't sell out to Len Myrtle."

"Jeff would have sold out to him, but the barn belongs to Bonnie. She walked out, stood under a tree, came back, and said it was not God's will. You didn't sell to him either."

She's using psychology, including him as an owner. Mike hangs his head and dread locks fall forward covering his face. He has come to tell her that he doesn't want a divorce in his family. Neither of them say anything and the subliminal persuasion fills the room like smoke from twenty joints. He is thinking of his mother writing about herself as a little kid. The tape ends in a long low trombone note. "Mom doesn't know Dad is your patient," he finally says in a Goodley headmaster voice.

"How do you know?"

He could have said, I smell "Moustache." If Mom had walked in here she'd smell it too. "I know everything!" That's what Goody-Goodley says when he wants to get out of a confrontation because his ulcer is acting up "And I won't have it!"

Ellen doesn't laugh or get mad. She narrows her dark eyes, the way she does in school when she is observing a disturbed kid and offers Mike a beer as though he were a man. This is a test. "No. But thanks ever so much, " this sounding too much like Dad. Her phone rings. Time to split. He makes sure she sees his six-pack when he slips the trash bag over his head and walks out into the storm. Mom's lights are on. She's writing away. Ideas he gave her really got her going. "What in fucking hell would they all do without me."

Chapter 14
COUNTERFEIT SMILE

Back in her own room, Liz gets up from her desk and curls up on the window seat to watch Mike leave Ellen's house with that Shoreland swagger she had first noticed when he learned to walk without holding on. Ellen has a way of making boys of any age feel more manly while she outsmarts them. In her way she is as generous as Bonnie. Helping herself to Chris just to be helpful.

No better place in the world for kids, Gramp would say. Santa coming into town by boat. Band concerts in the summer. The ocean, the woods, and great people. Gramp repeated the triumphant stories of his first pony, his first love, over and over, and rewarded her for not talking about herself with his hearty approval and admiration, which was, of course, self admiration. Why should Gramp have wanted to know that she had been picked for him by racial connoisseur Vogel since he was enormously proud of spotting a good kid, as he was of buying a good horse? "I think he'd like this chapter," Liz says to herself.

The novice played a game with the children while they waited for the Americans in the eye clinic. Twirling around between their little chairs, crucifix flying, she helped orphans to have their turn choosing letters from the charts on the wall and spelling their names. "Let's recite all the names now," she said. "So that you'll always remember to pray for each other!"

When the bell shrilled the orphans jumped up and ran to the glass door, pushing each other aside, while Jan and his troop arranged their little chairs in a half circle at the far end of the room. There was hardly time to sit down when Doctor Bunter and Sister Marie walked in with the two Americans.

The man was tall with bushy gray hair that could have benefited from Sister's wet comb. His raincoat, iridescent brown as a June bug, glossy shoes, the white shirt and blue tie all looked as though they had never been worn, while his sun-burned face looked as though it had been worn a lot in all kinds of weather but remained the face of a laughing boy.

The girl was even taller. Round gray eyes gave her a look of pleasant surprise. Dark hair falling over her shoulders, everything about her looked soft and rounded. The moment she walked into the room, the orphans ran over to stroke her soft pur-ple cape, which was fastened at the neck by a gold horseshoe pin. They grabbed her hands and clung to her arm. The man said something amusing and her laughter rose and fell.

Jan and the gang stayed in their chairs as though immobility would make them invisible and invulnerable before the ruthless cheerfulness of Americans who had come to take one of them away. The girl walked over to them and crouched down. "Are you afraid of us?" She spoke German like a newly Germanized child. "You aren't," she said to Liese. "Look at that sweet smile, Graham!" The orphans gathered around her.

"Liese always smiles," said Sister Marie.

The American took paper bags out of each coat pocket and handed them to the girl. "Candy will make everyone here smile!" She offered some to Liese, but the child shook her head because first Germans and then Americans gave you candy so that they could take you away. "Me! Me!" The orphans reached for the sweets, each one hoping for so much more than candy, they forgot the "dank you" the nuns had so carefully rehearsed.

"You might like an even younger child," the doctor said. "We have fine babies. They remember nothing and smile. Their fathers are often American military men." A sister came in as though she had been waiting behind the door to show off a comical baby with a big face, tiny nose and hands that grabbed frills of a frilly bonnet. The nurse chirped, "sweet, dear little boy!" tickling his cheek until he smiled, showing his gums.

"A fine boy. No problem with documents. The mother from the Sudetenland, a displaced person. Father, an American officer. The little one was only a month old when he was brought to us. The mother killed herself after the American wife arrived in Vienna with two children. Too bad."

The doctor talked fast; the orphans wolfed their candy. "She had him christened, John, after his father. A strong, healthy boy, but he needs a little hernia operation. No problem." The doctor took the baby, held its bottom in his pink paw which, was covered with red fuzz, and deftly lifted the diaper. The male organ, which looked large on the tiny body, stirred, the spout rose, spraying the doctor's face.

The American man laughed and whispered something to the girl. The doctor wiped his face and the nurse departed with the infant.

"Mr. Plant wants a girl." The young woman lowered her voice and spoke in halting German about Mr. Plant's son, back from the war, taking a holiday on his boat with his English wife and their twins. The terrible accident. An explosion. Only the little boy survived and he was badly burned, had to have a lot of surgery and was terribly lonely without his twin sister.

"How old is the poor boy?" the doctor asked.

"Four and half."

Liese had turned to the window and watched a butterfly flickering against the gray sky. Her butterfly! She thought of it flying all the way home to a field with wild daisies and poppies. She couldn't help wondering whether Frau Faser had remained in her cottage and was working in her vegetable garden.

Suddenly she was snatched up by the big American. She struggled. "Put me down!" but he held

onto her with one arm, while he reached into his
jacket for a photograph of a boy and girl standing
hand in hand under a tree. They had the same light
hair.

The doctor looked and said, *"Unglaublich,* unbelievable. Isn't that you, Liese? Could be you with
a brother!"

She shook her head and her fluffy damp hair
touched the American cheek. He kissed her hand and
she wiped it. He kissed her pink cheek, she pulled
away.

"He loves children!" The young woman said in her
funny German. He loved the little granddaughter
more than anyone in this world. He'd give this
child everything. He's got lots of money."

Then she turned to Liese and said that her name
was Dora, and she wanted to be her friend. Wouldn't
she like to be the little girl in the picture, live
in a big house by the sea, and have lots of toys?
How about riding around in a big car?"

Liese said, "No big black car. Put me down!"
But the man didn't understand German.

"The war children are not used to being han-
dled," the doctor said in English. "You've got to
understand. As I explained to you, there is an
advantage with a baby! Or even an orphan. War children do have problems. Besides, you never know,
parents might show up."

The big man didn't want to listen to the doctor. "What was she saying, Dora? Ask her how old
she is."

"There are no papers. We don't know the date of
birth," the doctor said.

"I am ten years old," Liese said because she
was scared. The young woman translated this and the
American looked puzzled and annoyed.

The moment he put her down, she fled to the
window. In Hitler School she had been in danger
because she was a useless baby. In America she
might be useless and in danger if she was too old.
What did they all want? Terror would grip her ever
after when she was questioned about her age.

The doctor laughed. *"Nein,nein!* Never. This
child is four or five years old."

Sister Angelica, who had been listening behind
the door, now came forward, introduced herself in

English, and pointed out that several mothers who had seen the search posters wanted to claim Liese.

"She's so pretty. That's why." The American relaxed, smiled, and sat down near Liese on one of the little chairs. The doctor took sister Angelica aside and spoke to her in anger. She flushed and walked out.

"Tell her if she doesn't like cars I'll buy her a horse." The American pointed at himself. "Graham."

"Gram," Liese said.

"Beautiful." The tiny chair made his long legs stick up and he sat there like a big frog. "Gramp, that's what the twins called me." He pointed at Liese, "and you?"

"Liese," she whispered.

"Liz," he turned to the young woman. "Did you hear that, Dora? Like our poor little twin. Chris and Sis, that's what they called themselves. I can't believe it! Tell her Dora. Our boy is going to love you, Liz!"

Gramp always heard what he wanted to hear, Liese knew that from the beginning.

Chapter 15

VISITATIONS

Mike finds the Myrtle ranch-style home locked, windows boarded up like a fortress under siege. He pushes the snow off the trap door, stomps three times, and waits. Elgar, gets the signal and opens the front door. He is taller than Mike. His neck is long with a protruding Adam's apple, his back long, legs short and slightly bendy. There is Elgar the dreamy musician and Elgar the madman. He's wearing a poison green T-shirt adorned with a big roaring lion head—glowing eyes of the beast on each nipple—to ward off any approval from his Mom and Dad.

"Is that you in that trash bag, man?"

"With a six-pack and a couple of joints." They are able to make it down into the shelter unobserved. Soon after Elgar was born, Leonard Myrtle Elgar's dad, the contractor converted the basement into a bomb fallout shelter. And fallout from weird building materials remains trapped down here all those years, smelly insulation and acrid paint; as well as fumes from new fireproof rugs, fireproof everything. Locked in a big vault are bottles of liquor, canned food, bars of silver, perhaps even gold to keep the Myrtle family going beyond the end of the world.

Elgar and Mike guzzle beer and eat potato chips. After they light up joints, Elgar has a blast improvising on the beat upright piano he got from the old timer volunteer fix-it man—the major of the dump. Gramp had given young Dora a Steinway grand, but she says "rock" ruins it and locks her music room. Then Mom and Dad gave Elgar the old Plant piano, but Dora Myrtle sold it to pay for Elgar's legal fees, although it was not their property.

"This dump upright is cool, but I miss the old Boeckstein."

"All my fault," Mike says. "I made you come to Jigger's send-off."

They had collected money for a keg. Built a fire up at Tompkins quarry. Sparks dancing in the wind while Mike made voodoo magic drumming on that chained-down, bullet-riddled trash bin. Jigger bowed his guitar with a piece of glass to make it squeal like a girl. Svenson danced on a rock. Caleb hung upside down from a tree above the flames. They weren't just guys getting together for the usual keg party in the woods. Jigger was taking off for California, deserting pregnant Del. They all knew this was wrong. Mike didn't have to drum up any Zombie demons: the male rotter in every kid was having a blast, hopping around the fire, stomping, sacrificing ruined girls.

Elgar had been guzzling down more than his share. Got up on this big boulder, started chanting insults at guys that go out to the coast and think they'll turn into rock deity because they do dope and bow guitars. Jigger was too high to react. By the time Elgar, stripped and pranced around naked. Mom's moped came buzzing up bumping over roots, he jumped into the black water. Mike yelled at her for butting in. She yelled back that she didn't want them all to end up in jail. The Chief and Dutch were on their way.

Mike hopped onto the back of the moped. She took the path around the quarry while the police were chasing kids. Most of them jumped into the water. Elgar had been too drunk to run and slept it off in lock-up. Svenson had passed out and had to be carried to jail. All the others escaped—thanks to Mom—or rather her crazy kitchen radio which will suddenly pick up a police message. She had taken that wild ride to warn the kids. After they got home she lost her cool.

It was not only mean and wrong of the Myrtles to sell the piano Mom and Dad had given him, it was stupid. Elgar is a genius standing at the keyboard making up a tune that takes you down and lifts you like a roller-coaster. Elgar is the kind of musician Robert Plant must have been when he was a boy, but Mike has all that Robert Plant hair. He plays along with

Elgar on old bongo drums, trying to think of lyrics, when the heavy door flings open and Elgar's mom Dora shouts, "Did you come in, Mike?"

"Yea, how are you doing?"

"You're smoking. It smells like skunk. Elgar! If you're smoking dope again, your Dad will lock the shelter."

"I can smell it too," Mike calls back. "It's the furnace. Better have it checked."

She leaves the door open. Elgar runs up and closes it. He looks like a skinny version of his mom. Dora was quite something when old Gramp picked her up in Europe. She still has a doll face and fuzzy hair, but she is big and shapeless now, wears glasses, and is the leading soprano in the Shoreland Community-Choir. Year after year at the Christmas Pageant she squeezes herself into her old angel costume, puts on cardboard wings that are pasted over with white chicken feathers, and belts 'Holy Night' out of the Tog Shop dormer. Year after year grade school kids are inspired to draw Christmas card angels with an O for a mouth and big O glasses.

Her husband and almost everyone else in town call her "Angel." She is tune crazy like Elgar but hates rock music, which she says comes from the devil, like drugs, and she gives Elgar a hard time when he wants to play his own kind of music and wants his own life style. In no time at all she opens the door again.

"Elgar, Mike! How about some cake?"

This is a summons. She invites them into the spray-waxed family room that looks and smells like Harrison's funeral parlor, dark with heavy drapes and silk flowers. There are smiling photographs of young Dora with Gramp; Mom and Dad as little kids. Dad says she lost her personality and put on weight after she allowed 'Myrtle Turtle' to have Gramp's old horses killed, and tear down Gramp's farm buildings, which she had inherited. Dora lost her looks, and Len made his first million building condos with a shooting range for senile types from the Shady Hill Hunt Club.

When she opens the TV cabinet and makes them watch the Nancy Reagan anti-drug commercial, JUST SAY NO 2, Mike dozes off for a minute. She prods his arm. "Wonder whether your mother has seen this?"

She is not going to get him to talk about Mom or Dad. He closes his eyes.

"What do you think of it, Mike?"

"Pretty lady."

"What do you think of drugs?"

Dora Myrtle, Angel, loves an argument with devilish Mike, but she has been totally uncool this evening; he is not in the mood. "Drugs, Angel?" he says, establishing a false intimacy. "It's like that caramel glaze you put on your cake. Perfectly good cake without it, right? But the glaze makes it so much sweeter."

Her glasses get steamed up. She takes them off and rubs them on her skirt, revealing a stout leg and fine ankles. "Well, I won't allow Elgar to ruin his life with drugs or drink in some fancy boarding school, where they don't even teach respect for elders." She sounds honestly pissed off. "I saw you on cable evening news. You have some nerve, Mike Plant. Getting up in front of the TV crew and telling a lot of lies to those strangers."

Eckert, the stranger and new owner of South Cove, happened to be in Harbor Square with his crew and a city-type TV hostess, taping a local interview with Garden Club beautification ladies carving their ice sculpture show. Two of them in their old foul-weather sailing gear were sawing big blocks of ice into flowers and birds to hide the sewer pipe.

Snow had been forecast. The air was wet and you could smell the stinking sewer fumes rising out of the pipes of the new sewer system that had raised local taxes. Mike had taken the opportunity to take Arthur Eckert aside and make a little speech about the pipes as sculpture as a work of modern art. One of the blue-haired beautification grandmothers started to titter. When the city woman asked asinine questions, Arthur invited Mike to come forward in front of the cameras and talk about the modern masterpiece. What a way to let everyone know that Mike Plant was back in town!

Elgar's dad comes bumbling into the room. "Mike, the TV star!" He is bald, wears a black wig and a dark suit, with a white shirt and crimson tie, and walks around hunched over wolfing a huge hunk of cake, dropping crumbs with energy. "What did your folks say to that performance?"

"We don't have cable. Dad's afraid I might watch the wrong kind of movies."

"Elgar doesn't watch that kind of movie," says Angel.

Len Myrtle does in secret. The boys know all about it and snigger. Nor would lying to strangers bother Len, who builds and sells ugly, damp condos to them, and they all get arthritic looking at the lovely ocean view.

"Don't they have a barber up in Maine, Mike? You sure need a haircut," he sounds off.

"Girls like my dreadlocks."

It's early, not much after ten o'clock, but L. M. makes Mike leave because he doesn't like to have any kids in the house after he goes to bed. Mike wears the trash bag to get the beer cans past L.M. and Angel who have no class. Poor Elgar.

Arthur Eckert has class. He had a good laugh after the Garden Club ladies wised him up about the famous artwork sewer pipe. He patted Mike on the shoulder. There was nothing like an insider joke, he said. Insider jokes helped Europeans survive the war. Mike patted him on the shoulder and told him that's how kids survived in Shoreland right now.

Coming out of the Myrtle house, you feel you're the last person on earth. The storm has dropped. Snow flies around in big white lazy flakes and Mike takes off his trash bag. No one is about; Elgar's roller coaster tune comes into his head and makes him think of summer and riding through the woods on a Harley one day with Karin on the back seat.

From the field near South Cove Road, Shoreland harbor and the town with its white church steeple and all the lights look like a Christmas card. Karin's house—the last light on Rooster Hill, twinkles through the snow. Her Finish great-grandfathers came here to work in the granite quarries. Finnish people on Rooster Hill eat together a lot, party together, and share saunas. By the time Karin was sixteen years old, she had been his babysitter for almost five years. She loved to play dress-up and baking cookies.

She was so much taller than Mike in those days, grown up looking with long braids wound around her head. Mom and Dad left her in charge while they had to go to a funeral in England. There was a big storm here. Lights went off all over Shoreland, a flying branch smashed the kitchen window. No phone. No heat. The fireplace smoked. A wave burst into the basement. The old house rocked; snow piled up and you couldn't get out the door. Mike and Karin curled up in bed together under two quilts. She was scared of boys her own age, but not of Mike, who had been reading every bit of sex information he could find in the recycle trailer at the dump. There was really nothing much to it all until they got used to each other. Not even Elgar knows what's been going on.

Since Karin went away to state college she has had to waitress all summer to make money. She goes to Yacht Club dances. Plants don't belong and don't sail because of that boat accident which is ancient history. Mom and Dad don't golf and don't belong to the Country Club because Dora and her "Myrtle Turtle" hang out there. Since Mom is writing, Mom and Dad are alone most of the time, go to few parties, and invite few people over. Dad sees mostly doctors, including Ellen.

A dog barks fiercely without catching its breath. Must be one of those barking doormats women bought after they had weird phone calls. A burglar alarm starts yip-yipping across the harbor. The end of loneliness and end of peace. More dogs, then police sirens. A cruiser goes skidding along looking to catch and punish someone. Mike ducks behind a tree, buries the trash bag with the empty beer cans in the snow, and hides his roach in his parka lining. He watches police cars heading for South Cove Point and Eckert's big house. What if the cable owner has been murdered? What if he murdered one of the foxy city women that come and go there? Or else he could be a big dealer and buying the cable station is just a front.

Mike zigzags across the wind-swept fields toward South Cove and dips into a barn. Someone grabs his hair. Mike swings out, the other one whim-whams and Mike punching every which way bangs his hand in the dark. "Fuck off!"

"Mike. It's you! Holy shit. All that perfume! Have you seen Caleb?" The squeaky voice identifies Tom the Tick, Caleb's cousin, who will fasten on and cause trouble.

"At Grove Academy."

"No way. He's here. Home for his birthday. His dad had to go out of town and so he left him money." The Tick sticks his head out of the barn door where you can see his fixed grin, wired-up teeth and, a squint enlarged by his dark-rimmed glasses. "Caleb, we're here!"

The response is the clatter of a copter in the sky. Something comes charging and pounding along. Mike jumps Tom and pulls him back in. A crazed black horse rears up in the dark and gallops on, kicking up snow. "Must have gotten out after I stuck that painting in the stable. No one in the house. Caleb split with Marilyn Monroe. No, no I'm not tripping my brains out. It's big as my Mom. Made of vinyl. Big boobs. And then there is that streaker running loose with a lantern and the Hound of the Baskervilles." Copter lights now quaver over the roof-tops, the raging sea and white beach, and hover above South Cove. Sirens shriek and cruiser lights twinkle through trees and shrubs back and forth from the big house. Copter lights hover above the stable. "Get down, Tick. Get in here!"

"No way! Holy shit, man, C.I.A. F.B.I. War! " One black horse in the middle of the field is pawing the snow, where dark figures struggle, waving and calling to another horse running scared from the copter.

"Some action. I'm not scared. It's fucking war! Wicked cool. "

"What's cool about war? Some old dudes wanting to take over another country they don't need, sending kids off to be killed for that." Mike tries to send him home, but Tick breaks away, waving his arms and shouting, "War! My dad was in Nam!" He races across the white field after one of the horses. A cruiser comes out from behind snow-covered pines, stops in the field and gets stuck. The cops get out and stand waiting for Tom Foster the second, son of a hero-loser veteran.

By the time Mike walks into the house his heart is pounding, his cheeks glow. Police sirens are in the house too. On TV. He stops at the glass door. There is Dad sitting in front of the set watching the chase. No idea of what's going on at South Cove. Lights and color from the set shine on his smooth face. No one smokes pipes anymore, but there he is, sucking on his English pipe. He looks stern, but great, like one of the British master spies he likes to watch, which makes Mike feel good about himself and hungry. He lights up his roach, feeds Ringo with a carrot to keep him quiet. Finds a small jar of caviar and crackers. Props Dad's new self-locking back door open with the doormat while he takes a leak. Then he makes his way upstairs, past Mother's room. You can hear her printer rattling through the padded door and her muffled voice reading something she has written.

He quietly opens his door to the usual evil, space-devouring mess. He can't even get to the light switch, stumbles over sneakers, shirts, and books, drops his jacket, lets himself collapse on a bed full of socks and sweaters. Junk always gets in the way. He doesn't bother to take off his clothes. "Creator of obstacles. That's me." Scaring himself by talking out loud and sounding so smart, he pulls the quilt up to his chin.

Chapter 16

CHRIS AND LIZ

Outside the doctor's office door, Sister Agnes, the teaching nun, let go of Liese's hand and touched the top of her head. "Mother of Heaven protect you."

Her blessing sounded more like a warning. And from this sad sister with the long chin, Jan and the troop had learned that the Mother of Heaven could not stop Roman soldiers from taking her son Jesus away, anymore than their mothers had been able to stop German soldiers. So why should Mother of Heaven save Liese from being taken away from Jan and the troop. She bit her lip and hung her head.

"I am glad you're praying," the nun said. "Never forget to say your prayers. If the American boy doesn't pray, you must teach him." She knocked, opened the door to a whiff of Dora's perfume and the doctor's disinfectant, handed Liese a small cardboard suitcase, and nudged her into the glaring light of two tall windows, where the American woman flamed up all in red. Liese dropped the suitcase. Ready to run toward her and desperate to escape.

The doctor was smiling. "Doesn't Liese look fine in this dress?"

The blue velvet dress hung down to Liese's old

shoes but did not hide them. On the big girls, like Martha, this dress would be short. Sister had told Liese to keep it clean. Such a beautiful dress was impossible to find in Vienna, and made all the difference when a child was presented.

"A lot of dress," the American laughed. Liese did not understand what he was saying, but she laughed because he sat straddling a child-sized chair, his face level with hers and legs sticking out like a big frog's. She would have to take the dress off the moment she got back to the shelter if the American boy did not like her. Even if the Americans decide to keep her for a day or so to try her out, they would be asked to return the dress.

The tall woman swooped down, kissed her cheek, "Dora, *ich bin* Dora." and handed her a small, wooden box. The child, who was not used to perfume or kisses or presents, backed away. The doctor came over. "All yours. No one is going to take it away." Then he took the box away and opened it. Liese went, "Ahhhh," snatched the small black and white china dog from red silk padding and held it in her hand.

The doctor talked about the shortage of toys and then the shortage of dogs in Vienna. *Zahlenlose*, innumerable animals had been killed and eaten. Even Bubi, the circus elephant everyone loved. The conditions were so bad right after the war.

Zahlenlose, numberless dead infants. He let his hand pass over the picture of a child's skeleton. War children had to be strong to survive. "For some reason they're terrified of being sick. Never complain when they have a sore throat. I have had to check their temperature and throat all the time. And then they often think they are being hurt when they are not, and panic."

When the American man wanted to know what the doctor was saying, tall Dora turned to the picture of the child skeleton and busied herself unbuttoning her bright red coat. "*Keine Angst*, don't worry." But the American kept worrying her with questions. "Mr.Plant wants to take her to Doctor Neubau, the child psychiatrist. The best he could find for his grandson. Do you know him?"

Dr.Bunter said he didn't have the honor.

"The English Queen Mother gave him a medal for

his work with little kids during the bombing of London," she said.

The doctor quickly told Dora in German that it was not a good idea to complicate matters by involving this Doctor Neubau. A second opinion from this 'soul doctor' was unnecessary. Herr Plant should take his word that Liese was mentally and physically healthy. The real parents had not come forward, but the Red Cross posters got all kinds of people interested in this beautiful child.

He leaned down to the sitting American as though he were a child, while he talked in loud school-boy English about a foreign man from a displaced persons camp who had come bursting in here this morning. Then he straightened up and told the lady that the riffraff at those camps would trade and barter for anything. Imagine a pork shoulder for a Liese! There was no need to worry. When the shelter closed, Mother Superior would take any of the unclaimed children back to the convent "In the French occupation zone. They will be safe and many of the girls they educate will become nuns."

When the young American studied her lacquered finger nails and did not translate, Graham Plant rose from the small chair and looked the doctor in the eye. "We better get going." But the doctor took his time writing down Mr.Plant's address in Vienna, the hotel room, his address in America, and his passport number. It would be in the best interest of the child to please return her at once if things did not work out. "My English is so bad. You speak such fine German, mein Fraulein. That is unusual."

"I studied German because I'm going to be an opera singer."

"You are connected with the Plant family?"

She laughed."No. Not really." She lowered her voice and told him that they'd only just met in Prague last week. "I was flying to Vienna to study voice. We were stranded in the Grand Hotel in Prague. I was singing for the other airline passengers in this cute little bar and someone stole my purse. I lost my passport and all my money, but Mr. Plant loved my voice and helped me out."

"How fortunate. But what a terrible experience for such a very talented very young Fraulein. And now all is well?"

"Just fine. I am going to see a voice tomorrow."

"If you are going to be a student, who would take care of the child? The nuns haven't had time to teach the children much English."

Dora beamed at him. "*Keine Sorgen*, don't worry. There is one of those travelling American grand-mothers and she is studying German. Great friend of Mr.Plant's. She'll love her."

"I want to stay here with Jan, the troop and the sisters," Liese said.

"You know that Jan's father is going to come all the way from Norway to pick him up?" the doctor asked.

"I want to go to Norway with Jan."

The doctor laughed and said, "How sweet." Then he lowered his voice and told Dora that the big boy and Liese had a slightly unnatural attachment. But under the circumstances this was quite natural. She was young enough to forget everything. "Always ready to enjoy herself," he said in English. When Gramp handed the doctor the dollar bills, the doctor put the money into the safe where he kept medication. He would not be smiling if Liese was returned, and he had to return money he needed to buy black market food for his own wife and five children.

He became quite angry when Liese sat down on the steps and refused to get into the car. "You will get the dress dirty," he bent down and hissed. "Get up, or you'll get a good smack!" She opened her hand, looking at the china dog. "If you don't go to see the boy, you're going to give the china dog back."

She allowed the American to pick her up, but when he took her to a big red car, she became fran-tic calling Sister, Jan, Holy Mary, Jesus, Heavenly Father,the Holy Ghost, even dead Adolf Hitler.

"She'll get over it," Gramp said to Dora as they drove away. He took the child onto his lap and let her hold the steering wheel, while they drove through the First District of Vienna, the interna-tional zone. Dora pointed out the statue of a seated woman, an Empress, fat as Frau Faser and mother of sixteen children. Military police- Russian, American, British, and French- passed by

in one jeep, keeping Vienna safe from each other
and from all kinds of displaced persons. Bombed
buildings were under repair.

When they drove past the ruin of the Opera,
Dora said that she herself would be an opera star
by the the time it was rebuilt. The hotel was just
across the street. Many famous singers used to stay
there. Now it was American. The flag at the
entrance decorated with stars and stripes instead
of the crooked cross looked new and bright, the
building old and dark. One horse-drawn cab and several bright colored cars stood lined up near the
entrance.

Dora carried the cardboard suitcase under her
coat, while Gramp whisked Liese past the guard, who
was used to seeing him with a child. They hurried
through the entrance room, crowded with men in uniform and a few women in bright clothes talking,
laughing and waving cigarettes. The hot, smoky air
was laced with cloying perfumes and the fragrance
of roasting meats. Two tall women came over to talk
to Gramp.

"*Sag kein Wort!* Don't say a word!" Dora whispered.

The women ogled the velvet dress. "Another
grandchild?"

Liese hid her face against Gramp's neck, which
smelled like cinnamon, baked Vienna rolls, and dog
paws. She clasped him tight.

"Shy! Just like me," he said to make them laugh
and get away. Upstairs, in his own rooms, he again
said,"Shy like me," to Sherry, the travelling
grandmother, who laughed out loud at everything he
said. Her short, round body and thin legs were
propped up on red high-heeled shoes that matched
her lipstick. Dark eyes wandered away from the
child to Dora and all around the room, as though
she had lost something. Gilt, crimson damask, crystal, glitter glow was reflected in two tall
mirrors. The room was too warm. The boy sitting on
the blue Persian rug playing with small trucks wore
a thin, pale blue short-sleeved shirt blue bow tie
and long, dark man's trousers. His blond curls
stuck up from a bandage that covered the right side
of his face.

"Here is Liz. Didn't I tell you she's just as

pretty?" Gramp said
   "Liese," Dora corrected as she took off her coat
and took Gramp's.
   "What's the difference? We like Liz." He
bestowed on Liese's cheek a terrifying kiss. "So
pretty, everyone wants you."
   Dora translated the "so pretty and "wants you",
for Liese, who already knew that being wanted could
be as scary as not being wanted. The boy seemed
comfortably disinterested and kept playing with
trucks and cars, following a blue pattern on the
rug towards the small girl in the big dress. "Grrrr,
grrr, honk, honk! Wrong shoes."
   Chris always noticed anything that was wrong
because he had been hurt, and Dr. Neubau had told
him to talk about his accident anytime he felt like
it. He started off by telling the girl that he was
a good sailor. His Sis had been allowed to light
the boat stove and so the boat blew up, killing her
and his parents. Nobody translated. When he took
her hand to pull her down to sit beside him, it
felt as though they had both been afloat in icy
water.
   Wounded orphans at the hospital shelter were sad
and angry, but the American boy sounded cheerful
and matter of fact. Liese sat beside him tilting
her head, listening for friendliness. She understood the word 'doctors,' and when he touched the
big bandage on his head and asked, "How do you like
it?" he sounded pleased with the bandage as she was
when she wore the old hat.
   He picked out a car, pretending it was taking
him to the doctor, quite contented to go on playing
his own game. And she played his game in her own
way, as she always would, picking up an army truck
to take her and the troop to a white farm house
beside a blue-green meadow patch.
   "Home," Chris said. "House by the sea. I like
staying in Shoreland with Gramp. He doesn't like
boats, he likes horses. I hate boats and I won't go
near water. I'm not allowed to ride, because of my
hands."
   The woman brought sweet drinks for the children
and cake cut up into small squares. "Don't drink so
fast." Dora raised her own glass slow as a priest.
Gramp was reflected in the sunny mirror, raising

his golden drink. Liese concentrated on eating and drinking slowly, without spilling anything on the carpet, while she took in the bewildering wonder of tall Americans all trying to please and appease a boy who was blond, but definitely sickly and unworthy. Instead of sorting the boy out, the grown ups in the hot, sunny room encouraged him to eat more with the litany of coaxing words and praise nuns used in prayer. When he handed Liz half his cake, she was the much-admired winner for stuffing herself, while the boy took away her truck and reached for her closed left hand."What have you got there?"

Liese stood up.

"We didn't have time to go to the P.X. to buy a toy, and Gramp found a little china dog in a shop on the Ringstrasse," Dora said.

The boy jumped up."I want to see it!"

"Why don't you let Chris look?" Dora said in German.

Liese opened her hand; Chris plucked the dog from her with his scarred hand. She knew it was going to drop, and it shattered on a marble side table. Dora was right there to pick up the pieces. "Graham will get you another one."

Liese did not make a sound. Tears she could not control ran down her cheek.

"You mustn't cry," Dora told her.

"Let's have that lovely smile," Gramp said.

"You were getting along so well," Dora said. "Look what you've done, Chris!"

"Sorry, Sis," the boy said.

"That's what he used to call his sister," Dora said in German.

"She is dead," Liese said. "Frau Faser called me Liese after her sister, and she was dead too."

Dora gave her a perfumed kiss on the cheek."What did the nuns call you?"

The child wiped the cheek with the back of her hand. "Engerl. And Angels are in heaven too."

Marble angels, children's graves, came to Dora's mind. She turned to Chris and told him about this girl's sad,sad life.

When Gramp said that he'd better be kind if he wanted her to stay. Chris quickly put his arm around the girl's shoulder. His bad hand, resting under her hair as if it were hiding, smelled both of infirmary and roses.

"See, he wants you to stay," Dora said, and then she and the American left.

Gramp and Dora went dancing, to concerts, or to the theater which was now the opera. They ate with other Americans. Chris had to be kept quiet with his new sister in the hotel room. The grandfather did not replace the broken china dog but brought more toys for them to share. Chris allowed her to play with the toys, but he did not share.

Chapter 17

RECKONINGS

By the time Johnny Carson puts on a purple satin turban and glares into the eye of the camera in his role of a hypnotist, Chris has settled down with his third drink and the pleasant awareness that millions of American drunks and insomniacs are ready to succumb to their nightly TV trance with him.

The first guest, a young pretty little monkey type actress, asks Johnny, the hypnotist, whether anyone could get stuck in a trance. Sure, he says. Just look at my band! It's a joke, a game. The child psychiatrist in Vienna put Chris into a trance by watching a windup clown go around and around until it wound down. As a four year-old he went under easily, but he also easily forgot the doctor's commands.

Chris swallows his Oban whisky, which is definitely medicinal. Closes his eyes to visualize the hypnotic windup clown moving slow and slower like a sleepwalker, when he is jolted by the kitchen phone. "Chris, darling!" The inimitable stage voice of Dora. An evocation of Gramp's nemesis. No surprise.

"The police came by. Kids stole a painting worth hundreds of thousands at South Wood, and let two priceless horses out of the stable. They couldn't accuse our Elgar. He never left the house. But Mike is running around dressed in a trash bag. Came to see Elgar, stayed for dessert and left half an hour ago. We didn't breathe a word," she says with an operatic breath and sigh of self-restraint.

But in his altered state of mind, Dora's busybody singsong insinuations, become superimposed on his picture of a young Dora in Prague singing, We'll Meet Again: a double exposure. "Don't worry. If any of the kids are in lock-up. Mike will tell them what their rights are. Liz will spring them in the morning."

"Not funny," Dora says.

But Dora is having fun. The storm—God's vandalism or God's will—with the sideshow pranks of bored kids provide entertainment in Shoreland, where nothing much happens and everyone knows about it. "Sweet dreams, lovely," Chris says like the seductive four year-old who had found Dora for Gramp.

Let kids invade South Point, which is lit up like cruise ship. Let the northeaster blast boats, devour land, rip away beach dwellings, throw cars into the harbor, and bury the town in snow. Let Liz bamboozle about a small boy clinging to a floating board. Once again, Chris commemorates his survival with Oban whiskey and Toscanini conducting Schubert's Unfinished festooned in his music room with the finest record collection in America. Sort of like Nero playing the fiddle while Rome burns. Danger is erotic, when you're safe.

Was it Bigfield or was it Ellen who told him to stop clinging to flotsam? But he never got over the shock of the explosions, fire, and icy water. That's why he could never forget the night landing in Prague, which changed his life. Flares lined up on the runway waiting to explode the plane, the giant red moon reflected on a black river. He had made believe his dead twin was sitting in the empty seat beside him during the noisy landing and later when the bus rattled them through empty streets past dark houses. He told her that people were asleep or hiding, ready to pounce. Finally, during the ride over the dangerous old bridge, Gramp had asked him to be brave and stop talking to ghosts, which was the best game a brave, bandaged boy could play.

Nor could Chris understand why Gramp was going to pay a lot of money to a specialist doctor in Vienna to get rid of the Sis ghost, who was far less trouble than the tiny black whimpering dog which needed talking to and kissing while it snapped at the stewardess and wet the seat. A dog was against regulations, a ghost was not.

The problem with the important American and her dog had made the Pan American Clipper late. They had to land in Prague, because the Russian occupation forces in Vienna did not permit night landings. If they hadn't had to stay overnight at the hotel in Prague, Chris would never have found Dora, and Dora would never have found him Liz. Gramp would not have left the farm to Dora and the house to Liz. Whenever Chris tries to think Liz away, or when he tries to talk her away during a therapy session or with Ellen, the fear of death comes over him.

Last year, during a session with Dr. Haupter, the Freudian, Chris had remembered how spectacularly grateful Dora had been to Gramp, while she took over and encroached, and, he had to admit, entertained. Dora's need for being rescued was sexual. She'd cling to her protector and overpower him. Dora was a stage name she made up. Her real name had been Sally Wood. Chris had wandered into the hotel bar and found her, but she always said Gramp was the one who had first heard her singing "We'll meet again" and fell in love with her voice. Actually Gramp would not have invited her to dinner in Prague if he had heard her quavering high notes. The Plants all have a fine ear.

Her audiences in Prague and everywhere else came to look rather than listen. Besides anything from the New World must have seemed bigger, better, more desirable in those days. She was built like the Statue of Liberty. Taller than anyone else in that piano-bar, until Gramp walked in during the applause. He saw her smile over the heads of all the dapper men who had somehow survived the war unharmed, and throw a kiss to bandaged little Chris. This made Gramp smile.

Her flight to Vienna two days ago had been late like theirs and passengers had to stay over in Prague. While she had sung in the cute little bar, her handbag had been stolen. She lost her passport and all her money. Gramp reminded her of the jovial old men at the Rotary Club in Iowa City, where her mother had to work as a cleaning woman and Dora had started belting out songs for dances when she was thirteen years old. After she graduated from high school, the club had raised money for her to study voice with a famous teacher in post-war Vienna, where a few thousand dollars would go a long way. She had learned to speak German to become a Wagnerian opera star, for she certainly looked the part and she did have a big voice.

She told Gramp that she was terrified of a Bulgarian who tried to force himself on her while she was stranded in Prague. The omni-presence of invisible passionate admirers had served her well with Grandfather, who did not believe in phantoms. So he took her along to Vienna, later all over Europe, and finally back across the Atlantic to Shoreland in a never-ending rescue mission. Chris had told Dr. Bigfield that Gramp had adopted Dora for himself, before he adopted Liz for Chris.

Loud banging now ruins the last exquisite cords of the Unfinished Symphony. Has to be a loose shutter as usual. Chris heads for the big living room, which runs the length of the twenty foot long terrace facing the sea. A crash indicates a shutter has fallen. The storm roars down the huge fire place. The painting above the mantle hangs crooked. There is not a living soul in that scene of palaces reflected in the Grand Canal of Venice, which has been the backdrop for his dreams of the dead father, mother, Sis, or the stiff, glass-eyed goat at English Granny's manor. Who would not prefer a ghost to a corpse? Better to be haunted than to be revolted by inevitable decay. If the wounded boy allowed himself to be hypnotized and stopped talking to the ghost of his twin, Chris has to keep himself and sister-wife, Liz, happy by talking to psychiatrists about his haunted past and his haunted present. What right does Liz have to butt in with her darned Stolen Child-Wounded Boy? Fantasizing in a book that would discredit years of Christopher Plant's psychiatric case histories? His life. Years and years of talking to doctors.

Chris flicks on the switch to light up the ten-foot black cross on the granite slab, where waves rise and explode, gushing over steps that lead down to the mooring that was never used again. The cold drafts swing the drapes, chilling his face into a tight mask. He grabs hold of the back of Gramp's carved armchair, holding on tight to the flotsam of Gramp's goodwill. Then he tears himself away, as though following a hypnotic command, and walks upstairs slowly. The attic door is banging, but a bomb blast wouldn't wake Mike or Liz once they are asleep. Her old room with her computer is next to Gramp's room, which is now Mike's, of course.

DEC MATE II sign flickers on the screen as he enters. "I haven't done a thing," he says. Liz has confessed that she could never have written this book without the word processor. Instructions from the screen warn her and tell her what to do. While she writes like one possessed, she talks to the computer in German, which is far worse than a four-year old talking to an invisible sister or Dora with her phantom Bulgarian.

Chris can't breathe in this room. "Using my hurt to concoct her story," he says to his shadowy reflection in the dark dresser mirror. "Stealing." He turns on the desk light. There is one of those brown envelopes with chapters ready for her editor. He fans them out. Little Procurer. What does that title mean? The invisible scars on his right hand start to itch the moment he reads a few paragraphs of a chapter that turns his tragic childhood into a farce.

He calls Ellen. "This is Shoreland personalized answering service. Will be back at seven thirty a.m. God bless and sweet dreams." Bonnie! He scratches his hand and dials the family number, using his three ring signal.

"Chris?"

"I don't think I ever told you how I kept talking to my twin after she and my parents were killed in that explosion. My grandfather called it talking to ghosts. Worried him more than my burned face and hands. I told you about that great child psychiatrist in Vienna. He was supposed to get rid of ghosts. He used a windup toy clown to hypnotize me."

"Did it help?"

"Not quite. He tried to program me to find girls to play with. So I found girls for Grandfather. I told you about the nurse when I was in the hospital in London, then that stewardess. Then I found Dora for him in Prague."

"I didn't know that about Dora Myrtle. Tell me—"

"Listen to this, 'Brave little fellow. Less trouble than a dog.' That's a direct quote from her book. Grandfather always said that to women we met. Liz makes it sound as if he kept me around the way prostitutes in London kept cute dogs." Chris swallows the wrong way and coughs. "Just listen! His grandfather looked as though he needed a hair-cut. Girls always liked to touch that wild mane. And a small boy with wild hair got a lot of attention. Especially when it stuck up from bandages."

"You still mess up your own hair to get attention, don't you? You have a lot of beautiful hair. So many men are bald when they're only thirty years old. And…"

"You don't understand. In her book, Gramp and I are weirdos. I don't know what's come over Liz. She never wanted to talk about herself or me. I told her, she wasn't supposed to."

"Chris. I'm glad you are able to talk about it. "

"I'm not." A sudden mood change drains him and makes him sad. "Sorry to bother you. Sweet dreams."

Ellen giggles. "Sweet nightmares, love!"

The sinking feeling turns into baffled rage. He stoops low, advancing towards the computer monitor. His dwarfed shadow follows him over the English wallpaper of field flowers. He eases the chapters back into the mailing envelope. The moment he puts it down where he found it, he feels the magnetic field winding him up with hypnotic magnetism, ready to feed the three boxes with the diskettes to the waves. Would they float like a bottle post? He can just see the headlines in the Eagle. **Fascinating cache of computer diskettes containing chapters of a memoir show up in a drag-net.**

But something has to be done. He gulps his drink with infantile burps and starts pacing back and forth like the mechanical clown. His fists rise and fall slower as his rage winds down. He descends to the kitchen, empty glass in his right hand, the envelope clamped under his left arm. The guinea pig starts to squeak and whistle in the dark, guarding food from strangers. Who would come into the house on a night like this? He turns on the light and it calms down. "Useless creature."

Chris gulps brandy from the bottle before stepping into the disgusting laundry room, which juts out of the house, refrigerated by snow and reeking of organic fertilizers, trash, and carcinogenic perfumed fabric softener. Tools are rusting everywhere. Mike takes them, never puts anything back. The wrench under the sink and the mallet were left out when Chris had to fix the plumbing. Since he does most of the repairs, Liz used to pick up after him. Now she is writing and doesn't have the time. She does have time for Ellen's boys, who decorated the trash bin with red and blue and yellow flowers and gave the big butterfly on the lid that awful bearded man's face. An incongruent omen.

The lid has been left half open to emit poisonous stench; Mike's candy wrappers decorate the floor with some fluff from the dryer and cigarette butts. Her house, her kid! Chris buries the envelope deep down under all kinds of wet papers. Beatrice Strout had spouted about "symbolic actions" He feels feverish, excited, really good about giving her a chance to reconsider her betrayal. But in his heart he knows that Liz has monster diskettes galore. Mate II will growl, and the printer will rattle out "Little Procurer" and all the rest over again. She prefers printing out to making love. Now that he has taught her a lesson, he needs to hold and comfort himself with warm Liz in his warm bed and heads to his bedroom. Regular lusty Shorelanders sleep in the altogether until they reach the flannel nightshirt stage. Chris modifies this tradition, wearing only the top of his black silk pajamas to keep his shoulders warm. In the morning he will take the top off and put on the silk pants. But he won't have Liz sleep in the nude. How can a man get excited undressing a woman when she is already naked? He likes perfume the way Gramp always did. The bottle on the dresser is open. That kid has been using his "Mustache" again!

Chapter 18

HOUSES DEVOUR WOMEN

The day starts white as a new page, and from her bed Ellen admires the trunk of a dead hawthorn tree sticking up from the snow in the Plant garden as a stark phallic symbol. The tree had died when forsythia, blackberry bushes, and wild maples were allowed to take over.

At one time, that garden had possessed Liz. The Plant house owned her. She was working her life away as though she had to earn the right to the property she had inherited. All summer long she would plant, weed and feed, water, and replant; growing vegetables had been an obsession. Not even Bonnie could keep up with her. Most of the Plant harvest had to be given away. Liz often left a bag of corn and squash and greens on Ellen's doorstep and fled like a thief. She never wanted to be thanked. Bonnie's influence.

But Ellen takes credit for giving her neighbors Liz and Bonnie each a copy of HOUSES DEVOUR WOMEN, a very liberated article by Beatrice Strout, which turned Liz Plant into a writer and Bonnie into a business woman. "Do you want a park, a farm, a picnic ground, golf course, or a Garden of Eden?" asks Beatrice Strout.

Last summer, when Liz allowed herself to work seriously on her book, wild roses and herbs, and new trees were taking over the Plant garden. Wild strawberries, blueberries, giant sunflowers reseeded themselves, yielding more seeds. But what good is a Garden of Eden to Liz when her Adam says it gives him allergies?

One day last summer, Ellen had come across the Plants lying in a hammock together under the big maple tree. He had put Liz to sleep talking about his allergies. Later when he came to consult Ellen about his symptoms, he refused to go along with her sensible idea that patients should sit up in a chair and be alert, while the psychologist relaxes on the couch. He said he was not feeling well and enjoyed himself stretching out beside Ellen.

Perfumed, dressed in white, he sounded more British than usual during his Sherlock Holmes self-investigation of childhood trauma, his terror of fire and water, a man in a slouch cap, while he had investigated her flawless breasts. Holding her tight while he talked about holding onto flotsam in the icy water and said she was saving him. Went on to talk about explosions, fire. New fire extinguishers. "Portable, potent ejection for putting out small fires." It was the only time Ellen ever laughed herself and a man into a climax. Can't be repeated. Nothing is ever quite the same. Ellen helped Chris to understand that he was turning his early childhood tragedy into a self-serving farce. And he had said, "Don't we all?" Chris and Mike both like to have the last word. So they don't get along.

Ellen's two sons, Billy and Jonathan, come toddling into her room with their eyes half open, curl up in the sun on her pink quilt. Eyes closed, they look average American like dependable George, whom Ellen can no longer depend on. She secretly loves anything solid and dependable, like this old cottage, which was built when women like Bonnie's great aunt Codgie kept houses, their home town, and America going no matter what, while men in charge governed and misgoverned as they always will, fighting little and big wars.

Listening to the distant sound of waves which is so common in subliminal persuasion tapes that aim to give a sense of soothing eternity, Ellen remembers falling in love with conservative Dr. George Burns and traditional Shoreland on the same day trip from Boston. George, the most predictable man she had ever met, made her feel wildly happy and liberated. She got him to run barefoot with her along town beach, below the old granite rock wall, the white houses, and churches, threw her arms around his neck, and proposed.

Two months later he had carried her over the doorstep of the proverbial little cottage with the picket fence. Everything proper. George, a surgeon, who had studied the female body to repair it, knew what he was doing. At first twice a day, then twice a week, and in the end, when Ellen decided they should be more experimental, every Friday.

She had her two sons, one right after the other, and became an experimental mother, letting babies run naked in the summer garden. Her cooking was experimental too. George accused her of poisoning him with wild flowers and roots, and mushroom recipes from the WILDERNESS SURVIVAL GOURMET. She would read feminist news letters while she was cooking and pots burned. George had married her because she was liberated and different, but then expected her to do everything his way. Al, her great helper, had appeared at her house like a gift from heaven.

Al might very well have become Liz's helper since he trespassed at her house first, to feed granola to hungry gulls on the rocks below the terrace. But Mike, the grade school expert on fugitive Aliens, took one look at Al's shaved head, the heavy chain jewelry, and welcomed him to earth with stories of settlers coming here directly out of European jails, ghosts of pirates, witch women, boats that burned and sank. Sharks, sea serpents, snakes, and Russian spies, anything far out he could think of.

Al escaped in his model A Ford, but just down the road at Ellen's house it stalled. She had taken an auto repair course during her second pregnancy, but she used psychology, stood by, and watched this young fellow take the engine apart. Perhaps he used his own kind of psychology when he didn't put the car together again for two years.

Al became the first house-boy on the North Shore. At one time there must have been about six or seven young guys who came away from California and became live-in helpers. Al was the best. He cleaned and repaired the house, shopped, cooked, despised money and social security, and worked for his keep without a salary. Ellen noted his fixed ideas as the natural aftereffect of mindlessness induced by hallucinogens.

Al, like most of the live-in boys who had come away from trying out drugs and crazed women in California, had turned to trying out religions that also left aftereffects. Buddhism had made him a fanatical vegetarian cook. He strummed his guitar in the evening when Billy, Jonathan, their friends, and even their enemies flocked around him for a chant-along against the President, against war, against the police, against pesticides and the hunting of animals. "Why not sing in praise of sweet Jesus instead?"

Bonnie had asked.

Since George performed open heart surgery in the morning and saw patients in the afternoon, he looked forward to a drink in the evening and hated vegetable juice. He liked a thick steak. Instead he got tofu and a lecture served up by Al: Didn't he see enough blood and suffering all day long? And didn't the doctor know he was poisoning himself?

And yet Al took over all the chores. Ellen was able to work as the school psychologist, went to hear Beatrice Strout lectures in Boston, and enrolled in Will and Desire, a consciousness raising extension course that introduced her to a lively young crowd, a dull young lover, and dancing.

Al waited up one night to catch Ellen in her fur coat and delivered a sermon on the suffering of wild animals and sin. George woke up. Came down the stairs in Christian Dior pajamas inspired by prison uniforms. He was a quiet man, but he yelled at Al. Then he got dressed and threw stuff into a small suitcase. Al told George he could not leave Ellen. Marriage was an eternal bond.

Ellen and George were divorced after Al dug a deep trench down the middle of the doctor's impeccably well-fed lawn. Ellen did try to get the other house-boys to come and talk to Al about the digging, but one had remained Buddhist, another was a former Catholic monk, and they didn't even talk to each other anymore.

After three weeks of rain that spring, baby Billy fell into Al's ditch and could have drowned in the mud if his father had not shown up to take the boys for the day. George threatened to take Ellen to court for neglect. Forcing her to choose between the house-boy and the kids.

George simply could not understand Al's artistic soul, the innocent childlike personality full of unconscious sexuality. How Al had worshiped Ellen, quite innocently, as his ideal: a mother. Even though he's been gone for years now, she continues to live up to Al's ideal and keeps her hair long. Snow covers the deep cleft he dug on the lawn, but each summer witchgrass grows around the edges like pubic hair, as Al's primitive work of art: a vulva symbol.

"*Schlamperei*, sloppiness." No better word, no better language for misery and scolding herself than German. Liz searches her desk, the file cabinet, shelves, drawers where the chapters she printed out yesterday could not possibly be. Her hands tremble. She throws old versions of chapters and notes into disorder.

"*Veruckt*, crazy! Did I throw the mailing envelope into the box and take it to the dump by mistake? No mistake, Beatrice Strout writes: Women will make bad things happen to avoid fulfilling their true destiny. After the call from Havelock Grimes, Liz had cleaned up with the frenzy of appeasing the unappeasable Frau Faser, the ghost of Codgie, Anika, one and all. As though fulfilling the expectations of the living as well as the dead would keep Mike out of trouble and safe.

The search creates havoc in her room as the lost manuscript and all she ever lost draws her into a maze of misery. She knocks a tattered dictionary off the book-shelf. A thin booklet falls out like a secret message from Gramp's mother, Rosalie Plant.

June Morning
Stray button near the kitchen door,
Mud on my Mother's braided rug
The dusty mirror doubles
Work that is never done.
A whiff of fragrance from a rose
Where beetles shimmer in the sun
The window glass doubles
Death that is never done.

Why should the booklet open to this page? An omen, a warning? Something to frame and hang on the kitchen wall? Rosalie's sweet, rounded letters embroidered all the other pages, not with such unusual poems but the daily lists of usual obligations. A record of all of Rosalie's tedium, the daily trivia. Monday, laundry day, Tuesday, upstairs rooms and kitchen. Wednesday, downstairs rooms. Then the garden. Vegetables in the vegetable garden, fruit. Everything had to be grown, harvested, preserved, put away on shelves for the winter, much of it given away at Christmas.

Every day of the week filled with duties to control dirt, dust, rust, mold, weeds and vermin, and tidy up after untidy men. Sew on their buttons, darn socks. She did not work with Codgie the maid. She worked for her to the end. There was no escape: the tyranny of meals, the baking, the pickling, marketing. Lots of relatives descending on Rosalie for tea, Thanksgiving, Christmas, birthdays. More to feed, more to please or displease. But that was not all.

When Gramp's little mother wasn't in church or working for fairs, baking for bake sales, or at the garden club plant sale, or at bridal or baby showers, or weddings, or visiting the sick, or at a funeral; when she wasn't writing happy wedding, or happy birthday, or Christmas, or Easter, or get well, or condolence cards and letters—she locked herself into the coat closet under the stairwell and wrote poems.

Liz would have to shut herself into her own room in order to print out again, before Mike and Chris got up for breakfast, but she can't go to work on the unpredictable printer in such a state. The author of LOVE AND LEARN says a creative sexual woman has to rid herself of stress and keep fit. If you get a sinking feeling, move, move, and feel the joy of your own power. Rather than looking for the lost envelop she should celebrate finding the poet Rosalie Plant.

To get the joy of her own power, Liz puts on her purple leotards and tights for the TV morning stretch. The teacher often grumbles out loud to herself, but she also laughs a lot, calling herself Joanie as she demonstrates and gives motherly advice on how to be healthy and thin. Joanie has been getting thinner and thinner and looking quite unhealthy.

On her way downstairs, Liz scoops up a shirt and a towel, Mike's sneakers in the hallway. She leaps over NEW YORKER magazines and OPERA NEWS as she passes through Chris's music room. The mess in the house is quicksand, something to avoid, or Liz the writer would go under. A sweater lies curled up like a creature in the adjoining dining room. On the table two orange-colored candles in unpolished brass candlesticks protrude from a deluge of bills, pamphlets, checks and tax records mixed up with trash mail gathering dust. Chris may not be handicapped, but doctors do take his childhood injury and symptoms into account and write letters for the yearly tax deferment. There is a stiff penalty he pays each year. She reaches for a banana, steps out onto the wind-swept terrace to take a deep breath of tangy air and watch the waves. No time, and then time stands still. A hawk circles down from the old commons over snow-padded houses, churches, shacks that sit on a fog bank above the sea. Clouds rising up like the sugar-capped mountains, which had towered above Hitler School Waldruh. The bird tilts over the graveyard and the woods. If there are nonmigrant birds, why not non-migrant souls of women? Old kitchen and cellar stones are all that remain of the village built by the first settlers on the old commons at a safe distance from the sea and pirates. After the Indians, pirates, and war, the town by the sea was built, and witch women stayed on up there in the woods in crumbling homesteads, guarded only by scrawny stray dogs that, like the women, were often punished rather than rewarded when they gave warning.

Witch women were not able to forewarn themselves. There is a legend of an old woman named Marcia who had warned seamen that their merchant ship would sink. When the seamen were afraid to sail, the captain got so angry that he took Marcia aboard and stowed her below deck. They had hardly passed Pig Island when a thunderbolt exploded their gun powder. Not one survivor. The ship with the crew, captain, and Marcia must have gone down near Pig Island, where the Plant yacht blew up. The dark reflection of the Plant house on the tidal pool often looks like a sunken vessel.

Weather has always been unpredictable, and there have always been unpredictable, ruthless men, and self-important women creating their own doom whenever they tried to save them with predictions and warnings. A Beatrice Strout would have fretted and starved up there on the old commons, and had her say.

Writing STOLEN CHILD is a warning too, in groping for the truth about the dutiful women who did not speak up about stolen countries, murder, starvation, children on the run, rulers murdering populations in the past, the present, and still to come. While now and always a woman speaking of predictable consequences has been suspect, an obstacle to ruthless males. A portent of evil, a witch. Something to berate, punish, and destroy. Liz the writer would have been banished to the old common too.

A good American woman was not supposed to predict but make life predictable from day to day as she tidied up the house for her family in this town, in this country. Women suffered and often died giving birth. It was the survival of the fittest. Rosalie Plant had started raising a family of men when she was twenty years old. But by the time she was widowed only Graham, her youngest and her favorite survived. Gramp often said Codgie cleaned his beautiful, boring, spoiled, barren wife right out of the house. His mother, Rosalie had shrank in size as her family shrank though she kept doing her daily work in the house to appease Codgie.

A modern woman does not sacrifice herself, says Beatrice Strout. Why be a good housekeeper when the worst world-keepers are on the rampage? Why struggle to raise children and clean, while the killer males are soiling and spoiling the air, the water, even the ocean?

Then, again, are housework and gardening self-sacrifice, or voluptuous self-indulgence? Liz thinks back to the days when she had learned to bake and cook and clean and garden—like all the Plant women before her. She enjoyed making gingerbread men with Mike. The taste of melons from her own garden with breakfast she carried up to Chris when he said he had a temperature, and then getting back into bed with him. Bundling under lavender scented sheets, like the small boy and girl in that Vienna hotel bed. Together they felt voluptuously safe.

The hawk circles over the old commons, down over the white woods to the graveyard, hovers above rows of snowcovered Plant and Codget graves—a predator hungry for movement of life betraying itself on the snow—a mouse, a sparrow. Under the wet snow roots soak, seeds will swell and sprout, crowding in on old trees. In no time at all it will be summer. There is no spring anymore. Everything grows fast, competing for space, as kids grow into teens too fast. No need for a Nazi doctor with needles for school girl Del to give birth to a little mistake. Roles have reversed. Children oppress both parents and teachers sorting them out as useless.

A new woman has to be at the helm of her own future, says Beatrice Strout. Liz flings the banana peel down into the dark water and plunges back into the house. You have to get your priorities right, or a day will float away like a ghost vessel.

Chris has left a pile of trash mail for her even on the kitchen radio. YOU LIZ PLANT HAVE WON A MILLION...Would it change her life if she had a million? The radio reports that the roads have all been cleared. Ringo stands up on his hind legs and makes himself heard. He likes to sit on her shoulder while she cleans his aquarium-cage and refills his food and water dish. Fifteen more minutes before her television keep fit.

Mike must have left a comic book on the old table. CLASSIC X-MEN. A woman dressed in green tights, flying away from a man covered with gold fuzz. Inside: PHOENIX UNLEASHED. A body builder in a red devil suit in attack stance is surrounded by leaping, hopping-mad killers in aerobic costumes. Liz in her purple tights could have stepped out of "Phoenix Unleashed", but her smile would have been odd among the angry grimaces.

THAT'S THE SPIRIT, TERRAN FOOLS! I AM GALACTUS, FORMER HERALD. HE WHOSE POWER IS LIKE UNTO THAT OF A RAGING SUN! I AM FIRELORD! ARRRGH!—GO AFTER FIRE LORD. KILL HIM. MY POWER—IT'S HITTING ME LIKE A DRUG, I'VE NEVER FELT SUCH ECSTASY!

Page after page of mindless fury. Fantasy of enemy after enemy, as a forewarning to kids programmed to expect having a good time in a world that is programmed to erupt into repeat patterns of mad violence. When Gramp was a boy there would have been Rosalie's Bible on the table, not a comic book. She must have read the scripture with pleasure.

In her days, the TV room had been a proper parlor, cleaned every week, but opened only for family gatherings at weddings, high holidays, funerals. Liz opens the parlor door slowly and tiptoes in like a thief. Then holds the door to avoid the self-slamming bang. For, stretched out on the big sofa, by television light, lies big Caleb, Mike's roommate, sleeping on his belly. His snub-nosed baby face looks grubby with rusty stubble. The red hair is short, to please his uncle, Emmet Gray. Caleb, breathing heavily, looks at home here, anywhere, usurping at all times, as the future will usurp the past. And one day another mother might tiptoe through the door in another time, to remember the legend of Caleb, stretched out like a dead boy washed ashore. Wet army boots, G.I.cap, Caleb, reader of CLASSIC X-MEN whose safety and education could not be bought; Caleb distrustful of the good, the safe future, as sailors and sea captains had been of danger. Awesome Caleb, in rags. Uncouth, unwashed, a refugee from marble bathrooms, white country curtains, prep school dorms. If Caleb can't hitch a ride in the middle of the night, he walks the six miles from his house to the Plants.

A log fire he must have lit casts a glow onto the portrait of pale Rosalie Plant which hangs above the couch. Round blue eyes, a pointed small nose and a straight mouth. Ageless like an archangel in the ruined Viennese chapel—neither happy, nor sad. She had lost her husband. Sons died fighting a war or fighting a disease. In the end only Graham had been left. Late in life, as a widow, she had a telephone installed in that airless coat closet, locked herself in to get time off from Codgie while she read her verse to a poet in Maine. Liz remembers old Codgie as angry and red in the face, on an inspection visit, hobbling around to check up on Anka, Gramp's Polish housekeeper and her husband Bruno, the gardener. Gramp the tease would say: "Codgie, you worked my poor little mother to death!" And Codgie, "Rosalie Plant died of poetry, and you know it!"

Poems must have been private as prayer to Rosalie. When Liz heard Gramp talk about his mother, he made fun of the poems which set the chimney on fire. He had made fun of religion too. As for Codgie, the house-keeper, Rosalie's last request to burn the poems would all be part of tidying up. And so was dying—passing away. Gramp recalled his mother laid out by candle light in the parlor, tiny as a doll in a fancy box, holding the single red rose sent by Carlton Higgins, the Maine poet. Her only kindred soul, and they had never even met.

The storm howls, but the TV is mute. Afghan rebels fighting Russian intruders shoot and die in silent pictures like cartoon X-Men. "Caleb!" He keeps his eyes shut. Does not want to wake up. Mike says Caleb is his own creation: army style designer cotton fatigues—willfully ripped, to allow Tahitian undershorts to blossom through camouflage green.

"Caleb. How did you get in?"

The hefty boy sits up to stretch and yawn. He likes to put on a show. "No doors are ever closed to a Grove Academy boy. Like five years ago that senior from Hartford—the convicted burglar passed it on down to new talent. Comes in handy. I'm good at working without noise. Didn't want to wake you up. "

This is touching, since he has no consideration for anyone. "Are you suspended too?"

"Worse, but Uncle Emmet has this awesome lawyer. And Goodley had already promised he'd let me out early for my birthday." Liz goes to the kitchen and comes back with two glasses of orange juice. They sit cross-legged on the rug facing each other, while the big boy talks in a conspiratorial little falsetto mimicking his gin guzzling mother talking about being neglected by her Mama, who just died in Paris. He pours half a glass of juice down his throat.

"Does your mother know you are here?"

"Drinking all day long in a bathrobe. That's why she won't fink—if I don't." His sister's away at school. Dad's off at a convention, or whatever. Left him cash and a fun card on the bar. So Caleb called his cousin the

Tick. They bought from the Cragleys, got high, feeling wicked good, running around in the snow. Got hungry. Hit South Cove. "All new, awesome. New owner's away a lot. Tick knows it for a fact, lights are turned on when they're gone.

The troop had hit an empty house too. "Did you find food?" she asks.

"Pistachio ice cream and Greek olives, tried on mink coats. Put one on a big naked statue in the garden to keep it warm. There were big abstract paintings of crazy, naked women spinning around like—Tick went back for it."

"Why?" Liz asks as though she didn't know that needy children take what they don't need. Somewhere in that cellar in Germany Jan and the gang had left a box filled with old medals, rusty nails, guns without bullets, a floral pin, golden rings, a dancing pump. Unforgettable treasures.

"All those pictures. They'd hardly miss one. And that owner is a dick. Buying a cool old house and fucking it up. Putting locks on left-over rooms. I got us into one with a big styrofoam box on a bed—kinda coffin. Inside, a doll in party dress, eyes wide open and huge. A real life looking Marilyn Monroe. I get into this shed with her like in a lot of mulch and leaves. Cops walking right past me. I am wet and freezing. Along comes this insane streaker, stark naked in the snow with a flashlight holding back a growling Doberman on a chain. Awesome. Then he yells "Go get!" Lets go of the chain. The Doberman whimpers and yelps. I'm ready to use Marilyn as a shield. But the attack-dog like spins around, deserts and fucking races back to the house. The awesome cold weather streaker beams his flashlight on the shed. With me shivering down under the freezing mulch clutching Marilyn. Cold finally got to him. He took off."

"Was it the new owner?"

"More the caretaker type, to jump out of bed, go streaking in the snow. High on something. Cops should have locked him up!"

"How about Tick?"

"The Tick? Juvenile. In lock-up."

"He will talk."

Caleb stretches again, "I'll swear he made it up to get me in more trouble. Or I'll just split."

"No. You can't!"

Caleb laughs. "If I'm gone for long enough, they're glad to have me back." He gets distracted by TV Joanie's leaping around on morning stretch. She's skinny and wears a skimpy furry leotard. Her face all smiles and tired. He turns the sound up. She spouts a little philosophy about warm up and cool down. The wisdom of preparing yourself. Keeping yourself and everything around you in good condition. **Shape up and tidy up!**

"Shape up and tidy up!" Caleb chants. "Shape up and tidy up—too much." He laughs so hard he rolls over.

"Your uncle is shaping up." Liz gets up.

Caleb straightens into a giant, and in one movement stoops for a kiss on the cheek.

From the kitchen window she watches him leaping off through the deep snow, just as the plow comes rattling along the road, followed by the black Mighty Clean van. A woman wearing a red parka jumps out with a shovel and pushes the light snow clearing Ellen's driveway.

Ellen has Mighty Clean service once a month. The president of Mighty Clean, the former Buddhist house-boy, hires housewives to come out of their own messy homes to clean others and earn ten dollars an hour. After they leave, Ellen's cottage is clean for about five days and she can entertain her single parents. But Mighty Clean imposes on Ellen the old Codgie standards. Ellen must have worked hard to pick up and get the house ready. Shaping up and tidying up!

Liz, who shapes up with morning stretch has been tidying Codgie style and losing her manuscript. The flames in the fireplace flicker and then shoot up hissing, where Rosalie's poems had burned like houses and farms in the war zone to keep them from falling into enemy hands.

Chapter 19
RECYCLING

"Mom!" Mike has climbed out of the upstairs bathroom window, onto the flat washroom roof—his vantage point for startling and entertaining Mother as he stages announcements, complaints, and demands. "Wait! You don't have to take that trash to the dump right now. "Too much blue sky and sun. I lost my shades and I need new clothes. You need a break, Mom. Let's go malling."

There he is half naked, draped in a sheet: a reproduction of the Etruscan reproduction she keeps on the wall above the tub. The Etruscan boy in that picture prances like Mick Jagger in concert, has a funky instrument and big, bare feet. Mike has stuck his big feet into unlaced sneakers, but snow on the roof is melting fast.

Mom drops her trash bag and laughs. She always has been crazy about anything Etruscan. Historians keep worrying and guessing where they came from and what happened to them, but they did enjoy themselves being artistic before they vanished into the unknown. In grade school Mike still had his own theory that they defected back and forth between planets looking for good times.

Bundles of papers keep slipping from Mom's arm. "Maybe later, I must have thrown out several chapters with some old papers yesterday. I'm going to check the recycle van. Might have to print out again."

"Master thief Caleb made off with it last night. Puts his name on it. Changes Stolen Girl into a trans-sexual and adds pornography. With my help it becomes a number one bestseller and is made into a movie. The name Plant isn't on the book or in the book. Dad is happy. You don't have to work so hard anymore."

"Get inside. You're going to get cold."

"I'll print out for you, Mom."

"Thanks, I'll do it myself."

"You don't trust me. That's bad psychology."

She feels ashamed, and at the same time she wishes she had locked her room. "Pancakes in the warming oven." She picks up the trash bag. It's only half full, but heavy when she lifts it into the station wagon. Rocksalt pelting the car as she turns onto Shore Road is wasteful, harmful and unnecessary; so is her fretting on such a morning.

Houses, the granite sea wall, the rocks above Town Beach, and boats in the harbor are flecked with snow and gulls. Etruscans, who had watched birds and water for signs, might have read warnings in the dark, choppy sea, the flurry of birds rising high above South Cove, and ducks dipping deep down and coming up in the far distance.

In Brenton Hall School Liz had become the best history and geography student, because her research had been a secret search for something familiar: her home, her people. She had found century after century of wars—lands changing hands—a repeat pattern of crazy emperors, taking over from the good murdered emperors, and kings. Warriors and heroes that were really grim Nazi-type killers, using their power to hurt the powerless, even women and children. On school trips to the Metropolitan Museum, she saw images of pagan gods who had to be appeased with human and animal sacrifice. Images of self-sacrifice, Christ on the Cross, pictures and statues of saints and martyrs, knights in armor. Finally, in the sculpture hall, where a naked Apollo made school girls giggle, Liz discovered the only smiling statues she had ever seen, the Etruscans. The monument of a man and a woman resting side by side facing each other looked like smiling twins.

Only a few words of the Etruscan language survived, but songs, music, and stories live on in bright pictures of celebrations on the walls of burial chambers, which like the smiling statues tell the story of a civilization that found secret meaning in life before they vanished.

Several big dogs race along South Beach, barking and romping in the surf, and chasing each other around the deserted bandstand. To a stranger Shoreland kids and dogs running in packs must appear unwanted, sad, rather like cats in Rome and dogs in Mexico, even children in a war zone. Outsiders wouldn't understand that kids and animals recycle themselves in this hometown, getting affection and food where they can find it, a home away from home.

Two boys are shoveling old Mrs. Libby's steps, while she watches them and waves her cane at squirrels on her bird feeder. Mr. Wittier is shoveling snow off his sidewalk. Houses on Hawthorn Street remain white, shutters black - none of that new canary yellow or Disneyland pink. Christmas wreaths stay on the front door well into summer. Anglophilia—genetic, or transmitted by Channel 2 Masterwork Theater, perhaps both—are endearingly odd in this part of the country which celebrates its proud history of having been the first to throw the British out.

No Emmet Gray at the window on his stationary bike this morning. Big footprints leading to his door and smoke coming out of his chimney indicate that Caleb has interrupted Emmet's unusual journey and vigil that brings speeders to justice. She can safely race to the Sanitary Landfill sign. The station wagon skids as she turns left at the gate, but the road has been plowed and sanded by Milton, who used to be a regular at the benches in Harbor Square. Always a show off. He's now wearing a bandanna. He waves to Liz from a bright orange compactor flying a black pirate's flag decorated with the skull and cross bone which had also been the Nazi S.S. insignia. The big metal foot smash—squashes the mountains of snow covered trash bags down into the sanitary land-fill with grinding roars and rattle of a tank in the war zone, while gulls screech and Red barks among a pack of dogs.

Today, Wednesday, with snow on the ground, the dump is deserted. Saturday is the day when everybody comes piling in, to look around and visit. Liz drives into the recycle area with its bottle shed, paper-van, and 'Boutique-Swapshop' shack, where Walter, the Major, collects and repairs broken gadgets: blenders, pressure cookers, disposal units, TV sets. Radios, irons, toasters. Some almost new, warranties barely expired, are displayed with a sign, "TAKE A GOOD ONE AND BRING A BROKEN ONE." An old radio is playing cheerful old country songs along with the rhythmic thump-clump grinding compactor.

"Nice day," Walter calls as soon as Liz gets out of her car. Stout, light on his feet, and never still, he comes over, swinging a cane he made from a branch of a fruit tree someone dumped after the Christmas storm. He has the clear blue eyes of a child; his face, like the cane, is pleasantly gnarled, the mouth a notch."How do you like it?" He pats a green knitted hat. "Imagine knitting me a hat for an old toaster. Quite a woman. Out of an old sweater she found here and unraveled. Bakes the best apple pie in town!" He loves to say nice things about Bonnie, but he won't name this friend who shares his invincible goodwill. "Hey, I almost forgot. I've saved something you might like." He produces three magnets shaped like tiny hands from an old bag he wears over his left shoulder." Handy. Get it?" They laugh. She feels honored when he singles her out, and he makes her feel that everything will be just fine.

"How about a cup of coffee and some pie?"

"I'll take a raincheck. Mike is home from school." Liz had to bring newspapers for recycling just to get past Walter, who would wear himself out searching the entire van if she told him she had lost a manuscript. She doesn't know whether he actually holds a job at the dump or officiates as a volunteer, collecting, arranging, repairing unloved objects lovingly—not to keep, but to give away to his favorites and to anyone who's unhappy, as though he could repair broken lives.

The major has shovelled and sanded a neat path to the recycle trailer, which stands where Anka Wronovska had grown vegetables, leaving parsnips and carrots to grow big and sweet under the snow. Empowered by hardy Anka, Liz now climbs into the trailer and starts pulling down bundles of magazines sitting on top of cartons. Her cheeks burn, her eyes smart, hands are black from newsprint, and her back hurts. "Not here. Not here." Having to lift and shift the heavy cartons deadens her panic. Finally one big box tips over spilling Play-Boy magazines addressed to Jeff Moonbins, Shoreland Hardware. Worry about Bonnie takes over. Liz carefully reloads the box and hides it behind bundles of trash-mail.

The Major is talking to a retired couple when Liz gets out, but there in the sun, a bearded stranger sits on the box marked "digital" reading her old German magazine, DER STERN. It's not unusual to get stuck reading magazines at the trailer when you recycle yours. "Excuse me, but this is my box."

The man looks up and stares. "You threw it out." He holds up the magazine. Her smiling face is on the cover. "It's you. Younger, of course. Very interesting story." His voice sounds slightly foreign, and familiar. "You should keep magazines with your picture on the cover."

"Are you German?" Liz asks the man.

"A little bit. Are you?"

None of his business!

"No. You're not," he answers his own question.

He has slanting blue eyes, wears a Greek fisherman's cap, a dark sweater and faded jeans. The suede boots are unusual, but all kinds of men do all kinds of work in Shoreland. The local garbage man is a Harvard graduate.

"But you were living in Germany when you got some of those letters. Are you sure you want to throw them out?"

None of his business.

He smiles and stares like a hypnotist. "Not a mistake?"

"No!"

"One mustn't recycle personal letters. Let's tear them up." He picks up a few he must have read and put down at his feet, and tears them without taking his eyes off Liz.

This is like a soap opera. How dare he? Well, she did want to get rid of the letters men wrote to her after *Der Stern* published a profile of the American model Liz Plant, who had once been a war child. Several men had offered to take her to Greece, or Spain or Italy. A fat Berlin plumber had sent his picture with his Mercedes and offered her marriage. A few iron curtain men and women had claimed her as their child, and asked her for money and a visa. Each time she had gone through the box, she had relived her old disappointment of failing to find her mother. Did the nuns not say that some of the mothers did not want their children back? Gramp had been right. No good came from publicity in Europe, only heartache every time she disobeyed him.

Who would want to read about a child stolen by Nazis in a world where at this very moment children are abused, forced to do slave labor, murdered, run away, vanish or starve to death? "Everyone," her editor had said. "You are writing a wonderful story."

"You haven't seen a large brown envelope with a manuscript?" she asks.

"No. Not in this box. Just few pages. Quite remarkable. I like this: 'Whenever Liz was alone with Gramp's new housekeeper, Anka, they secretly spoke German, which Gramp wanted her to forget'," he reads from the two pages in his hand. "Anka always wanted to know what really happened in Hitler School, whereas stories Liz embellished for Anka conveyed the eternal truth of children being sacrificed to adult obsessions, which must have touched the childless woman's heart."

He is about to hand her the page. "A computer printout. You won't need it." She can feel herself flush as she takes it from his hand. "I like the way you write, but I know more about scripts."

Impudent. Self-important. Cultivated accent. Typical unemployed actor. Good looking, but no longer young. Must be working at the dump in between small character roles or T.V. commercials. Bonnie would say, the poor fellow missed the boat.

"We do have the Shoreland Players during the summer if you want to get into summer theater."

He bursts into uncontrolled laughter. "This seems to be the kind of place where one can quite successfully avoid doing what one always wanted to do."

Liz has to laugh with him, thinking of those who come here to write a book without having learned to type, make music without ever having learned to read music or play an instrument. Then there are the artists who have never learned to draw, and the inventors of a super bottle opener that has already been patented. If they don't have money to live on, they'll subsist by doing housework, carpentry, fishing, even work at the dump—just to be able able to stay on and dream on.

"Are you afraid you'll never be published?"

"I have a publisher." This sounds defensive. "And a deadline."

"It isn't here, you must have mislaid it. You really should have filed the magazines. Important time of your life. Model. Cover girl."

She hears "How could you" and "You should" and backs away.

He picks up the box, ready to put it into her station wagon. "'Mementos are a roadblock.' I like the way you put that."

This quote from her notes make her feel she's been robbed.

"You're are not merely confiding and confessing to readers. You have something to say. I can't wait to read the book."

He must have studied the fragments she discarded, to read her mind and tell her what she needed to hear most. He opens her car door, helps her in like a valet, stands by until Liz gets confused. "Thanks." She tries to hand him a dollar. He doesn't want it.

In the rearview mirror she watches him pick up the box containing her memorabilia. Why not turn around, go through the box herself; make sure the brown envelope isn't in there? He is getting smaller and smaller as she drives away until, no bigger than a mouse, he jumps into the the paper van with the box.

At noon, at the Greenhouse, the man from the dump wears a blue blazer, white shirt, blue tie, and is paying for a bouquet of red roses, while she is consoling herself for the missing manuscript with daffodils and baby's breath. He takes her aside. "You are Liz. Liz Plant. I know." Then he formally introduces himself as Arthur Eckert, new owner of South Cove. "No one has ever offered me a tip before. I really love the way we met."

The change of costume, the new role, has not changed him. An inner rehearsal seems to take place before he speaks. The bright light carves his straight, sharp nose, wide forehead. Brown hair has receded into a peak with a white edge. He stands tall as a military man, telling her about boys who broke into his house last night and made off with a valuable painting and a display figure. He thought they might have possibly stuck it into a shed or even the recycle van to get rid of the evidence.

Could this be the notorious nudist in the snow with the cowardly Doberman? Liz, the pal of the Harbor Square gang, lifts her bouquet to hide her face, because she is certain that she has seen this man without the beard in a different role.

The painting, he says, a de Kooning, is insured but impossible to replace. One of these fascinating abstract paintings of threatening females. His voice sounds uncomfortably familiar. He interrupts himself with a smile and touches her bouquet. "How dainty. What do you call these?"

"Baby's breath. Nice with daffodils."

"Baby's breath." He stares over the rows and rows of seedlings and spring flowers. Ellen had said Eckert has the European habit of giving out strong sexual messages to every woman he meets. "I saw you in Boston. A while back. At an outdoor cafe."

He pulls a rose from his bouquet and hands it to Liz. "I know. Careful. Don't prick yourself." He wants Liz to remember the school girl stung by the thorn of his rose, and she feels trapped again as she had been at that table.

"You understand German. Don't you? It was really too bad. The way those young Austrians and I talked about you."

Liz retreats behind a table of potted impatiens from this wartime romantic. He follows her with his eyes.

"Our behavior in Boston was inexcusable."

Liz reads no apology or regret.

"I admired you; that's why I behaved that way." He raises his shoulders and drops them. "I admired you before we ever met."

She doesn't want to bring up the Catulle paintings of her face and the weird seductive child body. "Past life?"

He laughs. "Your past life." He turns away to a basket of rose geraniums, showing off his chiseled profile. "I'll tell you about it one day. By the way. Did you find your missing manuscript?"

She shakes her head. "I'll print it again." She only half listens when he warns her to be careful with her computer. Great help, but they can wipe out your work. A stranger giving advice like a friend, and at the same time, from the beginning—an intruder.

He interrupts the silence he creates, glances at his watch with an outburst of casual chatter, drawing-room comedy: he is invited to dinner with Dr. Ellen Burn's single parents' association. She has agreed to help him produce a program about the single parents groups on cable TV. Then he laughs, lighthearted, cosmopolitan, worldly. He is divorced. Not a single parent, yet he has a ward, at Grove Academy with Mike and Caleb Fairfield. "We have heard a lot about Mike Plant. Did you see him on our Garden Club interview yesterday? Come to think of it he told me you don't have cable. Too bad. We let him talk about the 'Pipe-Sculpture' in front of the camera. He's a natural. "Mike warned me that the single parents' club divorced women would try to marry me." He strokes his graying beard. "I should be flattered."

"This is a small town. Everyone talks."

"I already knew all about Liz Plant who married her brother. But I don't talk. As for you," he leans forward and sniffs the rose he just gave her. "There just wouldn't be any words."

Has he guessed? Does he know that his Old-World ways bring back the homesickness of a homeless child, dream memories of belonging and the nightmare pain of being snatched away? In LOVE AND LEARN Beatrice Strout says older men act like predators to prove that they are still young. Especially with married or divorced women. She can well imagine this man with Ellen and her liberated group of women, all younger than Liz.

"I like Mike," he says.

A hundred roses couldn't have been more seductive. She can feel herself flush with pleasure and finds herself running past rows of potted flowers, through the cloying, loamy sweetness of a mass of yellow-green leaves touched with crimson. Coniferous pitcher plants in a greenhouse? Perhaps a way of catching white flies. She escapes, taking three steps in one leap. Arthur Eckert has merely given her a head start.

Chapter 20
SCHOOLS

GROVE ACADEMY MEMORANDUM
To: Grove Academy Parents and Guardians
From: Charles Breed, Co-ordinator of Dean's Area
Services
RE: Restructured Dress Code
Ethics Rules and Regulations and Discipline v.
Punishment
1. Restructured Dress Code
During the periods from breakfast through dinner,
students should wear:
a. Men: Clean, neat slacks; collared shirt; socks
and shoes
b. Women: Clean, neat slacks; skirts or dresses;
stockings, socks and shoes.
c. This means: No trash-bag rainwear! No blue
jeans. No sneakers (must be shoe type). No T
shirts. No "muscle shirts." No tie-dyed or bleached
clothing. No head gear hats, caps, bandannas, etc.
In general, the students will wear clothing which
is neat and well kept and makes a statement about
themselves.

Regulations: rule or order issued by an authority.

Merely following the rules is not the intent of

Grove Academy; developing ethical behavior is. In
order to develop that behavior, it is the intention
of the Dean's area to impose a penalty for a fault,
offense, or violation.

Why should clothes Mike doesn't like develop his ethical behavior? The
kitchen faucet and icicles in front of the window drip, drip, drip away time
in a steady reprimand, while Liz, guilty of wearing old jeans and sneakers
in violation of the memorandum cowers at the old kitchen table staring at
the regulation. She has to remind herself that jeans—the American
national costume—adopted by men, women and children all over the
world, might well outnumber military uniforms.

She reaches for an "Outdoor Sporting Specialty Catalogue." The cover
is decorated with a solemn winter scene. Mother, father and son trudging
through a snowscape on cross country skis wearing the right outdoor
clothes, loaded down with expensive camping equipment. A picture of the
awesome ordeal of family fun in the wilderness. Far away and safe from the
drugs, hypertension, stolen children. Father chopping wood in a sweater
hand-knit by Canadian Indians, son wearing fleece-lined, watertight boots
made in Italy and carrying wood in a special log bag that is made in
Ireland. Mother wearing a pink wool and cotton shirt, popping popcorn in
the Best Ever Pop Corn Popper made in Korea. Pictures of house-cleaning,
cooking, outdoor sporting American superwoman with strong husband
and obedient, log carrying son, extraordinarily ordinary, safe, and right.

"The dress code is no problem," she says to Mike. "There are regular
cotton slacks here. Everything can be ordered from this catalogue and sent
directly to Grove Academy."

Mike looks over her shoulder and laughs. "You want me to look like
those geeks? No blue jeans, I like black ones anyway. You promised to take
me to the mall."

Liz can't laugh with him. She wants him to wear the right clothes and
be safe. What is safe? Would the German car have stopped to pick up a
shabby, grubby country child? And would Arthur and the Austrian students have scrutinized a woman wearing boy's jeans and a parka? And if
Ellen had not come home late that night, wearing her fur, Al, the house
boy, would not have made so much noise, her kids would not have come
downstairs, their surgeon father would not have walked out to get his rest
at a motel and then stayed away for good.

Chris notes that Liz has made broiled lamb chops for lunch—his favorite—because she is about to go off shopping with Mike. To please her, he keeps up with Mike and eats three chops. She hardly eats. Instead of cooking she could have printed out those chapters rather than worrying herself sick. Really, all her own fault. After any brotherly little prank, Chris always finds himself wallowing in devotion. "You've been working so hard. Buy something nice for yourself. Something you really want," he calls after her, as the door bangs shut the way it should.

Something nice he did to be helpful. He's always there to keep her house going. After they drive away, Chris goes to the music room, takes the jacket off and allows himself to sink into his soft reclining chair listening to the waves rushing against the shore in a fury. For every wave there must be someone drowning somewhere. He puts on Verdi's "REQUIEM" and lets the sounds of sorrow wash over him with memories of flames and of icy seawater, his father, mother, and sister disappearing forever—his own unfulfilled death.

The left back speaker on his hi-fi equipment does not sound right. He turns the system off, cleans his pipe. Mike told him that no one smokes pipes. So he gets up and calls Ellen. Both lines are busy. He smokes and keeps redialing her number.

"Dr. Burns Associates. May I help you?"

"Ellen Burns doesn't need you, Bonnie. She already has those darned answering tapes," he says.

"I know. Jeff is mad about my answering service too, Chris. And then I had a prayer group at my house on Sunday. You know the way he keeps ordering shoes. So he caught us praying in his shoe closet. He packed a suitcase and walked out. Now I'm glad I have a profession, Chris." Talking about Jeff makes her cough just like him. "You don't think he left me for good?"

"Hell, no, you're pretty, and you're fun, you're his bookkeeper and a great cook. He can't do without you. But Ellen can. She doesn't need an answering service."

"Someone has to answer her important calls while she's working at the school. I took one from Beatrice Strout. Can you imagine?" A giggle. "Ellen gave me her book. Jeff didn't like what Bea says about men."

"A lot of men call Ellen?"

"Men, women. She's very busy. Just gave her a message from Arthur

Eckert. He has invited Ellen's single parents to a party. He has to fly to New York tomorrow and left me his guest list. And I'm ordering for him from the Blue Jay caterers and the Liquor Chest."

"Did they all accept?"

"Who wouldn't? They all want to see his house and his paintings. And he's planning to have them on the cable "Doing Your Thing" talk show. Did you see the seals on the rocks in front of South Cove? They say it's like a circus. Something for them all to look at. The food will be great. And he's the nicest man. I pray for him. I always pray for my customers when they have to fly. You don't fly a lot?"

"I don't."

"Very wise. Hold on for a minute." There is a click, click." Ellen will call you when she gets back."

"No, thanks. I don't want her to call."

"Well, say hi to Mike and Liz."

"They're at the mall."

By the end of the day half the town will know that Liz and Mike went shopping at the mall! Bonnie believes in keeping everyone in touch and informed.

"Well, God bless. Have a good day!"

Chris goes out to see whether his Audi will start the way it should. The idle has been slow. Harry Davies is really good with foreign cars if you can afford him.This time the Audi starts at once. Chris throws it into reverse and it keeps going . A pleasant surprise, but the engine sounds like a jet taking off. Finally at the corner of Codget Lane, Chris can hear it shift. Must be a sticky transmission. He becomes distracted by birds around Bonnie's feeder, when a Mercedes comes skidding around the bend and they almost collide. They both stop and get out.

"Sorry. I was driving too fast. You're Ellen's neighbor, Chris Plant. Right? I am Arthur Eckert."

A bearded New York City type, wearing a mink coat here in Shoreland! On his way to see Ellen. The man has perfect teeth. No doubt older than he looks. Lots of money. If he had not bought South Cove, Myrtle might have turned it into condos. Eckert saved the property. No one should really be mad at him for remodeling South Point into a Miami fortress.

"I met your charming wife at the dump—of all places."

Must be cultivating a foreign accent. "She told me." Chris has an uneasy feeling that Eckert knows he is lying. They look each other over. "You were at the one-and-only parent-teachers' conference I ever went to. Riverbay Day School."

"You have a good memory," Eckert says.

"You look different. You've grown a beard. I remember your mink coat."

"Conspicuous," Eckert laughs. "One way of being a private person is to give everyone something obvious to talk about. Yellow Mercedes, mink coat. The foreign accent."

"How about three blond wives?" Eckert had arrived at the meeting with three very young women, very similar, very blond. The harem had worn perfect makeup, the prescribed fashion, and seemed to get along very well. There had been buckets of Irish coffee.

"Two ex-wives and the actress Bambi Skylark. All good friends. Girlish women. My type."

The three had moved along as a group from teacher to teacher to head-master while discussing a child one of them must have produced in her teens. They kept refilling each other's cups as they giggled their way from father to father, "You're British, Mr. Plant." Sticking their blond heads together with whipped cream on their lips. "We love the way you talk. Are you in films too?"

Eckert, the dashing European, old enough to be a grandfather, in a mink coat, with three showy young wives he had brought laughter, even flirtation—so rare these days, in these parts—as he circulated among all the pretty mothers like a big bumblebee. And how they all bloomed! What a nice change from the old in-group talk about boats, horses, kids, houses, divorces, clothes, and money.

"The headmaster wanted fathers to come that night. I was staying at Bambi's beach house at the time. She is an actress. We're very close, but Emerald is not my child. I went as a substitute father." He glances at his watch.

Who does this Eckert think he is? Telling Liz that he was making him-self conspicuous to be private, while talking about his private life openly, telling you nothing. What is this character doing here? Going on and on about Emerald and Mike at Country Day School together and now at Grove Academy with that boy Caleb Fairfield. All of them in need of Havelock Grimes. He rattles on about this founder of the school, starting urine tests to check up on drug use. No more smoking. Kids broke into his house during the night. A prank. Must have been on drugs. Made off with a valuable painting and a Monroe mannequin doll. Larger than life. Couldn't just vanish.

"You suspect my boy Mike?"

"No, no. But he might know something." Eckert goes on about Havelock Grimes's ideas of making kids responsible for each other. "We have got to get him to take charge!"

"Nothing but trouble I'm sure. And expense. I guess you got the memorandum. Dress code no less. Liz is off to the Linden Tree Mall just now." Chris has to sneeze. Might be allergic to something.

"Little bit of trouble now might prevent big problems later," Eckert says.

Chris gets annoyed with himself for talking about personal matters with this stranger in a mink coat, who is on his way to consult Ellen, or whatever. He mumbles something about having to see his mechanic and departs with a British "Cheerio."

Harry Davies, a happy fellow, pours Chris a drink and works on the Audi, although he knows there isn't much wrong with it. But he is well-informed about Eckert. This is a dry town. Men often drop in on Harry with their cars, to have a drink and gossip. It's more like a pub, if you can afford it.

Bouncing around bald, plump, and pink, Harry says you can't blame Arthur E. He just happened to be staying with that actress at the South End. When Violet had so much trouble with her kids, she decided to move into the True Bible Community with them. Sold South Cove to the Reverend Sorrel for a dollar. The evangelists put the house on the market off season. Leonard happened to be in Disneyland. Fairbanks wanted to buy it as an investment, but family problems with the boy—not to mention the Mrs.—slowed him down. So Eckert, a stranger, made Myrtle an offer and got it.

"Now," Harry says, "Edwin Fairbanks's problems with his Bentley are not the only ones. He had a blonde stretched out on the back seat sleeping it off."

"Are you sure?" Chris asks.

"Sure. She wasn't dressed for the weather. He had her covered up in a blanket. No matter what, Harry says, one has to feel sorry for Priscilla

Fairbanks. She's a good-looking woman."

Chris has his problems with Priscilla Fairbanks, the former Teen-age America beauty queen, who caused the Riverbay Day School rumpus when she was head of the parents' association. Chris doesn't say anything, because Harry talks. A stout old woman drives up in an old racing car. Chris pays fifty dollars to have a drink with Harry and have the Audi checked.

The roads are slippery so he drives home slowly, thinking of Priscilla, the president of the Riverbay parents' association. Secretly Chris agreed with Mike about the self-important parents who had forced the sophisticated, cultured, and witty headmaster to retire. The assistant headmaster, a hearty father of a large family himself, stepped in and tried to be jolly until they replaced him during Mike's final day-school year with Chester Pike, a proper humorless type, who had the right kind of false front.

Most of the kids simmered down, and settled down—but not Mike Plant. Hard to forget Mike's contribution to the Yearbook which the school turned down and mailed to Chris.

Liz had pleaded with Mike in the kitchen, tried to reason that this would never be published in the Yearbook, why get himself into trouble by insulting the school and his teachers. Mike did rewrite and tone it down a bit, but he took the original version to school. The downside of a good memory for music is that you remember the tune of words you'd rather forget: Mr. Worldly, this species is highly intelligent, which may make you ask why he is teaching English at Riverbay. The nicest thing I can say about the Riverbay School in all the time I have been there is that I don't like it. Why should Mike have been surprised when Mr. Worldly let this pass on to the new head, Mr. Pike? So Mike was suspended and became a hero. Kids kept calling him all evening long. Ellen called Riverbay and told them that Mike had the courage to be honest and a democratic place of learning should have the courage to publish what he has to say. Chris took Mike aside and told him to do himself a favor and keep his mouth shut or he'd be kicked out of Riverbay.

Both parents had to be present at the hearing. Liz, dressed like a Salem witch on trial, in a frumpy black outfit she had bought at the Yesterday Boutique. True to character she confessed at once. Mike had shown her what he had written. She should have stopped him; it was really all her fault. It had worked. Mike, humiliated by his mother's false confession, apologized mostly for her, and promised to rewrite, since even Hemingway rewrote all the time. The insolent parody Mike wrote of all the usual phony pieces in the yearbook raised no eyebrow. He was allowed to graduate, but one could hardly imagine the headmaster recommending Mike to prep schools.

As soon as Chris gets home he digs out his old checkbooks from the pile, to add up wasted tuition money. Marshfield, Shakerville, now Grove Academy. And there is a tuition insurance form for Grove Academy he never filled out. If it hadn't been for that year-book and Chester Pike, the new headmaster, Mike would have gone to Milton from day school, like Chris. His grades were good enough, but he was not accepted. After that Liz took Mike to an interview at four or five big-name schools, who had all called Chester Pike, took the application fee, interviewed Mike and turned Mike down. Finally, the assistant headmaster, a nice man, who had himself just suffered a rejection, telephoned Marshfield, where he had been a teacher, and Mike was accepted.

Marshfield, Mike's first boarding school had sent a list. Socks, underwear, shirts, etc. by the dozen. Sheets, pillows, blankets, quilt, bedspread, a nice curtain for the closet. There had been hundreds of shopping trips. Name tapes had to be ordered; Liz had sewn them even into each sock. Everything had to be just right to give Mike a good start.

But after two months at that school, Mike called and said he had no clothes. Even his trunk had been broken into and then thrown out of the window. Hazing. Liz got into her car and drove to Marshfield. Among several hundred kids, she went unnoticed while she waited and watched until some of the new boys from Mike's dorm came along the long corridor. A couple of big jocks pounced, knocking books out of their hands and ripping their shirts. Liz screamed and pounced on the jocks. One of them fell over backwards and said she kicked him down. No wonder they thought she was a senior girl on LSD. Liz and Mike both ended up at the headmaster's office. They did not like having a mother wandering around the school and interfering. Freshmen at Marshfield have always been hazed, a harmless old tradition. That's as far as the headmaster got. Mike spoke up: A boy was beaten and seniors stamped on his hand. That was not harmless. The headmaster said the kid should speak up for himself. Mike said the kid was colored and afraid of losing his scholarship.

After that Mike started to grow his hair. So did some of the other new boys. And Mike swore to Chris that the older boys had given them the idea of sending a bomb-threat letter to the headmaster. If nothing else, Mike developed his potential for a career as an unreliable government agent or a Mafia lawyer.

The bomb threat letter had brought the police and fire department on campus. Rooms were searched. The draft for the letter was found in Mike's waste paper basket. He was expelled, put onto the next bus without a jacket since all the clothes Liz had replaced during parents weekend had again vanished. What could Chris say? Liz used to lose everything when she was a kid. Chris got an appointment with Dr. Neptune, a top child psychiatrist in New York City that very same day.

Chris told the doctor that he was born in England. His own mother had been a very well-balanced, pleasant English woman. The terrible accident. They still had relatives in Norfolk. A British boarding school would be just the thing for Mike. That way his mother could not go rushing off to see him. He couldn't be suspended and sent home so easily. The school would have to take responsibility.

Chris sat on a pink sofa with Mike in the waiting room, while Liz had her turn. The door was closed, you couldn't hear what she was saying to Dr. Neptune in her soft voice to make the doctor laugh out loud. The doctor couldn't stop laughing, when he finally took Mike into his office and the boy laughed with him. For his final entertainment, the psychiatrist saw them as a family and allowed Mike to take over his job: Kids are sent away to school when parents don't want to have them around. There are loads of kids from broken homes; boarding schools have it made. The admissions people tell new parents that sex, alcohol, and drugs are not allowed on campus. And the schools over-enroll. Let the big oafs haze smart and interesting new kids, to break them. Then, they wait and catch a kid they never really wanted in the first place with beer, a girl, weed, or something, to throw him out and impress all the others and scare them and especially their parents. This helps with their never-ending fundraisings for building. They do this until they get the enrollment down to normal. The school has the right to keep the tuition. Mike said they took him because he paid full tuition. It was a jock school and he had been set up.

The doctor kept smiling, but Chris couldn't contain himself and yelled at Mike to shut up. No one had forced him to keep writing stupid letters; he did that all on his own. The doctor stopped smiling and told Mike to go on. So Mike went on and said American schools stink, outstanding Americans are really self-taught when it comes right down to it. And he named the old Grateful Dead and other drug-addicted rock musicians he liked. The doctor was interested in rock music to the tune of about three hundred dollars. He liked the idea of period costumes and boys giving girls roses.

Then the doctor gave them all his diagnosis and said that Mike had been provoked at Marshfield. He asked them to decide whether Mike should stay at Shoreland High or go to another prep school. Mike spoke up. Dad wanted him to go away. Boarding school was OK but not in England, and he brought up the old movie "Lord of the Flies."

The doctor said that Mike's reactions were natural and normal, and he recommended Shaker Hill School, which turned out to be an abnormal school. Old Shaker buildings, serene rooms, old Shaker school desks engraved with new foul words. Liz told the headmaster what had happened at the other schools. He was very understanding. Didn't seem to worry one bit. Mike was accepted.

Shakerville was set in the Berkshires, only a few miles away from Marshfield. It couldn't have been more than two months before another boy who had bounced out of the Marshfield School came to apply at Shakerville. That kid saw Mike and gave admissions his own version of Mike and the bomb-threat at Marshfield. The Shakerville headmaster, who knew what had happened not only from Liz, Mike and Dr. Neptune, but also from the Marshfield headmaster, had gone off looking for foreign students in Saudi Arabia. The assistant dean of the Shakerville school—an excitable woman, later arrested for embezzling funds—listened to the visiting boy. Someone had just tampered with stage lights. She couldn't take the risk of keeping Mike. These historical buildings had much value and meaning. She was terribly afraid of fires.

Schools willing to take a boy who had been in so much trouble were scarce. A professional consultant charged six hundred dollars to interview Mike. He had catalogues on beautiful handmade paper, with photographs of children playing in the sun, under the care of a staff of resident psychologists. Grounds fenced in. Gates locked. Windows barred. Liz shouted, "No. Never." The consultants came up with Grove Academy. An interesting Maine school.

Mike will no doubt have himself bounced again. And he'll go to another school, and another. If it takes every darned school for crazy kids in the U.S.A., he will have to stay until he graduates. Liz and her book, and Mike, it's all more than anyone can take.

Ellen, a psychologist, should understand that. Perhaps she knows, and she is waiting for Mike to drive Chris out of his own home. He fills his pipe, and steps out the backdoor although he hates the cheerless weather. From the end of the driveway he can look down to Ellen's house. Eckert's car isn't there. He wouldn't be her type. She likes a conservative man, preferably British.

Chapter 21

THE MALL

"Weirdos allowed to be weirdos. That's free enterprise, that's America."
Mike ushers Liz through the heavy doors into the mall. A policeman
standing beside the candy kiosk sneezes and keeps blowing his nose into
paper towels. "Won't bother kids here. Not supposed to spoil business."

"Maybe he's allergic to the mall. My eyes always smart here," Liz says.

"Could be the spray. See the girl in the green jumpsuit spraying down
there? Not just an air freshener. Subliminal persuasion music has been
around. Smells are new. The smell is supposed to make you want to buy
and spend money."

"You got that from some James Bond movie."

"No, I got it from Del. She works at Baby Land on Sundays. They like
to hire pregnant girls. But all this persuasion is getting to her. She spends
every cent she makes right away. See the long line at the Radio Shack?
They must be returning stuff they bought, pushing and shoving to get
their money fast. While they're waiting, they're already subliminally persuaded to buy again. But don't worry. We're not near the spray. And I have
awesome willpower. I'll restrain you!"

Linden Tree Mall, Mike's favorite, has more air and daylight and kids.
Shoppers strut around to rock music from their tune boxes. Girl and boy

watchers sitting on a circular bench under a huge, man-made linden tree, dangle their legs to a medley of sounds.

"See that guy with the thick-lensed glasses under the tree? He's holding a lace panty. He's happy," Mike says. "Shops for panties and pays with MasterCard. Pink lace for Easter. He goes ahead of the season, just like the stores. In August and September he already has red Christmas bikinis. Last Thanksgiving, before they started spraying, Drew put Ecstasy into his Coke when he was not looking. The little guy got all happy and went on a real panty-buying spree. They'd miss him if he didn't show at the Secret Garden Lingerie. Sort of fits in and doesn't bother anyone. Has a place to go to. Something to do."

Mike waves to the old panty collector as they pass the benches. He is in a good mood. A year ago Mike did not want to be seen with his mother and walked behind her or in front, shoulders hunched up, hands in pockets. Now he puts his arm around her. "Don't look so shocked. What's wrong with panties? I used to love hats when I was a kid. Your fault, you should have stopped me when I walked around here in my top hat. That poor old fellow, used to shake hands with me. Nothing but black panties for him in those days. You never even noticed. Time you wised up."

She does not want him to know that she is wise to loners desperately proving to themselves that they really exist in this exhibitionist world where nothing is private.

You can see older women go click-clicketing along in their high-heeled, painful plastic shoes, aimlessly weaving in and out of stores looking for the special outfits on special sale that will transform them into soap opera women in search of a role. A group of senior citizens march past in jogging suits, swinging weights, showing that they won't be shelved. Everyone demonstrates for something. Gays, minorities, animals, endangered predators, pro-life, pro-choice. How about subliminal persuasion rights? Or exhibitionist rights? A fetishist organization for lonely exhibitionists. Conventions for the unloved. And Liz, writing her own story, often feels like a lonely exhibitionist in search of every subliminal persuasion technique she can muster.

Mike is leading Mother past vendor stalls in the center of the mall. New England seascapes mass-produced in Korea. A sparkling crystal shop. MISS PAMELA READER ADVISOR PALM AND CARD READING. ADVICE ON LOVE, BUSINESS, MARRIAGE, HEALTH, STOLEN

OR LOST PROPERTY. LOST LOVED ONES.

A male voice on the intercom announces that a little fellow named Eddie has been found and is waiting for his mother at the customer service department. A young woman comes running out of the booth, yelling, "My Eddie!" Hard to know whether Miss Pamela had been consulted to find missing Eddie or his mother's future was so exciting she didn't notice little Eddie was missing. Liz slows down.

"Oh no, you don't!" Mike steers her to the food pavilion, McDonald's. He gets very hungry when he has to explain everything to everyone all the time. And he orders the usual, a fillet of fish and tea for Mother. For himself three big French fries and two quarter-pounders, with a large Coke.

Mike eats fast. "Remember the bank robbery a few years ago? Everyone was after suspicious strangers. And a townie could get away with robbing a bank. No problem. Take you, for instance. Everybody knows you. The entrance is dark. You quickly slip a mask over your head, charge into the bank, pull out a gun. Everybody in the bank flattens out on the floor. The teller puts money into your plastic bag. On the way out you pull off the mask, stick the money bag into your basket under some vegetables. The law shows up, the Chief and Little Dutch zooming around, chasing swarthy young guys in sports cars. You take your time and cycle back to the Plant House." He catches his breath. "Anyway, there is a good idea for you for a story. I'm off to get another Coke. Want anything, Mom?"

Liz sits facing the mall and the big discount bookstore, where pyramids of best sellers are piled up at the entrance and fill windows. The swastika on the cover of a new book about Adolf Hitler. Liz's editor, Robbie, who had been an investigating officer during the war, wants Liz to show how one thing always leads to the next, from generation to generation. She would never have found such an editor if she had not gone to the writers' conference. Chris chose it for her, to help her find out that she was not a writer, just as he had chosen her dates in New York City to help her find out she could not be their lover.

Liz had enrolled in Robbie's seminar, hoping to get a male editor's reaction to her story and her writing. But day after day a young man named Max read and reread his short story about a young man meeting the Archangel Gabriel in a toilet. What was a *Stolen Child* compared to an angel in a toilet? And on top of everything else Max was living with Beatrice Strout, the femininist author.

She had felt lonely walking around, carrying her unread, unwanted chapters in a backpack. She did not sleep well. Sat through seminars feeling sick. Waited and waited. Finally, she met Robbie on the way to the seminar. He politely inquired whether she wrote short stories. She took the manuscript of Stolen Child out of her back pack and gave it to him.

Two days before the end of the conference, he told her he would like to take her book to Thomson & Perkins. Her joy did not change the secret sorrow in eyes as deep blue as pit water and thick-lensed glasses magnified a resignation that can give you a sinking feeling. He is informal and polite like a good doctor.

Liz tries to imagine big pyramids of her book on tables out in front of the now-empty bookstore. Subliminal persuasion tapes drawing crowds in to buy it. Mothers all over the world reading it. And then again, she worries in case she might never get to finish it; no one buying it. An independent publisher at the conference had given a talk on the last night, inferring that big publishers look into the future and make good but not infrequently bad things happen with their predictions. It sounded like the witch women on Shoreland Common, who had relied on tea leaves, the clouds, patterns in the sand, and dreams, as publishers rely on sales figures and computers. A terrible longing for her desk, anxiety to reprint her lost chapters, tightens her throat.

Mike, on his second pile of French fries, is now talking about a great idea he just had for Leonard Myrtle of putting one of these big domes over the Shoreland inner harbor and all its quaint fisherman's shacks that are little shops. Make it into a mall.

"I thought you were against development and the Myrtle condominiums," Liz reminds him.

"But just think of all the tourists walking around without getting wet or cold. What possibilities! New England, warm as Florida. Not Disneyland, but the real thing and tourists the year round. Don't look so shocked. New ideas for buying and selling make America a great country."

A couple of blind people have come along beside Mike, she carrying a tray, he guiding her by the elbow and swinging his white cane. "Mike, that's your voice," she calls, and your nice cologne."

"Hi, Mrs. Wise." Mike takes her tray and empties it into the bin.

"Well, isn't this a nice surprise." She is a white-haired little woman dressed in white and pretty. He is tall, quite young. They stop and she looks straight at Liz. "I'm legally blind, you know, but I can see your outline. Very small waist. Are you his girl?"

"I'm his mother."

"Mike helped me with my tray; that's how we met. So kind. We enjoy him so much," Mrs. Wise says in a high-pitched little voice and introduces the tall young man as Mr. Vance Colby, former high school principal. "You must be so proud. Does Mike look as good as he sounds? I can see the outline of long wavy hair. Let me guess, blue eyes? A beautiful, strong face."

Mike had told Liz about meeting Mrs. Wise at McDonald's when he was in between schools. Someone who understood his private school problems through her friend Mr. Colby. And she then confided in Mike that she is over sixty years old but her friend doesn't know it, because he is blind too. She makes her voice sound young, and she has a weakness for expensive perfumes. They go dancing together. For the first time in her life she is really in love. She has time to do as she pleases, enjoys herself, and is so well looked after.

"You are at Grove Academy, aren't you?" Her Mr. Colby inclines his head towards Mike. "I met Havelock Grimes a while back when he started the school. Then I heard he left."

"He's come back. On a visit, we hope," Mike says. "Really harsh."

Mr. Colby laughs and Mrs. Wise laughs with him. "You know what, Mike? We will be at the Pine Inn for a convention of the New England Association for the Blind next month," she says. "You're near Portland. How about dinner with us one night?"

"Cool," Mike says.

Punctilious Mr. Colby provides a small tape recorder to get all the information. Linden Tree is a nice, safe place for walking, as long as you don't carry too much money. But there's something about this place that makes you want to buy.

"Subliminal persuasion," Mike says.

Mrs. Wise claps her hands and laughs and laughs. Mike is so much fun. She enjoys him so much. A buzzing sound interrupts her happy chatter. Mr. Colby's timer. Now they have to hurry. The van is picking them up. "We're going dancing, Let me touch your face, Mike."

Mike bends down, all smiles, to allow her small white hands to read his cheeks and nose. She caresses his hair, snapping one of his curls. "Isn't it nice to be allowed to touch. You're beautiful, a great fellow, Mike! So long.

Real luck that I ran into you."

Bad luck to be praised too much. Mike hurries Mom on towards the shoe shop. Since a great fellow deserves great Western boots. That's what kids will be wearing at Grove now that sneakers are not allowed in class. Mike wants a black pair. Reduced to $80.95, a steal.

The sales clerk agrees and struggles to help Mike into them.

"They'll get lost at school," Liz says.

"No, they won't. I'll wear them to bed."

"You'll have to. They won't come off."

"My feet have stopped growing so I can take them half a size bigger and have them for the rest of my life..."

The rest of his life. Died with his boots on. Where does that come from? She goes on paying with Mastercard in a daze of anxiety for those boots, socks, underwear, denim shirts, as well as a Grateful Dead button decorated with a skull and a feather and rose. Finally *High Times* magazine. Too much money wasted on that Plant kid, Chris will say.

A tune box in the Serendipity shop is blaring, "Go, Johnny go. Johnny be good." Pre-teen-age girls wearing stage make-up, high-heeled boots, and white jeans jig-hop and sing along. The window is full of masks. 50% off. President Nixon, Marilyn Monroe, and then there are apes, crocodiles, a turtle-faced monster with purple lips. A hairy beast head, very real. Mike tries it on, reminding her of his bank robbery scenario. Glitz-crazed kids mill around and laugh, shout-singing to the tune boxes. Mike helps girls spend money on feather earrings and glitter chains in the fog of incense, cheap flower perfume, whoopee cushions.

A wispy girl in a purple wig dances around Mike holding up the same poster Mike hung up in his room. "Hey, that's you. Are you Robert Plant?" The poster shows a boy who has curly hair like Mike leaning against a white wall lighting a cigarette. By now Robert Plant is old, Mike tells her; not dead like Elvis, but old. The Led Zeppelin tunes are great, but old. No one listens. They want Robert Plant now. A big, baby-faced girl named Sally buys the Robert Plant poster and asks Mike for an autograph. He looks into a mirror and then at the poster and laughs.

Girls line up with posters. "Not a forgery," he says to Mother, and invents a wild, curled-up autograph. "Robert Pant, get it?" The girls don't know the difference. Sally wants a kiss. The others line up making a lot of noise. A saleswoman comes over. Let's break that up."

"It's my birthday," says Sally. "We customers or what?"

Mike decorates posters for three more girls with a big authentic Robert Pant. And now, as though the incense and rock music weren't enough subliminal persuasion, the girl in the green jumpsuit is coming closer with her spray gun. She has reached the fur salon. Two men come out. One of them is wearing a mink coat: Arthur Eckert. Women stop and stare, jostling around him as they crowd into the store. "I'm going over to the pet store," Liz tells Mike and flees across the mall.

Dr. P Pet Store is unattended. Easter bunnies hop around in the window among colored plastic eggs. Noisy dogs are sedated, but birds chirp, flapping their clipped wings. "Hello! Hello!" the parrot screeches. "Need some help?" It did that six weeks or seven weeks ago. She never allows herself to cry, but when she had seen that puppy sitting up in the cage and staring at her with so much longing, she had burst into tears. There is the same puppy, still sitting up and waiting in the same cage after all those weeks. It picks up the same latex carrot for her, tail curled up, wagging.

It looks more like an angora kitten. A Tibetan dog, the manager had explained, bred by monks to be gentle and non-barkers. Champion stock, with the white spot of hair on the head. Perfect and deserves a good home. Was it Gramp or Dr. Finkle who had said that about Liese?

"Hello! Hello!" The parrot announces the girl in the green jumpsuit. "Need some help?" She sprays and the parrot tries to bark.

Liz says. "No. Don't spray. You're too close to the parrot."

"It's harmless, smells good and makes you feel good. Not available in retail. I'm supposed to freshen things up in here. Hi, Buddy." She scratches the parrot's head. "I'm crazy about him and that puppy is sooo cute! I always want to buy everything. Better get out of here. Gotta refill."

"Need some help. Need some help!" the parrot sounds off.

"How much are the Siamese kittens?" a young woman asks Liz. A grandmother with small children, a tired-looking man, and two couples rush into the store, setting off chimes and the parrot.

"What's going on?" The Dr. P manager, a gaunt, tall man, comes rushing from the backroom. Loud children clamor for dogs, cats, birds, even the parrot. The manager twirls around, white coat flying. "That spray again. I know it's Dr. P pet week, but we don't take pets back. No returns. Take a walk, all of you. After ten or fifteen minutes you can come back and I'll help you buy a pet."

He ushers them all out, keeping his eye on stragglers. "Those two suit-and-tie guys snooping on us again, Buddy," he squawks like the parrot, veers around and glares at Liz. "You're OK I remember. You were looking at this puppy a while back? This is a male Shih Tzu. Purebred with pedigree. We're having a Dr. P pet week. I'll give you a special deal." He turns and glares at the two men at the store front. "Difficult to do business when they hound us, Buddy."

Mike walks right past the two men and enters wearing a furry monster mask. "Hey, Nathan. That's my Mom." He takes the mask off. "She loves that puppy. It's been in the store since Christmas. I'm Caleb's friend. He works here. Doesn't he get a discount?"

The manager is not pleased to see Mike. "OK OK That dog used to be five hundred ninety-nine. If you take him right now, Miss, he'll be half price."

"Get him, Mom, or you'll start crying again," Mike says.

"We have to ask your dad."

"He'll let you get him."

"He might be allergic!"

"No undercoat. Doesn't shed," says Nathan. "Make it quick or there's no deal." He unlocks the cage. Takes the puppy out and hands it to Liz. Furry paws grip her neck. When he pries the puppy away, its teddy-bear legs paw the air trying to swim back to her. "Favorite dog of the old British Queen." He puts the puppy down and it splays out, crawling towards Liz like a turtle. "They can't walk around in the cage, but it'll be fine in a minute or two." He throws the latex carrot and the puppy gets up on wobbly legs to retrieve it.

While Liz picks the puppy up, Mike gets on the phone. Customers come piling in to buy a discount canary and noisy sightseers come and go. He puts a finger in his ear. "Why not, Dad? The puppy will give Mom a break from me and from her writing." Mike hangs up, turns around. "Dad says OK."

Arthur Eckert has quietly entered the store. Nathan glares at him. "One of them. Dressed up in furs to fool me. Get lost!"

"No, that's Arthur Eckert," Mike shakes Arthur's hand.

Nathan is unconvinced. "What do you want?" he asks.

"Buy the puppy for this lady." He reaches into his fur coat and pulls out a wallet. "How much?"

Liz says, "No, thank you. You can't."

"I insist. It's my pleasure, really." Arthur Eckert pays with fifty- dollar bills.

Why does this mad generosity make her feel deprived? Nathan shuts the register with a bang. Mumbles something about getting the papers and flees to the back of the store. Big Caleb comes out in a long white Dr. P coat, which fits like a straightjacket and takes over With a hug for Liz, "Hey man!" to Mike. Then he hands her a folder with the pedigree and some papers with feeding instructions. Turning to Arthur Eckert, he introduces himself as Fairfield Junior and shakes hands with him as though breaking into South Cove had been a social event.

"Are you under the influence of the persuasion odor, Sir?" Mike asks.

"This did not need any persuasion." Arthur scratches the puppy's head, and exits.

"You look as if you'd been mugged, Mom. He's giving us a present. He owes me. My awesome little talk like gave his boring local news program a lift."

"Now I feel I owe him!" Liz says, "but we can always send him a check."

Buddy the parrot screeches, "No deal. No deal!"

Nat reappears. "Quiet, Buddy. Let's be calm now. Here they go again, Buddy. Posing as customers." He turns to Liz. "Buddy and I, we have been through a lot, lady!"

Caleb pats him on the shoulder. "You were supposed to train the bird to talk, but you sound just like buddy-bird when you're wired. You worry too much, man. You and Buddy better cool it. Eckert in that mink coat isn't spooking us. Nat, you're like making us nervous." He pulls Mike's monster mask over his head and gets busy with papers. Nat hands Liz a shopping bag. "You get Dr. P. Diet. The best. Flea powder is in there too. Remember!"

"Does the puppy have fleas?" Liz asks.

"No," Nathan whispers. "No. Please don't use it! I give you the powder to keep on hand. Remember now. Just to keep on hand!" Color drains from his face. "Need some help, need some help?" the bird calls into the empty store.

Nathan looks around uneasily, snatches the puppy from Liz and hands it to Caleb. "Store policy. You hurry up, Caleb. Get this lady and her kid and everything out of the mall!"

Girls come rushing to the bunny window, shouting: "Cute. Cute. I want that one." Then they see Mike and shriek: "Robert Plant!" and rush the store. Buddy flaps his wings and shrieks with them. Nat shoves Liz and the boys out the door, bangs it shut and picks up the phone. Sally, the birthday girl who is high and happy and easily side tracked, hoists a giant iguana she always wanted out of its cage. When Liz turns around, the lizard has climbed onto the bush of her Afro style hair. One moment it perches there with the monumental indifference of a survivor, then it's gone.

"Come on, Mom!" Mike takes the shopping bag. They hurry out of the mall as two policemen come charging in. Caleb with the puppy rushes out. They ram into Mike and he drops a package. "Sorry, kid! Sorry, Mam!"

"What's up?" Mike asks.

"Security let an iguana escape from the pet store."

"Try the flower stand in about ten minutes," Caleb says. "That's where it'll go to eat, when it comes out of hiding."

The boys hurry on out into the parking lot. Liz runs after Caleb. "Give me the puppy!" Then she can't remember where she left the station wagon. There are white Subarus everywhere.

Two men pop up from behind a van. "Stop!" They are dressed like trendy boys in torn jeans and leather jackets.

"We don't carry money!" Mike says.

One of them flashes an I.D. " Security. This boy lifted the mask. We have to ask you to come back."

"It's my mask. I signed a poster for Sally and she bought it for me." Mike is in luck. "Over there, just coming out of the Mall. Hey, Sally!" he bellows. "Tell them you bought me a mask."

"We'll wait in the car. White Subaru station wagon," Caleb says from behind the mask. "The dirtiest one." The boys laugh as the men hurry toward Sally and her friends.

"That should get them off our back. But it is dirty. Over there. Give me the key. Let's run." He unlocks it. "I'll hold the pooch. Go for it, Mom!"

Big Caleb struggles into the seat. His head touching the ceiling "We did all right," he says like a tired businessman.

"I like the mask. Let's have it back."

"Did the girl really buy it for you?" Liz asks as she drives out of the parking lot.

"She'd buy anything for Robert Plant! Don't look so shocked. It's the persuasion tapes and spray. Makes you want what you want twice as much."

"They can trace us." She turns north and drives fast.

"Nat's in no position to fink," Caleb says with indifference.

Liz has written about the bruised face of a boy who lied and stole food and trinkets in Hitler School. She had called this harsh punishment for a five or six-year-old Polish boy, who had learned to chant, "Today Germany and tomorrow the world," and knew that German soldiers took what they wanted. Her editor's notes called this rather preachy and she remembers every word and phrase he questions.

She speeds on the way home, because she wants to get back to her writing. "My kind of driver," Caleb says.

Chris names the puppy Saki. "That chap Eckert wants to give you a dog, all right with me." That's what he would say in New York City when an admirer gave Liz a present. They stand in the garden with their arms around each other, watching Saki explore the glazed snow. "Look at him. He's already forgotten the cage," she says.

"Nice little chap. But we already have Ringo. Dora's dog comes every day and so does Bonnie's cat. I do hope Eckert doesn't give you any more animals. This place is beginning to remind me of the Manor."

"I have been trying to write about that. I think Gramp took us to the Manor after that man in Vienna tried to grab me away from Dora near the hotel."

"Nonsense! Sis and I were born at the Manor. We were four years old when my dad came back from the war and took us all to Shoreland. Granny missed us terribly. Wanted me back in England all the time, so Gramp decided to leave us with her, hire a tutor, and get you to learn English, while he took Dora to Italy to learn singing."

Chris has his early childhood down pat, after years of rehearsed sessions with psychiatrists, but he is clutching Liz as though someone might pull her away from him and is talking fast. They cuddle and he kisses her on the mouth. For a moment she succumbs to the pleasure of being held.

"And you are sure you don't remember that man?"

When Saki runs toward the road, Chris goes after him, turning a skid on the crusty snow into a slide with aplomb, and scoops the puppy up. "All yours!" Exactly what he always said when he went to fetch baby Mike back from the road, to keep her from getting hysterical about losing him.

Chapter 22

GLOBAL SEARCH

Police notices:
A gray and yellow cockatiel flew away from the
owner yesterday around 3 p.m. Police said that
there is a good chance they'll find it.
Police spoke to the owner of a rooster crowing on
Clark Avenue at 7:04 a.m
A woman who found a $1 bill outside the Lady Godiva
shop yesterday at 4 p.m turned the money over to
the police. The police will hold the dollar until
its owner comes to claim it.

If you can't keep up with world affairs, the daily bad news, old school
friends, social events, like church fairs and silent auctions to benefit stray
cats, save-the-wetland meetings, the police notices in the Shoreland Eagle
are a must, to keep you in touch with daily mysteries, mishaps, conflicts
and miseries that are universal. You giggle, you say a little prayer, kneeling
in that "back-chair." Shoulders relax in the stillness of the half dark.
Finally, *endlich*. But during the ritual of activating the computer system,
and giving the print command for chapter one, the system searches and
grumbles out loud and too long. The message PRINTER BUSY appears
on the screen. She goes back to the menu, tries again. PRINTER BUSY.

"You are lying, *Du luegst!*"

Gramp would say: "No more German." But the nuns had told Liz that she must look after the wounded boy. To make the poor American boy better she must say her prayers. At bedtime she knelt down in front of the big bed they shared and taught Chris to pray in German whispers. When the bandage came off and they were able to go out for walks, he was beginning to speak German with her. But the man in the slouch cap who pounced on them when they came back from the park with Dora had not learned to speak German or English properly.

Sauntering along the Ringstrasse behind the children, Dora was softly singing the blue Danube waltz they had just heard at the cafe in the park where the music played. Chris made Liz hop over the shadow of trees with him, pretending they had to get across deep water. They were already close to the hotel. The man was waiting for them. Jumped out from a doorway and flipped open the Red Cross poster with the picture of war children.

"I don't want to buy anything," Dora said.

Before Liz had a chance to tell Dora that this bad man had hidden behind Holy Mary, he grabbed her by the arm. "There. American lady. Picture of this blond child. You see!"

Chris screamed and tried to pulled Liz away and Dora stepped in front of him. "You are not the father, are you?" Dora asked.

He ignored that question and talked in fast foreign German, about a girl in his displaced persons camp, had her child stolen by Germans. A blond child like the one on the poster. He changed to bad English and he smelled of spoiled food when he came closer to talk about the pretty mother at the camp crying for this pretty little girl. He wiped his eyes with the back of his hand, but it was his thick nose that dripped. "You remember *Mutter*, girl?"

Chris shouted, "Come on, Liz. Run!" She didn't move. When Chris pulled her, she fell. The man came to pick her up.

Dora pulled Liz behind her. "Don't touch her! You can't just replace a lost baby with this child because a woman likes her face." But that's what Graham Plant had done.

Chris shouted, "Go away!" Dora opened her purse and handed him a fistful of Austrian paper money.

"Dollars!" he demanded.

"Stolen from me in Prague. I don't have any!"

An elderly couple and two young women stopped to see what was going on.

"The nun who is a teacher knows that the Americans have stolen this child," the man said.

The old couple stopped in front of the children. "Are you stolen, little one?" the man asked in German.

Nuns told her to always tell the truth. "Naturally", she smiled, showing off with a new English word she had just learned. Chris put his arm around her. "She's my Sis!"

"His little sister. How sweet!" The couple patted the children. Liz smiled so that everyone would be good to her. The old man and the two young women reasoned with the man. He seemed to be listening, when he veered around and picked Liz up. Chris howled. Tall, Dora yelled "Help, help guard" but the soldier had left his post in front of the hotel. So she pushed everyone aside, went after the man with her loudest operatic "*Zu Hilfe, zu Hilfe!*" Chris sat down, with fright. The man froze. She had Liz in her arms before he recovered.

"Americans—just like Germans—take anything they want!" He raged, after he had failed to take what he wanted. He charged through the crowd and grabbed Chris. "Now. You hand over the girl!" Two Russian officers walking towards a street car turned. The man pulled his slouch cap over his face, the poster flew up in the wind. Chris got away and ran to the hotel, Dora followed carrying Liz, just as the guard came out with a snappy salute." Let's not worry Gramp with this," Dora said.

Gramp had praised and rewarded Liz with presents for learning to speak English. Then, several presents and loud kisses later, the child psychiatrist, Dr. Neubau, told Gramp that the new Liz got Chris to speak German with her when they were alone. By now he even prayed with her in German, to God, to the mother of God, to baby Jesus, and to and for poor Adolf Hitler.

Gramp had the answer. Chris had to go back to his plastic surgeon in London. Why not leave the children in Norwich with the boy's English grandmother for a while? Hire a tutor. How did Gramp get papers to travel with two children instead of one? And how did he manage to adopt a stolen child within three months? Graham Plant always had his way. Suitcases were being packed. Liz and Chris drank delicious raspberry juice in the hotel room in Vienna and woke up in a taxi in London. She did not remember the journey.

In this isolated room Dec Mate II could not have caught a computer bug. She tries to print out once more. PRINTER BUSY. This has happened before. If a computer, like a stubborn kid refuses a command, just try another one and get back to the first one later. She needs to work on *The Manor.* The manual says, TYPE GS GLOBAL SEARCH AND REPLACE AND PRESS RETURN. She has just been given a new option: TYPE THE SEARCH PHRASE AND PRESS RETURN. It all seems so easy. Liz allows the pages to scroll, as GLOBAL SEARCH AND REPLACE changes, nameless stolen child, Hitler-School Liese, to Catholic shelter 'little angel' into Gramp's Liz, and Chris's Sis—into British Lizbeth. The dogma of computer language—like Nazi lingo with all those slogans—had to be invented to go with new power. "*Du bist tuechtig* you are efficient, Mate II. What you couldn't have done if you had been around during the war, computerized Himmler theories, lists of stolen children, bookkeeping of doom?" Great power put to the worst possible use. The sport and documentation of killings.

Liz remembers British great grandfather's study with the lists of all the wild animals he had killed. Dates, species, all the details. Walls lined with zebra skins and decorated with stuffed, multicolored exotic birds, the collection of guns in a glass case.

Did great-grandfather hunt birds because his wife loved them, or did she love birds because he hunted them? And how about Granny? His only child and all the cats she stole and locked up to keep them safe? The big drawing room in the Manor had been occupied by aged cats she had rounded up after the Norwich blitz. This had been her idea of war work. Any cat that happened to be out in the street had been snatched up, put into a wicker basket, and loaded into the old car. Since females in uniform were part of the war effort, Granny and her assistant, the housekeeper, had worn belted coats and boots and air-raid wardens' steel helmets while they rescued so many cats that a rumor spread someone was stealing the animals to make them into fur vests and hats, and the newspaper had warned cat owners to keep pets from roaming.

The troop of aged cats would sit around a glowing fire like a gang, conspiring to escape. No one knew their names. One big tiger cat, a leader, would leap onto a chair and claw the brocade. And Liz would beg Granny

to let them go and let them find their way home. Granny said they would-
n't remember where they came from.

LION ON WING

The emblem at the entrance to the big English stone
house was neither a hook-cross nor a Holy Cross,
but a lion with wings. And Liz, who had learned
about "mixlings" and "race shame" at Hitler School,
was fascinated by this Lion-bird. A creature not
merely of mixed blood but mixed species, pictured
on doors, plates, forks, and knives—even on a ban
ner.

And from the moment she arrived she found out
that there was a little war going on at the Manor,
because Great-Granny hated mongrels, and Granny,
her only daughter, kept animals of mixed breed.
Could emblems like the Lion with wings or hook-
cross bring about conflict? Or did conflict create
emblems?

When the taxi drove up with Gramp and the children, Granny was staking out her mottled herd of
goats right next to the cages with her mother's
ornamental pheasants, ducks, grouse, and geese. She
waved with her mallet, and came rushing over, tall,
stout, dressed like a camp matron in a dark raincoat and black boots, to greet Gramp and Chris;
then she turned to Liz. "Who have we here?"

The child bolted, tried to hide behind a staked-
out mottled goat, and worried out loud in German
about being locked up in this animal camp. The camp
director Granny came after her and said, "We speak
English here. You're our Lizbeth now." The child
had to accept another new name in order to be
accepted.

She had been made into Aryan German Liese, Gramp
turned her into Liz, and now Granny wanted her to
be English, exactly like Chris's English twin. But
Granny's mother, deaf Great-Granny the bird lover,
accepted the new Lizbeth as a mother hen will
accept a partridge or duckling. Great-Granny even
looked like a bird—tall with feathery hair tufted
on top of her small head—as she came tottering
around cages on thin, stiff legs. "Our darling,
darling twins," she chirped. Her cape, winging in

the wind, enfolded both children to keep them from
flying away again with that stranger. She scrutinized Gramp. "Who's that?" She raised her ear
trumpet and dropped it again. "They were born in
England. My good man. They're British you know.This
is where they belong and twins should always stay
together."

Great-Granny often told the story of how her own
twin sister felt her labor pains all the way to
India, where poor childless Lillian lived with that
military husband. "We should have been allowed to
stay together. Why should those who are born
together be torn apart? When my granddaughter
Sheila was blessed with twins. I was so thrilled.
Darling brother and sister." She shot a warning
glance at Gramp, who was leaning against the car.
Just like two little birds. "I hope nothing and
nobody ever comes between you!"

"Nothing and no one will. I'll see to that,"
Gramp promised. Great-Granny had already lowered
her ear trumpet. She must have been the only woman
in the world who didn't like Gramp. "She isn't his
real sister," he shouted."They can even get married
one day, keep everything in the family."

Granny said,"Do please lower your voice, Mr.
Plant. I don't want my mother to know any of this.
Besides, you are confusing the children."

Before Gramp left, he again asked Liz never to
speak German to anyone. But German remained her
language for worrying out loud when she was alone
with animals. She smiled so that everyone would be
good to her, and Great-Granny gave her sunflower
seeds when she smiled and called her darling little
fledgling."You are so pretty and so strong. The boy
is not. Same with birds. Some just never learn to
use their wings."

Old Great-Granny seemed to like birds, only
birds, but Liz did see her smile at butterflies:
"Darling twins on wing, swallowtail with swallowtail; sparrow with sparrow, robin with robin,
perfect. There is no mixed breeding among birds and
butterflies. She would lean out of her bedroom window and look at the staked-out goats, crying,
"Horrible, horrible misbegotten mongrel creatures."

Liese had learned German by listening to the
story of Frau Faser's sister. Now she was learning

English by listening to Great-Granny's story of how she had been persuaded into marriage with a stranger, who hunted and shot birds and tried to murder her doves.

In his study, the safari room, you could see pictures of Great-Grandfather, the late Basil Milford Jones, one foot on the carcass of an elephant or tiger, surrounded by natives who had driven animals out of the bush so that the English hunters could shoot them and be photographed. Guns were now locked in the glass case with multicolored exotic birds and two stuffed pigeons. Great-Granny kept her old parrot in the study where it perched on stuffed owls and hawks, leaving patterns of droppings on pelts of a snow leopard and a giant panda.

When the bird chirped,"Darling, darling bird!" in front of the mirror, pecking at its own image, it sounded just like Great-Granny, whose endearments had never been heard in this room during the days of the great hunter.

She had been quite lovely, and when you got used to the creases on her face, she still was. He had chosen her like beautiful prey, she said. He was a proud man, but Great-Granny was ashamed of him, and ashamed of having married him to please her parents. He had been her class, but not her kind. And he had met his end shooting her doves and pigeons.

After his return from a winter in Africa that year, the coo-coo-cooing of doves woke him up one morning and he went into a rage, opened cages and started shooting. When his wife appeared, he ran into the woods, where he kept on shooting birds. The sound of his gun had brought the entire household to the front portal. There they witnessed the great hunter breaking out through the thicket in a panic. Like a wild animal driven into a clearing for a quick kill, he fell face down. His heart had stopped.

"That's how he died, a stranger to the end. And then my own daughter married a stranger. I was not to blame!" Great-Granny considered marriage to strangers a family curse. "I did my utmost to spare her. The only time she ever saw men was at church."

Grandmother Beth was as used to the old stories

and the old tirade as she was used to the cry of caged peacocks. Whenever her mother came to the part, "And then my own poor girl married the vicar, a stranger from London, not her class, only five years younger than her father," Granny Beth would take her mother's claw-like hand, reminding her that the vicar had lived for only five more years, and there had been little Sheila.

Sheila, the granddaughter, had also been carefully kept away from boys in girls' school, where she had played only with girls her own class. She had loved to ride and was perfectly contented at the Manor while English boys were fighting the war, Then those American flyers had been stationed nearby. Two officers came and wanted to rent a horse. She went riding with them. Tragedy followed. "She went off and married an American. A flier, and I guess they've flown off together. We're lucky they've let us have the darling fledglings." No one ever told Great-Granny that Sheila and her American pilot had gone forever.

Great-Grandmother never knew about the tragic boat fire. Villagers who saw Chris and the new Sis walking hand in hand hardly noticed that the boy's cheeks looked mottled and scarred, his hands too. And if Chris's great-grandmother did complain that her darling Sheila had gone away and had even forsaken the little fledglings, Granny told the children it was better her mother felt betrayed than bereaved.

Chris and Liz were drawn into another conspiracy of silence with Granny when she moved them into the old nursery at the lodge, where she had hidden the dog Eileen. Meat was still rationed, but she secretly fed her chicken stew and took her for walks at night when Great-Granny and most of her birds were asleep. This half-Alsatian, half-Pekingese had murdered free-roaming Jack and Jill, two of Great-Granny's oldest peacocks, and had been condemned to death for exterminating all the hens at the neighboring farm on that same Sunday morning while everyone was in church.

Their Norwich nurse-maid had been in charge of the twins from the moment they were born, and the retired teacher Granny had hired as a tutor could be trusted to keep quiet about the new Lizbeth as well as Grandmother Beth's dog Eileen.

Granny secretly kept Eileen in the best room at the lodge, which had been furnished with white wicker and a French dressing table for Great-Granny's twin sister. But poor Lillian did not live to enjoy this sunny room with a perfect view of the bird cages, where the dog Eileen now languished on a silk quilt watching the birds and growled. Chris and Liz were ignored. She was their favorite.

Her yellow fur had been shaved, leaving a lion's mane because she suffered from mange. They much admired the way she squinted when she saw a fly or moth ready to spring, snap and devour it. They were ignored when they cheered. She had no time for children. Most of the time she crouched, ears pricked up listening to pigeons or doves—the wild descendants of birds that had survived Great-Grandfather's last shoot—calling,"Who, who, who. Who are you? from the roof and in trees near her window. She went wild, jumping up and down on the bed, snarling and barking, howling until they flew away. But they always returned.

One day when the tutor stayed at home with a cold, the children took their picture books into Eileen's room to entertain the bird hater with the story of Chicken Little. She just ignored them and kept glaring out the window, listening. A lonely fanatic, waiting to get into a rage.

The moment she heard Great-Granny's shrill quavering voice out in the meadow, the dog jumped up, scattering the story books. It so happened that Great-Granny was inside a cage with a wild goose and the winging bird had her cornered and was beating her away from the gate. All the other birds whistled, twittered, and squawked in their cages, beating their wings. The old lady was waving her cape with both arms, "Darling, darling bird be still!"

Deaf-Great Granny could not hear the terrible yelp, the crash of broken glass. She did not see Eileen fly through the window as if she had wings, and crash land on a straw-covered flower bed, roll over and race towards the bird cages, her yellow mane bristling and her war cry drawn out and high pitched as she shot forward. Great-Granny had collapsed inside the cage on a little stool trying to

protect her face from the wings with her cape, when
Eileen pushed the gate wide open. The goose snaked
its long neck and hissed. The dog pounced, was
smacked back by the powerful wings, retreated, and
pounced again as the goose rose with three trumpet
calls and flew out through the gate. The dog trembled as the wild bird rose and flew away over the
trees. She veered around in hopeless pursuit, racing alongside a row of poplars, leaping and howling
all the way through the field towards the vegetable
gardens of the neighboring farm.

The farmer heard Eileen yelp as she raced
towards his yard. One glimpse of the bristling yellow mane and he ran to fetch his gun. She jumped
over a fence, charged toward his gate, her head
raised—a perfect target—as she howled up to the
sky. Two shots rang out; Eileen jerked in one final
frantic leap and fell.

"*Krieg, Krieg*! War!" Liz ran out onto the road,
crouching behind hedges to avoid bullets from
fighting enemies, making herself small as a mouse
to hide when there was no escape. No shelter, no
safe place left, only the dark silence before the
next explosion.

Chris followed shouting, "Liz! Come back, Sis!"
When he saw her lying face down behind a hedge
trembling all over, he stretched out beside her and
held on, until Granny found them. Tears ran down
Granny's plump face. She grieved with the children
for Eileen until teatime, when nurse arrived with
fresh buttered scones and berries from the farmer.
Granny took tea with the children every day after
that. Graham Plant arrived at teatime two weeks
later.

He was more than pleased: Liz sounded every bit
as English as Chris, and the boy had healed beautifully. The children's stay in England had come to
an end. Great-Granny was in despair. "He's come to
take you away from us. My own dear Lizbeth." She
clasped the child in her thin arms and cried.
"Darling brother and sister. Our own little birds.
Nothing and nobody must ever come between you!"

"Nothing, and no one will. I'll see to that,"
Gramp again promised in a loud, clear voice.

After their clothes and toys had been packed,
Liz and Chris went to gather their storybooks in

Eileen's room. Doves had a big gathering in trees outside her window cooing and hooting: "Who, who, who are you?"

"What are they going to call me in America?"

"Liz, of course."

"No new name?"

"Unless you want one. In America you can do what you want to do. Gramp isn't strict. You'll like the food."

"Great-Granny and Granny want us to stay."

Chris handed her some of the picture books of English soldiers he wanted to take to America. "You'll like Shoreland. Dogs and cats run around there. They're not locked up. Wild birds are not in cages."

Someone had covered the bed and the broken window with floral spreads, but Eileen's china dish decorated with the family crest of the lion with wings remained under the wash stand. Liz emptied the water.

"She went wild," Chris said.

"Flying," Liz pointed at the crest, that fabulous mongrel: a lion with a dog snout on wing.

Does this ring true? The cadence of a story has to be a subliminal persuader. Liz scrolls back to read the last page out loud, when something touches her leg. She jumps. Saki stands under the desk wagging his tail. "I'd forgotten all about you." But the cat-face of the shih tzu-lion dog reminds her of the parlor cats, who had escaped onto a balcony and ran away soon after Liz and Chris left because forgetful Great-Granny, wandering around the Manor looking for the children, had left doors open. Most of them found their way home.

Chapter 23

MIRROR WRITING

Why put up with a drab day when you can imbibe magic? Take a happy pill and make summer for yourself on a cold terrace. Sea gulls circle above Mike's head shrieking, "Now, now, now!" Waves roll in and in, as the winds tear off his naked body the black silk sheet he took from Emerald's dorm-room. He holds on with both hands, letting it billow to sail him back to yesterday.

"Yesterday, yesterday, yesterday," he shouts into the wind. "Yesterday," to water boiling with sea serpents, squadrons of winged female demons all waiting to fly you to Aleister Crowley's satanic temple at Boleskin House on the shore of Loch Ness, over seas of yesterdays, to Jimmy Page magic. The Led Zeppelin group, partying at Boleskin house, dancing in the dark with shadows. DO WHAT THOU WILT. Crowley's words appear in two-foot-tall black letters on a huge boulder in the Shoreland woods. Did I, Mike Plant the Third write it? Did the wicked spirit of old Aleister make me do it?

Crowley spent one entire year staring into a mirror trying to make his reflection vanish. He couldn't do it. But Mike can see his own reflection right now—without any mirror: naked back turned on a waste land of hypocrites, looking out over an abyss of dead blue water, up to oceans of choppy clouds. In touch with demons, like old Aleister C., and trying to get hold of a guardian angel. He shout-sings "Stairway to Heaven."

Mike hasn't had much sleep. Karin ended up spending most of the night in the cellar in a sleeping bag with him. She showed up during the Suicide Four rehearsal and stayed on to tell him that rock music, pot, and Mike's perfume, unmarried sex, and AIDS are all from the devil. Prep school guys are all gay. She is crazy about Mike, but she had herself exorcised at Seal Rock Chapel, born again, and scared shitty. Mike told her that was ignorance and superstition, not religion. He tried to wise her up to the fact that recreational drugs are better than Valium or booze; AIDS did come not from the devil but from sex with green monkeys in Africa—monkey lovers and everyone sleeping around.

College dudes sleep around but he doesn't: He's not only the best — and has been reading Beatrice Strout—but also safe as a monk since Grove is not even coeducational anymore. The girls' dorm is off limits. And girls all have a curfew after Emerald escaped with aliens for a couple of days.

He had made Karin laugh and cured her of the exorcism the best possible way, but this morning he is beat. Everything has turned around. She stopped being scared and passed the fear of the devil onto him. It's like having a really lousy dream you can't remember hanging over you and making you feel it's still going to happen.

The mail slot slams after Mike goes back into the house, and Saki makes off with a letter because he wants someone to chase after him. Not so different from Caleb the thief, when you think about it. The letter turns out to be from Grove Academy, addressed to Mr. and Mrs. Plant. Mike leaves Saki listening to animal sounds on dog-and-cat-food commercials, as well as soaps when couples fight and have sex, while he steams the letter open.

Dear Parents:
Where are we now? Where do we want to go? How do we get there?

Grove Academy was founded to provide a full educational opportunity to help our students develop their unique potential. Help them learn to trust his or her judgments and raise a consciousness to world and family problems.

Mike holds the letter up to a mirror and that loopy illegible signature leaning the wrong way—Havelock Grimes in reverse—tells you that Havelock Grimes, mirror writer is a scary mirror thinker. Where are we now? Havelock asks. Answer: We are in a fucked-up polluted world. Where do we want to go? Answer: Nobody cares a shit. How do we get there? Answer: Against our will. Mike can feel mirror living zeroing in on him. And it would take a mirror big as the world for turning things around to make sense. He needs to read no further to know that Dad would simply hand this letter to Mom, who is already freaking out. So Mike tears it up and while he is busy flushing it down the toilet, the phone rings and keeps ringing.

"Liz! Pick up that damned phone or take it off the hook, for God's sake!"

Dad. Typical. He must be the biggest downer in the universe. Blowing his stack when it was his own idea to have extension phones. Mom unplugs hers when she is writing. Let him listen in and he'll hear every-thing to make him mad. That's what he's listening for. Never tunes into you, hears only the words, not what you are really getting at—never the tune. Mike drapes the black sheet over one shoulder. The day has just begun but he suddenly feels beat. Everything is always up to him.

By the time Mike picks up an extension, Mom is on the line saying, "OK, Bonnie, tell Priscilla Fairfield I'll be there." But she is not OK when he gets up to the computer room. Saki hangs onto the ruffle of her big white nightgown and she's grumbling in German to both the dog and the computer. Writing glasses Dad bought for her, as glare protection from computer radiation, enlarge her eyes and make them iridescent blue-green.

Mom says she just got the printer going again and is ready to print out. Now there is an emergency. Havelock Grimes has flown in from New York and Priscilla Fairfield has asked her to come to an emergency regional Parents' Association meeting at her house this morning.

Mike tries to calm her down: Grimes the terrible at the Fairfields! That is the emergency. He'll ask for money. Grove is always broke. "You'll never get Dad to go to the meeting. He's smart."

"I promised."

"Don't worry. I'll go with you, Mom! They can't ask me for money, and the food will be great. Fairfields have everything catered by The Blue Jay. Stuffed snails, stuffed eggs, stuffed oysters, stuffy everything."

"No kids!"

"What do you mean? We are the ones who are being shipped off to Grove. Prissy doesn't want us around. And Grimes has no right to make her president without an election. She'll try to have poor old Goodley fired, because he gave all those scholarships to blacks. Firing headmasters is her specialty. Remember? You better go and campaign against her and Grimes, Mom. Not in my old jeans. Put on a dress. And I don't mean one of those thrift store church sale specials."

"You look white and tired, Mike. You've been sleeping down there in the basement again."

Mike shakes curls that always mat up nicely after sex. "Dad doesn't like it when I play tunes in my room at night." The half truth.

He watches Mom tearing through dresses she keeps in her old closet in the computer room. Mostly old funky evening clothes from thrift shops and church fairs that she puts on when she is in the mood to be British with Dad at dinner time. Mike picks out a proper blue dress that Dora surprised her with at Christmas. The label says Christian Dior. She tries it on right over her nightgown. A size fourteen and much too big. "Angel" must have bought it for herself, gained another six pounds, and given it to Mom.

"Go for it, Mom. Great color, no style and therefore stylish. Take Dad's car. Yours is too dirty."

Wake Dad up early and he is likely to sleep until about two in the afternoon. Mom makes French toast for him and leaves it in the warming oven. Fresh orange juice and organic tofu breakfast sausage and eggs for Mike before she leaves. Mike drinks the juice, feeds the sausage and egg to Saki, and eats potato chips and raspberry jam in front of the TV, watching a soap where a young guy is making love to his former wife's mother-in-law, a skinny woman who looks like Caleb's Mom.

Priscilla Fairchild keeps telling Caleb she drinks because she has a horror of his ending up in jail with rapist monster criminals who will give him AIDS. But she has always been drinking, Caleb says, and "Parents who worry about kids together stay together." There is no doubt that the Plant brother and sister marriage is far more likely to split up while Mike is away and it is too quiet at home. Then there is Ellen, who really means no harm but has no morals. Being a psychologist is a good cover, but something has to be done before Bonnie and Mom find out the truth about Ellen and

Dad.

Mike's unusually developed social consciousness is not only raised but activated: It is all up to him. There would never be a day when Mike was more certain of his unique potential and doing the right thing. Doing your best, you can end up doing the worst, but Bonnie kept on telling him from way-back-when: You've got to keep trying.

The moment Mom leaves, he pours himself a double whiskey and soda, makes a Chris Plant face, and swallows half of it like medicine. Then he goes up to her room, where he kneels down in Mom's weird back-chair. It almost topples. Diskettes have been left in the drive to make it easy. Mike does check the quick look-up guide which says, "Always be certain your diskette has been initialized." He never has to read more than half a line to get the idea. He presses 'I' to initialize. The computer wants a six-letter name. He writes PWOPRO for Parent and World Problems. There is a time clock clanking away like the kitchen timer. A little grating sound. A big grind-groan and the menu appears.

If you put dates on letters, they get out of date and are thrown out. "Winter of Discontent" comes into Mike's head. Must have heard it on TV. He types fast with two fingers. Who needs to take boring typing or computer lessons? It's like learning the Olympic- style crawl in that little urinal of a chlorinated Grove Academy pool full of red-eyed sucker kids, when you can beat them all doing the fastest doggy paddle in the world.

Alcohol kills brain cells, but Mike is considered very brainy and cells must be crowding in on each other at this very moment. This letter is very important, and has to sound British. Ellen loves all those British TV programs, and she goes for Dad because he often sounds like one of those types. He looks it, too, when he gets dressed up. Mike drinks his whiskey and opens the phone book. The first name he sees is Renfrew. And then there is Oswald. Sir Oswald Renfrew. That's overdoing it.

Dr.Oswald Renfrew in transit Logan Airport Boston

Lonely Tuesday

Dear Dr. Burns:

I was so fortunate to be in New England when you appeared on the talk show "Doing Your Thing." I am a scholar writing a book about women and world

religion. I found your lively ideas as fascinating
as your beauty and free spirit.

I am travelling and doing research, but I will
write to you now and then until we have the opportunity to meet. This note is written in great
haste.

With respect and admiration...

The Cragleys will mail this from Boston. In Jamaica, Mike can get the
help of Harrison, a decent kid who was bounced out of Grove for selling
grass he brought from home.

Doctor Oswald Renfrew in transit Jamaica Hilton

Tropical Rain

My Dearest Dr. Burns:

Before I left America I went to hear you speak at
the Burnham Community Center. I was the only man at
the lecture and I stayed in the back of the hall
crowded with women. Your lecture was clearly positive. Some of the women in the audience were not. I
thought it prudent to leave as soon as the lecture
was over.

I am deeply impressed by your vitality, originality
and good sense. You are beautiful in every way and
I see in you a revival of female morality. Perhaps
you would consider a lecture tour in England and a
stay at my country house in Norwich, Norfolk. I
have lost my wife, and my interest in you is sin-
cere.

With respect and admiration...

Mike has heard Dad giving condolences to his English psychiatrist,
who lost his wife last summer. He changes "My dearest" to British "My
dear." Finishes the drink. Tries this and that and curses the DEC Mate.
Finally the printer rattles off the letters. "Wicked cool. Now lets do a
phony letter to a witch."

Michael Plant The Third
Shoreland MA, 01977

Full Moon

Dear Official Witch of Salem, Amanda Garlic

I picked up your "Witchcraft as a Science" pamphlet
at the Serendipity Shop in the Linden Tree Mall,
where I was shopping with my wonderful grandson. You
are a very striking looking woman. My daughter-in-
law, Liz Plant, could use some of your powers to
deal with my son, who is a selfish spoiled man.

She is struggling to write a nice little book and
could definitely use the supernatural power of Wicca
to get supernatural excitement into her story and
make it a supernatural bestseller. Your classes are
just what she needs.

P.S. This is confidential. Please send your material
to Mrs. Liz Plant at the
above address.

Mike signs this one "Your admirer." The drink is taking effect. He feels
aged, as though his life had turned around, and a happy grandfatherly low-
brain-cell mellowness comes over him. He keeps on writing letters and
printing them out without any problem. Finds a disk that has "back-up"
labels. No problem. You just switch disks and copy. "I'm psyched! What the
hell would they all do without me?"

Chapter 24
PARENTAL COMMITMENT

At the gas station Liz almost turns back to make sure she took her diskettes
out of the computer. Foreboding has made her late for the meeting. The
shortcut she takes to the Fairfield house gets her onto an unpaved icy road
in the South Woods. It is a Shoreland custom to paint or even carve slogans on Stone-Age boulders. DEL LOVES JIGGERS now has been
repainted with Aleister Crowley's DO WHAT THOU WILT in big, red
letters, which could stand as a slogan for the Fairfield southern mansion
with a driveway that runs through a colonnade.

Edwin had tried to appease his wife Priscilla, a former Miss New
Orleans, when she had the rooms decorated early New England-style.
With paintings of horses and inevitable tall ships. Shaker chairs, old portraits of someone else's great-grandparents. All of it brought to life now by
the fragrance of coffee and sherry and perfumes, the excited voices and
nervous laughter, of about thirty regional parents drinking, enjoying a
smorgasborg feast and worrying out loud about problems with their children without listening. "Liz, glad you could come." She doesn't remember
the well-rounded father. "Don't you look great!"—"How's Mike doing?"—
Greetings, kisses, and introductions. "Where did you get that smashing
dress?" A mercifully cloudy antique mirror gives Liz a glimpse of herself

which sadly reminds her of the oversized blue dress Liese wore when Gramp and Dora took her on approval. "Want you to meet—" "Guess what, Havelock's giving us re-admission interviews. Isn't this wonderful?"

A clever idea, for making himself popular with parents after humiliating them by throwing their kids out. Liz wants to feel wonderful. Silver coffee-and-teapots, cutlery, everything gleams. Platters glisten with Nova Scotia salmon. Tiny cakes, bejeweled with glazed fruit. She hasn't eaten much today, but anxious parents finding solace in food brings back a long-forgotten peasant funeral feast for partisans. The hazy picture of women cloaked in black fades from her mind the moment Priscilla Fairfield drifts into the room dressed in winter white. She holds her head high and her drink tilted. Platinum hair pulled over with a silver clasp to cascade over her left shoulder. Self-absorbed until she sees Liz.

"No. I don't believe this!" The glass drops from her hand, hits a side table. Crystal shatters with the fragrance of gin—not rose water. "How could you, Liz?" Priscilla hisses and draws her behind a potted palm tree. "That's Mother's dress. The Dior she was wearing in Paris before she died."

"I didn't know you lost your mother," Liz cries out. "I'm so sorry!"

"I'm not," Priscilla's mouth twisted in bitter sadness contradicts her words. "Don't look so shocked. Mike says yours was killed by bombs in London. Mine never wanted to have me around her young men. In the end she liked Caleb, no one else. He'll get her money when he's twenty-one. She left me her house in France and her designer clothes. Caleb promised to throw them into the Salvation Army bin for me. How much did you pay that awful boy for the collection?"

"I didn't buy anything from him," Liz stammers, trying to explain that the dress was a Christmas present from Dora Myrtle. A bar-tender is cleaning up the glass splinters and solicitous father, Jason Goldfarb, interrupts with two glasses of sherry.

Priscilla says, "No, thanks," and exits through a side door, while a thin, stern man enters from the adjoining living room and catches Liz downing sherry like medication. A whisper goes around the room. That's him. Havelock. Dark hair and a black mustache.

Their eyes lock. Liz quickly puts her glass away. "I'm Mike Plant's mother."

"I see. You came late." He looks at his watch. "We're late."

Fathers come over and interrupt with urgent questions. "It is essential to develop the higher self," he raises his right hand to finger the aura above his head, "in order to curb the need for instant gratification." He swallows coffee from a mug he holds in his left hand. "We are late!" he repeats to break up the chatter and is herding everyone away from the delicacies into the adjoining rooms, when Pat Mitchel comes bouncing through the door and gives Liz, her grade-school friend, a big hug and little kiss on the cheek. "I am starving. This looks super."

She now calls herself "Mitch." They stay behind and pick up smoked salmon in one hand, olives in the other. "Liz! I miss you. So you're still married to Chris." She laughs out loud. "Writing your memoirs. Ellen told me. I go to her parties. Then there is Mike. I don't know how you do it! Who am I to talk. My Bobo is no joke." Tears come into her round, blue eyes. Short, plump, dressed in pink, she again shakes with laugher. Two marriages. Her job as a legal secretary and the unhappy lawyer she dates. "Bobo is still a slow learner. Dope doesn't help. I don't know what I'll do if Grimes takes away his athletic scholarship." They let sherry console and warm them. "It's all Emerald Skylark's fault. That little bitch vanished," Mitch says. "Poor Goodley thought she'd gone to Paris, to her father. Two days later she is back and says she has been kidnapped by aliens. Now her dad—some kind of a diplomat—threatens the school with a congressional investigation. That's why they called Grimes back from his leave of absence." Mitch refills their glasses and moans with delight as she surveys the garden of vegetable platters. "I wonder what Havelock will do about her. Boys used to have their heads shaved if they broke the rules. One boy smoked dope after he had his head shaved. So Grimes kicked him out. No punishment nowadays. A lot of kids run away and they like shaved heads."

"What happened to the boy?"

"Havelock told the parents to lock him out of the house if he showed up. He vanished. Their only child. Years ago, but the Sorrels come to all our meetings. Must be lonely. Once a Grove parent, always a Grove parent, as they say. Sorrel does the accounting for Grove. Unreal. "She reloads her plate and shovels food into her mouth. "Kid went to Florida and worked as a clown in Disneyland then on the West Coast, but weirdos and Canada geese always come back to the North Shore."

"Could he be an animal rights fanatic?"

"Goes without saying, since his Dad is a furrier." They are giggling when Priscilla re-enters, puts down an empty glass, puts a finger to her lips. They follow her into a living room she had turned into a lecture hall by opening sliding doors to the adjoining library where Havelock Grimes stands facing parents who are glowing from good sherry with a fiery speech against alcohol and drugs that numb the mind or stimulate with dangerous illusions. She quickly sits down at an open window.

"It has to be stopped!" Havelock fumes, breathing out coffee steam. Liz can feel her head spin from both sherry and disbelief, when he talks about training leadership boys to bring to justice any student who breaks Grove Academy rules. "We need committed boys."

When he refreshes his coffee from a convenient silver coffeepot on a side table, the room is so quiet you can hear noisy sparrows outside the window chirp, pecking dry fermented berries, which Mike says give them a high. Who is going to decide what is just and what is unjust when it comes to betrayal? Mike being betrayed and brought to justice makes her throat constrict. German S.S. and S.A. boys had been committed to injustice.

The founder of Grove Academy repeats his warnings and threats on and on until the tulips on the wallpaper begin to jig for Liz like stoned kids at a rock concert. She looks out the window to calm herself, and there is Edwin Fairfield getting out of his white limousine under the colonnade and fussing around, spreading a raincoat over the back seat. Suddenly a shapely leg in a white summer sandal shoots out. He forces it back unceremoniously, slams the door shut, and locks the car.

Short, sturdy dressed in red tartan trousers and a blazer, he brags about prowess he developed from wrestling at Brown University. His carrot-colored hair, the grin, and the skittery walk have been passed on to tall Caleb, so has his ease of entering through the French window, the way Caleb had entered the Plant parlor. He looks around and pulls a chair over to sit beside Liz. Havelock stops pacing in front of books and veers around to face Edwin. "We all need the commitment to become the solution and not the problem," he announces. "The Grove Academy concept has to permeate each home. Parents will have to develop more time for their children."

"How about kids developing more time for parents? I never see Caleb or hear from him unless he's in trouble and needs money," Edwin speaks up.

"We will get to that." Havelock fingers the air above his head. "Never let self get in the way of accountability."

A father who wears his hair in the old Beatles style, raises his hand and stands up." Ben Willies, lawyer, single parent. Question: If the Concept is accountability and honesty, How about kids spying on each other? Is that honest?"

Havelock Grimes glares up at the ceiling. "Discussion will follow." His tone says that it will not.

"Interest in the common good is honest," a bearded father responds in a voice thick with emotion. "Reaching the unique potential as a group, giving up one's self to a higher cause. We need that. Our children need it. Only Havelock can help us out," he sobs. "I'm sorry, I always get this way. You see, Havelock straightened out my girl several years ago. Now, the boy from my second family needs help. We all need Havelock!" His young wife hands him a wad of tissues. There is a murmur of belief and disbelief. Edwin tells Liz he can't help loving those two.

"Why?" she asks.

"They are so devoted to everything,"

"Anything you want to bring up, Edwin?" Havelock asks.

"No. No. I'll let you explain the Concept."

Havelock Grimes bares his teeth in less than a smile, more like a dog guarding a bone. "Questions about the Concept will all be answered at the Family Learning Center. I'm here today to ask the big question: Where do we want to go, and how are we going to get there?" He turns to the Sorrels, who sit side by side, holding hands. "William, why don't you take over."

William Sorrel stands up, drab and lean in a gray suit, like a creature protected by the color of its pelt. He opens a folder to start a litany of an itemized Grove Academy deficit. A balding father in a bent-wood rocker sways back and forth to the report. Copies are being passed around and studied with coughing and whispers. One loud sneeze. "About half a million," Sorrel concludes in a loud expressionless voice. Mrs. Sorrel leaves the room. Papers rustle.

Edwin nudges Liz, "See that fancy fur vest she has on? Old Sorrel imports furs. Gave poor Edwin a really good deal last Christmas."

"But they locked their only son out. He's been gone for years. Would you ever lock Caleb out?" Liz asks Edwin.

"Useless. He's learned to pick locks at Grove."

Sorrel steps forward to stand beside Havelock. "What it all amounts to is that we have been offered a donation of six hundred thousand dollars."

This is the cue for Priscilla Fairfield to stand up. "The person offering this endowment demands that Havelock return as director of the school and bring back the Grove Concept."

"Who is donating all that money, Havelock?" Pat asks.

"The person does not want to be named."

"Is it a father?" she persists.

"I don't want an unknown man to control my child's school!" A frail mother makes herself heard in a shrill voice.

"Maybe it isn't a man. Priscilla, is it you?"

"Certainly not!"

"If we do not go along with this condition," William Sorrel speaks up, "the debt could be paid by selling the guard's house and storage building with a fourth of the campus."

No answer. Priscilla picks up an antique basket and sways a little while she hands out squares of pink paper and pink pencils. "A 'yes' vote is for Havelock, and the commitment to our Learning Center and higher awareness. Blank is a 'no' vote."

Edwin beams. "Just look at her. My very own Miss New Orleans. I just wish she'd take it easy like you, Liz. You have such a good time with bad kids down there in Harbor Square. Cute. Marilyn Monroe never grew up either." His wife hands them paper and pencil. "Don't worry, Prissy. I'm voting for Havelock and the Higher Awareness Concept."

"Do you understand what he wants? Do you believe in him?" Liz asks under her breath.

"Sure, sure. He promises to make Caleb shape up. More power to him, when he's trying to keep the sexes segregated. Boys will be boys. You know that a man thinks about sex every four or five minutes of the day—not to mention night."

Liz pretends to be writing; then she folds the blank paper and throws it into the basket. "Are you donating all that money to Grove, Edwin?"

"Me? I'm not that crazy. Prissy is spending plenty of money campaigning for this guy. Our kids are driving her to drink. The two girls are devils, too. Poor Edwin looks forward to the Learning Center and getting awareness, specially if you are there."

He'll say anything that comes into his head to women, wherever he goes. Caleb says it pays off. "Isn't the lady in your car getting cold?", she asks.

"Quiet, please." Priscilla stands up, beauty pageant straight, while William Sorrel and his wife count the votes. They beam and nod to her. Havelock got the vote. New York City has come out for him. California too. That is the majority.

Applause. Edwin cheers, everyone joins in. Optimism sweeps over the group of parents. Grimes will do it. After all, there is an anonymous millionaire backing him with hundreds and thousands. Kids will all become achievers of their unique potential and learn to follow the rules. The founder of the school has won. The money made it an easy victory. No one to convince, nothing to fight for at this point. He goes around shaking hands, looking suddenly tired as though defeated by his own challenge.

Mist hangs over the expensive ocean view. It has started to rain. Married mothers linger under the colonnade, while husbands and divorced women get cars from the back of the house. An east wind faintly laced with pollution sways the spring-flushed branches of a huge weeping willow. There is subdued talk of conflict Havelock stirred up with faculty since his return. Many of the teachers are loyal to the headmaster, Mr. Goodley.

"I can't get no satisfaction." The old Rolling Stones' gripe song drifts out of Caleb's window. "Someone's opened my car door and left it open in this weather," Edwin makes himself heard while he drives his limousine out of the way into the stable. Liz is walking toward her station wagon with Pat when Edwin comes skittering out, yelling, "Caleb Fairfield. You rotten thief, where are ya?" The volume of the song is turned up.

Chapter 25
LEAVE TAKING

Self-closing kitchen doors open and bang shut. "Watch out for Saki!" Liz shouts, as the puppy races around the house and out the back door with Mike and the Suicide Four band. Bang goes the self-closing door.

Chris storms in from the dining room, and bang goes the door again. "He's going to meet the Grove bus at the airport tonight, snow or no snow, even if I have to hire a taxi!" He had lost a quart of vodka and found the empty bottle in the cellar where Mike and the Suicide Four have been rehearsing.

"He was drinking because he doesn't want to go back to Grove," Liz says.

"Making excuses for him, as usual. And I've had it!" Chris goes to the liquor cabinet to mix himself a martini. "You've never been able to control him and he's bloody awful here. At school he'll have to behave."

"German-Americans sent their sons to Nazi German Hitler Schools to learn how to behave!"

"That book is turning you into a hysteric."

A pan falls from her hands with a clatter. "I'm afraid for him."

"You should be afraid for me. He's making me quite ill." Chris goes to the music room with his drink and the door bangs shut behind him.

Instead of keeping an eye on the boys and looking after Chris, Liz has been searching her own room like a frantic burglar. She doesn't want anyone to know that the computer diskette with her finished chapters has vanished and keeps hoping to at least find the brown envelope with the lost chapters. She has been searching her mind even in her sleep, then wandering through the house during the night like a sleepwalker from room to room.

Ellen thinks that Liz has a subconscious need to make her own writing disappear, because Chris and Mike have been making her feel guilty about being a writer. Bonnie, who invited them both to tea and oatmeal-raisin cookies, admitted she has had the subconscious need to make shoe catalogues vanish because Jeff orders so many shoes. She offered Liz her answering-and-help service free of charge, to give her more time to write. Then Ellen voiced the opinion that Chris would hate that, with such authority, Liz, his sister-wife, has to wonder whether she has not had the subconscious need to lose not only her chapters, but also Chris. So Liz asserting ownership rights to annoy her Chris, accepts Bonnie's service.

You can't move around fast in Shoreland Super, because no matter who you are, where you come from, what work you do or don't do; what you have or don't have, whether you walk, drive an old or a new car, ride a skate board, a horse, bike or stationary bike, go to committee meetings or prayer meetings, when a storm has been forecast everyone comes piling into Shoreland Super for food and a chat.

Bonnie's two cousins Gussy and Harriet have stopped beside the blockade of improved Ivory dish-washing detergent. "How are ya?" Harriet calls as Liz hurries by with her shopping cart.

"Good." Liz feels awful. The sickening perfume from the "improved detergent" makes her stomach churn while she shops with the list for salty and sweet snack foods and candy bars Mike calls his last request. "There. That's him. Eckert. Over there with Emmet," Gussy is saying. "Arrives on Half Moon beach in a big fur, under it a bathing suit the size of a postage stamp." Gussy goes on, "Not young, but has a fine figure. Must be the refrigeration he gets every day."

"You must have had a real good look, Gussy!"

"I watch ducks for Audubon."

"Odd ducks." Harriet Simons, the riding teacher, and Gussy, a complacent wife, dress in Dora Myrtle-style—pastel-colored pant suits—and have the same belly laugh. Behind a wall of that wondrously tasteless Wonder Bread, Liz can hear Emmet Gray, the solitary stationary bike traveler, telling Arthur Eckert that newcomers here best join in to fit in. "How about the Friends of the Library, Arthur? You should give a lecture. And there are all the churches, Jewish Temple, Masonic Temple, Shriners, evangelists, transcendental meditators. Town committee meetings."

"I travel a lot," Arthur says.

"So do I—in my own way," Emmet laughs. "I'm studying France at the moment, while I ride my stationary bike. Mile by mile. The things that went on there! The Revolution. Blood flowing in the streets of Paris. Worse than the German invasion." Arthur is a bit of a German and Emmet quickly changes to Hungary, where Turks came and did their worst and stayed on a couple of hundred years.

"My Hungary lecture at the library went over big. Thelma Nesbit took me into town and we had dinner at the Cafe Budapest. Paris is next. I'm aiming to get my mileage for an April-in-Paris dinner in Boston." Emmet stops to catch his breath. "I like my bike. I understand you are quite the swimmer. How about sailing? For someone like you there's tennis, horseback riding, hiking. Something for everyone in this town."

Arthur laughs and admits that he has been invited to join the Single Parents Association. Aerobics, support groups for the sick, the pregnant, the retarded, alcoholics. Historical and Art Associations. Garden, rifle, animal aid, and book discussion clubs. And that is not all. He has been asked to join golf, yacht, swim, ski, tennis clubs. Invited to volunteer, network, play in the Shoreland orchestra or band concerts. Sing in the choir. Circle dance. Go on stage.

If Arthur didn't want to miss out, Liz is thinking as she moves on to the cookie and candy aisle, he could join most everything, a sure way to avoid getting too close to her or anyone else and avoid getting too close for comfort even to himself. Best of all, Liz would like Arthur to know, you are free not to join. You don't have to believe in anything or anyone else here in Shoreland. She takes a big bag of pop-corn candy down from the shelf and moves off toward the soda, soft drinks aisle. "I Can't Get No Satisfaction", the song Caleb Fairfield was broadcasting from his window, drifts through her mind. And those who were young when that song was an anthem are now old enough to find satisfaction in this town one way or another. Keeping active during the winter, or going wild and crazy in little houses, big houses, apartments or rented rooms, everyone here lives the same—each in their own way. 'Landers' allow each other space.

Arthur waves to Liz from the flower corner. No need to start a lot of gossip; she hurries on. Even Dora, who had the head start among seven other hostesses notorious for telephone romancing by the hour with interesting new men, ends up talking to Bonnie. Arthur does not like to answer the phone, but he does like to call Liz. Long distance from New York, to ask her about the Grove meeting. Emerald is a problem. Another time, he called and asked how Saki was behaving, while he confided his problems with the trained guard dog, that cowardly Doberman. The moment he returned to Shoreland he called and told her a dream he had of hiding again in the cave where he had almost frozen to death during the war. "If we had not been so well trained we could not have survived that night." Chris, who has monitored Arthur's telephone monologues on an extension line, had voiced a sudden concern that this man—who could well afford a psychiatrist, or at least Ellen—has been taking up Liz's writing time.

She now quickly picks up a bag of Macintosh apples to improve on Mike's "Last Requests" and runs to the shortest checkout line; but Arthur follows and surprises Liz with foreign kiss on each cheek. He looks like a conquering soap opera hero in a gray Irish tweed suit, with his graying hair and beard. Gussy and Harriet, waiting in line at the next counter, give him the fish eye. He makes them laugh, but he's different, German or Jew or whatever, a reminder that what has been done in Germany to the likes of him, or by the likes of him, stirs up the dark side of the heart with what can be done.

"Could distrust of strangers come from inherent, self-distrust in descendants of strangers who invaded these shores, killed the natives and settled on their land?" Words from those lost pages. Questions she asks in her story keep resounding.

"Are you all right?" Arthur asks.

"Just fine." Because she has just remembered these lines.

"I called to ask whether I could drive Mike to the school bus for you, but you had already left."

If she couldn't find the diskette, or the finished chapters, would it all come back to her? How quickly could she rewrite? She could use the time, but—"Thank you. I do have to take him myself."

Emerald is flying in from Paris, and visits with her father unsettle her. Bambi is in New York and and won't be back till late. He'll be there to get the little imp onto the Grove Academy bus.

He is buying roses, candles, caviar, thick little tenderloin steaks, wild rice, frozen raspberries, and whipping cream for a romantic dinner. Shopping carts tell stories. Sandy, a fat high school dropout in front of them, has loaded up with potato chips, chocolate chip cookies, animal crackers, soft drinks, and candy. Her baby boy has torn open a package of marshmallows and sits in the basket stuffing himself. Arthur stares at the trash foods in Liz's shopping carts with impertinent curiosity.

"For Mike and his roommate," she says. "Kids hate school food."

"The diet should improve now that Grimes is back in charge. He has the right ideas. More discipline and order all around. A safer place."

Safer? Liz can't help translating order into German *Ordnung*, and tyranny. The baby howls while Sandy pays for her groceries with food stamps, and keeps howling as she hurries away.

"While Emerald is skin and bones, this young mother is about eighty pounds overweight; poisoning herself and her child. Food stamps should be limited to nutritious foods," Arthur says.

"Sandy is having a hard time. Her boyfriend was killed in a car collision two days before the wedding."

"That shouldn't keep her from buying milk for her child. Do you mind if I take a look at your bag of apples?" He opens the plastic bag like a customs official, holds up a glossy red apple with disdain. "*Gott im Himmel*! Waxed fruit. What next! Doesn't that remind you of that story of the tempting poisoned apple? *Schneewitchen*. Snowwhite. Allow me to exchange these varnished apples for you."

He had called himself a trained observer that day in Boston among Austrian disciples. Quickly, while he is gone, Liz unloads and checks out all the jolly sugar-or Nutrasweetened, or over-salted and nitrated kid-food packages, natural one percent juice drinks, sold by evil stepmother food companies. Then she can't find her money and is going through her wallet in a panic. She had eighty dollars in her purse; now there is only one ten dollar bill!

Checkout clerks at the Shoreland Super are mostly Mike's friends and her friends too. This one, a nervous, gray-haired woman, is a stranger. Liz says, "I can only buy ten dollars worth. Do you mind..."

The woman puts on oversized reading glasses, checks over all the junk food, and glares at Liz, who is wearing Mike's old jeans and a sweatshirt decorated with two dancing devils. "You got about thirty dollars worth."

"I had around seventy dollars in my wallet I can't find. Left my check book at home." Liz had also forgotten to put on her wedding ring.

"How about your food stamps?"

Her car keys drop. Arthur is back and picks them up. "I don't have any." She can feel her face glow.

"I don't see how you gals think you can feed yourselves."

Arthur steps in at once. Puts the replacement apples on the counter. "Just check us out together. I'll take care of it." He hands Liz one of his two bouquets of roses.

"No, you can't. I'll just run home and get my checkbook." Gussy and Harriet come over. "No need, Liz. We can help out." But Arthur has already pulled out a wallet thick with bills. Gussy and Harriet exchange meaningful glances when Liz thanks them. The computer register peep-peep-peeps, tttttuck, tttt.

He puts his arm around Liz. "Don't worry."

Her flushed face could be interpreted in many ways as Arthur takes over and pushes the shopping cart to her car as though he had done this for years. "No one should be ashamed of being without money."

"I'm ashamed of being ashamed," she says foolishly.

He comes to a dangerous stop in the parking lot. A car swerves around them but he doesn't even notice. *"Ich scheame mich das ich mich scheame. Mein Gott.* A girl said this to me during the war. I remember conversations, documents I read only once. But it often takes me years to get the meaning. Emerald says I have a computer mind, because I remember everything she promises and then forgets." He takes charge of her car-key. "You look tired." Loads her bags into the back of her station wagon. "The weather's dark. Let me drive Mike to the bus?"

"No. I really have to take him. I'll have to pay you back tomorrow."

"Never. *Niemals.* My little present for Mike."

"This is too much. The puppy and now this."

"My pleasure!"

Why does he make her feel as though he were taking something everytime he gives? He is waiting for her to confide in him—say something intimate—she leans over the long stemmed rose, breathing hothouse perfume laced with the odor of decay and smiles good-bye.

She finds Mike stretched out on the carpet too close to the TV screen. He doesn't want her to know that he still watches Charlie Brown, and quickly changes to a wildlife program on the public television for her, which she abhors. Always the same beautiful shots of lions or tigers or other predators, and then fleeing gazelles or other non-predators with their young. You already know you are going to see a squealing young animal torn away from Mother, ripped apart and eaten. She turns her back to the screen. "Do you know what really happened when that girl Emerald vanished from Grove?"

"Her dad, an asshole in the foreign service, sent a lawyer. There was one of those Grove emergency meetings. A congressional investigation. Goodley had an ulcer attack and Grimes arrived with his monster secretary. We thought we might get rid of Grimes again, if we got Emerald back. Caleb knew she was go-go dancing twice a week at the Golden Oar. She bought herself a false ID and Caleb has one too."

"How about you? Do you have a false ID?"

"I can't afford it, Mom. Besides, one of us had to stay. We filled Caleb's bed up with clothes and a soccer ball."

"Caleb found her?"

"Yeah. Frying her brains out, go-go dancing in red bikini pants and string bra. Got her back to her dorm. The next day she tells the Screw Crew aliens zapped her and she doesn't remember anything. Then she stops eating, because earth food makes her sick after that great experience. You don't have to get into outer space to get sick of Grove food. Em is a dancer. She's been on TV even as a baby. Does commercials, but all her money goes into a trust. You should see the way she dances and she sings songs she makes up. Grimes says to her she can't do any dance, music or drama, unless she eats. So they put Em between him and Mrs. Berry, that overstuffed mummy, his secretary. Goes wherever Grimes goes and drinks buckets of coffee with him. Between them they practically force feed Em. She gives in to them because she wants to dance and get back into communication with Aliens. These wired goons spot her in town, and stalk her. Man, were they ever from outer space!"

"Are you planning to get a fake ID?"

"I don't have enough cash, and—"

"—About seventy dollars is missing from my purse," Liz says. Mike gives her a slanting glance. "I often lose money too. I lack role models in my home life. It makes me irresponsible in some ways."

Ask Mike about missing money and he goes on and on about his own lifestyle. How awful it is to be poor when you are young and can really enjoy money. Other kids have uncles, aunts, grandparents who come to visit them at Grove Academy and take them out to dinner, give them extra money.

When the African wildlife program changes to tribal customs he stops his lectures and gives all his attention to fascinating topless women. They smile into the camera, showing magnificent white teeth. There are three stages in the lives of males: getting old enough to fight, fighting, getting too old to fight.

"Women should take their spears away," Liz says. "They are the ones that give birth and raise the boys." Liz is furious—mostly with herself for not simply asking whether he has been in her room using her computer, and not simply demanding that he return her missing money. "They should stop them! Shouldn't allow them to kill each other! Beatrice Strout is right. Women should take guns away from men."

"Men have always been fighting. I should have been toughened up too. But you hauled me out of public school."

Now the topless girls from the other tribe have painted themselves red and start dancing around inside a circle of seated male warriors. They choose a man by putting a foot on his shoulder. One man can be chosen by several women; then he has to perform for them all in one night. The women go back to their own tribe and have babies.

"All right," Mike shouts and rolls over laughing. It prevents in-breeding, just as the kill prevents over-breeding. He likes the idea of a woman from another tribe choosing a man. Boring the other way around. He is watching his mother, trying to start an argument. Liz closes her eyes. Did the young women have any choice during National Socialist tribal mating rituals? Did the German SS studs perform with more than one Lebensborn volunteer girl in one night? Girls gave birth and left infants behind. Why does Vogel's young adjutant stand out? Could he actually have been a stud, at Lebensborn? And if "Stolen Child" is made up, not her own story, is it less valid? And where does it all come from? Why am I so scared? Where could the manuscript and disk have gone? Why would Mike take them, when he was hoping the book would make him rich?

That take-a-bite-out-of-crime dog comes on the screen. Saki and Ringo start chasing each other. Mike picks up a slouch cap and pulls it down over his face, adjusts his earphones. "I want you to give me back the money you took out of my purse!" Too late. Mike has put on his earpiece and turned the Walkman on. "You haven't used my computer?" He drums on the floor to a song only he can hear.

After the station wagon has been loaded, Mike is shaking hands with Dad, and Liz has made up her mind. The moment they pull out, she'll insist that Mike give back her money. He gets into the car, she has already started the engine, when the Dr. P Pet van pulls up, screeches to a halt, and Caleb jumps out. Nat, costumed in riding boots and breeches, follows right behind him.

"I've got to have it back!"

"No," she says."It's our puppy, we love him."

"Nat, doesn't want that pooch," Caleb says.

Chris appears on the stoop impressively attired in the blazer he wore to Mike's hectic hamburger farewell dinner. Nat turns to him. "I need to have the flea powder, sir. A mix-up. Dangerous mix-up. I'm very absent minded these days."

Liz runs into the house to get it, but the flea powder isn't on the shelf where she keeps Saki's brush. Not in any laundry room drawers. When she comes out the back door again Chris is talking to Nat about hypertension and neurology, his inability to concentrate on his income tax.

"The puppy did have fleas, but the powder didn't work. Must have been old. It was half empty," she says.

Nat slaps his own face so hard tears come into his eyes. "You used it?"

"I showed it to Dr. Belmont, the vet. Maybe I left it there."

"Holy Moses," Nat flies back to the van. "I better get there fast."

"They are closed. You'll have to wait," Liz calls after him.

Rain is turning to sleet. Caleb chases after the van, a tattered burlap band—his magic good luck hat—covering his left eye. "Hey, Nat, throw

me my duffel bag!" He catches the bag before it hits a puddle and carries it
to the Subaru. "My Mama is in no shape to take me to the bus. Nat got
mixed up and came to my house first. She thought he was an FBI man or
something. I'll ride to the Grove bus with you."

"Is there some kind of poison in that flea powder? Could it have hurt
Saki?" Liz asks.

"No, no," Caleb laughs and rolls the window down.

"What kind of flea powder is it?" Liz asks.

"Who cares. It's lost. Gone!" Mike says.

Gone are chapters of her book, the diskette. Lost. Money missing from her
purse. The radio is playing "Don't give me no hand-me-down shoes...Don't
give me...no hand-me-down world." Mike turns it up, but you can't make
out all the words against the drumming, blasts of amplified instruments
and the rush of air in the car. Boys shout-sing of wanting or not wanting
this or that and Mike sings along with them in his deep voice, drumming
on the dashboard. Then Liz forgets everything and sings with him.

"All right," says Caleb. "You two are good. Forget about Grove. Let's go
for the Big Apple. My cousin plays with The Purple. He'd put us up. How
about it, Liz?"

And for about fifteen miles they are a troop escaping to New York,
rock bands, great food, wild people. "Hey," Caleb says, "You're taking the
airport road, Liz! Why not Big Apple?"

"Can't leave Saki," she says.

"Dogs, statues, women, cars, always something to keep everyone back.
My dad hangs onto that Marilyn doll. I can't take it away. He keeps it
locked in his office. Mama is jealous of a vinyl statue."

"You'll have to give it back," Mike says.

"Dad will get sick of it by the time school is out. The way he gets sick
of secretaries and cars, and lady lawyers. He gets sick of everything, I told
Mama."

"She should turn herself into a multiple personality," Mike says.
"Like me," says Caleb.

Or me, Liz is thinking. A mother who should ask boys to return what
they have stolen, but plays along with them. A writer who is into everything and out of it at the same time.

❀ ❀ ❀

"Chris Plant!"

Priscilla Fairfield draws him behind the imported wine shelf. "I usually have them deliver, but I needed to get out of the house after Caleb left. I felt so awful. I really wasn't up to taking him to the bus. He wanted to ride with Liz and Mike. She doesn't drink." Tears tremble on her remarkably long lashes. "I let him down."

Her long white fur coat, more suitable for a sleigh ride in Siberia than the three-mile drive from dry Shoreland to the Liquor Chest must be Eckert's influence. She goes on and on about Grove Academy. How she had to back Havelock Grimes because he is the only one who can control kids. Sending children away to school is abandoning them in a way. "Caleb, my baby, is leaving." Tears and eye makeup run down her cheeks. "Now we are alone. No kids in the house."

"Thank Heaven," says Chris.

A tipsy little smile of complicity plays over her mouth. "You are a beauty." Gramp used to say this to his horses as well as to middle-aged women who needed cheering up. Nowadays, in this part of the world, you don't talk like that until you are in bed. And the moment kids leave, parents get horny. Chris has discussed this with Dr. Haupter.

He carries Priscilla's bottles to her old Jaguar. She might not have the right husband, but he did pick the right car for this tall and vintage beauty queen. Chris opens the door for her, puts his arm around her and says, "Kids away, time to play." She cuddles up against him, making herself small like a kitten, and laughs and laughs, showing her beautifully capped teeth. A wildly sexual beauty going to waste, but too much of a problem. One little kiss and the stale taste of alcohol is enough to change Chris into an English butler, carrying her gin and easing her into her car. "Drive carefully."

Women shouldn't drink. Liz never did. It puts her to sleep. Health-conscious Ellen always eats a lot when she drinks wine, and considers safe sex with a healthy partner a beneficial exercise. Chris refers to her as 'Edith' when he talks about her to a psychiatrist. He has always been discreet. Dr. Braggert, a child psychiatrist, has made Chris aware of his continued dependence on doctors caused by the early childhood injury. Handing over the responsibility for his well-being to doctors—and especially to "Edith"—with his prepared and carefully timed monologues, or her rehearsed and carefully timed orgasms.

She takes charge, telling him what she is doing with her fingers, her mouth, even her feet, following Beatrice Strout's sex technology, preparing him with grotesque and irresistible expertise. He does not love athletic "Edith," he has told Dr. Braggert. She is a habit.

Chris goes to the last of all the good old phone booths that cut off your oxygen supply, but function as one of those old psychiatric orgone boxes for recharging yourself by shutting yourself in. Here the booth and walls are constantly redecorated with sexual graffiti and "call me" phone numbers. JIGGERS CALL DEL URGENT. Inside a lopsided heart MIKE FUCKS KARIN. Quite a shock. There might be nothing to it.

The summer Chris graduated from high school, the "Chris and Mary" painted in large letters on the water tower actually got Chris interested in Mary for a while. Graffiti curses, slogans, names of enemies, lovers, rivals can have a powerful effect. Mike might get ideas. Chris takes a pen out of his pocket and ruins it blackening the inside of the lopsided heart.

He inserts his dime and then can't even remember Ellen's number. An Alzheimer symptom brought on by paternal penis envy, fear of aging, terror of early impotence. He has to squint trying to read the dogeared directory in the half dark. His eyes are going. SAVE THE ENDANGERED SPECIES is written right across the B page. SAVE THE PREDATORS. And someone has used the bottom of the page as a sketchbook drawing ugly cats.

He deciphers the number and dials, fully expecting telephone graffiti. That nasty "bug off kid" tape on Ellen's private number answering machine. He dials Ellen's other number, and gets a bitchy female voice, "The number you have reached has been disconnected."

"Damn you to hell!" he yells and dials 0 and rages at an apologetic operator who has been programmed to be polite but does get Ellen's phone to ring.

"Good evening."

"Sorry, I must have the wrong number, the damned telephone company."

"Chris. How are you, darling?"

Why does she talk like a Boston debutante? Chris says he must see her now.

"Well, we really should talk. But I'm not sure…"

He persists. Liz is taking kids to the bus and won't be back for hours. It isn't snowing too hard. Perfectly safe. A ten-minute ride to the Whale's Jaw. No one they know would be caught dead there. Well, he is wrong. The bar is closed and for the first time ever the parking lot almost full. Snow has piled up on two big, black, hearse-style limos on the far right. But you can't allow the Boston Mafia to get in your way.

Ellen drives up while he is paying for the room. Always cash. The owners aren't around; the horse-faced woman behind the desk wears a big black cross and is busy answering a new switchboard-type phone.

Chris signs in as Mr. and Mrs. Micheals. Ellen is waiting in the snow. She looks great in the London Fog raincoat he gave her because she likes anything British. And he likes the way she usually wears it over some flimsy transparent little nothing when she comes to meet him here. The white gloves are new. She carries a picnic basket with a bottle of chablis, cheese, and crackers. Chris takes the basket from her and they walk arm in arm. He unlocks, holds the door, and takes her coat. "A dress!"

"New. English. Liberty print. You like it?"

"Nice." A Sunday school teacher's outfit buttoned up to the chin. He tries to undo the top button. She gets him to open the chablis instead.

Over a glass of wine she holds forth about creative women. How writing must be very good for Liz. "After all, she did have a great career as a model before she married you, had Mike, and moved to this village. Eckert showed me a couple of Catulle paintings. Definitely a Liz face. He collects art."

"Walt Disney art, one of the critics called it."

"You had a great time in New York City, didn't you?"

"Perfect. We should never have left. You wouldn't understand."

"You were living with a nurse and Liz was getting engaged all the time. Pretty obvious. She was type-cast as a child-woman. Strout has written about those preliberation years—The Russian artist was painting the American male fantasies of wicked virgins."

"Has Liz been talking to you?"

"No. You have been talking to me. Remember? The brother and sister days, when you even picked out the men she dated and got engaged to."

Usually Chris talks and Ellen listens before they get serious and undress, but nothing can stop her tonight. She goes from Liz to the enslavement of women. Beatrice Strout writing about the survival of female slaves as a class that was linked with their ability to be productive in a manner and form determined by others. Dependency as their way of life. Immaturity fostered.

He gulps wine. "Plant women were always well taken care of, and Liz doesn't have to earn her living like you." He takes hold of Ellen and kisses her ear because she likes that. "I want to do something for you too. I can afford it. You need someone to take care of you."

Ellen squirms a little and sighs deeply. "How perceptive of you, Chris. You are changing. My needs are changing."

Chris massages the back of her long neck to give her a change, stop her jargon, and to lie down, but she stays on the edge of the bed going on about recycled "Playboy" magazines her two boys find at the dump, turning them into lewd male chauvinists.

His hand explores her back. "Nice back. Lonely back. Heavens! You're wearing a bra! What's come over you?"

"I'm going through a fabulous new phase." She shrugs back her hair. "I hope you won't laugh at me. Something amazing has happened. Out of the blue, I just got the most wonderful letters from a British doctor. He heard me lecture, and he is really interested in me. Almost too good to be true! But no one I know would go to all that trouble for a practical joke. You don't know anything about that?"

"Don't be silly; I wouldn't waste my time." But time is being wasted while she talks about fate, destiny, and her need to believe in this wonderful man. Chris tries swinging the room key like a pendulum. She ignores this. He downs another glass of wine and devours cheese. "Are you making those silly letters an excuse to get rid of me, because you're after old Eckert?"

"Arthur? We all like him, but no." She gets up and goes to look out of the window. "It's really coming down hard now. And look at the cars. This place is busy tonight. We better get out of here, Chris. She sighs and reaches for her coat. "Snow is getting heavier. At least we had a chance to talk."

The fabulous new phase, of course. They hardly got together. She did all the talking—playing with him—pretending there is someone writing to her, to stir him up. He jumps to help her with her coat and gives her a powerful hug which produces a shudder.

"No. No. You mustn't."

He can already feel it working when he catches her at the door, lifts her hair and gives her nape a Saki nip. She responds with a squeak and runs out into the snow. When he catches up with her, they walk linked together like Siamese twins. Her face looks young and happy. She shakes snow off her hair and it stings his cheeks. "I can feel the key in your pocket."

He kisses her wrist three times, and she slips her arm under his tweed jacket, lifting the back of his shirt to scratch his back in just the right place. He kisses her pink nose, "I know you want to go home." Then he presses her against a tree and they carry on like kids who have no place to go.

Suddenly a bus drives up, all kinds of people pour out. A couple of wheel chairs. Mothers carrying infants. "Good heavens. What's going on here?"

Ellen points to the big, blinking sign. WATER BED has been covered over with JESUS SAVES. A procession of men and women carry covered dishes. "There's Bonnie. The one with the basket."

"You forgot yours in the room. And I don't want her to see us." As they race back to the room, Chris feels his heart race, possibly too much. No sooner does he shut the door and fasten the safety chain than the three big spotlights come on in the parking lot, and the WATER BED sign keeps blinking and winking JESUS SAVES.

Chris stretches out on the bed. "My heart is racing."

Ellen laughs too much. At the far end of the corridor someone is playing a guitar, to the clatter of dishes and chatter. The congregation preparing a feast to follow redemption, while Ellen undresses Chris quickly, methodically—no arousal technique—just getting him ready for bed like a child. He can't remember the last time anyone folded his clothes. Then she hesitates, holding his clothes in her arms, and rests her cheek on the pile the way Liz used to when she was folding Mike's baby clothes.

"Take that dress off," he says.

"I feel I shouldn't. I know it's crazy, I haven't even met this English doctor."

He lifts her onto the bed and pulls her down beside him, swooshing the water bed, and takes off her dress. Fiddling with the bra turns out to be fun.

"But I keep thinking about his letters..."

Chris switches off the lamp. Should he tell her he is thinking of Mike and Karin? In the blinking light from the shrouded water bed sign, he admires his growing lust with infantile amazement and senile pride. "Do you think my heart is racing too much?"

She puts her head on his chest, her long hair sweeping over his belly. "It's normal." But she stays there, listening, studying his wild heart, while Chris studies himself. He hasn't examined himself like this since his school days when he turned to the dictionary and memorized answers to his curiosity and anxiety. Erection 1: The act or process of erecting; construction. 2: the state marked by firm turgid form and erect position of a previously flaccid bodily part containing cavernous tissue when that tissue becomes dilated with blood.

It had sounded like a disease that could have been caused by early injuries from his first American pants, that zipper that got stuck when the boat blew up. He rests a sly hand on Ellen's breast, feels the nipple turn hard as a bullet. He may not be in good health, but neither was the composer Chopin, and women were wild about him.

"I think of the English doctor so much, he might as well be in this room. It's wrong to think of this man and have intercourse with you."

"Intercourse 1: connection or dealings between persons or groups. 2: exchange especially of thoughts and feelings: communion. 3: physical sexual contact between individuals that involves the genitalia of at least one person—Webster—Dictionary, better than Beatrice Strout. Isn't it?"

"This is fantastic." She wants him to repeat it.

He does, while he peals off her bikini. "Final, brutal act of procreation which is redemption. I wonder where I got that."

"You made it up."

"I didn't make up *Webster's Collegiate Dictionary*." A fog horn clamors. And Chris does the honors without fuss. They sing out together, and for a minute their voices blend with the unrehearsed hymn of praise sung by the congregation down the hall.

Chapter 26

BREAKFAST WITH A SERIAL MURDERER

Police Notice:
A telephone worker descending from a pole on Summer
Street spotted a wallet in a tree yesterday. He got
it and notified police at 11:02 a.m. The worker
gave the wallet to the police who returned it to
the owner.

"Do you think you have a conscience now, Henry Lucas?" the male voice
on the kitchen radio sounds hushed with reverence. Liz can hear Lucas—
the serial killer of women—slurp during this breakfast interview in jail
while Liz, alone in the house by the sea, is drinking morning coffee topped
with whipped dried milk. Ringo is munching a carrot in his cage. Saki has
finished eating dried organic biscuit with chicken and is lapping water, and
the sea laps the shore with sucking sounds.

"A conscience? I think so, but I guarantee nothing," says Henry Lucas.

Then follows the aside comment of a psychologist: Lucas's mother was
a prostitute and she had sex in front of her son. He was beaten as a child.
Could have been beaten on the head.

Hundreds and thousands of mothers must be listening to the radio this
morning. Mothers who are spied on by their kids as they spied on their
mothers having sex before them. Hundreds and thousands that had been

spanked and now spank their kids can hear Lucas declare that he murdered his Mom, and it was all her own fault because she had spanked him and she had sex. Mom's fault that he kept murdering both in fact or in fantasy after she was dead.

The Shoreland foghorn keeps moaning while Lucas talks about pictures he paints in jail—anything that comes into his head. "I'm quite an artist," he brags. "No telling what I might do." Painting with words, as he creates images of blood and mutilation, a manual of mother hate: how and why you kill hateful Mother over and over again.

"I hate you!" Mike had said from the steps of the school bus, after Liz had finally asked him about the money missing from her wallet. The bus had just begun to move. Mike simply turned his back on her and went to his seat. Mitch, her school friend had heard it all, threw her arms around Liz, bursting into tears. "The kids have been passing joints around. They're stoned. He doesn't mean it."

An unsolved prank. Not funny, Chris said, leaving a mother without drivers license and money. Kids getting away with murder. Chris warned her, and that's why Mike is turning against her now. Chris had turned away too. She noticed telltale tire tracks in the snow. Chris reeking of perfume with the aura of a hearty embrace, a certain sheen of satisfaction and well-being he could not hide.

When she decided to sleep in the computer room, he came in, woke her up, and told her once again that it was unhealthy to sleep with all that electronic equipment. "Not as unhealthy as sleeping with you," she finally said. In some African tribes men perform with several women in one night, and the SS had performed as studs for volunteer girls at Lebensborn. Serial sex and liberated sex is simply unsanitary and repulsive. Chris had changed the subject to her chum Arthur Eckert with his harem of blond ex-wives, a live-in movie actress and her child. A stranger, playing up to married women with flowers and presents, telling them his dreams on the telephone. She reminded him that he believed in open marriage. "Especially when your wife is your sister!"

While Chris had gone to the phone and left an emergency message in Dr. Braggert's answering machine, Liz had locked herself into her old room for the first time ever.

Dr. Braggert responded to the emergency around midnight to give Chris an eight o'clock appointment. It was somehow all her fault that he had to drive into Boston at this unearthly hour, in all the morning traffic, through fog, on icy roads. On his car radio Chris, who had refused breakfast, might hear Lucas, the abused and abusive son, say his mother never fed him. Lukas says he hates prison food but loves sweet milkshakes. Liz can imagine policemen supplying frothy shakes, allowing Lucas to mother himself, just to keep him talking about all his murders. Claiming murders they know he could not have committed, allowing a multitude of mutilations to inspire those who want to put him to death, while inspiring potential mother killers waiting to become famous just like him.

In prison Lucas subsidized by taxpayers to paint in oil instead of blood, will in time inspire, or even write, bestseller horror memoirs and be paid for a TV series or movie. Getting away with mass murder and getting rich. Liz uses one of those You Liz Plant Have Won Ten Million fraudulent trash mail letters as a notepad and writes, "The infamous become famous every minute of the day. Lucas wants all the mothers in the world to know what he has done. He awaits punishment as a lonely lover waits for love that never comes. Killers, like lovers, reinvent themselves.

"Does that make sense?" She is thinking of mothers she invented when she was in boarding school. And you could add it all up into serial mother love.

She turns the radio off and runs up the steep stairs to her room. She did turn the computer off last night. The moment she reaches under the bed for her dusty old Valentine chocolate box her heart begins to pound. The chocolate had been sent to her by a Brown University student many years ago, but its contents, the photographs in there, are sweeter than the sweets or he had ever been.

She dusts over the hearts and roses on the lid and opens it. There they are, all those smiling mothers. Unwanted pictures of hated mothers she took away from roommates at boarding school and college. Vicky and Norma had actually been sent away to school because they could not get along with their mothers. They never even noticed when photographs vanished. They didn't care for mother pictures, but Liz did. Some of the tone has faded. Norma's mother, the favorite, a tall and sturdy woman dressed in a suit like Chris's English mother and Granny, has a round, pretty face.

They were already in the third grade, when British Granny during her one visit informed Graham that it was time to separate the boy from the adopted girl and furnish this sunny room for Liz with lacy white curtains, dainty as a bridal veil. Properly British. A girl's room, not a woman's. The kind of room one of those chocolate-box mothers would have furnished for their daughters and kept up for them to come home to anytime. Liz feels like a girl who has come home when she looks at her secret Mother pictures.

Chris has always been mothered and consoled by women who enjoyed him one way or another, but anyone trying to separate Chris and Liz had only brought them closer together. There had been no need to turn on him. She could have told him that she did not feel well last night. And that was no lie. Arthur Eckert had stirred up her painful need for approval with his admiration and scrutiny.

The moment the mail slot snaps, Saki runs down stairs and she runs after him as he tries to make off with one of those cards advertising a trinket on one side and on the other, smiling little blond Peter Welch, the missing boy, who had made radio news the day Mike came home. Today there are more self-improvement pamphlets. SUMMER RETREAT 1986. The picture shows young men and women dressed in karate pants, legs apart, arms poised in attack position. More and more self-improvement pamphlets have been arriving lately. Chris doesn't usually throw trash mail out, but her own kitchen bulletin board, behind the fragrant rose geranium, has been stripped, leaving plenty of room to tack up the new self-improvement opportunities.

INSTANT MEMORY
YOU ARE GREATER THAN YOU THINK!
A QUANTUM LEAP IN UNLEASHING HIDDEN ABILITIES,
TALENTS, AND SKILLS

GUARANTEED TO IMPROVE YOUR PERFORMANCE IN EVERY-
THING YOU DO! USED BY OVER 200,000 FOR INSIGHT,
CREATIVITY, KNOWLEDGE,
AND PROFIT. SUCCESS.

Super success comes when you transform the way you look at yourself! The discovery of a more powerful self guarantees a richer, more rewarding lifestyle.

INSTITUTE OF ADVANCED THINKING

And a full money-back guarantee. Like most of the self-improvement pamphlets from California it makes you feel backward and left out. Liz, in genuine need of MINDSTORMING, INSTANT SPEED READING, INSTANT MEMORY, pins this pamphlet up at once on her bulletin board, mindstorming about "I hate you, Mom," Chris on icy roads, the lost manuscript, the missing diskette —anything at all that makes her feel awful. SUPER-SUCCESS COMES WHEN YOU TRANSFORM THE WAY YOU LOOK AT YOURSELF! But breakfast with a serial murderer has transformed her into a scared woman. Saki lies at the door but refuses to go out, just waits there and listens. Finally, when Liz warms up the coffee, the bell shrills and a spoon drops from her hand, clattering into the sink. The window she tries to open is frozen; so is the back door. The bell keeps ringing urgently. She has to push hard to get it open. Salty air and snow rush in.

A snow-covered van faces the back of the house, and Nat, the Dr. P. manager in a black riding habit, stands waiting in the freezing drizzle. "Mrs. Plant. It's me again. I came yesterday, or was it the day before? Don't know where I am these days."

When she lets him in the back door, he ignores Saki, who nips at his heels. He chews his fingernails. "The vet's secretary remembers you put the flea powder into your bag, because she liked the big leather pouch."

Liz runs upstairs to check her bag, but can't find the flea powder.

"Oh, my God!" He stares into space, hollow eyed and unhappy. "How about your kid's room?"

"It isn't just flea powder, is it?"

He seems to age before her eyes. "Could we look?"

"It's a mess. I haven't cleaned."

"Good, good! If you'll get me a broom and dusters. I'll clean up for you."

Mike's room is littered with pennies, tape boxes, comic books, candy wrappers. A small white skull. Saki picks up a tissue, shakes it, and tears it up. "Vacuum cleaner would break down. Just give me that broom. I can't stand dirt or any kind of litter for that matter. I clean up and lose things. That's my problem."

"Mine too," Liz says.

Mike had decorated the wall facing his bed with the dark old portrait of William Plant, whom he resembles, and the poster of Robert Plant as a boy, lighting a cigarette, his alter ego. The old Indian blanket crumpled on his bed is full of cigarette holes. Terror of fire has passed on to her from Chris, and she has been asking Mike far too often not to smoke in bed. Now smoking is forbidden at Grove Academy.

Nat starts right in, emptying paper cups full of butts and ashes, sweeping frenetically. He creates piles, searching every corner, shaking out old sneakers, lining them up, while Liz collects empty wine, beer, and soda bottles. No cleaning help Liz ever hired has worked hard as this. On the floor, among T shirts, comic books, dirty tissues, and old socks, Liz finds one of the pamphlets from her bulletin board:

THOUGHTS HAVE WINGS
You Can Influence Others Without Thinking

Try it some time. Concentrate intently upon another person seated in a room with you, without his noticing it. Simple mental energy which can be projected from your mind to the consciousness of another. Do you realize how much of your success and happiness in life depend upon your influencing others? That thoughts can be transmitted, received and understood by others is now scientifically demonstrable.
THIS FREE BOOK POINTS THE WAY, "THE MASTERY OF LIFE ," explains how you may receive this unique wisdom and benefit by its application. Write: Cribe N.G.S. THE ROSICRUCIANS San Jose (AMORC) CA. 95191

The pamphlet smells of Polo Cologne. Liz leaves it on Mike's desk and stacks OMNI magazines, trying to keep up with Nat, who is sitting on the floor folding and sorting pants, socks, dirty sheets, clean towels. Why? She hardly knows this Nat, nor does she care about his flea powder or whatever. He, Mike, Chris, Saki, Ringo, impose their will on her like Rosicrucians. There was no need for her to give up her writing time and punish herself with cleaning Mike's room just now. There are societies for child abuse and elder abuse, but Mother self-abuse should be the biggest society in the world.

Saki, wagging his tail, retrieves another pamphlet.

WITCHCRAFT AS A SCIENCE
In Witchcraft One, Amanda Garlic Official Witch of Salem,

Massachusetts, guides a select number of students on a passage through the first psychic doorway to performing effective magic. Designed as an introduction to all witchcraft classes.

Could witchcraft classes be co-educational? She dismisses the far fetched notion that Mike took her money to help pay for a summer course in witchcraft. Nathan is shaking a pillow slip. Feathers and dust fly around the room. He keeps sneezing, knocking down a pile of quarters he just stacked. His black riding habit is turning gray, his gaunt face red. He dips under the bed, comes out with the box from Mike's new boots, a plastic Buddha, and a computer diskette. "That shouldn't be on the dirty floor!"

She snatches the diskette. COMPOSE ONE, her handwriting on the label. The master diskette for the lost chapters! It just can't be. It couldn't possibly have happened. What would Mike want with it? He just wouldn't do this! She leaves Nathan searching Mike's closet. Runs to her computer.

"*Lieber Gott!* Dear God." She feels sick as she sinks down into the chair. Her hand trembles. The drive won't accept the diskette. She has to try three times. The mumble-grumble responses are slow, ominous. A diskette flashes onto the screen. A warning. She must have done something wrong. Or was it Mike? She takes the disk out. Starts up again, listens to another grumble, grinding computer self-test. Holds her breath. The menu appears.

"Mrs. Plant. Mrs. Plant!" Nathan is looking for her.

"In a minute!" she shouts and presses **I** for index. PARENT AND WORLD PROBLEMS. Only one document! Fear grips the back of her neck, her throat. She chokes. She can't breathe or move, her heart pounding. She hears herself sob and bites her own fist like a Nazification school kid to keep herself from howling. Raging, she chastises herself for not having made a back-up copy. She stays bent over, as though she had taken a terrible beating.

"He didn't do it on purpose. *Nicht absichtlich.*" Saki keeps licking her hand until she gets up and dries her wet face on the tie-dyed shirt Mike has outgrown. She faces up and opens the document PARENT AND WORLD PROBLEMS.

Letter to the official witch of Salem. Both printed and deleted. She scrolls until a letter to the Sea-Shore Retreat and Healing Center growls onto the screen.

My son Christopher Plant is always depressed

now. He drinks and he smokes and he thinks he is
sick all the time and takes pills. He is the
biggest problem. Please put him on your mailing
list. Especially for the Firewalk. Mind over matter. I believe everyone has a unique potential and
I feel you can help my son achieve his.
   Cordially yours,
   Michael Plant, The Third

Mike impersonating a worried old father has deleted her manuscript.
Words blur as she rereads the letter. "Where are you?" Nat calls outside her
door in a desperate, high-pitched voice. "I can't find you!"

He is carrying the broom under his arm when she opens the door. "It's
lost. Lost..."

His cry echoes in her soul. "I used to lose things all the time," Liz
remembers. "Never used to worry about it. One really shouldn't." Nat
hangs his head like a wounded bird, dusty, shattered, unconvinced. "That
lost flea powder can't be that important!"

"Better you don't know anything, Mrs. Plant. Please find it
for me!"

What she has lost cannot be found. They walk downstairs and out
through the mudroom in silence. He shakes hands with her at the door.
Gulls are shrieking behind a skiff putt-putt-putting toward the harbor. "At
least the fog has lifted." He shouts to make himself heard. "And we did
clean up Mike's room!"

The mudroom is a shambles too. Mike's first and most favorite stuffed
toy, a rag-doll dog, droops over the edge of a basket full of old gloves.
Threadbare, a fantasy creature Mike loved, abused and wore out. Just like
me! She walks up the stairs painfully. Sits down on the rug in her work-
room with her notebook, to look at the very first version of her lost
chapters, but her head begins to nod. She stretches out on the chaise, trying to think of what she will say to her editor, and is dead to the world
until the phone rings.

"Will you accept a call from Michael Plant, the Third?" asks
the operator.

Mike usually calls once a week to complain about injustice—other kids
in trouble—when he knows the school is about to call Shoreland to complain about him. Liz is only half awake when he reports on the new
male-female segregation at Grove Academy. Everyone is getting edgy.

Friends are fighting. Klein not allowed even to walk with Marge and they're in love.

No response. In the muffled tone of a ransom caller Mike demands chocolate bars, socks, cookies, summer sausage, potato chips, and thirty dollars.

Silence.

"Are you there, Mom? What's up?"

"How could you do this to me!"

The sob in her voice shocks Mike into a moment of silence. His mother never cries. "What are you talking about?"

"My diskette. You wiped me out!"

"I did not! You left that old diskette in the drive and I followed the instructions."

"You never follow instructions!"

"I did so. Remember the course in letter writing I had to take at Marshfield? You and Dad were all for that."

"We were not for the bomb-threat letter."

"History. And you're not wiped out. No big deal. Use your back-up. You don't have any? Shit! Than you're not following instructions. Now you're blaming me. Everybody backs up. Even here at Grove." A pause. "Sorry, Mom. I hate it here. I'll come home and help you retype." A silence. "Shit. You lost the manuscript as well! You can't blame me for that." He lowers his voice, whispering about stinking climate, sleet, ice—a code—letting her know someone is listening. "Talking to my Mom! OK! Hands off, Emerald, and bug off. Still there, Mom? Emeralds hanging around me. Leadership narc just stopped by. I bet Grimes made them take a vow of celibacy. They've all dropped their girls and now they're watching to catch us and report us for our own good. You have to be so careful." A stony silence. "I'm not a bad person, Mom. I was practicing my letter writing, to develop my unique potential." A girl interrupts to make an urgent call. "That's Lila, Caleb's girl, Mom. Leadership kid narced on them. Really harsh." A pause. "I could help, you know. But you don't want me around. I'll only get in the way. Don't forget the care package, Mom! I'm waiting."

His need to be consoled when he has caused her pain is not new.

Chapter 27

SUN ON ICE

A pale morning moon has been left behind in the primrose sky, and gulls hovering to attack the dark mountain of trash bags look black as bats. "After all you've been through, Liz. So kind to come along." Bonnie's nose is pink. There are tears in her eyes when they get out of her van at the Dump Boutique on this frosty morning. She is wearing a belted raincoat like Ellen's with the collar turned up. "I'm glad you didn't tell Chris. It would just make him sick and Mike didn't mean any harm. You all right, Liz? You look tired. Just couldn't go it alone. All week I've been drivin' around like a nut, with around thirty-three pairs of shoes. They meant everything to Jeff. Imagine, now he tells me, to just throw them away. One pair is all he took in his overnight bag: dancing pumps with tassels. This should have told me something."

Walt makes Liz stay in the repair shop by the electric heater with a cup of coffee while he and Bonnie come and go carrying the boxes of Jeff's shoes into Walt's swop shop. Liz has come along gladly to get out of the revolving door of her own distress. Gulls perch on the mountains of trash bags lifeless as decoys. Does everyone regret what they have thrown away by mistake? Most of life is forgotten waste. If you write your forbidden story you are a decoy on mountains of waste.

Years seem to have gone by since she came here to look for her lost manuscript and found Arthur sitting on her box of old magazines, letters, and manuscript pages. She might have salvaged the early version of her chapters, had he not provoked her with advice and prying question. But did his questions not give her new ideas? She keeps going from certainty to uncertainty in her writing, while the weather changes from spring to arctic winter. Rewriting is like taking dictation from a new tyrannical self. Hours go by like minutes. Shoulders and neck ache. She keeps the radiator low in her room. On a cold morning like this when feet are cold, and toes numb, she remembers the bitter winter of German defeat when Frau Faser lined their boots with bits of old German newspapers that had once announced Hitler's victories.

Liz had held onto those old boots. Anka had decided to throw anything she had outgrown out, but she liked the sweet little worn boots. Bruno had picked one up and discovered the lining, cornered Liz behind the weather house holding up the yellowed fragments of victory news, calling her a liar in German, English, and Polish. He had whipped her bare legs with a switch, ordering her to remember that her mother had been looking for her in Austria and the American simply snatched her away. He was dressed like any Shoreland working man in a flannel shirt and green pants, but when he came close to her, she recognized him as the man in the slouch cap, by an acrid smell. Before long he had vanished. Gramp often said that Bruno was trouble, Anka was better off without him. Did Anka miss Bruno and his trouble the way Bonnie misses Jeff? Liz can't imagine life without the legacy of Chris.

When the Major and Bonnie stop to have a cup of coffee, she says that she is glad the UPS-man doesn't stop at her house anymore. "Used to make me sick. Jeff placed the orders for shoes from the hardware store. And they cost a mint. Had to be made in America. The finest. Like the ones they'd made in the shoe factory where his dad had worked as a foreman. Imports did the factories in. Unions too. When the factory died, his dad lost his job and he died too. "Once in a blue moon I'd refuse a package and send it right back. He never found out. And wouldn't you know, the pastor, Story Gusswell, and about six of us, we were all in the shoe closet praying for deliverance when Jeff walks in unexpected. Fit to be tied. That did it. Imagine him walking out on all his shoes."

"But Jeff was already mad about your telephone service," Liz speaks up.

"Whatever." A response Bonnie must have picked up from Mike and Elgar. "Never even came back for his shoes. This lawyer O'Hara called and asked me to come to his office."

Walt grins. "I know him. He brings his own trash."

"Bald as an egg with a wart on his nose. He has an office that's real dark except for a heat light for Boggles, a big iguana he keeps under glass. There was Jeff, wearing sneakers and asking me for a divorce. Lizard nodding and nodding when Jeff got to the ownership of Moonbin Hardware, which I bought with money Aunt Codgie left me. But not one word about the shoes. He's got an apartment overlooking our neck of the woods. Keeping an eye—not on me, but on Ellen. Could be he moved out so he could get into her dancing and meditating group. All divorced and lonely. You've seen him jogging down back bay trying to catch up with her and Red. Jeff's lost a lot of weight and looked so handsome at the lawyer's office. Able to get back into the pin-striped suit he bought for his father's funeral. He now wears sneakers. I told him he could pick up the shoes anytime. So he shows up on Sunday afternoon and eats half an apple pie."

The Major grins. "Don't blame him!"

"Just imagine. Jeff used to polish those shoes every day, during the evening news and weather reports. Always kept them on shoe-trees. Now he shows up and tells me to throw them in the Salvation Army bin. My prayer group has been praying for his deliverance. He's delivered all right, Walter. He thanked me for the pie and said he'd call me sometime before the divorce. No hard feelings. And not only that, the Lord delivered me. I used to hate all those shoes. And after he left them, I'd take them out of boxes, to look at them. They are beautifully made." She takes a deep, deep breath and sighs, opening a shoe box, picks up a glossy brown pump, and sniffs. "I even love the smell of new leather. Imagine his precious shoes in a Salvation Army bin. No way. Bringing them here to Walt is the right thing. Walt, you see they'll all get a good home." She bestows on the shoe a kiss goodbye for Jeff. Tears raining down. Then she giggles. "Isn't that silly! What's over is over, but I just couldn't go it alone, Liz. I'm so sorry I bothered you. Honest."

Liz sits in a rocker among broken-down food choppers, an old manual Royal typewriter, old radios. Warranties expired. Hers must have run out last night, leaving her drained and broken. Scared of being sorted out as an unworthy writer, as Liese might have been of being sorted out as *wertlos*—

unworthy to live. Gulls squabble, clacking like hens. In the distance you
can hear the notorious rooster Homer, a solo among morning sounds of
irrepressible renewal. A radio Walt repaired plays a Noel Coward-type song
Sing for your supper.
And you'll be asked for breakfast-
If the song is sweet.
Song birds always eat.

Liz is humming the tune when she goes to the bedroom to get warm slippers, and finds Chris sitting up in bed wearing a Dior pajama top, volume
four of his complete Casanova has dropped onto the floor. He is studying
one of those hospital newsletters, MALE HEALTH. "All this writing, worrying about the darned book. You have not been looking after yourself.
You're not getting enough sleep or fun." Liz doesn't want Chris to know
that Mike overwrote her diskette, so she talks about Bonnie and Jeff.

"Dump in this freezing weather. That's no fun. Shoes. Typical New
England frustration. Lack of healthy passion. He draws Liz into bed and
makes her laugh as he undresses and seduces her with the deft determination of the boy hobbyist he had always been, and the experience he had
gained first from Geraldine, his live-in night nurse, now from Ellen. There
is both the slight insult of being manipulated and mechanically coaxed,
and then the self-forgetful oblivion of being overwhelmed by joy. They go
to sleep in an embrace.

The alarm clock goes off at 10:30, because Chris has to fulfill the
dietary requirements and vitamins which are essential before and after great
passion. He rattles off information about the prevention of impotency,
while they feast on ham and eggs. Over his second cup of coffee, toast, and
English ginger marmalade, Chris explains to Liz how Casanova never lost
his head over a woman and knew what he was doing in bed.

When Liz points out that Casanova bragged and no doubt made up his
adventures, Chris says, then her story is a lie too. "You don't know anything about my story," she shouts. "I don't brag."

Saki, the non-barker, usually bellows ten or twenty minutes before anyone rings the bell. No surprise when Jonathan and Billy arrive at the back
door carrying hockey sticks and skates, wearing thick sweaters and matching gnome hats Bonnie knitted for them. "Want to come skate, Liz? Take a
break?" Sounds like Ellen's idea. Women who indulge Chris often feel

obliged to give Liz the consideration they don't get from him.

"Mill Pond? Why not," Chris says and opens the *Wall Street Journal.* "You really want to go. I can tell by your face. Come in, boys. I'll make you some toast while she gets ready."

❀❀❀

The sun is out and Mill Pond has turned into a glass platter loaded with kids in candy-colored clothes. The Norwegian great-grandmother who lives in the old Mill enjoys being pushed around on the ice in a chair wearing the ethnic red coat trimmed with braid. When dogs chase each other and slide in front of her chair, she calls Barney, Hudson, and Red by name, but at times can't always remember her own. The barking, shrieking, and laughter resound and the waterfall gushes from under the ice down into the churning basin feeding the creek which rushes past the giant weeping willows, past the deserted swings, down under the road, gurgling out over frosted pebbles on the beach into whipped seafoam.

Ellen used to sit by the creek in that little playground with books, studying sexology while Billy and Jonathan climbed trees. They still climb like apes, even with their skates on, to swing on branches, dropping down in front of girls to make them shriek and scatter. Ellen's fearless boys somehow make Liz aware of her own fear of failure. The pain of losing her chapters never quite goes away. She is skating by herself in the far end of the pond, when Arthur appears on the foot-bridge and stops to take a picture. A black duffel coat with the hood up, rather like a monk's, makes him unfamiliar. He sees Liz, waves, and watches her skate towards him avoiding hockey boys charging their puck and senior girls, who are showing off skating on one leg.

Great-grandmother is swinging her cane. "Stop, stop that at once!" she shouts in a manly voice, which does not stop her great-grandsons from racing after girls from their class who are so much taller.

Near the bench where Arthur is waiting, little ones on double runners hold onto mother's hand. He holds out his hand to jump Liz over the water at the edge. "This is unsafe."

"There is always water at the edge when it's sunny."

"Yes, indeed. Sun on ice." A continental hand-kiss. "How cold you are. No gloves." Sneakers and boots are lined up behind the bench. He helps her take off the skates and slip into boots. "You're shivering. It's warm in the sun, but jeans and a sweater aren't enough." He takes off his gloves, rubs her hands, and, with the fur lining still warm, slips them onto her cold, red hands.

Chris's *Male Health* Magazine explains how easily women who have been hurt succumb to deliberate kindness. Her words pour out like water under the ice. The manuscript lost. Mike trying to be helpful, overwriting the diskette. An orgiastic lamentation. "All by accident," she quickly says.

He puts his arm around her shoulder. "Nothing is ever an accident."

Chris would agree, since he considers hazardous Mike and the hazardous computer somehow both her fault. "I'm to blame."

"You didn't overwrite your own disk."

His arm around her shoulders tightens as though her involuntary tremor were amorous and not mere reflex after the erotic games with Chris. But it's Arthur who now listens like a lover and also shares silence with her, in the midst of shrieking laughter, barking, the cry of gulls. "What do you remember of those pages I threw away?" she finally asks.

"That day at the dump? To be honest, I became engrossed in reading the German letters to you and then the "must-do notes" you wrote to yourself. 'Tired, not feeling well' was scratched out. Then there were shopping lists—mostly for Mike. You must have been running around like an errand girl. I was impressed by the liquor you had to replace in a hurry because Mike and Elgar drank it and you didn't want Chris to find out. Your worry that they might use drugs on top of liquor. But Mike and company never worry about hurting you. As for Chris—I doubt that you even told him that Mike overwrote your diskette. No. No, I have no right to say anything." He gives her time to speak before he changes the subject to the wonderful dinner at her house. "Veal cutlets, no less. Pie made from cherries in your garden. When I drove away, you and Chris in evening dress at the top of the steps, under the light, arms around each other. Everything just right."

Chris had suggested that Liz invite Eckert, who had given her Saki. So she took time off to prepare a European meal. She wore Priscilla's mother's Dior dress. Chris a blazer. Arthur had upstaged them when he arrived in a dinner jacket. The rose had the thorns removed, he assured Liz. The Veuve Cliquot Posardin champagne he gave to Chris was already chilled and rare. Living up to his reputation with stories of adventures on the Riviera

Levanto, an Italian Countess; bathing in African waterfalls in very special company. Finally he had raised his glass to toast them and declare that he would rather be here than anywhere else in the world just now. That was before Chris started going on about *Male Health*.

"A perfect evening. The beautiful old house, a little bit of a moon—not a big obvious one. I got the picture, as they say. A perfect pair in a perfect home—not the usual compromise. I got the impression that you'd wave good-bye to anyone who got too close for comfort."

"Sometimes Chris and I are just too much."

"He probably thinks I am too much." Arthur laughs and gives her a hug. Definitely too much, but she doesn't even care who is watching.

He sighs and clears his voice. "Sun on ice. If you listen carefully there is rumbling under the ice like faraway guns. That graveyard up there reminds me of the time we had to hide in an Italian family crypt at the end of the war."

Gulls, perched on headstones of the old cemetery slope face the wind, others screech on the roof of the old mill, where smoke blossoms out of the chimney. "It was safe as long as ice and snow sealed us in. We were ter- rified that the sun might melt the ice. We froze and we starved and it was dark and it stank. *Schrecklich.* Terrible."

"Terrible," she repeats. "Just terrible." German boys freezing in a tomb. War children hiding in a cold stream. Waffen SS executing German refugees because they were inconvenient and unreliable. What if not the American scouts but Arthur and his troop had come across a ragged troop of inconvenient, unreliable children?

"We had no more ammunition, but we had guns," Arthur says. "I was no hero. I was scared, but I had been trained as an investigator and I spoke English. An actor is used to overcoming stage fright. I didn't know who was out there. Melted snow and ice running off the roof had formed a bar- ricade. I pushed and jumped out with my unloaded gun and roared. My best act, totally wasted. There were about thirty Italians passing bottles of wine around. They held onto the bottles but dropped their guns. It so hap- pened they were out of bullets too, but they had wine and prosciutto and bread. No heroes. The worst soldiers and the best company, an end to killing. They were supposed to be our prisoners, but those Italian boys held us captive, singing and laughing. We celebrated the victory of having sur- vived. During that last week of the war we hunted for civilian clothes, food and talked about girls."

"Have you kept in touch?" Liz asks.

"I'm still in touch with Juliano. He returned to Rome and became one of the best tailors. Having him make suits for me is an excuse for a reunion. Italians live in the present. I, of course, have even gone back to that crypt to film the snowdrops among graves. Before long spring flowers must be coming up there among the stark New England slabs. Unrelenting spring. You wrote that somewhere. There is something unrelenting about the way you write. You will not give up. That story was in your head for a long time. The artist Catulle knew about it. He'd adjust his repertoire when he talked about you in the gallery to make 'his brats' even more fascinating." Arthur stroked her hair absent-mindedly. "That's all long ago. It's writing your unique story that is important now. I know it will all come back." He draws her closer. "One of my ex-wives, a young opera singer, knows both music and words that aren't even her own, in several languages." He takes his glove off her left hand and holds her cool hand against his cheek. "That's better." Then puts the glove back on her hand. "What will Chris think of the disaster?"

"I don't want him to know."

"How about your editor?"

"He doesn't have to know. I'm rewriting as fast as I can. This has changed my style. My editor calls it understated. Maybe he's trying to tell me that my story is too understated. I have just read about German soldiers killing Jewish babies by bashing them against stone walls while their mothers looked on. Not monster Nazis we have seen in all those movies, not demons, just boys. In uniform."

"My assignments were more devious, but you won't ever let me forget that I was one of those German boys in uniform?"

"Do you want me to?"

He has no answer. "There is Elgar with Tick!" The boys are wearing Myrtle company caps and are carrying a long company ladder. "Just in case someone falls in."

"Jacob's ladder," Arthur says under his breath.

"What does that mean?"

"Bonnie's friend, and you don't know about the dream Jacob had of angels going up and down from heaven on a big ladder? According to St.Thomas Aquinas, there is a hierarchy of angels."

"Some angels more angelic than others?" Liz has an absurd vision of angel inspections, Hitler School-style. "Leadership angels trained Grove Academy-style?" She laughs. "As long as we can laugh." But he isn't laughing when he gets up and leans over her. "How would you recognize your mother? "

"You really want to know?"

"I'll keep this to myself."

"Her smell. "

"Perfume?"

"The scent of her skin." She hands him his gloves. He refuses to take them back as though he were compelled to provide her with comfort. He makes his exit with the hood up and hands in his pockets. Later, eating hot dogs at Jimmy's place with Jonathan and Billy, Arthur's car passing by reminds her of the gloves, the puppy, and roses he has given her, as though doomed to serve her. German reparation. Dismissing the Hitler time as an evil spell to obey orders, like a Fifinella in a crystal flask. And Mike under the evil spell of both dope and the Grove Concept, had followed a higher dictate of a brother's keeper, overwriting her diskette while serving a good cause.

"Shame is like a frozen crypt!" Liz says it out loud facing her computer. She sounds off like Svenson the drunk when she takes her own dictation this way. Typing at top speed, like a secretary. No doubt hitting the wrong keys, making mistakes as she recovers lost phrases and finds new words by picturing her story and getting into the picture. She closes her eyes, allowing herself the feeling of being held warm and safe. The fragrance of mother's skin, while being carried towards a creek swollen with cold spring water. Mother scolding and coaxing, then the quivering reflections of a child clinging to her child-mother among bathing women. Naked, all of them, screeching, laughing, splashing ice cold water. Soaping mountains of rosy flesh. Then floating on their backs, hair floating above their heads as the rippling current whirls them around, carrying them downstream. She clings to Mother, feels the belly quiver with her laughter as they drift together, holding to each other tight, too tight. Mother's loud scream, "Dead man—dirty corpses in my clean water!"

A mother who is still a child, screaming because war turns young lovers into foul corpses soiling her river, spoiling the spring of her life. The echo

of this outcry will either wash over the prosaic world or stir the soul of
readers. Arthur is right. She does remember cadences and words and
phrases as they flow into thought.

     She gets up in the dark to steal from the day the quiet hours. It all comes
back sentence by sentence, page by page and much more. Her impetus gathering force like the water under the frozen Mill Pond. Rapids of the mind
will spin her around from yesterdays, today, tomorrow, beset by the maniacal
hope of women who sense danger, getting high on dread. The pain a
German-American mother must have felt after sending a son to German
Hitler School has been documented mostly by her own dread of Mike being
sorted out, suspended or expelled and running away. If German-American
parents really sent boys to gain discipline in Nazification School, their sons
might well have been held hostage during the war, sorted out, sent to child
labor camps for their own good. Or died for the common good of the Reich.
Secret shame remains walled in like a crypt with ice.

Chapter 28
PRAYING MANTIS

"Would you believe it's warmer here than in Florida, Chris? My sister's freezing down there." Martha Willies, at the Shoreland Regional Bank, never changes. Her prim china doll face remains the same year after year. And as long as she is at her window, Chris feels his money is safe year after year.

"But you do have to watch out when Shoreland gets this warm from one day to the next: pneumonia weather. And they say TB is back again, big."

Chris becomes aware of all the coughing in the bank, while she counts his money a second time.

"President Reagan is just over a virus. Isn't he a hero? Bullet passed through his heart. Urinary problems. Polyp in the intestines—not once, but twice. And skin cancer. Back in the saddle again. The way he keeps going and keeps us going." She hands Chris his money. "Most precious thing in the world is your health."

Chris makes off with what remains of his health, stuffing twenty dollar bills into his wallet as he flees through the heavy door that was installed after the robbery. He feels threatened and susceptible to infections. Xanax doesn't work anymore and he'll have to install a good burglar alarm.

From the Audi in the bank parking lot Chris can look down to the grade school playground, where kids dressed in psychedelic slickers run wild, acting out shoot-outs they have seen on TV. When Ronald Reagan was elected president, there had been Marc Fowler, head of the FCC, all for consumer sovereignty. Liz had to coax Mike away from GI Joe, Thundercats. What happened to all the anti-war activist parents? Chris feels old as Ronald Reagan, observing all the war games down there. But the twin girls dressed in the same sand-colored tunics and matching tights keep to themselves as usual. He hasn't seen them for a while and they've grown tall. You can't tell them apart as they spin around and around a climber pole, faster and faster, side by side, long brown hair flying out. They mirror each other's movements the way he used to mirror Sis. He rolls down the window to hear them call out and shriek with laughter and he laughs with them. A couple of old lady artists pull in right next to him in a new sports car, stay a minute too long.

Nowadays a youngish man who is too interested in other people's kids can become suspect. You have to be careful. Chris pulls his checkbook out and props it up on the steering wheel to look busy. In Shoreland twins are allowed to be twins. The Hillford twin brothers are now around sixty years old, and you can't tell them or their watercolor landscape pictures apart. They live together, dress the same, and drive the same American cars. It had been wrong to separate him from Liz and to send them to different boarding schools. He should have been allowed to feel like her real twin. He told Dr. Bigfield how he suffers with her like a twin. All the rewriting she has to do is killing his natural lust and making him sick. The moment the bell rings, the children disperse into the granite buildings, but the twins stay behind. Ellen comes out of the administration building wearing the English raincoat Chris gave her. The tall man who holds the door for her is dressed the same way. Chris drops his checkbook. Bigfield!

The doctor stands by and smiles while she says something to the twins that sends them skipping hand in hand to their classroom. Bigfield and Ellen stay behind under the three magnificent old trees that arch over the empty playground. Ellen, the traitor, reaches up and holds onto a branch Chris and Liz used to swing on when they played Tarzan. Then she tilts her head toward the doctor, using her long, glossy hair to touch his cheek. What is going on? What is she now whispering? She must have seduced his doctor. The idea of them discussing Chris Plant on her trundle bed is disgusting and serious. There must a law against a doctor taking over a patient's lover.

Chris clutches the steering wheel in helpless rage. His horn peeps and he speeds out of the bank parking lot, almost hitting a white mongrel named Jezebel. The big toe on his right foot starts to throb. It has to be gout! With this new pain he forgets about Ellen and worries about the pain all the way home; his head and neck ache by the time he gets out of the car and his heart races. He hobbles into the house, where Saki is running around with a letter he pulled out from the mail slot. Could be from Ellen, but he will never be able to forgive her. Chris has to chase Saki. "Give me that letter! I'm in pain." The dog understands what he is saying and drops it, stands by and watches while Chris tears it open.

Dear Chris:
We hope you have benefitted from our Male Health *newsletter, but the purpose of the healing center is manifold. Astronauts discover outer space for us. They bring back pictures and films and scientific measurements which increase our knowledge and satisfy our intellectual curiosity.*

The great astronauts of inner space, Christ, Buddha, Lao Tzu, etc., brought back from their journeys beautiful maps, hints, and metaphors, but cannot do the journey for us. Their blissful statements are encouraging, and we can make it our own experience only in as much as we put these beautiful ideas into practice. HEALING IS TRANSFORMATION. It is creating harmony you want in all areas of life—your body, heart, and soul. It is opening up to the energies of the universe and the people around you. We have been asked to help you. Come join!

Chris likes the musky perfume on lilac paper and calls the healing center. He can hear a click. "This is Chris Plant." A sweet, low female voice chants, "Chris, this is Pauline. I was expecting your call. Your wonderful concerned father wrote to us, Chris. A very caring person. It is healthy to be caring. This is what the center is all about, Chris. I do hope you will join us."

"Father! My father died when I was four!"

"Unusual things happen, Chris. We have a beautifully caring letter from the late Michael Plant the Third. Someone could have received the message. It is really, really inspiring. I do look forward to meeting you, Chris, and I will show you this meaningful letter. Very caring."

Chris slams down the phone. He needs a drink, but the moment he opens the refrigerator to get ice for a martini, the guinea pig stands up in the old aquarium and whistles, sniffing the air. "You're over-fed," Chris says. "You'll get gout! You'll have a heart attack."

When he calls Dr. Fox he gets Bonnie's answering service. "It's you, Chris. I always know your beautiful voice. Reminds me of Upstairs, Downstairs." The doctor is out to lunch already. You all right?"

"Liz is at the Boston Public library and I have an attack. The gout!"

"That can be so painful! My father-in-law—" A deep sigh. "Well, this is private." She coughs nervously. "I'll get Dr. Fox for you."

Chris feels deserted like Bonnie after he hangs up. Liquor is bad for gout, but he refills his martini glass and is getting some ice when the phone rings. "I'm in pain. I need an appointment," he blurts out at once.

"I could feel your pain, Chris." That soft chanting again. "That's why I called back. I know you need the healing center." Chris doesn't want to tie up the line, but can't resist briefing her about his many symptoms: fluctuating temperature, gout, pain in his big toe, the right one. His digestion. Agitation from having experienced a terrible betrayal (Ellen). Pauline wants to set up an appointment for a free consultation and acupuncture. Chris says he has had too many needles as a child, but he'll think about it and call her later. He hobbles up to the computer room. It seems as though a century has gone by since he sat up here, read her manuscript, and then threw it out. He walks in quickly and closes the door; Saki scratches to be let in too.

"I'm not doing anything," Chris calls out in the high-pitched panic of Granny and Great-Granny trying to control creatures who controlled them. He opens the door and says "Go away!" But Saki wags his tail and with a little jump comes in and follows him to the desk. The computer has not been turned off, and the light glares, onto the clipboard Liz left on the desk.

FRAU FASER IN VIENNA

Sister Agnes, the teaching nun, and Dora sat on the park bench watching the children play at an ornamental Greek temple.

"This park gives you an idea of the old Vienna.The beautiful little ones.Girls in embroi-

dered dresses wearing white gloves. Boys in sailor
suits. Beautifully behaved children played here.
There are not many children left in Vienna now, but
plenty of women in mourning," the nun said, as two
women dressed in black came along the path.

"Have any of the war children found their parents and left the shelter?" Dora asked.

"Several." The nun stood up, looked around, and
sat down again. "But the doctor is in too much of a
hurry to hand the orphans over for adoption. They
should go to good Catholic families." Since Dora
did not respond,the teaching nun went on with a
little lesson about the Hapsburg monarchy and the
benevolent Christian emperors who had created park
lands for the people of Vienna.

Dora felt like asking the nun why Christian
emperors put all those fun statues of naked Greek
gods and goddesses here,there and everywhere all
over Vienna, but this teacher, who spoke English,
French, and even Russian, made her uneasy.

"You get away from all that dust and noise of
tearing down bombed-out buildings here. It's rest-
ful," the nun went on while her dark eyes kept
looking around restlessly. She got up and sat down
again several times, before a woman wearing a brown
hat and brown-belted leather coat came through the
wrought-iron gate. The sister stood up and waved,
went to her. They shook hands and stood side by
side watching Chris and Liz from a distance. The
woman took off the wide-brimmed hat. Her hair was
the same brown color and pulled back; everything
matched, but when the nun brought her towards the
bench, Dora again noticed anxious protruding eyes
that did not go with her placid face. "Ja, ja." She
gasped, "*Ich bin sicher*. I'm sure." But she wasn't
too sure of anything at all, when she suddenly
turned back towards the children and shouted:
"Liese, Liese!"

The child looked up from her game and saw a big
bad boot step on three snowdrops. "Look who I
brought for you," said the nun.

The child got to her feet with her mouth half
open and her eyes half closed and retreated.

The woman turned her head toward Dora. "My
child! *Sie haben mein Kind!*" Her voice quavered.

"Your child?" Dora spoke up in her clear, loud

English. "A young girl in a displaced persons' camp says she's hers."

The woman either did not understand or ignored this. "*Schone Kinder.* Beautiful children. Pure blondes, both of them," she half smiled. "*Aber was ist los mit Dir Liese?* What's the matter? Look at me! Little run-away? Trying to hook up with Americans like all the big girls in Vienna?"

Dora was on her feet. "We better get back to the hotel."

Sister Agnes stepped in front of her. "We must allow her to talk to Liese."

"Who is she, anyway?" Dora demanded.

The blasting of a nearby ruined building drowned out an answer—if there was one. "Boom, Boom. House is gone," shouted a toddler walking between two women who held his hands and swung him in the air. "Boom, boom!" after a second explosion.

Liz hid behind Chris and held her ears, moving her head from side to side in panic. "We don't like explosions," he said. "I was in a terrible boat explosion. I'm scared too." Chris smiled to get the attention of the big woman, who seemed more interested in his Sis. "When the boat blew up, there were flames. I—"

He was silenced by a third blast, closer to the park, followed by the thunder of falling walls. Sis let out a shriek. Dora tried to pick her up, but she shook her off. The woman opened her arms wide. "Come to *Mutter*. Come *Kind*. Come to me!" Chris, who needed to be hugged when he was scared, ran to her, while his Liz turned, darting into the temple, around a naked God, out the side, where she raced along the path past the two women swinging the boy, past empty park benches. She got as far as flower beds, before long-legged Dora caught her and picked her up. "Why are you shaking like this?"

"She stepped on the flowers."

"Is she your mother?"

Liz shook her head. She nodded right after that, but Dora had already turned to the nun and Chris, who had caught up with them.

"You must excuse this," the nun said. "Frau Director Faser found us through the Red Cross. I checked her credentials. She is a certified matron who ran a school for homeless children during the

```
war. Since she came all the way from Munich, I
couldn't just send her away. She told us that she
had adopted Liese and the child was abducted. She
has a photo of herself with a child who looks like
Liese." She sighed and bent down to Liese. "No
child would ever run away from a real mother."
     "Let's run!" Chris said and took the lead.
```

Chris puts the pages back on top of a folder. The nun and the fat woman must be fantasy, just like her version of Chris, but Dora did take them to play in parks. He remembers what it was like having a new twin sister who went along with your games. But when people shouted in German and tried to go near Liz to pick her up, she ran. Now she has changed and sometimes speaks German to Eckert on the phone.

Spending so much time in front of the unhealthy computer must be making her unstable. You can hear the exhalation of magnetic radiation, but the diode he is about to place on the computer is in his right pocket and so he is safe. Liz had laughed when he showed her the Ener-G Polariti-T Products catalogue, and he had laughed with her. But he sent away for a diode to protect himself and her from the low-level radiation and magnetic fields one is exposed to all the time—especially in front of a computer. The diode protects against 47 different frequencies, is made of nontoxic material, and will hold energy patterns and polarities in balance. If you smoke and carry a diode in your left pocket, you are protected from lead, mercury, cadmium, formaldehyde, and arsenic. He takes it out of his pocket, crouches to get away from the screen, and places it against the brain-box of MATE II. Then he jumps up in shock and surprise.

A monster creature—a long grasshopper body, minute triangular head, and long antennae—sits on a stack of chapters on bent wire legs, waiting, dead still as though it had been exhaled by the system to guard printed pages.

Chris can feel his heart pounding in double time to the throb of his toe. The phone rings. For a moment he is paralyzed and can't move. But the phone keeps ringing, so he crawls past the light, gets away from the creature, and picks up the receiver. It's Dr. Fox's office. The nurse wants to know whether this is an emergency. When he has been betrayed by two of his shrinks! She better believe it! Yes, he can be there in an hour. Or can he?

The forelimbs of the creature rise slowly. Bathed in the eerie, dangerous light from the monitor, poised to spring, will it fly, leap, attach itself, suck blood? Definitely a bad omen. A praying mantis, of course. But how did it get into the sealed room? Could it all be a hallucination caused by radiation? Should he send the diode back for a refund? What if all of Liz's writing is a hallucination brought about by computer radiation and the diode protection puts an end to it? He carefully closes the door behind him.

After Dr. Fox tells Chris that there is nothing wrong with his toe, or his heart, he speeds home and settles down to watch open heart surgery on TV in the parlor, where the reflection of the procedure flickers on the glass of the portrait of Rosalie Plant. She had died of heart failure. Then Gramp had died the same way. He can feel his heart racing again. Stress. Too much daily stress. The medical program is making his heart race. He turns the program off and looks up the mantis in the dictionary.

Praying Mantis. Mantis,(NL fr. Gk lit, diviner, prophet and akin to Gk mainestai to be mad—more at MANIA): an insect that feeds on other insects and clasps its prey in forelimbs held up as in prayer.

When he turns to the encyclopedia for more information he finds out it's a she. You seldom see males; they are small, and the female eats the male during mating. Disgusting. The encyclopedia falls from his hands and hits his foot. When he staggers into the kitchen for the first aid of a little brandy, who should be interviewed on the radio but Beatrice Strout? Going on and on about her new book "Be Sensuous and Be Psychic." Already a number one bestseller. The way she laughs when she is trying to be serious reminds Chris of Ellen. When she is asked how she is able to write her books so fast, she talks about female psychic power in a breathless, seductive voice: New Femininism—non-competitive with men; using sensuous psychic magnetic power to attract the right mate. Singular not plural! Pluralizing is out.

A man-hungry femininist, like Ellen, ready to clasp prey—plural! He feels a stinging bite in his toe just thinking of the female mantis sitting up there and waiting. Chris rushes up the stairs, ready to throw the disgusting creature out into the garden, the toilet, anything, but she had the psychic power to know he was coming after her, left a few droppings on the manuscript and has gone into hiding. He hunts for her on the floor, in the bookcases, on the table, even checks the tattered hat Liz keeps on a bottle.

He knows the creature is waiting somewhere, feelers trembling. He didn't see the mouth, but it must be curved into a smile of anticipation as saw-edged limbs lift, resuming the ominous prayer position with all the innocent monstrosity of a starving female waiting to devour a male.

Chris notes that Ellen's mouth turns up at the corners—not smiling but in smug anticipation—while Red, who's not used to a lead, drags her along Beach Street. An unexpected 65 degrees this Saturday puts everyone into a giddy mood. That school-teacher dress with the demure cardigan she wore last time at the motel billows in the wind. Her hair flies up behind her. On such a sunny day, Shoreland men wave to her from their cars. Chris gets excited and stops his Audi to invite her in, but she shakes her head.

"I know you've been calling me. I've simply not been available, Chris. I told you a while back that an English doctor was writing to me—"

Chris leans out of the car window and his blue eyes light up in a rage. "Those damned Oscar letters..." Everything makes her laugh this morning.

"Dr. Oswald Renfrew. Subconsciously I was on the lookout for this English doctor and that's how we found each other."

"Harold Bigfield happens to be my doctor! I saw you with him. I know he lost his wife. Must also have lost his mind if he wrote those letters."

She laughs into his face and dimples annoyingly. "It would have been simply fantastic if he had written them to me before we ever met, but he didn't write any letters." She takes a deep breath with the look of mischievous expectation he knows too well. I thought you might have—But, of course you didn't. She turns her pert profile and gazes out over the water. Red sits down on her left foot panting and slobbering, "A hundred years ago a young woman here expected the right man and knew he would come sailing in. Or swimming in. She just waited. Living by the sea makes for longing."

"And drowning," Chris says.

She has learned to ignore Chris when he is morbid. "A true story. She was walking along the shore and came across a sea captain who had to swim ashore. She nursed him back to health. They loved each other and married. Women waiting and longing developed mystical power. I was talking about the fact that femininists want to regain some of that faith in their own mystical power. Beatrice Strout calls it 'leap-frogging into the future.'"

"Spare me the lecture, Ellen. How did you get hold of my doctor?"

"He came to hear me lecture. He was standing up in the back. Quite conspicuous in his suit, shirt, and tie. In front there were the usual old-fashioned feminist hecklers. One of them asked whether I had been reading Jane Austen lately. The doctor called out, "Let's hope so!" Don't you love that? Oswald Renfrew mentioned that he had heard me lecture in one of his letters. So I naturally thought he had materialized. I was so excited and nervous when I got down from the podium to hand out some pamphlets that I tripped and fell."

"On purpose," Chris says with conviction.

"I think there is a Jane Austen young girl who falls and then this wonderful young man helps her up and they fall in love. Anyway, Harold helped me up! I thanked him for his beautiful letters. He didn't say anything when I called him Dr. Renfrew, but he has such a wonderful boyish smile. When we were having coffee, he said, 'No better way to find your identity than through mistaken identity.' Don't you love that?"

"Typical. He's always quoting something."

"After his wife dropped dead in the garden, he sank himself into his work on depression, environment, and change. Through me he's proved his own theory on taking a chance. He's bringing his manuscript and notes along for me to read."

"Staying over with you?"

"We might go to Maine. I'm off to meet him right now. Boys are with their dad. I've got to go!"

Chris rolls his car window up, steps on the gas, and the Audi stalls before it shoots forward. In the rear-view mirror he sees Red, who has been amazingly calm, chase after the Audi trailing his leash and Bigfield will no doubt get a chance to admire Ellen, that show- off, chasing after the dog, skirt and hair flying.

Chapter 29
THE BLIND BRIGADE

Icicles outside the window drip, drip-drip, on and on while Havelock Grimes goes on and on about the Concept. Repetitious like one of Ellen's persuasion tapes, only it isn't soothing and subliminal, but loud and boring. Mike goes to sleep and dreams of shaping a sand-mermaid on Myrtle Beach: sea grass hair, green beach-glass for eyes, and rare pink ones for a bellybutton and a nipple. Amazons had only one, but they were mean to men. Mike doesn't want a mean mermaid so he runs around searching in a panic trying to find pink beach glass for a second tit.

A man shouts, "Mike Plant," and an icy wave washes over him and washes his amazon mermaid away. "Wake up and stand!"

Mike stands up and shakes himself like a wet dog.

"Napping during leadership-class—"

"I closed my eyes. You hear more with your eyes closed. It helps you think. The blind hear better. I have this blind friend—"

"Your ideas do not belong in leadership training class."

Mike stands up before Havelock Grimes. They are both thin, the same height, tense as actors at curtain time. "Leaders have to have their own ideas." (Karin could not disagree with that!)

Havelock Grimes picks up his mug to swallow black coffee, but it is cold. "You just say anything that comes into your head. You talk, talk instead of learning."

Mike keeps saying anything that comes into his head about Hitler, and about Jesus, who shouldn't have allowed Judas to narc.

Grimes hitches his pants up and bellows, "Get out, Plant!"

"I was making a point. If you can't express your own ideas you might as well be dead."

Havelock Grimes picks up a chair and bangs it down. "Out. you don't belong here!"

Weird, but awesome. Mike is ready to follow orders and walk out just to get away. Then the devil gets into him. He ambles toward an empty easel to the right of Grimes, leans up against it, arms spread out as though he could not pry himself off the wooden cross. (He doesn't need Karin to tell him that this is no better than Madonna, the godless rock deity dangling a crucifix between naked boobs. Anything for a kick.)

Boys gape. A current of icy air blows in through the window Grimes opened. A siren screams off into the distance followed by dead silence. Havelock Grimes comes down hard on the chair and it slides with a squeal. "You have it coming to you!" he says under his breath. And for once every kid in the room—even Mike—believes him.

Mike expects to be sent home again, but a week goes by. Wednesday night two lanterns at the back of the Student Union got smashed. No one owned up. Not one leadership "brother's keeper" comes forward to inform. "Then let it stay dark," Havelock Grimes tells the assembly.

This time Mr. Goodly, the headmaster, did speak up to point out that vandalism invites vandals. And he was right. The lights should have been repaired. In the meantime everyone enjoys coming and going unseen at the dark back door, most of all Havelock Grimes himself. He walks in unobserved, following the beat of Mike's drums to the stage of the assembly room, where he finds Mike Plant on the podium, stripped to the waist, his head adorned with a red rag and head phones, pounding and bashing his drum set to tunes from the Walkman that only he can hear.

Havelock Grimes has made up his mind to put an end to the self-induced deafness of the Walkman craze, an end to the stupor and madness induced by dope.

"Enough!" he bellows.

Mike pulls the headphone off.

"Get your shirt on at once, Plant! Where do you think you are, in Africa? Your aunt called. She is staying at the Inn. There is a convention for the blind. You're invited to dinner."

Mike responds with a drum roll to the news of clever Mrs. Wise coming to rescue him from a Grove Academy charred chicken dinner. "My favorite aunt. And the food at the Inn is great." Why did Grimes show up here, when he could have sent a leadership stooge? Mike lets go with a reckless attack on the drums. Wild hair, wild eyes. "Lined my drum with aluminum foil!" When there is no rebuke, he yields and slips into his shirt.

"They'll pick you up in a van, here, at the back door."

"How come you're letting me off?"

"Letting you off?" A pause. "Shirt and tie, jacket. Comb your hair. Six o'clock."

"You're setting me up? Are you?" Mike's voice booms and is full of laughter. "Grove Academy boy leading a blind aunt in to dinner at the convention of the New England blind." Mike can well imagine the picture in the local papers. "I'm good enough for a publicity stunt, right!"

Havelock Grimes bangs the door against the wall as he walks out, and it swings bang, bang, bang, drumming an answer that echoes. Loud girls in the hallway fall silent, watching the founder of the school hurry out the back door. Then they rush the stage. "What's up, Mike. What's up?"

"Dinner at the Inn!"

"Your Mom. Cool!" Emerald sidles up to him. "Take me!"

"An aunt. She doesn't know you. And you don't eat!"

"I'll eat at the Inn!"

"You look like hell with green hair and three earrings in one ear." The blind would not be able to see what Emerald has done to herself. Emerald might forget to starve herself and eat a good meal, talk about her mother the actress, and make Mrs. Wise laugh. Somehow he feels he should not turn Em down—but he does.

❀ ❀ ❀

At ten to six Mike smokes a forbidden cigarette at the dark back-door of the Student Union, where the light was smashed. On campus roadways old fashioned lanterns shine on trees that sway their lacy shadows like stoned go-go dancers. There is not much traffic out on Holly Road at dinner time. Staring at the moon will drive you mad. Make you walk in your sleep, wet your bed. One of baby-sitter Karin's sayings. "In Finland," Mike would tell her. Moon- gazing is not the same without her chanting. It's only a half moon. Nothing is the same. He is deprived of his girl when he most needs her to get along in this mad school, this flaky world.

When you stare up from the dark to the half moon long enough you can see it jiggle to get loose from its dark side, trying to break away and come crashing down like a comet. For once, Mike is early. He has done everything just right. New white shirt, black leather tie, new boots, and leather vest an overstatement with the leather flight jacket. Why did Mom sound so worried when he called to get parental permission to go out to dinner with Mrs. Wise?

Too much country peace is interrupted suddenly by the smell of threat-ened skunk. Mrs. Wise will be sorry he is kept waiting around in the cold. Natalie Wise is very knowing, so Mike put on plenty of Polo cologne to smell dressed up. And when she asks, "Mike, what are you wearing, what do you look like?" he'll say, 'Robert Plant.' She'll want to know all about Led Zeppelin and rock musicians. Mike could sing "Stairway to Heaven" for her. This will make her laugh like a little kid.

Snowflakes large as moths fly around helium lights in the empty park-ing lot, and wood smoke stays trapped in ground fog around the guard's cottage. Frank, the guard, a Vietnam veteran, is in a permanent fog. No one could blame him for washing tranquilizers down with a few beers, which he has been known to share. He has shown his wartime experience by shooting down creatures of the night so that garbage and trash can be lined up for collection at the kitchen door. Those all purpose plastic trash bags used to keep kids warm and camouflaged, before Havelock banned them..

Inside the Student Union, the work crew of kids clatter dishes while Kline plays classical piano, pounding the wrong keys. Mike, like his dad, can unfortunately hear each mistake. But Kline's Mama flies up from New York at least once a month just to hear her boy play and thinks he is another Bernstein. They eat at the Inn every time she comes.

Other kids get taken out to eat when relatives come to visit. Mike lost his Aunt Melissa when he was still in grade school. The rest of the Plants scattered and died out. Now he has found himself a blind aunt! Mike is starving. He digs his cold hands into pockets: his gloves always vanish. Finally, headlights come through the gate, but they stop. When the vehicle gets going it makes up for lost time by swerving around the bend hitting the frosted mountain laurels. The blind people might not know they had climbed into this rusty old battered VW, but they would know that their rotten driver is speeding and slamming down brakes, as it skids to a stop.

He quickly douses his cigarette in snow, sticks it under dead leaves, and steps into the half light. Three guys tumble out. One of them stops, hacks his heel into a frozen puddle. "Hey, you. Where's Emma?" An embryo on growth hormones, monstrous and fat, eyes and mouth stayed small. The other two are thin, shifty weasels. "Emerat, stupid," one of them squeals. All three of them ugly as they come and making the most of it by wearing blond wigs.

The big guy slips and glares at Mike's leather flight jacket, the western boots. "That chick, Emerat. Where is she?"

"Emerald. Her name is Emerald." A loud TV preacher type chants out the driver's window.

A dealer, Mike tells himself. "No such kid around."

"Where are you from?" inquires the polite driver

"Where ya from?" echoes a weasel.

The big guy hitches pants up his paunch, spits three times. Then, fast as a viper, he twists Mike's left arm, yelling: "Where ya from!"

Mike is overcome by the stench. They've been drinking and tripping, peeing in their pants. He's seen that type of loser before. He stays cool and shakes him off. "Massachusetts."

"That's where they locked you up, Big. You hate Mass. Big, don't you now!" the careful voice broadcasts from the car.

"Hate Mass!" A putrid weasel comes closer and sniffles, "Perfume! A queer!"

"We hate queers!" says the voice.

Big pounces on Mike, pins him against a tree. The two weasels, doing their bit, kick Mike's legs and the tree. The kitchen crew are bashing pots and pans, and what with a tune box blasting "Johnny be Good," and Kline banging away playing his classical piano, who would hear Mike? His roar—which is famous for making cheerleaders fall over in fright and go into a two-minute coma—gives him the chance to kick at shins and punch

Big in the mouth. They expect him to run back into the Student Union, but Mike turns and runs toward the guard's cottage yelling, "Frank, Frank. The gun!"

He even gets close enough to hear the car chase of a TV shoot out, but the road is glazed with ice and he skids on his new leather- soled boots and falls. "Frank, Frank!"

The weasels pounce on Mike and he twists fast, this way and that, kicking them off, cursing himself for taking this wrong turn. He grabs a leg as a lever, pulls one of them down and gets up.

"What are you waiting for, Big?"

The stage voice comes from the bashed-up van. Mike has his legs kicked out from under him. Snow stings his hands.

"All rrright!" the voice again.

They drag him. Mike turns himself into a dead ox. The light is out, smashed. Grimes had said, "Let it be dark." A weasel tripping into a vampire movie, bites his neck. His partner pulls his hair. "No wig. It's real!" It hurts. Mike punches and bellows for rabies shots, bites a leg and then a hand, shoves one of them against a frozen bush, and runs toward the kitchen door.

"Go, Big, go!" chants the voice from the car.

Mike thunders back to the ground again and pain splinters at the back of his head. Somewhere on a flickering screen above him hovers an embryo face on a monster body; eyes half closed, snotty button nose; lips drooling with infantile lust.

"Go, Big, go!" sings the voice. "Biggy, be bad!"

"Bad trip, or what is it with you?" Mike is silenced by a jab under the chin that makes his left ear ring. He forces his knee up in a rage, kicking left and right with a thud, thud, thud, gaining the space of a second, a glimpse of the other one, leaning against the van: mop of hair, dark clothes. A familiar on a bad trip following some outer dictate, to coach a twisted losing game.

"Kill!"

Mike is pinned down and a black boot hovers, dripping mud onto his mouth. He turns his face from side to side as it comes pounding down. "Johnny be good. Johnny be good," he roars the song, tasting mud and his own blood running from his nose into his mouth. Then the weight of the world crushes down on his chest. Agony turns dread into desperate longing for an end, any end. Thin guy leaning against a van, long, curly hair, lighting a joint: another Robert Plant. He's me. He's I. I'm he. I'm dead looking at myself. "I want daffodils!"

Daffodils bloom in memory of the Shoreland dead in the big field on Raven Hill. Plant daffodils for grandfather the pilot, English grandmother, and Dad's twin. Gramp's daffodils in full bloom have taken over. Aunt Melissa sitting up there, rosy cheeks, white hair curling down to her ice blue eyes, stuffing herself on little cucumber sandwiches and big raisin cookies with sounds of appreciation: I want my daffodils. Now don't you forget! And she reaches for another cookie.

"I want my daffodils. Karin, my daffodils!" Mike hears an elephant roar from hell. "That's his voice. I smell leather. New leather. That's Mike, Mike!" Mrs. Wise is interrupted by a hyena's laugh.

"Take the skin, take the leather!" The voice again.

Stripped, ripped, dragged for trophy, the dying elephant roars from hell of turning into carcass.

"Mike—It's me. It's Mrs. Wise. Driver, what's going on, driver?"

"A fight—A dirty fight. Guys beating up on a kid. Hey, you over there. What are you doing?" He stays put, but the blind men have clambered out of the van, all three of them. "I can smell action. I can smell the enemy!" The Colonel, blinded in the Korean war, swings his cane and hits a tree trunk with a big smack. "Colby, Kempt, Burns, follow me, men! Driver where are you!" The driver, a local man, doesn't budge.

"Which way?"

"Go straight ahead. Along the road. Stick to the road, sir!"

"Leather. The smell of new leather. Mike! Oh my God!"

"You're the one started it. Go get some help," shouts the driver.

"Go yourself!" says the voice.

"Can't leave those blind folk. We're picking up a kid."

"Blind. Holy Homer. You say he's blind?"

The Colonel and his men rush forward, swinging canes from side to side to avoid trees and shrubs. "Two feet to the right, Colonel!" The driver calls.

"You can smell them. They stink," Colby calls out.

The Colonel moves forward at an even pace, tilting his head and sniffing. "There is garbage." Then he takes a right turn, charges forward, lunges, striking out and his cane thuds, a yelp, a burst of filth. He wields then, towards foul words of Big, the foul odor of Korea, Vietnam, obscene cruelty of war taking hold of him, hitting and punishing enemy apes that had blinded him. "God, do I love this!"

Mrs. Wise gets out of the van. "Mike's cologne. I'll follow the scent!"

"No, lady. You don't go nowhere!"

Mrs. Wise ignores the driver and follows the path, swinging her white cane from side to side. "Leather. The smell of new leather. That's Mike!"

"We're coming!" Kempt calls out. Burns has found the garbage bags. "Ready for orders, sir!"

What could it all mean? Mike no longer knows or cares. "I'm here. No, I'm standing there. He is here. " Mike opens one eye and there are men swishing scythes, while he floats off into Mom's computer screen. "Mike, Mike! where are you?" Mrs. Wise again.

"Kid's on the ground!" yells the guard.

"Watch out for Mike. His cologne and leather. Smell of new leather."

"You come back here, lady. Come back!"

"Natalie, Natalie, be careful!" Vance Colby, slips on the ice. A confused weasel bumps into him. The former headmaster grips him, takes him over his knee and uses his cane to deliver a good old-fashioned licking. "What's going on here? What have you been up to?"

"Nooo. Nooo! Stop. Fuck you! Let me go."

"Won't talk. We'll see!"

"Stop. Stop it, man. Big did it. Big's the one!"

"What did he do? Talk! Talk!"

"Killed. Killed a queer!"

"Blind queer punk."

"Murder one!" squeals the other weasel, trying to break away from the Colonel.

Vance Colby pushes the weasel away. "You stinking devil. Go, go clean yourself up!" Gives him a good push. "Go, get, out of my sight!" His hand holding the white cane trembles from the illusion of beating the devil out of boys.

"Mike, Mike where are you? Are you all right?" Mrs. Wise bumps into a tree and stops. Car doors bang, boots pound over the asphalt. The Colonel follows the scampering. "Did I stop them? Have we cut them off, driver? How many are left?"

"You beat a couple of them up. They're running to the van. Kid is on the ground."

"Cut off the retreat, driver. Block them." The driver follows orders. The van blocks the road and the rusty V.W. swerves into a footpath, hitting shrubs. Weasels run after it and one of the doors bashes against trees and lanterns. Then it bangs shut. They drive through a thicket and get stuck. Big Will gets out to push the V.W. out of the mud. They are right behind a faculty house and he is mad, scared, crazy enough to throw rocks through the window aiming at a faculty wife cutting pie for her young children. It misses, but breaks a jar of pickles. She telephones her husband, interrupting a meeting with Havelock Grimes. He tells her to calm down. The window is broken but she is not hurt. Probably just a snowball. An accident. Why get kids into trouble? This is not a matter for the police.

❀❀❀

The driver, satiated with violence, tears open the door to the Student Union with a fixed grin and leaves it bang, bang, banging, behind him, "Get the cops. Call the police and an ambulance."

"Campus under attack! We have a casualty!" The Colonel knows how to make himself heard. "Call an ambulance!"

Kids pick up chairs, forks and knives, anything as they pile out the building swarming all over the campus. A white-haired woman wearing a white coat sits on the road, holding Mike. His eyes are closed and his face covered with blood.

Emerald and her friends screech and howl, "Mike!"

"Get away!" the woman raises a white cane.

Girls back off and go looking for baseball bats and sticks and rocks. The siren of an ambulance sends Emerald down the road towards it, shrieking, "Help, murder. Help!" tearing her hair. Men who had been called to Grove Academy to subdue Caleb Fairfield see another crazy kid, and get out of the ambulance with a straitjacket.

"Lay off me! It's Mike. He's dead! At the back of the building. This blind woman killed him and she tried to kill me!"

By the time the police get past Emerald and get things straight, the old van is racing along River Road, where Brenda, a local high school senior, is walking home from her baby-sitting job.

"Emma. Emerat! There!"

"Git her!"

The rusted car screeches to a halt. They grab her.

"No. Help! Let me go. Why me?"

They shove her into the car.

"Liz Plant? It's me Priscilla."

Silence.

"I'm your official Parents Association contact. Mike did not want us to call you. He wants to tell you about it himself, but Havelock thought I should be the one, because of all I went through with Caleb. Everyone is very upset. You know about Mr. Goodley's ulcer. But it was nobody's fault. Havelock says.

"Mike just happened to be out there in the dark waiting for this blind aunt to come and take him out to dinner. And you did give parental permission, you know. Well, this local gang drove in through the gate and they were violent. Mike happened to be in the wrong place at the wrong time.

"He's well taken care of in the hospital. Havelock says not to worry. Mike will be back in school in a few days. He has contusions and a rib is broken. Kidney bleeding a little, but kids heal fast, you know. Jaw cracked a little. You should have seen my Caleb when they took him to rehab. You mustn't worry. He's angry. The school psychologist isn't getting anywhere with him. He hates you for sending him back to Grove; blames Havelock and the school. We think it would be better if you stayed away just now.

"This blind couple and the local blind people are there all day long with food, spoiling him with all kinds of presents, you know. His new jacket and boots were stolen. He has three new jackets and two pairs of new boots. Best you stay away. He's getting to be too much of a hero. Are you still there, Liz?"

A clock ticks. Something drops and shatters.

"Are you all right?—Well, don't worry. I'll be in touch with the hospital for you, and with Mike, the doctor, and Havelock. Be strong, Liz, and stay away. Let him be a man. Stay out of it. That's Jake's opinion." There is silence. "You O.K?"

"O.K." An echo.

The phone rings. She picks it up. "Mike!"

"Mrs. Christopher Plant? This is consumer research, I would really appreciate it if you could answer some questions."

"I can't."

"You could really help me out! Only take one minute. When have you cooked turkey parts the last time?" The female singsong voice lilts to the serene "Gold and Silver Waltz", which conjures up stout German women waltzing in pairs while Liese, the mascot, winds and rewinds the gramophone for the celebration of a brief victory—an evocation of sacrificed sons.

"How often do you buy turkey breast in one month? Eight times, four times? Two times or less?"

Nice voice, stately waltz, while squawking turkeys strung up by their legs go waltzing along assembly lines to be sorted out scientifically, and mechanically chopped up.

"Three times? Five?" Mike stripped of his new jacket and boots, bandaged Chris, Mike in a hospital bed. These images torment Liz in three-quarter time. Her face is wet. No crying. They won't have it. The receiver falls and dangles spinning around.

Chapter 30
HARM'S WAY

"You were lucky," the nurse's aide says to Mike." The poor little girl they picked up was half dead. They had her tied to a tree under the bridge. A dog found her and barked. Worse than rats, those guys. She would have frozen to death if it hadn't been for the dog. The girl's dad, a local businessman, doesn't want anyone to know what happened to her. No good ruining her future, or his own; won't allow her to press charges."

"So, how come you know all about it?" Mike says.

"I gave her the dog, when our dog had a litter."

"So the dog is a better man, it talked." Mike said.

The doctor gives Mike painkillers. He goes to sleep. They wake him up with broth. The nurse helps him out of bed and wants to stand by while he takes a piss. "Get out! Please get out!" In the mirror he sees a blue and red monster face. They've tied his hair back with bandages, didn't cut it.

Mr. Goodley walks in and thinks he's in the wrong room. "Don't call my mother, Mike says." Just leave me some change and I'll call her myself. I don't want her to come rushing to the hospital."

In the evening Mike drags himself to the pay phone and calls home. His father answers. "Got a cold, Mike?"

"Sort of." Dad has been drinking and his voice is hoarse with suppressed emotions because he can't get himself to talk about Mike's injuries.

"Mom at home?" Dad shows he cares with a long lecture on how to prevent and treat the common cold. "Can you please get her?"

"Mom," Mike says. "Dad doesn't want me to wise him up. Just as well, or he'd get started on that old boat explosion. How he was almost killed. You better fill him in. This was no accident. They tried to kill me. He's got to take the school to court for negligence. The guard is a drunk; there's no protection here. I'd be in the morgue right now if Mrs. Wise and those blind men hadn't gone after those punks. This place sucks. I really hate you for sending me back here. Are you there, Mom? You probably think I did something. I was asking for it. Deserve it for taking your money, right? Goodley says you're planning to show up here tomorrow. Well, don't bother. This is not the time to take me out of Grove!"

"Hey, Mike." A girl cuts in. "I need to make a call. Make it short!"

"You don't have to make calls from the hospital, when you're not even supposed to be here. Beat it! Sorry, Mom. That's Emerald."

There is a scuffle. The phone clicks. Liz has been cut off. She gets the hospital phone number from information. Dials and gets: click. "The number you have dialed is not in service." She tries again and gets a busy signal. Hangs up.

The phone rings. She picks it up. "Mike!"

"Mrs. Christopher Plant? This is consumer research, I would really appreciate it if you could answer some more questions."

"I can't."

"You could really help me out! Only take one minute. When have you cooked turkey parts the last time?" The female singsong voice, the serene "Gold and Silver Waltz,"

"How often do you buy turkey breast in one month? Eight times, four times? Two times or less? If you can only complete our consumer report and answer a few questions, Mrs. Plant." Subliminal persuasion music, to program you with a desire for turkey meat? "You love turkey. You cook it once a week, twice a week or more. "Do you buy name brands?"

"No branding!"

"I have put your name on our list."

This breaks the spell. "No list!" Liz bangs down the receiver. When she calls the hospital, the operator passes her onto the repair service: The line is already on the list as out of order. She finds herself writing: listed as out of order with a red ballpoint pen on a telephone notepad, below the list of tranquilizers Chris left jotted down for a report to the doctor that he is out of order.

At first he had orders to make lists, the Herr Doctor Finkel. And he sorted children out and he would do it again because sorting out children for Fuhrer and Fatherland, sorting out unsuitable, unworthy ones, had been his job. And the Inspector was not to blame. He had his orders and he had to give orders.

Have you ever awakened from your own murder, surprised to be warm under your cover in bed, safe? And doesn't that make you think of all of God's children: Polish, Russian, Jewish, Gypsy—wrong color, wrong size, torn away from Mother—sorted out, listed according to orders, worksheets? You think of all the papers, declarations condemning the world to wars, lists of recruits, soldiers. How about the executioners? Boy soldiers following the orders of old men who condemn the world to war. Sons ordered to kill sons or be killed before they had ever known love. Prisoners of lists—one and all.

Then there's no hiding place, no shelter. You run and run on a forlorn, deserted plain. Then you hear the rustle of papers, something sliding behind you, coming closer, a mountain rumbling, thundering toward you with furnace blasts, whirlwinds of stench. An icy claw fastens onto your nape, a giant branding-iron scorching the flesh, with a number. Why, why, when there are no more lists?

"Mike. Why Mike?" Liz calls out and Saki jumps up and puts both paws on her knee.

No more records, no more lists. The doctor burned all the lists and secret records. The children left behind to march in the parade ground were neither chosen nor rejected. They did not exist.

"Does God have a list?" Liz asks herself.

The phone rings. "Is this the Plant residence?"

"No turkey!"

"Mrs. Plant, Liz. Are you all right?" Mr. Goodley's secretary. She is sorry to call so early. Mr. Goodley thought she would want to know that the police arrested three gang members. The leader, the one who drove the car, got away. High school dropouts and unemployed, that is the problem. Those gangs torch buildings and cars. "There's concern for Mike's safety, and there is the safety of the school. Juvenile offenders get out in the street in no time. We've got to help him understand that this is a community problem. Grove Academy does not want Mike to take any risk. He has been asked to appear in front of the Grand Jury. We want you to know that we don't think it is safe for him to testify. Best to stay out of harm's way."

"Mike Plant will testify. Not I, nor anyone else, will be able to keep him quiet," Liz says.

Later, she can hear the kitchen timer ticking in the music room to snatches of old anger, grief, and needs, Mike's injuries making Chris talk fast and faster as he rehearses to fit all of it into one session with Dr. Nathan, a psychiatrist who has not had his turn for several weeks. She is on her way to her computer when the mail arrives with a note from her editor to remind her that he is waiting for her final chapters.

That night she walks in her sleep, dreaming she is her own mother looking for a lost child, every mother of the world defending and avenging her child. Liz wakes herself up shouting , "*Nein!* no, never, neeeee!" to male thrills of seeing someone bleed. No! to doomsday, uglification, pollution mongers, and serial murderers that brutalize the land, the sea, the air. No! Neeee, *nat*, NIEEEE! to skinning newborn seals alive in front of their mothers. Animals will devour their newborn young to protect them.

History repeats itself. Part of everyday news, daily entertainment on the tube. Mini-series Nazis making both serial killers and actors famous. Do you think you have a conscience now, Mr. Lucas? Secrets of the Serial Mother-Killer. His picture will be on the book-jacket. 'How-to books' are most popular. And war books, of course, and murder stories and horror stories. The memoirs of one serial murderer could turn into an army of copycat killers out there.

Grove student attacked by gang. The gang was unarmed, said the paper. Free country. And everyone has the right to bear arms. A hunting season on Grove students might begin. No list, no uniform, anyone in the wrong place at the wrong time is the enemy. On Friday night she wakes Chris, shouting foreign words in languages she was told to forget, or is she speaking in tongues? Words of warning before sinking into a bog where screams are stifled, the mouth is gagged by mud. Silent screams preceding the end, the ultimate progress of the modern world, the doomsday heritage of gaping. Stifled screams: "*Nein!* no, never, neeeee!" to cheap thrills of seeing someone else bleed. No! to doomsday. Neeee, *nat,* NIEEEE! to making pain into news.

What if mothers turned off the TV sets and radios demanding a moratorium from the atrocity barrage? Demand good news, good people for a day, a week, a year? What if Lucas got no attention, no picture in the paper?

The abuse Mike suffered passes onto Liz in waves of anguish and uncertainty all over again. Havelock Grimes told Mike that anything you survive makes you stronger. "So, if more gang members come after me, will that make me into Superman?" Mike had raged on the phone.

Icy doubts grip the back of her neck and twist inside her belly: not being read, not being heard—and the endless nonexistence of a nameless, unprotected motherless child.

Mike's hurt makes Liz remember how *der Laborant*, the Lab Man, at Hitler School had dragged her by her hair out of the hide-away cot in the matron's pantry. She had cried out for an end, any end, as he let her dangle, until hellish pain turned her into a broken puppet. Did this happen just before she escaped? Did it happen at all? Or is her writing a self-inflicted wound in front of a looking glass?

THE LAB MAN

The children knew him as *der Laborant*, because the Hitler School workers were known by their job or rank, not names. The war was not going well for Germany; an able-bodied handyman was a real find. Nobody cared that the Lab Man spoke funny German when he could repair even the Doctor's car.

He started wearing a white coat, as a kind of uniform with a cap and his hob-nailed boots. He added an American pilot's medals after he advanced to assist the Doctor, and they jingled when he jabbed children with needles, helped to cut and sew

them up to make them better, or worse, or dead like
the pilot.
    He could fix anything, even a good-for-nothing
child hiding in the matron's pantry with all the
food and spying on him when he came looking for a
snack.
    What do we have here? *Raus!* Out, out. Won't
move? Long curls *verboten*, but good for grabbing!
We'll get rid of this little rat!"
    Then he roared with pain. The child dropped from
his grip and lay on a rug which was patterned with
roses and drops of blood from his cheek. "Killing
my child!" Frau Faser shrieked, stabbing his face
with a nail file.

"Liz!" Chris bursts into the room. "You better come; your Harbor Square
pals are in the kitchen. They are in a state. Elgar thinks his mother lied to
him and Mike is dead."

    Mike murdered! In Shoreland bad news turns into terrible news wicked
fast. Non-violent Svenson, threatening to skin those killers alive, ended up
dead drunk. Karin calls long distance and then just sobs and can't go on.
For several days the back door bell and front door bell keep ringing. Mr.
Wilson, who delivers fish, always comes to the back. His deep-set blue eyes
anxious. Not in a coma. Out of the hospital! That's good news. His wife is
a grade-school teacher and he dresses and behaves like a nice school boy.
His fish filets glisten on white paper. He does not trade in lobsters because
the local lobstermen would not like this.

    From backdoor Mr. Wilson, Mike learned how to be nice and polite.
But he got his worldly, wordy know-how from the Professor, the garbage
man who is a Harvard graduate. The Professor comes around to the back
and announces himself by flipping the heavy metal lid at the garbage hole
in the back garden a few times. At nighttime, the raccoons flip that lid.
The Professor is a tall man, has a short neck and wide shoulders, strong
nose and chin, and wears a cap. From him Mike learned to sound serious,
important, and win an argument before it ever gets started. "Not as bad as
they say. I knew it." He deliberately changes the subject. "You can try to
weigh that lid down with bricks, but the big raccoon, he'll lift it off every
time. I know that cuss from the Whale's Jaw Motel. Tourists kept feeding
them. The big one got bigger and stronger. Opened a window and moved

his gang into a two bedroom unit. Took over waterbeds, they had a litter or two. The new owners were afraid to shoot them because of the Save the Predator, Endangered Species notices. They got Erikson to trap them, take them over to the woods. Now they're back here."

Kids beating up on kids, raccoons; the Professor has studied it all. He is a philosopher. The smell is bad, the conversation good. When Mike hung around during the garbage collection he learned about dictators like Napoleon and Hitler, as well as peacemakers like Gandhi, before he was five years old during the garbage collection. Backdoor and front-door people, who put up with Mike from way back, all have a vested interest. Especially Ralph Poach the electrician, a real genius and very natty dresser, who always comes to the front and allowed a six-year-old Mike to carry his bag asking questions to learn all about the wiring and fuses. While Randel Gordon, the refrigerator and washing machine repair service could teach lessons in how not to be bothered and hurry. He is a member of the rifle association, and the rumor that Mike has been shot brought him to the front door in a hurry since this could provoke a lot of bad feelings against guns. Farmer Noland, on the other hand, gives Liz his personal condolences. Boys messing around with rifles almost shot him when he still delivered milk.

Unexpected and unannounced Jehovah's Witnesses, a stout mother in a fur coat and shivering teen daughter, ring the front door bell seven times, choosing this moment to convert Liz. Finally politicians running for town elections come to talk about safety in Shoreland. Prissy Girl Scouts selling cookies Mike might like if he lived. High school girls selling raffle tickets for a TV set. For Mike —if they get the bullet out of his chest. The census taker. "Still three of you?"

Over and over again Liz and Chris have had to repeat: only a broken rib, bruises (she leaves out the bleeding kidney). Not so bad. Could have been worse. By the time Bonnie walks through the backdoor with her Elgar and a basket full of her blueberry muffins, Liz has been consoling herself by consoling.

No thanks, Chris says, to tea and muffins. Let them guzzle! In the midst of the commotion he has been forgotten. A huge bouquet of roses arrives for Liz. From your Arthur. "You'd think this is a funeral," Chris says.

Chapter 31

CONSOLATIONS

No one has asked how Chris feels. Not even Dr. Nathan understands that
Mike's ordeal and Liz's writing about his own, which had been far worse,
brought back the terror of the explosion and flames, the icy water. Loss of
father and mother and Sis. He keeps playing Verdi's Requiem, abandoning
himself to soaring sounds and orgiastic grief for the man he might have
been.

Carried away in exaltation of his near death, he jumps up to conduct
the finale, waving his arms, leaping up and down like Leonard Bernstein,
when the phone rings. Not Eckert again! Chris darts into the dining room
and grabs the receiver before Liz has a chance.

"You are under great stress, Christopher. I feel that." Pauline's singsong
voice. "The Healing Center can really, really help you!"

Unpaid bills stare up at Chris from the dining room table. "I can't
afford treatments and I hate needles!"

She titters. "Consultation is free and since you don't like needles, we
will give you a little shiatsu. Wonderful. Healing."

"Nice, but we already have a little Shih Tzu and my wife is calling me
to have blueberry muffins." Pauline is against muffins although they are
home-baked by Bonnie. Sugar is ruining America. He should change his
diet. He does like her voice and promises to get back to her.

Chris consults his dictionary: shih tzu= Pekingese dog fr shi—lion+tzu—son +kou—dog) A small, alert active dog of an old Chinese breed.—Face that is sometimes compared to a chrysanthemum. No mention of healing. The medical association wouldn't allow that. Chris starts luring Saki with so many dog treats that they begin to collect in the dog basket and are buried under carpets all over the house. When they walk along the beach, Saki holds one in his mouth like a cigar. Then Chris will tell Saki about Ellen and the terrible betrayal with his psychiatrist. He tells him of the book, of Liz making fun of him. How Gramp wanted him to become a financial expert and how he hated Wall Street and money people. He has run out of Xanax, but driving to the drugstore with Saki he calms himself down by talking about doctors, who never ever give you the kind of help you need, and all the side effects of medication, which then requires more medication. By the time he meets Priscilla in the drug store he is relaxed enough to offer her some of his Xanax.

He invites her to have a drink with him. Saki quietly withdraws to the backseat. They drive all the way to Salem. "Havelock has been endorsed with half a million the school needs desperately. If you take them to court, that money will be gone." She's the president of the Grove Academy Parents Association, but she does not know who gave all that money.

"Let's not discuss the school and what happened to Mike. It makes me quite ill," Chris says. What does she want to talk about? Beatrice Strout. Femininism. Witchcraft.

"Do you believe in crystal magic, Chris? You know about my husband. I bought a lot of amethysts and put them in every room of the house."

During her gin-flavored goodbye kiss he can feel the sting of a crystal pressing against his chest, which makes his heart race.

"Witches are taking over the world," Chris says to Saki, when he gets back to the Audi. The following day Chris receives a pamphlet decorated with the picture of a bewitching, wide-eyed, Mediterranean-type beauty made up to look oriental.

Anna Cicoria, the only certified shiatsu expert on the North Shore. Shiatsu acupressure therapeutic massage. One-hour treatment only thirty dollars.

"Shiatsu massage. Nothing to do with with dogs. Saki, you're just another fraud. But at least you won't talk or write about me," Chris says.

❀❀❀

By the afternoon Chris is looking forward to his massage so much that he gets a speeding ticket as he races past Merle's chicken farm. He gave up the "Shoreland Eagle" since he has to keep up with medical news letters, and nobody had told him that Merle's chicken farm had been taken over by the healing center and retreat. Hen houses have been converted into treatment rooms and meditation chambers. A big sign above the egg storage room, where you could pick up fresh eggs and leave the money in the basket, says

WELCOME TO THE HEALING CENTER.
Touch the wind chime and enter.

The office is empty. Just as well. Chris hates registrations and filling out forms because he can never fit all his medical history into those idiotic questionnaires. The narrow room reeks of sandalwood, but incense can't quite kill the lingering smell of thousands of hens that laid eggs here until they were killed. This would have bothered Chris if he hadn't calmed himself down during a week of walking and talking to Saki.

The hatching room door DO NOT ENTER has been covered over with

SHIATSU CENTER
Take off your shoes and enter in peace

A purple doormat sets off a startling fasten-your-seat-belt chime. The door sticks. He pushes it hard and stumbles into a darkened room. "I've been expecting you." Anna Cicoria, the only certified shiatsu expert on the North Shore, rises from meditation and bows like a geisha. Soft features, sensuous lips, and a bosom no karate suit can hide. Better even than her picture. Chris sizes her up as an old-fashioned Italian daughter who has traded in her ethnic restriction for self-imposed new-age rituals.

The room is full of incense. Gigantic aloe vera plants twist like fugitive octopi towards light which is kept out by bamboo blinds. Her smile flickers white teeth and is gone. She hopes he is wearing cotton. Flickers again when she apologetically demands he take off his watch, his wedding ring and belt, unbutton his pants, and lie down on a purple mat. When Arlene kneels at his feet he is expecting subliminal tapes to help him re-experience Ellen at her best.

"We need to find your pressure points," she softly promises and points
to a door covered with notices which reminds Chris of the one at Whale's
Jaw Motel. Instead of rates and check-out time and warnings against
smoking in bed, this one is posted with a really ugly textbook picture of a
bald, naked man. Sexual organs are omitted and the body is marked all
over with lines and colored dots like a Bionic Man repair chart. Mike had
loved that TV series. Chris had resented the Bionic Hero, who was so easily repaired.

Anna lunges without warning to pinch and poke his left leg. He lets
out a scream. "Hey! That hurts!" That smile again, "Good, good. I found
the point. Now, where does it hurt most?" One powerful hand kneads the
pain around. "Here, here, or here?" He moans as her other hand nabs his
pinkie hard—to help heal his heart. Then his toes are attacked.

"God, this hurts!"

"That's your liver." She keeps checking his pulse. Anna pinching a man
all over—even inflicting pain—is more effective than aerobics in bringing a
man's heart rate up. But she spoils the obvious male side effects with com-
ments about each sore point as it is triggered by this and that dilapidated
internal organ. Poking him hardest when she talks of "Vital Energy
Points," his weakest. He feels abused and injured—definitely on his way
out—and then her smile flickers and she starts poking around his face. She
is taking a course on shiatsu facial lifts. "Not that you need that. Your face
is beautiful, Chris. Just working on that chin line." A deep sigh. The smile
has gone out. "A new Chris Plant. Now I'll let you listen to this chant, for
inner peace; then we'll discuss diet to increase your energy and joy."

He hears promise in her voice. There is only one way he could now
have some inner peace. Chris is quite hopeful when he hears a shower
gushing and rushing along with the droning chant "BAAAAAAA,
OOOOOOGGGGGGGGGARRRRRRRRRRBBROOOOAAA."
Hundreds of sad Buddhist monks, survivors or victims of Chinese invasion. Another holocaust." BAAAAAAA, OOOOOOGGGGGGGGG
ARRRRRRRRRRBBROOOOAAA." Mike beaten up. Thousands of
monks in their Tibetan monasteries butchered by the Chinese. The
Chinese eat dogs. Saki's ceremonial ancestors must have been devoured.

"AOOOOOOOAOORAAAAAAAA." The chant drones on persist-
ently, while he persistently waits for the lovely Anna Cicoria his mind
begins to wander from chant of the dead or their mourners, to the strange

moaning he hears when his Audi backs up. And then to the right speaker of his hi-fi system which is definitely out of sorts. By the time Anna reappears his mind has turned into a repair shop.

"You look spiritually refreshed." She turns the tape recording off. Helps him up. Firmly fastens his pants for him and buckles his belt. "Olivia Haversat, our nutritionist. A beautiful human being. Expecting you in the Nutrition Center. Don't forget your jewelry."

Olivia Haversat wears her Titian-red hair in a single short, lopsided braid which she flicks around like a horse tormented by flies while she studies Anna's computer printout report. Chris is convinced by now that one of Ellen's pranks got him into the Healing Center and starts composing another new will in his head, cutting her out.

"Let us look into your soul. "Olivia puts on a pair of tinted red-rimmed spectacles to study his face. "Open up, Chris. Talk from your heart." She activates a tape recorder to record his lies: no drinking, smoking, or medication. None of her business! He has his psychiatrists, medically trained experts, when he needs to talk about stress in the home.

"The acupressure diagnosis tells me everything I need to know, Chris. A nutritional malabsorption problem." She asks about his meals. Chris takes out his pipe. "No, no. This is very harmful!" She frowns and writes in her book. "We might have to change you over to a macrobiotic diet. Well-known to both cure and prevent cancer. One does have to consider a reluctant family." Olivia flicks her red braid and suggests that he start off by eating small meals many times a day. And even during the night whenever he wakes up.

In the evening, he has to explain all this to Liz over a drink in the kitchen. Make her understand that he does not demand a macrobiotic diet, but needs to be fed every three hours from now on. This starts at seven in the following morning when the alarm or timer sounds off. Chris hurries to the kitchen, or her computer room. Finally, when he knocks on the bathroom door he finds it has been posted with: "Sandwich in the refrigerator."

This isn't fair. He needs to be cared for, so he calls Ellen. She denies having anything to do with the Healing Center. Never wants to believe that there is anything wrong with him. As for eating every three hours, this is worse than a newborn. Liz should put him on a formula, like Tiger's Milk.

He can hear a man laughing in the background. The doctor! Chris has a schedule to keep. When Ellen breaks up with the doctor, Chris won't have any time for her or for Bigfield. And she may very well have been a terrible nutritional drain.

In the kitchen he tells Liz, "No more sandwiches. Meals should be freshly prepared. Vegetables lose their nutrients in the refrigerator." The refrigerator defrosting itself grinds and crackles while he talks. She is busy going through trash mail. Suddenly she laughs out loud. "For you." She hands him a folded pamphlet from the Salem Crow Haven Corner Witch Shop and leaves for her computer.

```
Dear Chris Plant:

Amanda Garlic, Official Witch of Salem,
Massachusetts will be offering, to a select number
of students, intensive classes designed to harness
and expand psychic potential through witchcraft and
magic. Each class meets consecutively for five
weeks and the advance tuition price, $350.00 paid
in full, is non-refundable.
```

While Chris reads this out loud, Saki stares up at him expectantly. "Female frauds, all of them," Chris tells him and Saki wags his tail.

Chapter 32
RETREAT

The pitcher plants behind Grove Academy are encased in ice. "Look how delicate, shaped like an orchid, and hardy," says sweet, sturdy Sylvia Bell, who teaches girls' fitness and botany. "The color of the blossoms will be green suffused with red, just like the leaves. The nectar attracts insects."

Her fifteen-girl botany class, clustering around both the plants and Mike, the only male, are quite a lure—if you ignore anorexic Emerald and Donna the blimp. But Mike took the class out of genuine interest in growing herbs and mushrooms.

Emerald gets down on her knees to photograph the pitcher plant. Someone should really take her picture: spiky green hair, ears mutilated and decorated with five crystal earrings, painted cheeks and lips, a hunk of crystal dangling from a long gold chain. Emerald's mother, Bambi Skylark, has the lead in "The Return of the Sea Serpent," which has a lot of mirrors and magic crystal to ward off evil. Emerald got Grove girls into magic crystal to keep them from getting caught with a boyfriend, and to ward off Havelock Grimes, bad tripping, and rape by murderous local gangs.

"Tubular leaves are shaped like urns, trumpets, or small pitchers. From the lip along the outside on the ventral wing are stiff, downward-pointing hairs."

Sylvia Bell, who has lured sex-starved Mike into her class of hazardous girls, hands him a dry pitcher plant which makes him think of a mummified uterus.

"Insects trying to garner nectar here almost always fall into the pitcher and are trapped and digested by liquid secreted by the leaves," the teacher sweetly concludes.

Back in the classroom, Sylvia delivers an erotic lecture on the fertilization of ferns, which gets Mike aroused into mentally unbuttoning her big, ugly sweater. She notices the look in his eyes and picks on him, trying to trap him with questions, so he is forced to improvise the kind of lectures he is famous for: reckless deforestation, over-building, greed and violence, and harsh treatment of nature which hurts plant life, animals, and children. Mike's deep male voice and fanatical stare make his irrelevant generalities sound relevant. When he stops to catch his breath, it is so quiet he can hear ice crystals pelt window panes. "So much cruelty," he sighs.

Havelock Grimes, who has been listening into botany class on his newly installed monitor radio, hears the teacher give way to a sob, an example of the shocking lack of self-control in her classroom.

❋❋❋

"Mom," Mike says on the phone, "Havelock Grimes has had the entire school bugged by an alumnus-in-residence called Nigel. Regular kids have been forewarned by Caleb Fairfield and me.—Dad, are you on the line?— Guess not. We keep tune boxes blasting in the dorms to safeguard our right to privacy. Caleb taped my snoring and it sounds like an adenoidal rhino. He sells copies for ten bucks, and he deserves every penny and a medal. He keeps locks well-oiled for scouting around on his own business during the night. That's how he spied Nigel doing his installation job in the Grimes office.

"Can you imagine Havelock guzzling coffee at his desk and listening into classes? OK with me. Let him hear what I have to say. At least he won't get bored. And Mom, Eckert got his cowardly doberman, Buddy, back from a trainer and gave her to the school. Supposed to protect us from gangs, we were told. But guess what! She has been reprogrammed to sniff for drugs." There is a silence. "Mom, you there? No, my scars don't hurt, Mom. My inside is OK but I'm traumatized! and it's bad to be under surveillance day and night. Isn't that what your book is all about?" By the time Mike hangs up he is late for math, which he hates. "You wouldn't have missed me if they had killed me, Mr. Bornson," he says and successfully delays a test by talking about the sociological ecology of computers that are making arithmetic obsolete.

Havelock Grimes keeps the evidence of those small plastic bags locked in a rolltop desk on the locked porch adjoining the director's office, where old files of students are kept in a tall old wooden filing cabinet. Six years ago Al Hollowell had to wash the glass walls of the porch as a punishment for being late to classes. For some odd reason, the boy had painted big pointed teeth on the handles of the file cabinet, adorning the double-locked drawer which held his file with a crocodilian grin.

Evidence that Al was a bad egg locked in that cabinet. If anyone took the trouble, they'd learn that Al Hollowell set light to a stuffed squirrel, a bear rug, and a moose's head during an LSD trip. They'd find Al's formal letter: I had no choice. I had to do it. God told me to.

Havelock's office could have gone up in flames. Old books that nobody reads would now be ashes. The boy himself could have burned when his hair and sweater had caught fire. He came running out of the building. Ez Barrel, a young insomniac art teacher, saw the burning boy explode into his sleepless night as an alter ego erupting from his own abused brain cells. A confrontation, a challenge: Jacob wrestling a blazing angel. Ez burned his hand as he rolled Al in snow and mud.

The next day, Havelock Grimes had Al's scorched hair shaved off as a punishment. Instead of going to his hearing, Al went straight to the dorm, where he stuffed a few belongings into a backpack, made his way around the shack, and vanished out into the world, or underworld. Anyone looking at letters in that old file would find a copy of one of the first restraining orders served by a parent on a Grove student. Evidence that Alan senior, a furrier and importer of leather and furs from third world countries, had followed Havelock Grimes' advice to banish his only child, Alan, from the Hollowell's grand old colonial home.

The moose head, which had hung on that wall since the turn of the century when Grove Hall had been a summer home, now wears a mink toupee and patches that were donated by the boy's father. Mr. Hollowell remains on the Board year after year and brings to the meetings his wife Fiona, in yet another magnificent fur coat. They attend plays, recitals, and graduation ceremonies. Remaining part of the Grove community helps them live with their loss, loneliness, and regrets.

They don't like to talk about themselves. Neither of them ever has much to say, but they make a statement just by being around, especially at the yearly parents' talent show, when they perform their little tap dance to the Beatles' song "When I'm Sixty-Four." Their loyalty to Havelock Grimes and the Concept, which he could never get them to understand, has never changed. You have to believe in something.

When Havelock gets up and looks out of the window, there is Buddy, the doberman bitch, who was supposed to be tied up, pointing at the shed like a retriever and holding in her mouth that can of pet store flea powder she has been carrying around. Minutes later, the suspects Mike and Caleb come along to feed her. She drops the can; they pick it up and lure her away. Eckert must be told that she needs more retraining.

He brews fresh coffee in order to compose one of his famous briefs to all the Massachusetts parents. His mind is made up. He will no longer invite the Hollowells, who can be neither consoled, nor retrained.

We have found the quality of growth demonstrated in Grove Academy education is significantly increased by family involvement and resulting growth in our unique family-learning curriculum. Participation in this three-day learning program at the Silesian Sanctuary is required of your family. The cost is only $60.00 room and board.

The prorated tuition for this term is $5,750.00 plus a $50.00 damage deposit. The payment is due on or before the day you register for the retreat.

"Come in. Come in. It's cold," the old priest says to Liz. A striped kitten rubs against his long white apron and purrs. He stoops to pat it and blood rushes to his face. "Stray boys, dogs, kittens. They all find their way to our backdoor. We keep this shelter going by catering." He smiles rubbing his red hands. "A few years ago a boy from Grove Academy came here. His head was shaved and he was all stirred up. So many wild ideas!"

"What happened to him?" Liz asks.

"He stayed with us for a while. Worked in a garage until he had enough money to go to California. After a couple of years he was back working as a handy man in a doctor's house. Kept talking about saving wild animals."

"Was it Al?"

"Who knows? Troubled boys often change their names. Called himself Francis. St. Francis left the home of his wealthy parents."

"Isn't this a wild animal refuge?"

"The night before the hunting season starts, deer come into the park. They know. And so do the foxes."

Some of the nuns in the shelter had cared for the needy with that same cheerful resignation. He ushers her through a passageway to hang up her coat. "Roast pork or baked haddock and apple pie. Our own apples."

"I can smell it. Making me hungry."

"Kitchen on the main floor, not the basement. Unusual in an old house."

Liz is late. Heads turn when she walks into the conference room. She is used to being watched for all kinds of reasons, but the attention she is getting as the mother of Mike, a victim—belated words and looks of sympathy—in this assembly of fathers and mothers, makes her heart pound.

Priscilla comes to meet her. "Where's Chris?"

"At the Healing Center. Having his awareness reprogrammed." Everyone is staying for the weekend, but Liz is allowed to come and go because Mike was beaten up and Chris has had a bad reaction.

"We saved you a chair." Priss hurries back to hers.

The one empty chair is on the right side of Havelock Grimes, who sits at the head of a big circle of Massachusetts Grove parents. On his left side sits the coach; big chest, massive arms, bulging out of a red muscle shirt Dora gave Mike last Christmas.

Students are no longer allowed to wear muscle shirts. Liz herself tried to comply with the new Grove dress code for this retreat, in an understated, plain, sand-colored cotton shirt and matching skirt she bought for $22.99 at the Yesteryear Boutique. The Bergdorf $299.99 tag she forgot to cut off scratches the back of her neck as she walks around the circle. Pam, the plump mother of the skateboard artist, reaches out to whisper. "So sorry about Mike. That's Emerald's mother, Bambi Skylark, over there beside Priss. Beautiful! I must have seen her on TV, I think."

A gaunt, stylish mother Liz has not seen before is standing up in front of her chair talking in a loud, breathless voice, while Bambi Skylark moves her lips as though she were an understudy learning
a part.

"I was an unwanted child and never really wanted any children. My husband was an only child and wanted a large family. I was thirty-two years old when my boy was born. And I decided to have my tubes tied." Bambi even mimics the downcast eye at the end of the confession. "It's my fault that our Henry is having problems in school. I didn't give him brothers and sisters, and I refused to adopt," the mother goes on. "He got bored and lonely, took a car out of the garage, drove it out on the highway, and crashed. My fault. That's how the marriage broke up." She sinks into her chair casting imploring glances around the circle, tears in her eyes. Bambi's green eyes shimmer and flood, but her face remains expressionless, picture perfect.

Everyone in Shoreland thinks they have seen Bambi on TV but no one can remember just when. She is one of the many bland, expressionless sleek blondes. No one is invited to Arthur's house when she is staying with him. She is said to be shy.

Could Havelock Grimes be under her spell? Liz takes the empty chair beside him and is ignored, but the young father on her right, wearing curly replacement hair and reeking of Polo cologne, whispers: "Ben Hacket, lawyer. I'm divorced. Judge gave me custody of Ben Junior. A junior offender." He hands Liz two pamphlets:

OBJECTIVE:
NURTURE INTELLECTUAL GROWTH AND ACHIEVEMENT WHILE ADDRESSING ISSUES SURROUNDING THE DEVELOPMENT OF ONE'S CHARACTER. PROVIDE CONCRETE DIRECTION FOR PRESENT PARENTS AND MANY PAST PARENTS; TO ENABLE FAMILIES TO RESUME OWNERSHIP OF THE GROVE CONCEPT.

"You missed number one, 'Why am I here?'—That was supposed to open us up. They are now doing Who am I? Number two," Ben whispers. "The retreat is consciousness-raising. "

"Next!" says Havelock Grimes.

Priscilla, head of the parents' association, stands up to a round of applause for arranging this retreat at the sanctuary. Food is very good here, and it is all very cheap. She wears lilac-colored suede, seems quite sober, and has the perfect modified southern drawl for the story of a New Orleans girl stuck into a convent school by her mother. Condemned to wear an ugly green uniform, while her mother adorned herself in Parisian gowns.

Bambi soundlessly savors each word of Priscilla's lament: stuck into bed by nine o'clock when there was a party going on. Fifteen years-old and sent to stay with Grandmother during Mardi Gras. At convent school nuns declared any interest in boys and fancy clothes a sin you had to confess. "I thought of nothing else," Priss confesses. So does Bambi.

"As soon as I could, I entered the Miss America Pageant, and I won. My mother left for Europe, and Father died of a heart attack a few weeks after that. He was laid out in his coffin, one eye half open. I'll never forget that. I had gone against my parents and I still feel guilty. If my children ignore me, I do believe that is my punishment."

The room is two stories high, paneled in dark wood. Up in the center of a gallery stands a Christ figure exposing a bleeding heart—in reproach it seems to Liz—the way her Chris exposed the new red rash he has developed since Mike was hurt.

"Next!"

"I hated my father," says a stout, gray-haired father, who becomes disconcerted as he sees Bambi mouth his words. "Imagine taking me moose hunting when I was not much more than five-years old. Making me fire an air-gun at the moose. I was supposed to get the feel of the kill. The moose cried out. I have never forgotten that sound."

Liz, who never forgot the radio story of a moose hopelessly in love with the cow named Jessica, has a sickening vision of father and son murdering a lover moose.

Then the saddest of all the parents, Anthony, a dear, kindly, elderly Italian from a poor Italian family, says there had been too much love. Too many children. His emigrant parents had six children in a one and a half room apartment. He had to go to work when he was fourteen years old. And he did all right. Supporting his poor parents and an ailing wife, he had been both the boss of an oil delivery company and nurse at home. Then his wife died and left him three ailing children. Poor Peter, the baby, is a handicapped Grove student. A couple of mothers sob, uninhibited.

Anthony covers his face. So does Bambi.

The circle game of soul-searching fathers and mothers are making Liz drowsy and hungry like a child who stayed up too late. Even the notorious coach seems lovable; and Havelock Grimes, who is himself a father of sons and a divorced man, leans forward, holding his coffee cup with both hands like an offering—to himself.

"Next!"

Jason Goldfarb, a tired-looking father, is holding hands with little red-headed Gloria, the new wife that Jason junior, his only son, couldn't adjust to. This new mother—nervous, pretty, wearing little red pants and little red, high-heeled slippers—confesses that she is only two years older than Jason, and he was really crazy about her in high school when he invited her to party at his house. His dad was supposed to stay over in New York, but he walked in around ten o'clock. Gloria was the only one who hung around to clean up the mess. That's how she got to know Dad. They talked all night. She wised him up about drugs and sex. They drank left-over beer. "Dad and I—we fell in love."

"That's so beautiful," Mitch says with a sob in her voice.

Havelock cuts her off with a sharp, "Next. Bambi Skylark."

The actress draws herself up and takes a deep breath. "I could never please my father although I even married someone he liked. And then I could never please that man either." A trained voice. Her trained body revealed by a tight green dress, she speaks softly of her father's death. "He was lying in his big, carved bed and he turned his back on me and refused to speak. When I was leaving, he suddenly dragged himself to the top of the stairs. Stood there without a word. We never talked. I never told him how I felt. Now it's too late. I have bad dreams of him standing there, looking down, watching. And the only way I can get away from him is when I have a good director. Someone who reminds me of him, telling me what to do." The appeal of weakness in someone so perfect reaches a climax when her voice becomes inaudible, forcing you to read her lips for the ultimate confession, "I was never much of a daughter, and am not much of a mother."

She makes an unhurried exit, to sympathetic sobs. Who are they weeping for? Liz has to ask herself. The relentless ghost of a father? or the relentless daughter to a ghost? A moment of silence is interrupted by the racing engine of Bambi's getaway car. Ben turns to Liz. "You'd think she had it made, a lovely blond like that. You look as if you had it made too."

Most of the mothers at the retreat are blond—perhaps by choice. Those who cannot choose are noticeably absent. Mr. Goodley had given about twenty scholarships to negro students, but there are no negro parents at the retreat. Are they too poor or too proud to come here and tell their tragedy? They had stayed away from the Grimes election too. A few came to parents' weekend to watch their children distinguish themselves in games and shows. And one Jamaican couple had driven up in a rented white limousine. Perfect pair—handsome, laden with gold chains, adorned with glittering bravado smiles, displaying themselves like tropical birds.

"Betty, ready." Havelock says.

Betty Miles stands up, pale as though she spends her night with a vampire. Her scholarly husband watches, waiting, listening, and draining her with his intense sympathy. She bites into a tissue and gags herself. "Betty had a breakthrough at her group therapy session," he says. "She thinks a young uncle tried to rape her when she was in the second grade. When she told on him, her mother slapped her face, told her she had a dirty mind."

Liz has a breakthrough looking out the window at the park, remembering horse-and-buggy and sleigh rides here in this park with Gramp, Dora, Chris, and sometimes Bonnie. The Sanctuary is only a mile from the Black Stallion Condominium sign Leonard Myrtle put up when he converted Gramp's horse farm into a retirement home for members of the Shady Hill Hunt Club.

Gramp used to give the children turns holding the reins. After a sleigh ride there was always dinner at the Gray Fox Inn, where they could order anything, even two desserts. Does anyone else in this room remember the luxury of such good times? Bambi might have good times at South Cove. When she stays with Arthur, he does not call Liz.

"My turn," Ben, the lawyer stands up. "What would you say if you came home and heard Junior howling; your wife, a karate expert, beating him up?"

Caleb's father, Edwin, comes skittering into the room and laughs. "Karate, Priss. Just the thing." He perches on a side table swinging a leg.

"I was beaten as a child," Ben goes on. "It has left its mark. I took my son by the hand and we walked out on violence. I don't believe in corporal punishment."

Liz's editor had told her that middle or upper-class Americans are the book buyers. But how could such wounded mothers and fathers ever get engrossed in the understated story of one stolen child in Nazi Germany where bad news had been forbidden and complainers exterminated?

"I'll bet you are against the death sentence, Ben," Edwin speaks up. "Doesn't it save you a lot of time and money to stop a kid with a good karate kick before he goes out and gets into big trouble?" He is showing off and smiling across the room to Liz.

Havelock Grimes glares at him. "No debates. Next! Liz Plant!"

What could she say? Liz looks at the question, "Who am I?" What could be said that hasn't already been said? Mothers and fathers, reminding themselves of how they have all been abused, are beginning to droop, as though they had taken a beating. A spotlight of sun shines on Jesus, who looks like a mutilated flower child.

She considers herself privileged, not deprived. She had been that little disgrace. Hidden away at times by her little mother and later by Frau Faser. Not knowing where she came from, she did not have to resent any parent or be a rebel. Liz remembers kind and cheerful Gramp, Granny and Great-granny, Nanny, then doleful, faithful Anka, the encouragement from teachers, and never without her brother-husband Chris. "I am lucky." She sounds shockingly cheerful. Out of place, smiling, indecently healthy and happy.

"You were late. Let's go back to question one, "Why am I here."

She blurts out the truth, "We're afraid that Mike will have himself thrown out before the end of the school year."

The room echoes with laughter. Heartfelt truth often sounds slapstick. Grove parents keep laughing, especially Edwin. She feels like a clowning kid. "I wanted to ask Havelock about Buddy. Mike says the school now has a marijuana-sniffing dog."

Grimes is up on his feet. "Mike says. Mike says. That's your problem. It's all I ever hear. He talks too much. We know what happened to him, but he still has to follow the rules. And there is a rule against coaxing a guard dog into your room and keeping it there all night."

"He must feel he needs the protection!" Kindly, plump Pamela makes herself heard.

Grimes paces back and forth, fingering the air above his head. "I demand commitment to the Concept, loyalty. Do you as parents have the self-confidence and maturity you want? The formulation and implementation of a sense of purpose?" He is staring at the coffee urn. "Where are we as parents? " He's off into a lecture: parents as a team. "Where are we as a team?"

"Divorced, like our leader, Havelock," Ben mumbles.

"Where do we want to go, how do we get there?" Havelock brings in a Concept question, which allows another wounded couple to respond by accusing each other of violence, followed by a solo from a divorced mother about a husband who beat her each time her daughter misbehaved. By the time Harrison has his turn, Liz, who has been trying to write about physical violence, is beginning to wish for a law against indecent exposure of bleeding hearts.

"My girl had a fall on the dark steps behind the student union and broke her arm." Harrison leans forward, peering at the founder of the school through thick-lensed, dark-rimmed glasses. "Mike Plant waiting for a blind aunt almost murdered back in the dark. To hell with concepts! We don't want theories. We want our children safe."

Havelock is up on his feet pacing with an abrupt turn, as though caged "We! We! We! Each man for himself. Your girl was using drugs."

"Prescribed by her doctor!" Harrison jumps up and confronts Havelock. "Someone gave you more than half a million to improve the school, Havelock. Or was it an interest group? We should be told whether there are any strings attached. "Who's that man? If he's here let him stand up." He glares at Edwin Fairfield. "We need some straight talk. Less theory!"

Havelock fingers the air. "We! We! We. Speak for yourself, man!"

"You talk for yourself too much. 'Let it be dark!' We heard about that. And two of our children end up in the hospital. Imagine!"

"Get out, man!" Grimes bellows and hitches up his pants. "OUT!"

Portly Harrison pulls down his camel-hair sweater and sticks out his chin, steps out into the ring with Havelock, who is wiry and thin as a young man. The big coach is up and ready, bulging in the little red muscle shirt. Harrison's gentle wife, Brenda, goes to him, whispers something and takes his hand. They leave as a team.

It is not over. Havelock hoists a chair onto his back and walks around the circle, like a wrestler in the ring. "Control, control. We have here a manipulative controller! That's why his child is out of control."

"Awesome," Ben whispers to Liz." Last time he did that stunt a mother fainted."

"How about Harrison and Brenda?" she asks.

"They're out," Ben concludes.

"What does any of it have to do with our children?" Liz softly asks.

Havelock couldn't have heard her, but he veers around, lowers the chair and confronts her. "Mike's father was absent at my election. Absent again at our retreat. How about that absent husband?"

It's like being fully dressed in a nudist colony and asked to disrobe. Someone setting tables in the adjoining dining room chimes with silverware. Outside, a flock of starlings, a perfect community of birds, has landed on the trees.

"He's also her brother." Edwin, father of Caleb, speaks up, creating a little uproar of questions and involuntary laughter.

Havelock Grimes shows his teeth. "Not your turn, sir!"

Fluffy, the stray cat, comes walking into the middle of the circle with unhurried grace, sits down, and displays herself washing her tail end. Fathers and mothers laugh and keep laughing. "Here kitty, kitty, kitty." The cat jumps up and runs to Liz, who didn't coax. The luncheon bell rings.

Chapter 33

MILLION DOLLAR VIEW

Bonnie calls herself a Sunday painter. There are Sunday drivers—horseback riders, snowmobile types and Sunday sailors—like Jeff. Painting to her is getting away from it all; she doesn't make much of it. But the view she used to paint from her window of the old Hodges house with the widows walk was snatched up by local historians and collectors. Even Leonard Myrtle, the contractor who ripped the historic house apart, has one hanging on his office wall. Her watercolor landscape and flower paintings shimmer with the delight in what is here today, before it's gone.

When Liz looks at Bonnie's painting of the grand house, she can almost hear music drifting across the water. Gramp used to take Dora to house concerts there and dancing parties at South Point that had been going on for two generations of summer people, but ended with Violet. The daughter with long dancing legs and the longest red hair in Shoreland, who married Cod Spiral a dancing carpenter. They lived at South Point the year round and had two sons in a row, by the time Del was born Cod already drank a lot and stopped dancing and started drifting. Violet stayed on at South Cove with her kids. The two boys took after their father and went wild in Florida, driving a stolen Bentley. So, like several other divorced women on the North Shore, Violet sold her home to the

Reverend Sorrel for one dollar and a permanent cottage in the True Bible Christian Community where kids are taught to pray, play the flute, the harp, or the piano, sing and circle dance like Shakers to stay out of trouble—if they don't run away. Del Hodges, the pregnant high school dropout, now hangs around Harbor Square, and is planning to run off to California to find her boyfriend Jiggers.

In the meantime the Reverend Sorrel had quietly sold South Cove to Leonard Myrtle for two hundred thousand. Only a month later, Myrtle had quietly sold it to Arthur Eckert, a stranger, for three hundred and fifty thousand and a contract of equal value to rebuild and insulate. The racket of hammering and sawing had annoyed Chris in warm weather, when he likes listening to his records on the terrace.

Arthur wanted to have privacy and space. Walls had been taken down to create a fifty-foot livingroom, expanded by mirrors reflecting sky and water, winging birds, and fragments of the small collection of modern paintings everyone who is anyone in Shoreland is now dying to see and ready to deplore.

Too much color, too much light for Liz, who arrives flushed, breathless, and furious; dark as a shadow in black jeans and a black top. "How could you back Grimes with all that money? *Sie kennen diesen Menschen nicht!* You don't know that man." No better language for anger than German.

Arthur bends over her hand, barely brushing it with his beard. Then he picks up the dog he gave to her and kisses him, gazing into her eyes. "So, that did it. Too busy rewriting to come to parties, a cup of tea, or a drink. Now you come running to scold me... All I asked was that the trustees keep their mouth shut."

It has been foggy and warm for several days. Now the afternoon glare shivers on white walls, rounded white modern furniture imported from Rome. Arthur, leaning back in a white wing chair, dressed in a white turtleneck and trousers, blends in like a winter hare, while Liz, stands out. "Little Emerald is now terrified that the gang will come looking for her again. Always liked to show off dressing up, dancing, singing. Now she wants to go around in a trash bag. Bambi keeps her jewelry in the safe. Her furs have been hanging in the closet out here until Hollowell picked them up just now. An animal rights fanatic has painted a slogan on the Hollowell van. His driver got scared. So Hollowell gave Bonny the list to call his Shoreland customers and came to pick up furs himself. Opened his mouth, told Bonnie and God knows who else that I gave money to keep Grove going. On top of that he had the impudence to turn around and say that he had to pick up furs for storage so early because I brought an infestation of moths to Shoreland from abroad!"

"I wore mine only that one time when you saw me in Boston. That day a woman had a fake fur cut up in the parking garage."

"Where is the freedom? It's getting more and more dangerous to show off in a fur coat, as I do. Just look! There goes the Hollowell fur van now, with a police escort. Perfect view. You see what's going on and hear nothing."

"Only Bach," Liz says. Len Myrtle, insulating specialist, has done it again: Arthur can listen to Bach, behind spaceage window walls made of insulated one-way mirror glass. No boat, bird watcher, tree-climbing boys like Jonathan and Billy, no trespassing peeping Tom, spy, or thief can window gaze at South Cove. Noise is shut out. Gulls circle without shrieking, Ralph Poach, the electrician's truck rattles soundlessly up to Myrtle Knoll condos that sit above Rocky Beach like warts. Paul Deed's outboard lobster boat bobs on the choppy water from empty trap to empty trap, while the scuba diver's black van drives away with lobsters. And four public works men stand around in Main Street watching a fifth one drilling.

Liz, the writer, would describe this million-dollar view as a gigantic TV screen—its sound cut off—giving an unrelenting picture of endangered beauty, prevailing deceit. Until you raise your eyes to the gilded illusion of angel-hair clouds in the ice-blue sky, setting you adrift to the end of the horizon where the ice-blue sky meets ultramarine water.

Arthur talks along with the well-tempered ripple of the clavichord about the Eckerts, who had been wonderful parents, but not very musical. "My mother's young sister was an actress and she loved Bach. By the time I was about seven years old she had become quite famous as a film star, but my parents did not approve of her lifestyle. She was living with a married man. A famous director. I was walking home from school. She got out of a white car draped in white fur and sparkling with jewels, drew me aside, and asked me whether I might want to be an actor one day. She was a bewitching beauty. I never forgot the way she bent down to kiss the top of my head and said *"Auf Wiedersehen*, don't tell your parents!" I loved her, and had dreams of being a child star in one of her films. I kept waiting for her to come back, day after day. Finally I saw her picture in a newspaper. She had left Germany and was on her way to Hollywood with her Jewish film director, Schreiber, a married man. And the article said that she was going to make films with all those Hollywood Jews. Then, as I grew older I was told Jews were mercenary and they had destroyed Germany.

"When I told my father I wanted to go to America and live with my aunt. My parents put me into the Hitler Youth to give me discipline instead. You had to follow orders, work out, march. The discipline actually made me strong."

"You became an officer?"

"I was a young actor when the war started. Believe me. I used my talent. And abused it too." He takes her hand as though he were on stage and playfully brushes it with his beard as she pulls it away. "You are such a good listener. *Genug.* Enough. I'm talking too much," he says and goes on to talk about New York women who start talking about themselves the moment they hear his accent because he reminds them of their analyst. "I find myself appalled by that kind of self-centered chatter." While he proceeds to fondle Saki, he hems Liz in with his glances and his smiles and that million-dollar view.

Binoculars on a side table would facilitate both bird-and people-watching. Light ripples over white walls and white furniture. When the shadow of three gulls glides over the wall Saki jumps down and softly growls. "What happened to your parents?"

"They were killed during a bombing raid. Our home was destroyed. Nothing was left when I came back. Then, a Red Cross telegram came from California, signed Aunt Ursel. Schreiber had done well in Hollywood, but she didn't have a chance to make the most of her talents in America. They had no children. I went to live with them. We got along well as long as they didn't ask me about the war. Nazi films were popular. I didn't want to be cast as a Nazi villain, so I learned to direct from Schreiber and worked with him until he died. After my aunt died I inherited their wealth. I have a good life." He waves towards the million-dollar view, in a gesture that includes Liz. "I'm happy just now… Why are you laughing? Why is that funny?"

"You smell like Mike. Polo Cologne."

"Present from Emerald. Her father lives in Paris, he is a diplomat. She has turned to me. And doesn't Father Bach give you the feeling that all is well? His children were trained musicians. A true German father and a perfectionist. Masterful structure and harmonies. Do you know that the sound waves can control both animal and human behavior?"

"Through subliminal persuasion? Not that new. Just think of the Nazi marching songs at those big rallies and now the rock concerts. And if Havelock Grimes forbids rock music, you can always make up for it by piping in the right kind of subliminal music to help him control the kids."

"It's no joke, Liz. Here we are. Just think of us sitting up here. We see what is going on in the village but hear nothing but healing harmonies. While thanks to me Havelock Grimes, the old fox, sits in his office at Grove, sees nothing, but listens into classrooms. That seems to be his style. Fanatics do have blinders on. And there is small difference between a dedicated educator and a fanatic. But you can't allow the young to become a threat."

"Grown-ups have been a threat to kids century after century."

"You can't consider discipline a threat, Liz."

"Can't I?"

He closes his eyes for a second. "Those pages from your book I read at the dump went too far. You write well, but I'm not sure that you can link our teenage hoodlums who have not been disciplined and are out of control, with Hitler Youth. We were trained—"

"To death!" Liz can feel herself flush with annoyance. How could he judge her writing from the pages she had thrown out at the dump? "Of course you shouldn't have to justify the story you're working on," he says without apology. "But, *Kind*, you and I were exposed to monstrous over-simplifications under Hitler."

Does he indicate that she is writing like a simplistic Nazi? What is there to say? He doesn't like the idea of her writing any more than Chris does. She sits quite still in the blinding light, clasping her hands tight with a smile, to hide the dismay like hunger pangs she feels when she is torn away from her desk.

"I often thought how nice it would be to have you here—not at parties, but by yourself. And here you are, disguised as a teenage boy. He averts his eyes. "You wouldn't have come to see me just now, if Chris hadn't listened in on another line and butted in, telling me you couldn't come. He is possessive isn't he?"

"He thinks you are." Saki stands up and puts his front paws on her knee possessively.

Arthur laughs like a boy, but frowns like an old man. "Before you were married when you both lived in New York, were you free to go out with other men?"

"Of course! He often introduced me to someone he liked."

"You shared an apartment?"

"No. Mine was at Grammercy Park. The size of my first class cabin. Chris and I usually met with our friends at Pete's Tavern. The bartender always said, 'Welcome aboard.' He was right. The young crowd behaved like shipboard acquaintances. Never kept in touch after we left." A sunbeam reflected from mirror to mirror flames up in the unpleasant tempest of a purple and black abstract painting.

"Catulle said that you ran away to Europe and didn't want to keep in touch. He adored you. After I bought two paintings of you at his gallery he told me how he first noticed you with Chris at a penthouse party, and asked you to sit for a portrait. This made your career as a model." Arthur gets up. "I keep his paintings in my office since the burglary. Come and see."

He hurries ahead of Liz in fast, short parade steps and unlocks the door to an old New England bedroom made over into a Madison Avenue gallery with a huge black desk that has lion's paws, a chair which is a theatrical throne, and an occasional chair in the shape of a giant hand. The Catulle oil paintings on the wall facing the desk are not real portraits but cartoons. A Liz baby-face with huge, sad eyes and smile, but the body of a wispy child. Costumes and setting were Catulle's fantasy and formula. A lace slip that is about to slip, a purple yo-yo, the inevitable sliced pomegranate, a few scattered seeds on a dark side table look exquisitely real. Then the same girl in ballet tights holding a hoop, bubbles drifting. In the third the slip has dropped from her left shoulder exposing a minute nipple, which is the same translucent red as the drop of blood on her finger and the rose in her hand.

"Technically flawless details, rather like Salvador Dali—definitely a good investment—I told myself when I bought the paintings. Bambi says it's my worst investment: giving in to my fixation with that face. But trained observers can never observe themselves. Bambi says that my two ex-wives and she are all the Catulle type. You, of course, are the real thing."

He stares not at Liz, but past her at the paintings. *"Unwiederstehlich,* irresistible," he says and takes a step away. "Catulle knew how I felt. The one with the rose, and the drop of blood on her finger was a commission. When I met him he was already living at the Pierre. After a few drinks he'd always confess that he simply took advantage of a trend. What with Nabokov's best seller, 'Lolita'. My Fair Lady on Broadway. Followed by 'Breakfast at Tiffany's'. Skinny kids like Audrey Hepburn were fashionable. So he got rich by assembly line painting you as his 'brat.'"

"Chris thought he made up the stories of the family estate, when I posed for him."

"Half naked?" Arthur asks with a sly glance.

"Never. I didn't even have to change my clothes. He invented the body and the costume. At first, when I sat for him, he painted one or two pictures a day. When they started to sell, he could not turn them out fast enough. Chris helped with titles like 'Alone', 'Waiting', 'Forsaken', 'Lonely Game.' Catulle would have ten canvasses or more on the rug in his room at the Hotel Pierre. Starting with the eyes and the smile. The props were a formula too: a spider's web here, a rose there, and the famous pomegranates."

Arthur picks Saki up and holds him like a baby. The puppy relaxes in the sun and closes his eyes. "I was invited, Liz, and I arrived at his big opening when you were trying to bounce Ethel Merman, who had paid for the champagne but didn't have an invitation. She was furious. Then she saw the Catulle girls all had your face and started shouting, 'That brat! Here's that brat!' The crowd gaped at you and the pictures on the wall and started to buy them. I later met you at another party, and wanted to talk to you, but you were besieged and Chris acted like a bodyguard."

"We met Jarret, the magazine editor, that night, and he wanted to use my face for a cover. He would have loved this room, especially the 'handchair.'" Liz tries it out. Fingers yield and comfortably cup her.

"No one can ever resist this chair." Arthur comes over to show her how it turns and swivels. "Usually I buy something I really like at once, but I was going through an expensive divorce at the time. A year later, when Catulle had his own gallery, I bought his paintings and commissioned the one with the rose. You were in Europe. He didn't need you as a model anymore."

"He bragged how men bought a painting and left candy and flowers and pomegranates because they thought the child looked hungry in the picture. I was in the gallery when a Texan bought four 'Lil Gals' and wanted to feed you big steaks in the worst way." He laughs and he keeps on laughing, when Liz tries to get up, but can't get out of the ridiculous chair. "Trapped again. Caught in someone's fantasy." He enjoys his own joke, and can't stop laughing, while he holds the chair down. "You must have been well trained to be someone's fantasy."

She can feel herself flush."You were someone's fantasy too when you put on Nazi uniforms. The New Order in Germany was all theater. You said so yourself."

"An oversimplification. When you write about this you must make it clear that Germany had been defeated and humiliated by the first war. Hitler's fantasies of a New Order, a great new Germany, revived pride."

"Arrogance!" And arrogance made Arthur buy a New Order for Grove Academy. Liz walks away from the paintings and out. Arthur locks up. "So you went to Europe. Catulle said you ran away from him."

"I was turning into a Catulle Brat. He became impossible. I had turned into a type. It all got to be too much."

"Zu viel, mein Kind, too much, my child. He guides her by the elbow as though she had suddenly become frail and aged, and leads her back to the million-dollar view where Bach reverberates from insulated mirror glass. She stands at the north end of the room, looking out over the water to Harbor Square. Saki jumps up on a chair and looks out with her. Arthur, the trained observer, follows her eyes. Mike's friends are specks of color.

"Whenever I see you at the benches with those kids, you look so happy. It make me sad and lonely as a ghost. Always trying to protect someone or save something I can't control." He gets up, stretches. "Enough. We have both earned a Campari and soda."

She didn't give him any warning. He didn't have time to stage her first visit. He is gone for awhile. Leaving her alone after drawing her into a story full of echoes. She closes her eyes to the glare of the million-dollar view which is reflected in mirrors. The harmony of Bach, that sublime perfectionist, and Arthur have drained her. He has chosen the music, as he had planned the decor of this room, this house. Timing now his absence from the room could be staging, leaving nothing to chance, as Bach—master of definitions with the well tempered clavichord—overpowers the soul with subliminal persuasion. Mike would say, "wipes you out."

Shut away here in his controlled environment with this romantic stranger, the million-dollar view of the ocean, without the sound of rushing waves. A million-dollar view of Harbor Square without the sounds, the thrill of jarring discords from tune boxes, the excitement of bashing and grinding skateboards. Their gossip and worries and secrets.

She can hear Bach prepare harmonies of a prolonged climax like a fatherly lover, while a trapped fly bumbles around a window and glasses tinkle discreetly in a recess.

Liz and Saki get to Harbor Square in time to interrupt a fight between Svenson and the biker. Barney drops his Frisbee and barks. Can that be Tom the Tick trumpeting a string of commands like a football coach from the vantage point of the sewer pipe? Liz doesn't even remember exactly when Mike's voice changed. "Where is Del?" "Finding God!" The biker shouts back. A staring Neighborhood Watch eye painted on his glossy black leather jacket has been enhanced with three big tears that could be something a gull did. Saki pulls away from Liz and runs around and around the chopper trailing his leash. "Jesus loves all creatures!" The biker's chopper barely misses Saki and flattens Barney's blue Frisbee, roaring off past the Candle Den, scaring the gulls on the Sweater Shop roof. At Miss Maureen's Beauty Nook he brakes so hard the big gold crucifix dangling down his front hits the handlebars with a ping you can hear in the square.

Kids settle down. You can hear the steady hammering of carpenters renovating historic fishermen's shacks into gift shops, the clamor and shrieking of gulls and, grinding saws.

"Del isn't like hid'n out at your house, is she?" You can hear Elgar's grief in his voice as in his songs.

"No."

"Her mom kicked her out." Always half in love with someone's girl. Elgar bites his fingernails. "I did put her up for a couple of days in the shelter. Tried to talk her out of hitching a ride to Frisco and Jiggers."

"Ends up in the hospital." New voice, but the same Tick. "Baby was dead. Never lived."

Elgar lets his head droop. "Her Mother like wants to pin the kid and everything on me. Just because I'm here and Jiggers split. Shelter is locked.

I can't play my tunes."

Tom jumps down from the bench. Sneakers unlaced to "look cool" make him trip and fall forward and get up cursing the biker, who is having his curls done at the Beauty Nook practically every day while Del is missing. "A queer and a nut like that shouldn't be running around loose."

"Unfair. Free country," says Svenson, who has been called names and told he shouldn't be running around loose many times. The boys would blame the stranger who rides a chopper they would like to own, the way German boys blamed Jews. Gypsies they executed because they knew how to enjoy themselves and make music through life, unencumbered by wealth, stealing without malice, whatever took their fancy—even blonde babies—long before Himmler had that idea.

The blue water sparkles between the one-story shacks turned into shops, the sawing stops. There are a lot of FOR RENT signs every fall after they go out of business. Rents are too high. Some of the new tenants are already busy scrubbing, polishing, painting everything up so bright and expectant, it makes you squint. Sights and sounds of renovation, beautification on the neck, and in the Beauty Nook, are accompanied by old and new ugly gossip broadcast in the loud voices of women under dryers, which is a convivial form of spring-cleaning.

Gulls go GEE GEE GEE and then cackle like hens. Women setting men right. It has happened before and it can happen again. Everyone knows the story of Anne the patient seamstress, who lost all patience and organized an uprising of women in 1856. The Beauty Nook had been her home and women brought to her with their clothes for alterations their sadness, because husbands spent money they earned on rum, while children starved. Anne led women in a rampage, swinging hatchets against rum barrels. A famous picture of the event shows men lapping up rum from the gutter.

In the Beauty Nook, the biker sits motionless as granite, while Miss Maureen rolls his hair into her usual curlers. Just give Miss Maureen time and she'll cut and bleach his hair, Tom says to Liz in his new manly voice. Even his own Mom has turned into a fuzzy blonde at the Beauty Nook. The moment Dora comes out of there, the boys duck, and Liz instinctively takes cover with them. But you don't have to worry, Dora does not look around. She walks with that disgruntled look of disapproval that goes with the angel style, and those big rimless glasses from handsome Dr. Turner, who teases the women, makes them all laugh and love him, and wear prescriptions that make them see every speck of dust, or crack on the wall, or line in faces, enlarging all that is imperfect and flawed. Just before Dora turns the corner she looks up to clouds that are perfect for her in their own way, she starts to sing to herself. Her face softens. You can see her as Elgar's mother, and Gramp's brazen filly.

Kids on the bench start talking about Crunchy seated on a rock above a cove, grinding his mother into hamburger, the way Hitler School children had talked about the Inspector—just to make themselves sick. Elgar thinks someone should check and see what's inside the dead mother's pocket book, which Crunchy carries all the time. Might be a clue.

What would boys be without spooks and spooks without children? The ugly Herr Inspector, who ate mountains of scrambled eggs may well have put on a monster act, with the intention of saving children, while a deranged Lucas, who stalked and killed might not have known his own intention. Should people be judged by their intention or their deed?

"No one cares," Elgar says.
Del's missing. Mike almost killed. The boys sit stunned into silence. It might all happen to them, they might be alone, on the run, hurt, murdered by a gang. Get the disease.

Tick starts passing around pills like candy. She's left out, ignored, as they flaunt information, also misinformation, about pills, sharing what they can find from medicine cabinets. They share anything good or bad: Anything is better than nothing. Why put up with feeling beat?

This troop will test Liz—the cross-over mom, when they want her to get lost, disappear, *verschwind*. But now, as she obliges and walks away with Saki, a million-dollar view of herself, affords her the perspective of leaving boys to gulp pills a mother should grab from them. When she turn around at the corner, they have already formed a circle and are playing Hackie Sack. A game that excludes her.

Chapter 34

FAKE ECSTASY

The ups and downs, beginnings and end-alls of Shoreland and the world flit by the great stationary bike-travel buff Emmet Gray, retired banker, senior senior citizen. By 9 a.m. on the dot, he makes his rest stop and goes outside his front door to put a fifty dollar check for his grand-nephew Caleb Fairfield the Third into the slot for the mailman to pick up.

He feels younger by the minute standing on the stoop in the warm sun, showing off his new sky-blue Spandex outfit, when Liz Plant waves to him from her moped. He flags her down to let her know that things seem to be looking up at Grove Academy. Caleb had serious problems. Now the dorm master's wife got the boys to make brownies and send them to their families. The idea is to give something instead of always expecting to get. "When I made a rest stop after the first two miles for my apple juice, I ate a couple of those goodies."

Liz lifts her helmet visor. "I just got some from Mike. They are deli-cious!" Cookies from Mike gave Liz the boost to finish correcting, then print out and mail those rewritten chapters with pleasure and pride.

Emmet chuckles. "I seem to be getting a lot of presents these days. My friend Thelma Nesbit, that tease, gave me this Spandex outfit. I foxed her and put it on. I always wear the helmet in case I get dizzy and fall off. And I'm glad you're wearing yours on that dangerous vehicle. I always know you by that jacket. You look like a delivery boy. "

Cars and trucks used to almost force Liz off the road when she wore jeans and that motorcycle helmet on a low-speed moped. She had tried a skirt and helmet, and that made certain drivers slow down, honk, and whistle. The Pizza Parlor jacket Mike found at the Dump Boutique turned out to be the best protection—for him too when he illegally rides the moped—because someone on business is treated with respect.

Emmet says she should get rid of the noisy moped. A regular bike is far better exercise, a bike like his by far the safest. "I'm doing Compiegne now. Having a ball studying the history of that old town. A peace treaty was signed in the castle. Which one? I read about it yesterday and now I can't quite remember. Bonnie called the French tourist office for me, and they are sending pamphlets and posters for free. The castle is a must. Napoleon the Third lived there."

Liz turns off the noisy engine. "Compiegne? Isn't that where Joan of Arc was locked up?"

"You sure know your history. That poor child. I have just put a brochure picture of her statue in the mail for Caleb. Better than any card I could buy. Only a young girl, but what courage! Caleb's a big boy, but not much of a go-getter. Grew too fast. His father is hard on him. That's why Caleb sent the brownies to me. Best I ever tasted."

"The best!" That's what Liz told Mike this morning. He usually calls collect and a direct call from a pay-phone spells trouble. Liz did try to tell herself that the Grove Concept was taking effect, but she became uneasy when he wanted to know how she was feeling, how many brownies she had eaten, whether she had been able to rewrite.

"Find out how Caleb is doing when you talk to Mike, will you?" Emmet asks. "The boys don't like that fellow—the new principal—no, the first one. He started the school. Can't think of his name. Hammock?—No Havelock. Funny name for an educator. What business had this Eckert to pay out all that money to bring him back? A mistake in my opinion. Well, on to Paree! By Friday I'll be on highway A1."

"Did the German army take that road during the war?"

"I wasn't in the war, but I suppose so." He hesitates. "They moved fast. Didn't stop to study history or explore."

Emmet doesn't seem to be studying and exploring the history of Hitler's Blitzkrieg, that earthquake of bombs and the rapid invasion, an

infestation of France by a plague of conquering boys in uniform, raven-
ously vengeful vandals, destroying whatever they had been told to dislike,
stealing what they considered valuable—like blonde children. The French
boy they had named Rudolf at Hitler school was almost as tall as Jan, but
had no talent for the German language. He kept speaking French even in
his sleep. When he was beaten up by Frau Faser, the children didn't care.
Why should he get away with it? Then he had vanished—not the usual
way. He somehow escaped. But how?

Emmet says he'll do OK if he does 50 kilometers to Paris by next
week. That is about thirty-one miles. "Got to beef up enough French to
show off and order dinner for Thelma and the right champagne at the
Chat Noir. Black Cat, in Cambridge, you know. Last year—that great
Hungarian feast—Thelma ordered coffee at the Cafe Budapest—not to
drink, just to sniff. Have you ever heard of such a thing? Can't remember
the name of her hundred-dollars-an-ounce French perfume. Well, must be
on our way. Have a good one now."

Emmet closes the door. His outfit makes Liz smile, and Spandex does
show his paunch, but also his good legs. Today he did his duty to report
that red speeding Corvette to the police. Then back to pedaling around
Compiegne. No sight-seeing American riding on a tour bus would get as
much history. He is smiling to himself, thinking of that French dinner in
Boston—the end of this journey—perhaps his last. Caleb says it's good to
let it happen in your head just the way you like it. Emmet set him straight:
not with drugs and alcohol! You have to use your own steam to get the real
feel of all that terror and beauty of life each single God-given day.

Liz is still smiling when she leans into the curve on the wooded stretch
of the shore road with pleasure. She had found it easy to rewrite this
morning and mail finished chapters to Robie. Sunlit water sparkling
through pines and young silver birch; the empty road ahead, she buzzes up
the hill, with the one upmanship of being lucky, perhaps too lucky and
comfortable in this rare part of the world. Such a rare hometown self-con-
gratulation, always containing the silent warning: enjoy this sunny day
while it lasts.

Chris was happy with her this morning. He didn't eat any of Mike's
cookies, because sweets were not allowed in his new health regime. When
she had trouble starting the moped, he leaned out the upstairs bathroom
window telling her to check the gas, try the tickler. She was thinking how

well he looks and how pleasant he always is when he becomes interested in anything that is out of sorts. It was thoughtful of him to make her wear the motorcycle helmet Mike picked out, really more for himself. The dark visor always makes Liz feel like a female knight. She put on an Evel Knievel act for Chris, rolling the moped to a start, jumping on and riding right through the sheets she had hung up to dry. It is OK to act like a clown, not OK to feel like one, she had told Arthur Eckert. You have to be careful. He admitted that there was that same difference between a man in uniform and a uniform. "Once you allowed yourself to become 'a uniform,' a type, hurting and killing becomes clowning around."

Thoughts spin through her head as fast as the fast ride on a slow moped. A travelog view of South Cove flits by for her at a clearing. Gulls shriek as they fly back and forth from the sea to the top of Witches Hill. Etruscan seers might have read danger signs in the turbulence of winging birds and heard warnings in their shrieks. Or could warning signs merely indicate fear the seer passes on, promoting bad luck with warnings? I have to stop worrying about Mike, Liz tells herself.

A rescued greyhound lies waiting in front of a converted church. She stops at the old Riverbay Pharmacy and Variety Store. The dog turns around and races back to the antique store. Animals find their way home. Miss Nesbit's lazy pig, had been the daughter of a legendary sow who was sold to a farmer in New Hampshire, escaped and showed up thin and tired on her Shoreland home farm two months later.

Elated with the idea that she might be writing her way home to Mother, she breaks at and almost hits the hitching post in front of the weathered old clapboard pharmacy-variety store building. Crying out for a paint job which the new self-help gas station—that eyesore in front—should help pay for. Liz opens the door to a whiff of home-baked blueberry muffins. When Mike and Elgar were in grade school and had their first bikes, Liz used to ride over here through the woods with them along the old fire road.

The ceiling fan in the pharmacy section turns at half speed with a plaintive squeal. Harry, both short-order cook and pharmacist, keeps it running summer and winter. And summer and winter he wears his red checked overshirts and his red hunting cap to protect himself against drafts from the door.

Liz takes off her helmet. "Hi!"

"Look who the wind blew in." Harry says. "Long time no see."

She orders coffee and a blueberry muffin.

Old-timers sit along the counter nursing cups of coffee and talking about the rumor that Myrtle wants to build condominiums up at Tompkins quarry. Harry points out that Myrtle does bring rich people like Eckert into town. Harry brings Liz coffee and a big blueberry muffin. "Everyone enjoys a lot of sweet stuff at this time of the year," he says.

"How about those darned seals," says Boomer, a stout man leaning against a glass case filled with a mess of combs, curlers, nonprescription drugs, cosmetics, and candy. There is usually someone in the pharmacy aisle waiting for prescriptions or medical or personal or legal advice from Harry.

"The seals didn't have to be lured, they came to be extras in the movie like you, Boomer," says Dick, the retired mailman.

Boomer, who has been teased too much about his new career as an extra in the movies, ignores this remark and goes to study the bulletins pinned up to the right of the door. "Save the endangered predators," he scoffs. "What the hell! I was working at Benton Club for the drag hunt. No fox, but this nut shows up dressed like a circus clown with a SAVE-THE-FOX sign. Pulls a woman off her horse, rips up her fox-fur hat, and everything."

"There was an endangered-animal-rights clown in Boston and he—" Liz fails to make herself heard.

"That clown was one of her three endangered ex-husbands, if you ask me," Boomer speaks up in his growly voice. "That's why she didn't report nothin'."

Everyone knows that his wife Ruth walked out on him after his fishing trawler sank. One of several boats that went down since foreign factory vessels started emptying the sea. Now Ruth wants some of the insurance money and Boomer hangs out at the Variety to get legal advice from Harry on how to keep it. "Struck it rich three times. Women like that are asking for trouble," he says with feeling.

Lucas the serial murderer had made it clear that women are always asking for anything bad that happens to them and have no one but themselves to blame for what he did. **DEL NEEDS TO HEAR FROM JIGGERS URGENT!** stares at you from the bulletin board, where it has hung all winter. The door opening in rain, snow and wind soon curls notices that are not pinned down on all four corners. Old faded notices are taken down by those who need a thumb tack to put up their own, but a rare love note is left on the board. Some, like Del's, have phone numbers at the bottom that you can just tear off. Isn't Del asking for more trouble? What are the intentions of either one Jiggers or other lonely man, who tore eight phone numbers off? The intention of those who had responded to a war child in search of Mother was perhaps not even clear in their own minds.

Twin stroller. Brand new. Never used. $60.00

Phone numbers at the bottom of the note have all been torn off. There must be plenty of newborn twins around.

Widowed Young Grandmother will Babysit.

Find help! Premenstrual Stress Syndrome Support Group Meets Monthly. $5.00 donation accepted

Found black cat wearing orange ribbon. Very pregnant.

Emily Jones. Proud mother of six sons and two daughters running for selectman

Selectman has been scratched out "Why not select *women*?" someone wrote under it. Two girls are hitching horses to the old post in front of the store. The tall girl has a beautiful white pony, the short girl a big old nag, which she pats, then reaches up and kisses on the nose. The horse bares its teeth. The girls laugh. They have kindly, round faces.

"Good girls, the Baker sisters. They ride up the hill every chance they get to help take care of their Grandma," says one of the old timers.

Come and enjoy fried dough and coffee Saturday at the Whale Harbor First Baptist Church $1.50

Witches League for Public Awareness, working to protect civil rights.

The Witches of Eastwick is a defamation.
P.O. BOX 4337 Salem, Mass. 01971

Early chilly spring is a time for brownies, fried dough, and conviviality. Why not turn the Unitarian Church coffee hour into a magnificent swap shop event? A bereaved mother who never used the twin stroller might adopt a kitten; the widowed young grandmother could give helpful home remedies to the girls with menstrual stress syndrome. The sisters come in and order chocolate milkshakes. The din of the blender cuts into their easy talk about Maggie, the horse their Dad had to buy, because it turned out that without that big nag, the white pony refused to leave the stable. Grandma likes to sit at the window watching the trail for their horses.

Harry goes around refilling cups. Liz loads hers with sugar. Those brownies, now the sweet blueberry muffin—all that sweet stuff turn life into one big bulletin board for those who want something and those who have something to offer. She can feel her heart beat to a new tune.The horsey girls might meet and share some of Del's jiggers. A rusty truck drives up. Violet—the mother of pregnant, high school drop out Del driving the truck her dancing carpenter mate left behind. She climbs down and hurries into the store, ignoring the men. "Liz, I'm glad you're here." Her violet eyes full of tears, as she leans over Liz. "Do you know where Del is?" she whispers.

"No. I don't."

"I'm going out of my mind! Had to try and get my ex out of jail in New Hampshire," she goes on whispering. "While I was gone, Del emptied the house, sold the furniture, and vanished. She must have had help." Violet stifles a sob with an embroidered handkerchief. "Some of the old furniture from South Cove. What's left is all out on Route 1 at Agatha's Flea Mart. Money I keep in an old clock for an emergency is gone too. I was too ashamed to say anything to anyone. We were sleeping on a mattress on the floor on Thursday night. Walt has been helping out with furniture from the dump."

She turns to the bulletin board, pulls a piece of paper out of her pocket, pins it up in an empty space below the Witches League for Public Awareness.

Kids in crisis. TOUGH LOVE parental support group will meet at Benton Community House Wednesdays at 7:30. We don't talk about

how it happened. We don't blame ourselves, the school, our town. We use proven methods to stop kids that hurt us and themselves and have become a threat in our homes.

"I don't know what I would have done without Tough Love." She wipes tears with the back of her small white hand. "If you see Del, or hear anything, please call Bonnie. I don't have a phone anymore." At the door she turns back. "Mike doing all right? You should come to the meetings, Liz, and be prepared."

"Take care now, Violet," Harry calls after her.

The old-timers turn around and watch her drive away. It's a shame. Her husband an odd duck, a drunk, leaving her with the kids. She was a beauty. Nice lady too. Liz pays and "More coffee?" asks Harry.

"No, thanks. I've had too much."

"Look at that fog rollin' in."

"You're leaving us, Liz? Have a good one now."

A suddenly blast of air flings back the door, tearing at the notices on the bulletin board. The Tough Love notice flies towards Liz. She pins it back up on her way out. Old-timers sitting around the counter when Gramp brought Liz and Chris and Bonnie here never seem to have changed, as the young grow old, take the place of the dead, and talk the same way. Watching Liz vanish into the fog on her moped, they'll say. "Asking for trouble. Crazy world. Woman riding around on one of those things. Nothing the way it used to be." But they all wear hats, Harry recommends, to avoid the drafts and keep going to eternity.

The sun has gone behind a mountain of dark clouds as she rides away, and so has her sunny mood. The dense fog smells of dead fish when Liz goes around the bend of the road. She can hear a powerful engine swerve out of a picnic area, tires skidding on sand. She turns and looks. Nothing behind her but fog. She can't see ahead on the road, nor can she see ahead in the isolated life she has been leading since she started writing her book.

Against the racket of her three-cycle engine, you can hear an invisible car coming closer and the cry of invisible gulls sounds like warnings. She wipes the mirror. Nothing. Opens the throttle and leans into the curve, following a road she can't see. Full speed is only thirty, but it feels like ninety. The road ahead is a white cloud.

"Hi, Mom."

Not a collect call. He's paying! "What happened?" Liz cries out in alarm.

"Not much. Just want to know how you're doing." An uneasy pause. "Are you all right?"

"I fell off the moped."

"You got home OK? You're not hurt?" He takes a deep breath. "Those brownies. Did you eat them all up?"

"They are very good. I ate quite a few. Caleb sent some to Emmet—"

"He would."

"How's Caleb doing?" Liz asks.

"OK considering. Nose job had made him into a withdrawn nut. That's how his Mom decided he should go to Grove, because I'm here. His face was perfect, but he feels scars and the old snout, the way amputees feel the leg or arm they lost. Spent his time either fighting with someone or playing tunes on glasses and empty bottles with a knife.

"Coach got him to change over to pumping iron. Getting to be really overweight with muscles. But tripping on PCP could be fatal." Mike rattles on about Caleb in the hospital that time. Then in a rehab."

Liz can tell Mike is high on something when he feeds coins into a pay phone and rattles on like this, without reversing the charges. The operator wants more money. Mike has it ready and she can feel the drop of each coin as a pang. Her stomach begins to churn as he goes on and on and on about Caleb's problems, avoiding the real reason for this direct call. "Anyway, go easy on the brownies, Mom."

"Wait. Don't hang up. What's the matter with the brownies? "

Mike says it all happened the other day because Coach brought Caleb back from the AA meeting and warned him that Grimes had ordered dorm inspections. Caleb got high to try and clean up his room, so he emptied his ecstasy into a sugar bowl, and forgot about it. Later when they were all in Coach's kitchen making brownies with his wife, she ran out of sugar. Caleb, always trying to be helpful, got his sugar bowl, which was dumped right into this tub full of brownie mix.

Cal always feels he has to give something away, and afterwards when he was looking for the Ecstasy he couldn't find it. He did find a bag full of white pills in his drawer. He has come a long way interacting with other kids, so he made the pills vanish before the inspections by handing them out.

"The entire dorm was insanely happy. You should have been there, Mom. Like everyone, everybody's friend. Except for that one leadership narc who hands his pill over to Coach. Since the Killer has this powerful dad, Coach decides he better have proof. He drives to Portland, has the pill analyzed. It turns out to be vitamins B+C and Cal really thought he was giving away Ecstasy. But it happened to be vitamins they gave him at rehab. It all worked out nicely."

"You mean you sent us brownies poisoned with dope?"

"Not poison. It's good stuff. We had no idea. Coach had already put the packages in the mail when we found out. Mom, health-food stores in California used to sell Ecstasy. It's harmless mixed into the batter. Just gives you a little buzz, and there are no little kids in our house. Dad drinks and takes all kinds of pills. Don't give him any. Watch out for Billy and Jonathan. Ellen ate them? Bonnie is naturally switched on. Won't make much of a difference. You felt good, didn't you? I bet Ellen had a blast."

Could kids get high on vitamin B+-C while getting parents to crave ecstasy? Liz does not dare tell Mike how great she felt after she ate the brownies and how easily she corrected her manuscript.

Mike says that fake-Ecstasy happiness comes from expecting to be happy, but those awesome brownies will give happiness to anyone who doesn't expect it—for a while anyway. Enjoy it while it lasts.

Chapter 35

TOWN MEETING

Must be the weather. Possibilities of another storm gets everyone out of their shell. There is nothing like an urgent emergency to lift the spirits. Townies buy too much food and too much liquor, and then there was the usual letdown: Nino the barber has no real disaster to report to Liz his early customers. Only a few fallen shutters, a few uprooted trees. The traffic sloshes around, temperature rising to a record breaking 70°—tempers rising too, bringing resentment and anger to the special town meeting. Animal control seems to be the big issue. The school gym is packed when Liz gets there. Some are sitting on the floor, others have to stand up. Liz takes her place in the bleachers among kids, who have no vote, but side with the animals because they are against any control.

Bonnie's phones have been ringing and she wants Liz to attend, because animal rights are in dispute. There have been complaints about dogs barking, also against Homer the rooster, a late sleeper who sounds off around 8 a.m. The barking at South Cove is reported as starting precisely at 6:55. A mutt bit a mailman, who had run out of dog treats. Three dogs supposedly murdered an angora cat. Owners are not picking up after dogs. How about horses? Animal control officer Herb Mouser is only on part-time duty. There is one suggestion from a stout angry newcomer, to have meter maids carry cameras and catch the culprits in the act of putrefying the sidewalk as well as mean canines on the loose. Strangers and strange animals increasing the population causing a water shortage. And then, the latest. About 63 seals gathering on a small island off South Cove causing a fish shortage.

Those who are vehemently in favor of a strictly enforced leash law have arrived early to complain about dogs roaming in packs, face the town fathers in an angry front-row pack. Two rows behind them are taken up by their reinforcement of dog lovers, who groom and restrain their dogs at all times, brush their teeth, and dress them up in coats and hoods. and cute boots and are afraid of encounters with flea-infested free roaming town dogs.

No one is supposed to have more than three dogs, but those who keep as many as a dozen cats are against dogs, and have joined forces to barnstorm with the barnstorm troop of angry ones. While the Audubon Society bird-watcher types would like to restrain cats as murdering predators.

Before Bonnie's cousin Gussie, the riding teacher and a fine speaker, has had a chance to mediate, plaintiffs start shouting "Control. We need more control." Stomping and booing erupts in the bleachers from kids. There is a call to order.

Donald Spittles, a professional dog trainer is allowed to have his say about owners who do not train their animals. His well-trained son hands out bookmarks with his phone number and rates. There are those who'd like to send him kids on liquor and drugs, since they use foul words and deface the pretty town in their get-ups.

"They say you've even trained wild animals for the movies, but your llama makes a big mess on Bilford Lane," a house owner makes himself heard.

"I'll scoop it up anytime. Fine manure." The owner of the local vegetable stand is out of order. Gussie waits for the microphone to declare that dog races are not much better than cockfights. Gamblers exploit greyhounds then put them down. The lucky ones that are rescued have earned a right to go bounding about. This leads to Walter, speaking up for dogs that find homes away from home, playing with kids and visiting old people who can no longer own pets. Both Barney and Jezbell have been visitors at the nursing home.

After Walt, other calm voices speak up from different parts of the room. Liz, whose childhood had been affected by extremists feels her heart race and her belly churn, because those with good sense and good will never seems to get organized to collect signatures and form a troop, so that decent and sensible people are often caught off guard by extremists in Shoreland, as they must have been in Germany before the war.

But here in New England, the owner of Homer, the rooster, raises his hand and has his say to quote an old law that allows Shorelanders to keep chickens, even sheep, goats and cows and horses in their backyards. His rooster keeps hens from fighting, and they lay much better. Homer might crow all day long, but he is a fairly late sleeper. Seagulls make more noise than Homer and he doesn't poop on windshields. The village is just getting too citified. How about a call to the police from some folks on Shady Lane, when one of Homer's big bossy hens wandered and stood at a front door. Owners were scared to set foot outside the door.

Loud laughter. Kids cheer. Liz cheers with them for her home-town where rage can be followed by laughter and a call to order, and further entertainment for a report about a missing pet boa constrictor. Police having had to perform minor surgery on a brand new Volvo before finding the snake.

"Put it on a leash!"

Raccoons and skunks have always been around, but now they moved into a house that was on the market and listed with Better Homes and Gardens. They raided the fridge and ate everything they could find. Slept on the waterbed and left it in a disgusting condition. Loud laughter, although this isn't so funny for the owner of the waterbed. Homeowner insurance nerds are sure to declare the hole in the wall was an act of God.

A count is taken. The animal-control motion has to be studied by a committee, but the organized troop demanding animal control storms out in the same rage that has brought them together, and had brought their ancestors together and torn them apart, in little and big wars here as in the old country.

Conflict dealing with the lack of control of the sea is the last on the agenda, gathering a new pack of angry citizens to discuss the infestation of the ocean with seals who have gathered on a tiny island north of South Cove and devour tons of fish, while they entertain tourists. This has brought the interested troop of fisherman to the meeting.

Anna Tazzioti, a fisherman's wife, had called Arthur after all those seals showed up on the rocks by South Cove. He was in New York, and she got

Bonnie instead. Anna was in a state because her husband Paul was out on the headlands with an assault weapon ready to shoot all the seals, although he had never fired a gun in his life and was drunk. Anna was terrified he might shoot one of the seal-watchers by mistake. Bonnie had been worried about Shirley, Arthur's housekeeper, and called the police. The Chief and Little Dutch raced out to the headlands, persuaded Paul to come along, and took him home in the cruiser. No shots were fired. Arthur Eckert might somehow get the blame for everything.

"Arthur Eckert imported fifty or more seals?" asks Arthur's attorney, Barbara, a pert young redhead, her suit a somber gray. "There is not one witness who saw them being unloaded. There is no law against Mr. Eckert's camera crew filming seals. Plenty of tourists were out there with their cameras, too." Just like Eckert to hire Barbara, who has been on TV and is famous as the first woman to run in the originally all-male Boston Marathon, disguised as a man. Hard to imagine how she got away with it, because she is really built.

Charley Shelby, a science teacher turned lobsterman, has the floor to point out that the camera crew was on the spot the moment the seals showed up, because Eckert produces experimental subliminal persuasion tapes that could have lured the seals.

Leonard Myrtle has the last word as usual: What difference does it make whether the seals have been lured or just came? Eckert's Cable Vision did everyone a big favor getting the seals onto national TV, which attracted busloads of tourists and brings business to Shoreland during the dead season. Seals putting on a show around those rocks are as good as the New England Aquarium and increases the value of waterfront real estate. He points out that the lobstermen were able to retrieve traps without any problem. And there are plenty of fish in the sea.

Tazzioti jumps up, waving both arms. "You go out there, Myrtle; go get your ass froze off, try to fish for a livin' with foreign factory fleets, and a hundred or more seals poaching!" Fishermen's wives shout that fish are already scarce and far too expensive. The meeting is called to order again and the microphone is passed to Lesley Hollowell, the out-of-town furrier who has come up with a helpful idea for Shoreland. Wouldn't cost the town a cent. Perfect solution. A humane killing of seals, in exchange for their pelts. "After all, people are more important."

Svenson shouts, "Not a snowball's chance in hell!" down from the bleachers. "Unfair!" he says to Liz in passing as the chief escorts him out of the meeting. "Unfair!" echo high school dropouts around her. A word that had no meaning to stolen children. Lesley Hollowell, repeats his offer, and promises a donation of a thousand dollars for a children's aid fund.

Bongo Dryer and Fatty Kent, overweight high school dropouts who have been turned down as extra aliens by the casting director for The Return of The Sea Serpent, stamp their feet yelling "Shithead," and are thrown out by Chief and Little Dutch.

The door opens. "God help you all," shouts a loud youngster. The icy draft from the door and the chill of godlessness—that Hitler School children knew so well—now passes over kids on the bleachers, who are fascinated by demons. They sit quietly now while the usual parents and grandparents have their say, repeating what has already been said in their own way. Others know how to keep their mouths shut. The animal restraint laws will be appealed. Bonnie is already collecting signatures. Her answering service will come in handy.

Outside town hall in the warm sun, Ed Flame, the biggest man in town, leaves the meeting with tears in his eyes for the seals. Although nothing has been decided, he is ready to reinforce the local police by going after three skinny fellows wearing camouflage jumpsuits and long hair in pony tails, for selling Save-the-Whale T-shirts without a permit.

The Cragley twins stop in their rusty old car. Right behind them, Thelma Nesbit, Emmet Gray's friend. Never wants to miss a thing but is always too late because it takes her so long to get ready, in purple from head to toe even the eye make-up. The Harvard graduate garbage man, the Professor, parks his smelly truck behind her and gets up to the top of the Town Hall steps where he delivers a lecture on atomic waste as everyone comes piling out.

The clown carrying "Save the Endangered Predator!" pamphlets is surrounded on the sidewalk by Episcopal Church ladies who have come away from preparations for a Saturday rummage sale. "You a volunteer for Greenpeace or something, honey? Cute clown costume. How about working for us on Saturday?"

"Predator, endangered. What does that mean?" Anna, the fisherman's wife, asks Liz.

Perhaps a furrier being put out of business by animal lovers is an endangered predator as much as fish-eating seals, or fishermen killing fish?

How about developers? How about a clown stalking fur-clad females? "They're all predators," Liz says.

The clown, a tall, skinny person hiding inside huge baggy red and blue bloomers, has a white face with red circles on his cheeks and nose, and wears a small hat with a big red paper flower. The sneakers are quite small, old and dirty. "Do you ever sell balloons in Boston, wearing a yellow clown suit and purple wig?" Liz asks him.

At that moment Paul Tazzioti punches Leonard Myrtle, Leonard's fore-man acts as a bodyguard and shoves Paul, and two fishermen, trying to pull them apart, gets punched. The Chief shouts "Break it up!" He takes Paul Tazzioti by the arm, but the angry fisherman breaks away and rams the clown person, who stumbles onto the road and disappears in the confusion. Little Dutch finally stops the scuffle with a roar he developed before he dropped out of karate.

Priscilla is calling for help, because someone has sprayed red paint on her fur coat and it looks like blood. Leslie Hollowell, who custom-made the coat for her, has noticed the damage and promises to clean it free of charge, while the Chief and Dutch nab the noisy dropout kids at the back of Town Hall, to question them about ruining the coat and plastering cars with "Save the Predator" stickers.

"They couldn't have done it," Liz says to the Chief. "Must have been that clown with the SAVE THE PREDATOR banner. Some kind of organization. One of them assaulted a nurse in a parking garage in Boston and cut up her fake fur."

"You're always trying to get kids off."

"They don't have any of those stickers, do they? They don't have any paint."

"What's all that with the clown?" Dutch asks. "You sure Mike Plant isn't in town?"

"Wrong feet!" says Svenson who always sees more than you think.

Chapter 36

THE CLOCK STOPS

The night before the meeting with her editors, Chris woke up and needed Liz for his health. They went to sleep holding each other and slept until ten. Liz, in a hurry to catch the 11:00 train, put on the blouse and skirt she had worn to the retreat. Understated secondhand elegance, which might have come from an unhappy woman, or unhappy mother with hand-me-down bad luck.

She was certainly off to a bad start at the station. Usually there are students on the platform with their backpacks. Now there isn't anyone around. Finally a man gets out of a discount oil truck. She asks him about the train. "You missed it. There's another one in half an hour. The clock? Ignore that. Just hasn't been reset. Electricity went off during the storm last night."

Robbie sounds annoyed on the phone as though he didn't quite believe her. He will have to change the luncheon reservation. She arrives half an hour late at the charming old Boston Town Hall. The restaurant is quite dark, crowded with business men in dark suits. Robbie gets up, takes her coat, and holds her chair. He is tall, strong, around 60 years old. His dark hair might be a wig. Black-rimmed glasses stand out and make you forget his face. He enjoys his drink, smokes, and asks about her family, and relatives in Europe. Questions she avoids by asking about his experience during the war, which he avoids by ordering another drink and persuading Liz to accept a glass of wine. Ted Swift, the assistant editor, has sparse blonde hair, a full beard, and strong opinions. He says once too often that he likes her manuscript quite a lot. Which indicates that he hardly likes it at all. Liz gulps the wine while forcing herself to eat. Repetition, Ted says, is a flaw in prose writing. With beer foam on his beard, he talks about a course in editing he took at Yale and the importance of good line editing and cutting. He names his famous teacher at Yale. By the time they get to the Boston office of the publishing house, Liz has forgotten it.

They take an elevator to the top floor, where her manuscript is spread out on the table in an empty office. A story has to be gripping, Robbie says. Readers do not care whether a remembered story is factual, or a factual story is really actual, they want to be absorbed. Mike would say, wiped out, which is an escape. She allows herself to be distracted by sparrows totally involved with each other on the roof with their ritualistic, repetitious chirping, aggressive hopping, pecking, advancing, and retreating.

"Do you have any questions?" Robbie asks.

"Do you think my book will be published in Europe?"

The birds chirp during his silence. One cock sparrow pretends to take off and flaps his wings, then turns to stab another one with his beak and drives it away. A pair of finches landing in the gutter scare the sparrows off.

Robbie keeps smoking a lot, and her eyes are beginning to tear. Ted, the assistant, does not lift his eyes from her manuscript while Robbie explains that foreign sales, all sales, depend on publicity. Another local publisher did spend about $15,000 on publicity for a first novel by a young woman author. Her photographs and TV interviews helped sell about 30,000 books. Very rare for a first novel. Her next book is almost ready. Fast-paced young American books like that always do well in Europe too.

He pauses to light his last cigarette. "How about your next book?" When she hesitates, he goes on to say that this is an unfair question. Some writers do get discouraged after their first book, because they don't understand that the average first novel doesn't sell well. Another woman author, an older woman writing about her experience in the theatrical world, spent her own money on publicity, but all kinds of things went wrong. If a book is well-received by the reviewers and there are signs that it is really taking off, the publishers will get behind it. "Well, you and Ted better get busy." Robbie leaves his last cigarette smoking in the ashtray.

Ted cleans his glasses with a tissue before he starts going through the manuscript, with the pompous authority of someone who is new at this game. He shows her how he has had to scratch out anything that seems like repetition, while Liz could have written a short descriptive piece on the repeat pattern of aggression, of birds hopping around in courtship, fighting for a mate and space on the roof.

The editing course at Yale has also taught Ted that good writing shows rather than tells. And he has crossed out in pencil any direct statement or summation. The surgery he has performed on her manuscript gives Liz a belly ache. After half an hour his educated, slightly nasal voice, his conde-scending affection for the manuscript he has been cutting down, has a subliminal persuasion effect. He has been trained to do what his teacher believed in; and Liz can feel the stupendous dread of backing off to her outer limits, like a sparrow without wings. "You're saying, my book has to blow you away, or it won't be translated and sell in Europe? I want to find my mother." It sounds pathetic like Del trying to find Jiggers.

Ted's glasses enlarge the annoyance in his round, stone-gray eyes. The tone of her jabber is too personal. Defensiveness by an unknown author is like the chirping of a weak sparrow. Writers don't usually ask for a working session that takes up editorial time. Manuscripts are mailed to them for final corrections. A phone rings in the adjoining room. A welcome inter-ruption. Ted jumps up.

"A message service wants to speak to you. Someone called Bonnie."

Has to be important. The phone in the adjoining room sits on a stack of book boxes. "Liz. Mike and Caleb have been expelled. Mike left the school. Please don't worry. "

And at that very moment a puffed-up finch, red feather helmet ruffed in rage, hop-hop-hops towards a schoolboy sparrow, who retreats, walking backwards onto the gutter, feathers ruffled and fluffed up too. Did it fall? Was it expelled?

"Mr. Grimes doesn't want you to let Mike into your house. Imagine that! I told him Shoreland is Mike's home town. Mike could come and stay with me, or Ellen. The Myrtles would take him in too. That's his order. He doesn't want to discuss it. The Fairchilds hired a driver to bring Caleb and Mike home, but Mike didn't wait around. Had an argument with Mr. Grimes. Smashed a valuable glass door and left. Must have taken the bus to Boston. I thought you would like to go and pick him up."

* * *

Liz sits in the bus station among travelers and homeless people, waiting with their packs and bundles in a fog of cigarette smoke, pot smoke, and dismay. An arrest breaks the monotony; children cry. The Nubian beauty of a black teenaged mother, who wears her hair in many beaded braids, enhances the landscape of an unhappy dream, as the bus from Maine pulls into the station. A boy carrying a guitar gets off. Liz runs to him. "Mike!"

The kid backs off. "I'm George! Want to see my ID? What's the charge?"

"I'm not trying to arrest you. I'm a mother!"

An hour later. Bonnie comes in from the street, towering over the crowd. It is her pleasure to pick Liz and Mike up. Chris was out when she took the message from Grove Academy. Mike not here yet? Last bus. You've been waiting all this time? Not to worry. Mike will be home by morning.

"The gang. The leader was never caught!"

"Mike looks out for himself! And I've been praying. Just close your eyes." Liz sits back and sleeps all the way home. Chris has been drinking and is in a fury. "Your fault, all of it. Cuddling up to all those psychotic kids. And then when you're really needed you're in town having lunch with editors." He paces back and forth in front of the television set, turns to the bookcase. "Books. Books, while your family is going to hell." Frantic about the missing Mike, he starts throwing books out of the bookcase. Some of the old ones come apart. Saki thinks it is a game and picks a cover up here, a page there. The Tell Tale Heart. A Dickens first edition. Chris downs his drink, stomps upstairs, and will soon be asleep.

Liz calls the Portland police. Ran away from school in the afternoon? That's not a missing boy. She is told to wait for at least a week. "I can't, I can't wait!" The officer hangs up on the hysterical mother.

Liz stretches out on the sofa in Rosalie's parlor looking at the portrait above the fireplace. "Did you write poems about the sons you lost?" A serene face, the mouth relaxed in resignation, large, knowing eyes that have passed on to great-grandson Mike.

Liz curls up with Saki and wakes up to the loud theme song of "Love Boat" to watch an adopted young woman find her real mother while the purser plays up to another handsome young woman who turns out to be his college roommate, Paul, transformed by a sex change into Paula! Finally, when the Captain lectures his daughter about the adversity and complicity of love, Saki rolls over on his back, legs sticking up, and Liz allows her eyes to close again.

She thinks she is dreaming when she sees Mike stretched out on the rug in front of her with both Ringo and Saki. Light from the TV screen falls on uncombed curls, soft cheeks, strong nose and chin. He is watching a TV commercial: a wisp of young girl walking all alone along a dark street. "All right," he calls out and Saki starts leaping back and forth over his legs. When the girl looks behind her, Mike sits up. The camera slithers up her long leg, playing around the lace of the full petticoat as she walks up dark stairs; garments drop discreetly. She sinks onto the big, sunlit curtain bed and closes her eyes. Mike sinks down on the carpet and closes his eyes. The soft music reaches a crescendo while the camera circles down to the haunting face, playing over closed eyes and half-open lips. The sensuous voice of a female pedlar speaks of the pleasure of coming to your safe "daughter-room" softness, caresses—the camera closing in on a dreamy pattern of field flowers: Laura Ashley bed sheets.

Pattern of wild flowers, visions of Mother embroidering flowers on pillowslips and dresses, using cross-stitch while her child wanders out of her life. Mike running away but coming back home, resting on his back, his eyes closed. It's like a happy dream.

"Tiny body, but everyone wants to look at her. I guess you've never seen her. That's Emerald. The way she dances, and she makes up her own songs too. Isn't she cool? Eckert gets her these jobs, but the money goes into an account to pay for her detox. I told her she should get a lawyer, but detox in Cal costs a lot of money and made her worse." His mouth turns down at the corners. He frowns. "She likes listening to my tunes. Not all the time. Knows how I feel, but makes out with creeps. Result, they like come looking for her and try to kill me."

Saki shakes a bag of potato chips, sprinkling him, the carpet, even the sofa. Ringo is feasting. Guinea pigs can exist without mothers and feed themselves the moment they are born in order to survive among predators. Mike looks helpless and vulnerable, when he is safe. The laughing boy, has come home sad. "Why didn't you call?"

He sits up, startled; still thinking of Emerald. "You aren't even pleased to see me!" Everything is Mother's fault. "I don't have to hang around here. I can go back to Portland and stay with Rick."

"Who's Rick?"

"He was kicked out of Grove a couple of weeks ago. Does OK dealing. Dropped me off on his way to Boston."

"What if he gets caught and spends years in overcrowded jails?"

"Jails are overcrowded with kids who've done recreational drugs. Criminals are running around free." He sits up and pats her on the shoulder. "This isn't Hitler's Germany, Mom. They tried to keep old Timothy Leary in jail for possession of a little weed. Weathermen gang came in with a copter and he was rescued. He's doing just fine. Getting rich, designing software. He even plans to have his head cut off and frozen when he dies. Then later they'll find a way of putting it on a new body so that his genius won't go to waste. I hope Leary remembers to get an auxiliary generator, in case there is a brownout and his head defrosts."

He turns around, his mane blocking the television picture of a man shot in the head in Boston. "No good in this case. The head's damaged. The weasel's head was crushed by the coke machine. I don't know what Grimes told you, but we didn't kill that weasel in the supermarket, Mom."

"Who was killed? What happened?"

"One of the dudes who tried to kill me. You've got to believe me. We didn't go after him. I didn't even see him. We were at the variety store on a rainy afternoon. Bought candy. And then, after that, one thing led to another. Grimes tried to connect it up and blame me."

"You OK? You look white. Relax, Mom. It had nothing to do with me or any of the other kids. Take nitrous oxide, Mom. A balloon filled with it wouldn't float. It's not lighter than air. It's used in cars to make them faster and also in cans of whipped cream. Nitrous is a drug to be enjoyed in moderation and on occasions. Suppresses and kills bone marrow even faster than it kills your brain cells."

Worn down by guilt, she feels her fingernails tear at the inside of her palm. Whether it is cruelty, trust, or a need to just talk. She must not interrupt.

"If used in a dumb way it can kill you. The inventor of the drug died of exposure to it. At concerts, balloons are fairly safe because you're not breathing from a tank." Mike was not after revenge. Had no idea that one of those rabid weasel-types was out on probation, working at the supermarket to earn money for his part of the $600 hospital bill for the injured Grove Academy boy. The judge thought that Jim, the fifteen-year-old, had been influenced by the gang and gave him a chance to make good. But Mike says the kid did bad, simply because he missed the gang and didn't like to be by himself.

"Having to take off his female wig and having his hair cut, must have been harsh. You couldn't recognize him. On probation, he had to get cleaned up, wear a white shirt, a green tie, and a green dust coat, and work as a stock boy at Daninger's Superette."

"Why did the gang wear female wigs?" Liz asks.

"So that you'd notice the wig. Not the guy. Get it? Like the SS men. Police. You just see the uniform. Emerald got herself an Afro wig, so that the gang wouldn't spot her. Since I was hurt there was never less than six of us allowed off campus. Lousy day, the store practically empty. At the candy aisle this stock boy falls off the ladder right in front of me. We hadn't touched the ladder, but he yelled at me 'You blind?' I didn't get it. But the kid thought I was blind, like Mrs. Wise and her blind brigade.

"Big Caleb, walking around with a fistful of bills, didn't like the way the kid kept following us and sent him to the back to get more Pringles. There were two chicks in the store with us: Emerald, wearing that Afro wig, big Babs, bowlegged from riding all her life. Then the guys. Dudley, the black Jamaican, and Emerald start sucking the whipped cream cans. She hands me one to try. Stock boy must have watched us get high at the dairy case."

"Didn't he report you?"

"No. He never knew about the brother's-keeper concept and he was more interested in watching us stagger around laughing. Em dancing. You should see her. There was all that loud, piped-in bunny-cotton-tail persuasion music, and she started everyone off hopping down the bunny trail and even with her big, black wig. The kid shows up yelling 'Emma.' She jumps him, bites his ear. Goes right back to hopping."

Mike turns the sound off a Colgate-white-smiles commercial, cutting off at the same time any maternal, "How could you, why did you—why didn't you" with the complicity of a long minute of silence between them and the ticking clock and hush-shush-slosh of the sea.

"We even checked out and paid for cans of whipped cream—not all of them. Quite a few. That made it worse. Weasel must have gone to replace them and sucked every can they had in stock, to prove that he could do better than us. And if you overdo whippets a kind of tickticktick starts up. Head rush and tingling fingers. Ting-ting- ting—from far, far away. You feel your hand and head are about to drop off. He just didn't stop. Hard to see this skinny weasel topple the Coke machine.

"We were already back on campus when we heard sirens. But they go on all day long. How should we have known that it was that weasel leaving the world in an ambulance? No one told us. They kept it out of the papers, Mom. The big ape who did most of the damage to me is now locked up in some nut farm. But the driver, the maniac with the big voice, Kill! Kill! He looks a lot like me. The checkout woman is elderly and deaf, so she didn't hear the crash, but she said she saw me running out the back. His hair could be a female wig, but it looks like mine. We think he was the one who helped topple the Coke machine on his buddy to keep him from talking.

"And Mom, honest, I didn't even testify against those guys. One look at the grand jury and I could tell they'd hate my long hair too. They'd think I was asking for it all in some way. When I told them my story, I made it into a kind of joke. In a way, the judgment against them went against any long-haired kid. Me too. As for the that pathetic supermarket weasel, working to pay my hospital bill for having bitten me and help beat me up, Em bit his ear hard."

"And you didn't even testify to get them off the street? Just think of what they did to that babysitter. "

"I had no idea the kid was dead when I got his $110 compensation check. We would never have gone ahead with the business idea Caleb got after we had fooled around with those cans."

The words come fast again, like Chris rehearsing for a psychiatrist, "Caleb has the idea of getting a restaurant tank. The Jamaican kid, Dudley, wanted to invest. Thinking ahead to a summer job selling animal-shaped balloons at rock concerts filled with nitrous, one buck a hit. Harmless. Buzz over in five minutes. I didn't like the idea of selling such boring, pre-dictable hits. It's been around for a long time. Dentists have been doing hits with their own nitrous for years. Lousy job being a dentist. Who can blame them?"

"Don't look so shocked, Mom. Wise up. The balloons. Animal shapes? There is that dude Grimes kicked out way back at Grove. He has all those balloons and the tank was easy. Emmet, Cal's uncle who rides his stationary bike all over the world. He sends Cal money. But listen to this, Mom! While monster Cal gets high and does his body building, no one was looking out for Em invading the shed. Helping herself. A beautiful chick. Making a move on me one moment, then staggering and crying not to leave her all alone. The shed was getting smaller and smaller. Next she's on the run to the football field squealing like a pig."

"I thought they had a new guard."

"At the other end of the campus, Mom. A cop car like parks behind the student union after dark. There Em has a sudden Brother's Keeper narc attack. Told them about the nitrous tank in the shed. We would hardly have taken the risk of investing in a nitrous tank if we'd known about the whippet OD in the super market.

"Grimes had his chance to kick us out. Gets the others to own up and makes out we are potential mass murderers like the Nazis with their gas. Em said I bought the tank. So I lost my cool, Mom. I threw a chair. The way he does." His mouth goes down, changing the boy into a sad and angry man. "They'll sure miss Caleb and me at Grove. The Jamaican kid, Dudley. He was like hiding in the bushes with little fat Daisy Grossman. If Dudley is thrown out of Grove, he'll send Daisy the fare and she'll follow him to Jamaica. Caleb and I we're invited. Grass is better than nitrous."

On TV someone is selling persuasion tapes with a money-back guarantee to make you thin. "Just a skinny, mean kid." Mike turns to his mother. "Pathetic!" His mouth begins to twitch. "I didn't kill him. We didn't see him."

Liz holds him and rocks with him, absorbing his hurt, while the Ashley sheet commercial is repeated, letting guilt to pass onto her for leaving him vulnerable to be enticed with millions of consumers into a sweet safe daughter room, where Emerald offers herself up to the multitude of gapers on soft, floral 100% cotton sheets.

Chapter 37

SOONER OR LATER

Gulls cry out as they circle Pig Island where they nest. Song sparrows in the gardens warble against the metronome of mournful mourning doves, the blaze of the cock cardinal, and the combat twitter of small birds defending small nests; the moist air carries the scent of buds and decay, sweetness and salt, sea and land.

Cardinals have their nest in the quince bush just outside the sheltered kitchen window where the tawny hen-cardinal with the orange beak sits on her eggs day after day, while the scarlet male swoops down to display himself, snapping open the red wings and offering her a morsel. Then he perches on the top of the crab apple tree, his call brilliant and piercing as his red against the blue of the summer sky.

At night, when the kitchen lights are on, Mike likes to watch the cardinal hen sitting on her eggs so close you could reach into the nest. Mom keeps the side window closed, but the bird does have a good view of the crazy kitchen with Mom dancing back and forth between the stove and the sink, Saki hanging to her long skirt or playing games, rattling paper bags; she must see it all, and she must hear classical music change to rock when Mike changes radio stations, hear Ringo whistle, the self-closing doors banging. The mother bird stays steadfast on her eggs while the red male, who according to Bonnie is supposed to take his turn, trills and shows off.

Mike has to wonder what has happened to birds in Russia now after Chernobyl poisoned vegetables and milk all over Europe. How about insects? Nobody seems to know or care.

After the eggs hatch, it's mostly the mother bird who stuffs insects into open beaks while the male sings, claiming his territory. Finally his trilled whistling coaxes fledglings to try their wings. Mike comes home and sees the fledglings lined up on a comfortable branch among the crab apple blossoms. "Mom. One bird is missing." Mike runs out, squeezes into a narrow space to crawl under bushes to the west window, finds the last fledgling on the ground, and puts it back into the nest. "Use your unique potential. Fly!" A Havelock Grimes imitation that could discourage any bird or kid. "Won't budge," he says when he comes back. "Weak bird." He taps on the window. Saki starts running around wagging his curled up tail.

"Leave it alone," Liz says. "It'll get scared and fall out again."

"What difference does it make? A weak bird is dead. Del's baby was too weak to live. No one's fault. But Del had herself born again."

Dad comes into the kitchen wearing his new black helmet for the bike ride to the Healing Center." Everyone gets wasted sooner or later," Mike goes on, "Those guys could have wasted me. The moment they get out of jail, they'll trace me and come after me. That's why I should have a trail bike, or at least that beat moped."

Chris opens drawers looking for sunglasses. "You need driving lessons."

"I don't want to drive a car. A motor-bike is perfect."

"Too dangerous," Liz says.

"Who cares? Good or rotten, sooner or later you die. That's life," says Mike and closes the drawers Dad left open. "I might be dead too, any-time."

The picture of life, but always talking about death to his mother in the kitchen. Chris takes note. Mike has a dark tan. His hair, bleached from the sun and water, keeps growing like the grass. His tattered pair of small boy's cut-offs—all torn and frayed with long strings of thread—show off his bulging male parts. Karin, the wholesome babysitter girlfriend, has been absent lately. Now there 's Nadine, an Aussie fashion model—at least eight years older then Mike. Wearing the serene resignation of a stone martyr and always the same Sea-Snake sweatshirt, which exposes stilt legs as she descends through spider's webs to noisy rock music and noisy romping in the cellar, which Mike has furnished with a lumpy Futon. "Stop that. Stop worrying your mother!"

"Get real, Dad. She hears about hijackings, bombs, nuclear energy explosions, acid rain, poisoned water and air on the radio and TV. "

Mike picks up a page Liz had been correcting from the kitchen table. "Clusters of clouds. Doesn't mean anything, Mom; you want the name of the cloud. Like altocumulus. That's good writing."

"No, nimbus clouds," His father says.

They are still arguing about clouds when they leave. The self-closing door bangs shut. They keep telling her what to do, throwing ideas and words around, as Chris throws new cotton clothes around and leaves tools and medical books everywhere. Just can't help himself. When he loses something in that mess he goes out and buys more clothes and tools. As he and Mike compete for space, messing up room after room, staking out territory, they lose space.

There they are side by side, the same height, walking across a field of clover and dandelions. Ask Mike to cut grass, he suggests dandelion wine. Ask him to pick up his socks and his sneakers, you get a lecture about his injuries. Chris no longer takes his own temperature several times a day, and he no longer checks and controls all the electrical equipment in the house. Ask him about getting help in the garden before the grass goes to seed and he starts suffering from hay fever and he'll ride off on his new bike to continue reprogramming his system at the Healing Center.

The moment Liz is alone with Saki and Ringo, the reliable old toaster clicks and goes down. A minute later it comes up again. Each time it clicks and goes up and down the radio buzzes. After Liz unplugs it, loads the dishwasher and turns it on, the new refrigerator starts its endless gnashing and grinding defrost.

But who cares on a day like this when roses spill over stone walls? The fragrant, warm air wafts through the open windows with all the lure and sadness of enchanted Shoreland. On the radio President Reagan is saying with such cheerful conviction this is the greatest nation on earth and the economy is in great shape that you can hear him smile. On Frau Faser's radio Adolf Hitler's hoarse voice had shouted the same message about the German Reich.

Cardinals fly, dive, and shriek when Bonnie's cat Garfield scampers around the side of the the Plant house proudly carrying the weak fledgling. Since Garfield is rewarded with chicken livertreats he has stopped killing and acts as a courier for her bird-rescue service. Spring and early summer you can often hear the chirping of a weak or injured bird she is nursing, as well as Garfield's loud purring while he basks in the sun among her phones and geraniums.

❊❊❊

In the afternoon Mike is in the garden assuming responsibility by taking his mother's moped apart. "It's too slow, Dad. Mom was trying to get away from a car and had a fall." Some of the moped parts have now dropped into the dandelions and tall grass. The end of the moped—unless—Chris would be tempted to show the boy how it's done, if it weren't for his new, white 100% cotton tennis whites and the three young women from the stress management group waiting at the tennis-courts to play doubles. Then there is Ellen, the traitor, who saw him playing doubles with a young female lawyer, a baby-faced software designer and a dancer from the Boston Ballet. "How about learning about engine repair? I can speak to Davies about giving you a summer job?"

"Work for minimum pay when I can make a fortune as a psychic?" Mike waits for a reaction, but Dad keeps himself calm by returning an invisible ball. "It's true. Two days before takeoff I saw the spacecraft blow up. Acid makes me psychic, but it makes Caleb crazy. As for Em. We were like standing on this drawbridge in Bath, when I saw the explosion. I could have saved that cute teacher in space. But Caleb thought the draw-bridge was opening up and started yelling for help and clinging to the rail, although it hadn't moved an inch. Em starts taking her clothes off. If I had said anything about astronauts blowing up to the police, they would have locked all of us up." Mike twirls a wrench waiting for the usual rage against illegal drugs from a Dad who is a prescription addict. Nothing hap-pens. Dad uses an unripe apple for a powerful serve and makes his getaway quietly on his new stress-balanced sneakers.

Later on, during supper, Mike again talks about all the money that can be made from predictions. Especially if you have a career as a channeler. Like J. K. Knight—this woman out West making millions channeling. It makes a lot of people happy. Mike produces a magazine with the picture of a crowd on a brown hill gathered around J. K. Knight. Thousands seek spiritual guidance through channeling. Rathma speaking through Knight at sunrise in Yucca Valley, California. For $400 you can get words of wisdom from the Cro-Magnon Age.

"Mom, you can get some really sad people to believe that they have a lot of power and that they are really God—each one of them—and then you get in touch with a good guiding spirit who talks to them and they turn around and begin to do well and you do well too because they give you lots of money and they really love you. There'll be all those chicks waiting to be hypnotized. Chicks, hypnotism. Get it?"

Talk about psychic power now, or talking about death, leaves Mom speechless.

"Your English great-grandfather was a parson. You might end up studying theology, Mike." Dad says.

"What for? American tuition money has become the biggest rip-off in the world. Who needs to study religion? You just meditate. I could even take witchcraft as a science from Amanda Garlic, the official Salem witch. Lots of money in New Age religions and they make people happy."

Chris has seen the impressive picture of Amanda Garlic pinned up on the kitchen bulletin board among all kinds of crazy pamphlets.

"There's nothing queer about a man taking a witching course. That's integration. The witch girls might all make a move on me. What's wrong with that? No, I'm not about to get tangled up with witch women. Not with Nadine the Aussie around. And I've not broken off with Karin. She's just working and eating too much. Putting on weight—" Mike waits a second, but no one takes the bait. "I'm sexually active. Doubt that I'll ever get married. Look at you and Mom! If it weren't for that funky bit of incest…" No reaction from Dad. "Everyone is splitting up, so why bother getting married? Just for overpopulating purposes? If you're lucky you have your meals cooked and house cleaned. When I get to be old, maybe around thirty and I want a servant, I can import a beautiful, rich oriental girl who wants to become an American. They really treat you well."

Dad does not tell Mike the channeler, witchcraft student, future owner of a Japanese heiress-serf, to shut up. Dad smiles. Mom does not. Roles have reversed. "By the way, there is a summer kid who wants to sell his trail bike. A steal. It's only 200 bucks."

Chris is in a good mood. He takes out his wallet. Produces his checkbook. "Might as well get it over with." He's already writing the $200. "Now who should I make it out to?"

Mom, who's dressed for dinner in a slinky long dress she must have picked up at a church fair, leaps up. "No. No motorbikes."

"I just promised." Dad keeps smiling.

Liz finds herself reaching for the checkbook, tearing the check out. She rips it up, and can't stop tearing it into tiny pieces. During the night she wakes up, leaves Chris and Saki fast asleep, and quietly goes downstairs to get a glass of milk. There she finds Mike lolling around in the parlor in shirt and underpants and one sock, drinking brandy and burning a candle on the floor, watching some vampires on TV. He leaps up when he sees her, lets out a shriek, grabs great-grandmother's high chair and, loading it onto his back in a Havelock act, turning around and around, then swinging it out at her. When she backs off, he trips over one of his sneakers, stumbles and falls onto the candle with the chair. She puts it out and rescues the bottle.

"I'm sorry, Mom. Bad trip. The vampires. I didn't mean to—"

Then she grabs him by the shoulders hard. "No one ever means any harm. You were almost killed by boys on drugs. The boy in the grocery store died. I guess no one could be blamed for anything." He allowed her to shake him back and forth. "Lucas killed his own mother on and on. He didn't mean it. Do you hear me? Are you listening, Mike? I know, I know, Caleb smokes opium, lots more grass than you do, because he has the money. Do you think this is great?"

"You don't have to think when you're on acid. You have all that worry about your book. Here, Mom. He actually reaches into his pocket and holds a pill on the palm of his hand the way you feed a cow or a horse. "Try it Mom."

"I did. Those spiked cookies you sent. That's when I fell off the moped." She runs to the toilet and flushes the pill down.

❀ ❀ ❀

On Sunday afternoon Bonnie waves to Mike from her garden, ready with admiration and sweet treats for him on her day off. Wearing a straw hat among all her flowers, she'd make an awesome commercial for hay fever remedies. But he doesn't get off the bike, because praise and admiration you don't deserve is worse than a lashing.

He is quite glad when Ellen flags him down, big orange sleeves waving

in the wind. Wants him to meet the English doctor she's hanging out with.
They're drinking sherry under the concord grape arbor. She's wearing this
cool toga. Nothing else, it seems. You can see her nipples. All cozied up
with the English dude, who wears shirt, tie, and tweeds, like Dad. Sounds
like him too, but is older and taller. Mike congratulates himself on this
perfect replacement. "How was Memorial Day, Mike?" Ellen asks as
though he were a child. He makes a grimace thinking of Mom and Bonnie
decorating old graves. Dad putting up a flag. Old guys marching in old
uniforms, baby girls in white dresses carrying flowers. Boy Scouts and the
police department. "I'm not into Memorial Day. Cookout at the Fairfields
was cool."

The English doctor has materialized from those great English doctor
letters with pink cheeks and sharp blue eyes and a firm hand-shake. But
why after doing something so amazingly good do you feel bad? Mom. Her
fault. She really has herself to blame if he freaks out, when she doesn't even
want him to have a trail bike. He deserves a Harley for getting Dad to the
Healing Center. Mike reaches into his pocket for the leather pouch and
rolls a joint, offering it first to Ellen and then to the doctor. The
Englishman smiles and refuses for both of them. Not for moral reasons, he
says at once.

Mike takes a hit and points out that a joint helps you pass exams. The
doctor laughs across a ten mile table and keeps laughing until it clicks.
Bigfield of course. Sort of making a house-call. Old Dr. Green used to
come to the house. Mike talks and talks, trying to get across the miles of
misinformation that his hypochondriac Dad must have given to the polite,
healthy looking doctor. "If you are in the wrong place at the wrong time
and are almost killed, there are some people who'll make it God's will. Like
you deserved it or even worse. Anything you survive makes you stronger."

The doctor seems to be lip reading with too much understanding,
exchanging glances with Ellen, which tells Mike that they have talked
about him. What if this is a plot to have Mike misdiagnosed as a multiple
personality or something? Would Ellen be naked under her robe? To live
up to his reputation Mike lectures about the benefit of recreational uppers.
Ecstasy. Which used to be sold in health food stores in California. No side
effects. The best. The anecdote of the brownies. Then Timothy Leary.
What he has to say seems so important when he is high and enjoys himself, that he hardly notices the doctor's departure until he sees him in the

downstairs shower room, which is usually the only clean room in Ellen's house. The window is open. The doctor stooping over the basin to wash his hands. A faucet squeals. The doctor soaps his hands again and rinses for a long time, while Ellen picks up glasses and puts them onto a tray table. Another squeal.

Why feel sad for him? Dad must have talked about Ellen to this psychiatrist. The awesome Dr. Renfrew letters worked too well. But by the time the doctor has finally dried his hands, Mike feels sorry for Ellen and just as much for himself. Two psychologists should be able to analyse each other. But Ellen likes to have all kinds of people coming and going.

She puts on a tape playing the old "In a White Room," while the doctor is upstairs in her white bedroom, white curtains billow out the window and wave. She refreshes her gin and tonic. The doctor comes out carrying a medium sized black suitcase, heavy with his books and manuscript. Mike likes the way Ellen helps him carry it, falling into step.

A minute later she is back. "He rented the car," she tells Mike, "Because he didn't want to leave me at the airport." Before the car turns off onto Shore Road, she jumps up and runs out to the end of her drive and waving, calling, "Harold! Harold!" Sleeves winging like a frantic butterfly. She follows the car with her eyes. It does slow down at North Beach. "That's where we first met." Tears run down her cheeks when he drives on slowly. She wipes her face with her long hair. "Last July his wife was pruning roses, fell over, and died. He was fearfully lonely all year until we met."

Mom would notice her British, "fearfully lonely" Ellen picked up from both Dad and the doctor.

"An English doctor heard me lecture. Wrote to me." She fills Mike's glass. "Then I met Harold. It was all so dreamy for us both. In fact Harold's writing a book about taking a chance.—But right now. I'm just not sure. He wants to live in England."

Mike gets up slowly and offers her the roach. She would like to get high just now, but the doctor would not approve. She refuses. As his car disappears around the bay, she sheds more tears and wipes her face with her hair.

"There goes Oswald Renfrew," Mike finally says.

"What!" With the shriek of a witch, she grabs Mike's mane with both hands and tugs. "I should have known. You! Those letters!"

"Let go. Let go. This hurts."

She lets go. Her anger gives way to that wicked slow smile. "The Health Center. I've seen that "Father" letter. You wrote that too!"

"It worked, didn't it? I got Dad to change at the Healing Center, but he's changing too much."

"I've been neglecting him," Ellen says.

"Good! Good!" Mike starts composing a phony letter in his head to keep Dad safe from Ellen. A Harvard Medical School health letter, warning against sexually liberated sex partners should do it. When you have so many great ideas, you just have to calm yourself down with a smoke.

"You overwrote your mother's chapters!"

"Her fault. Not mine!" He always gets hungry when he is accused of something he doesn't want to admit. So he helps himself to cheese and crackers. While she goes to fetch a smoked salmon platter, he treats himself to wine from the doctor's glass. She absent-mindedly refills it, while they feast in the sun. He allows himself to bask in the false pride of his own amazing creativity. His letters seem more important than Mom's book. "So are you going to move to England?"

"Everything might have worked out if I hadn't asked you in just now. It made him feel old."

"So why did you?" Mike looks up at the trees where a flock of starlings are hanging out. "You got lonely alone with him? "

She ignores this. "I was going to England in August with the kids, but now—"

"Go by yourself. The boys are too much. Put them into a summer camp."

"It was a dream come true." Ellen laughs, but a minute later tears flow down her cheeks.

Is not a dream come true a dead end for a dreamer? Like Karin as the half naked mermaid in the sand. The pink tit missing. Karin soft boobs and long legs. Mike stumbles over a sneaker while he runs to find Ellen some tissues, and quietly pockets an envelope with the doctor's English address. So he'll have to express an "I miss you, can't live without you" note together with a copy of Mom's tape of Ellen's lecture "New Feminism—Old Devotion." Perfect! It might even get to the old country at the same time as the doctor. He drains the doctor's glass, savoring the sweet power of a great-grandfather parson. "Mike giveth!"

Chapter 38
THE PARADE

Bonnie's favorite day of the summer. The Fourth of July. The weather is good and hot, the parade better than ever this year. Six marching bands. They must have had a competition for the tiniest majorettes. Swishing their flip skirts, stepping it out in place on strong short legs as the parade comes to a halt. The police force staring straight ahead and marching in place too. The Chief his best in gala uniform. Many women go to town meeting just to see him stand up and have his say, while men think he talks too much. It's thanks to the Chief, Bonnie says, that little officer Dutchy has really turned out. Wasn't easy for him in school. Whether you are too small or too tall, kids will give you a hard time. Now he is the one who looks out for the teenagers in this town. There's Denise, Bonnie's niece, in her uniform, towering over the men, hounds strangers, or anything that seems strange to her. "We're lucky. Our police are dedicated." Bonnie waves to Boy Scouts and Brownies, calling kids she knows by name. Then she stops waving. "There's Jeff's Shore Road Hardware. No float this year." A red Corvette. Jeff with a couple of fellows who work for him stripped to the waist and wearing black sunglasses. Right behind the police," Bonnie says. "He always likes tall girls. Denise is the one."

The Major wanted to rig up a float for Bonnie, but she loves watching the parade so much she even turned down a giraffe costume for Story

Gusswell's Evangelist Community Noah's Ark float. She claps her hands and cheers for an out-of-town band—musicians of all colors, all sizes, all sexes, and all ages—playing a rumba, followed by the Gray Panther Senior Citizen float, which displays Emmet Gray cycling to the music and active couples dancing the rumba in great style under a big LOWER YOUR CHOLESTEROL THE FUN WAY sign. Walter passes out to them Bonnie's PERSONALIZED HELP AND ANSWERING SERVICE. THE ANSWER TO YOUR PROBLEMS pamphlets.

The Major quickly angles himself in such a way that Bonnie can't see a clown dressed up in a fur fit for a movie star when it must be ninety degrees in the sun, has a down-in-the-mouth white face and wears a big trap splattered with red tied around the neck, balloons and a big animal rights sign board.

"Harriet, Harriet. There's Harriet!" Bonnie waves to her cousin, the riding teacher Harriet Simons, dressed up in her Roy Roger's costume. "Hot as blazes. Just look at her." Just then, the clown in the fur coat crosses right in front of the riding school with his bunch of balloons and his billboard, scaring their horses. Harriet's posse of horse-crazy preteen girls shriek pointing at him. She shouts a few orders, trying to quiet the girls and calm the horses.

"Didn't mean any harm. Poor clown must be feeling the heat in that crazy fur coat." Bonnie says. "There should be water for the horses in this heat." Mothers carry coolers with lemonade for the skinny little girls from Evita's School of Dance, who tap step along and perform cartwheels and back flips whenever the parade comes to a stop. Bonnie pours water from her cooler for the three mongrels wearing hats, and for Barney, the frisbee champion, following behind the Myrtle float which is decorated with plastic models of condominiums Len Myrtle wants to build around the Tompkins Pit.

Dora in a pink satin gown adorns Len's float, but saves her voice for the band concert by lip-singing her tape of, "Home Sweet Home"—nonstop. Len, in his dark suit, white shirt, and red silk tie, sits arm in arm with Smokey the Bear, to show that Myrtle is an environmentalist and thinks ahead to the next generation. He throws lollipops with his left hand. The sign on the side of the float says CREATE CLEARINGS AND PREVENT FOREST FIRES. CONDOMINIUM OWNERS ARE SMOKEY THE BEAR'S BEST FRIENDS AND FIRE WARDENS.

Walter notes that the Smokey the Bear suit is fake fur. The only possible animal fur in the parade is the white rabbit-ermine trim on the red satin cloak worn by Queen Karin. A crazy clown would have a hard time getting near her up there on the Buzz Landscaping truck surrounded by the usual pushy, pretty cheerleader types who display themselves dancing on the float, skirts and hair flying to the jungle sounds of Mike's Suicide Four rock band.

"Where's our Elgar?" Bonnie calls to him.

"Grounded for something he did or didn't do," Mike shouts back. "Wait till you see Mom, on Ellen's float." Caleb Fairbanks has taken Elgar's place as vocalist. Lucky rag flying around his head, he staggers in a permanent Elvis knee bend, abusing an electric guitar he can't play, shouting anything that comes into his head. Sonny, kicks up his legs playing backup, Mike drums a loud and lazy bush telegraph.

The cheerful crowd lines upper North Street sidewalks, all the way down to Harbor Square. Pink or red is the big color. Hundreds of children with balloons or waving flags, activated by any kind of music that comes along. A huge turnout this year. Many out-of-towners have come to see "The Return of the Sea Serpent" star on the Cablevision float. Bambi Skylark, what a beauty—what boobs. Are they real? Costumed as Clarissa, the good witch, a black leather mini-tunic bespangled with mirrors that keep the evil Sea Serpent at bay by dazzling it with its own reflection, casting back its evil spell; her silver helmet sports a glittering wind chime. "There, there, look. A sparkling mask and those pretty wings. That must be little Emerald. Pretty little pixie. Poor little skinny thing. All that jiggling. Just look at her go." Arthur Eckert, Mr. Cablevision himself, wears his safari jacket and holds a video camera. His crew throw healthy peanut butter and popcorn candy, mostly to the float behind them, where Pearl's Oyster Bar waitresses in bikinis are sitting on Styrofoam oyster shells that are propped up on old toilet bowls from the dump.

Silvester Marching Band with overweight sway-backed girls weighed down with heavy drums, followed by Ellen's nuclear peace float. "Liz, Liz! Such a good sport. Always was. There she is."

Liz waves to Bonnie and the Major from Ellen's anti-nuclear float. She happened to be in Harbor Square feeling both at a loss and relieved since her book went into production. Ellen came to interest kids who loiter as well as Liz to help promote better understanding in our endangered world with her antinuclear peace float. The boys all wanted to be Einstein. When they had to draw straws, Svenson the alcoholic won. He is much too tall, but Ellen told him she would allow him to wear the latex Einstein mask, if he stayed sober. Ellen's setter Red never acts sober and adds to the confusion with his barking and slobbering on the hectic peace float.

Ellen's boys made Liz and themselves up as victims. Green and white stage make-up, eyebrows—penciled Japanese eyes and plenty of lipstick wounds. Ellen dressed Tom the Tick, Smithy, and her boyfriend Quail, as atomic scientists in white coats and wigs and black-rimmed glasses. A black wig and a green silk kimono decorated with a big Hiroshima sign complete her disguise. Their explosion tape had to be turned way down because they unnerved Liz, but the brothers fall down dead on a futon at regular intervals, turning nuclear explosion into a clown act. Little kids, used to cartoons and disaster comedy from TV cheer along with the disbanded, but loyal and noisy single parents club, shouting "Ellen! Ellen!" while antinuclear people throw pennies to show their support.

The KEEP SHORELAND BEAUTIFUL float right behind the nuclear explosion gets the applause. Flowers and the Garden Club beautification old ladies in blossom-trimmed straw hats, dainty and sturdy as their potted plants. "Now, that is pretty." And "Cute! Just darling!" The Doctor P Pet Store float has a standard poodle wearing a nurse's uniform, standing up—each time the parade stops—front legs on a baby carriage full of toy puppies. There is Nathan, in his white coat, smiling nervously.

When the parade comes to a stop a lot of girls in tight white satin uniforms play Dixieland music, while The Horribles come jigging along. Every year some of those serious men get this chance to dress up as wild crazy women. Big guys like Rusty, the cabinet maker, bulging out of little frilly skirts. The crowd cheers, claps and hoots. Bill Laird, an accountant, wearing his wife's see-through beach robe and Mexican hat, Ralph Poach, the electrician, in a see-through black negligee; Dr. Daily, the dentist— sweating in red velvet. Pete, from the funeral parlor, showing off his fine furry legs in short shorts. Is that...No. Can't be! The appliance repair man, Lester Gordon, wearing harem pants and cheesecloth veils, performing a jelly-belly dance, while male ballerinas throw salt water taffy to children, kisses all around, and squirt water into the crowd. What d'ya expect?

Liz sees something she did not expect: a clown in a big white fur coat

with those animal-shaped SAVE THE PREDATOR balloons. Children
run over to get some, shriek, and back away. The clown turns, and Liz sees
a big bloody animal paw ear ring. A steel leg-hold trap is a broach holding
a big sign: GOD'S CREATURES STRANGLED, BEATEN, GASSED
OR ELECTROCUTED AND SKINNED ALIVE FOR THEIR PELTS.

There is always a just or unjust cause to bring out such idealists to send
a personal message into an impersonal world. But who would notice this
clown in the midst of the dancing and prancing Horribles and their noisy
marching bands and the amplified Suicide Four rock group?

Liz, under the influence of the Grove Academy brother's keeper
Concept, grabs Ellen's megaphone to summon officer Denise Codget who
hounds strangers, or anything that seems strange to her, but the fire
engines of the volunteer fire department sound off at that moment with
the biggest racket as they always do. Everyone's favorite, Ye Old Engine,
which only the conservationist selectman can start, lets out forceful unique
laryngitis monster blasts. Mothers cover babies' ears, dogs go crazy, Red
howls. There they are. Everyone throws a little money into the big dropcloth.

Liz can't see the clown anymore, but when no one was looking, Ellen's
boys, tired of playing nuclear corpses, have climbed like apes from the float
onto one of the last elms left on Main Street, where they perch with their
backpack of illegal New Hampshire firecrackers. Ellen takes the megaphone from Liz: "Billy, Jonathan! You two get down from that tree! We
need some corpses." The boys wave from a big strong limb and start
throwing firecrackers, zipwang, zap-crackling towards Melon Street.

Liz sinks down on the futon and covers her ears. Arthur hoists himself
onto the atomic float and produces a brandy flask. "Are you all right? I saw
you fall. The explosions. Understandable. No wonder you don't want to
come to my fireworks party this evening. But why on earth did you get
yourself into this?"

There is talk in the crowd. "Did you see the way he's holding her?"

A young woman wearing a sky blue sari comes up to the nuclear float.
"I'm Anna from the Healing Center. Anything I can do?—Sure? In case
you haven't had our mailing." She hands Liz a perfumed pamphlet about
stress relief and trauma treatment. "We have much to offer. First visit is
free. Do come!"

When the rest of the firecrackers hit a side alley and the top of a
parked van, a mule called Snow White starts acting like a billy goat and

backs into the crowd. Anna flees. Snow White throws March, an overweight junior. Mothers shriek and pull children to safety. "How come you let your kids cause accidents, Dr. Burns?" asks sober Svenson in his Dr. Einstein mask.

Lines Liz should have written and lines she has written, all kinds of ideas keep coming into her head: those who come to see and be seen, then, make it all happen. In celebration as in desecration, spectators create the spectacle.

The bagpipe is already serenading Bonnie Prince Charlie in front of town hall, when the Jehovah's Witness woman with her frail daughter approaches the Hiroshima float to hand out pamphlets to Liz predicting the end of the world, while Hubert Nolan, the farmer, leads the mule and they slowly move on towards Beach Street, where the parade ends the traditional forty minutes late. Liz wipes off her makeup and runs to the bandstand with Ellen's boys who enjoy startling out of towners with their painted wounds.

The crowd has already gathered waiting for the fireworks and the bonfire. Some sit on their folding chairs just above the beach, others on the sidewalk or stone walls. A great crowd this year waiting for the bonfire and the official fireworks by the water. Others gather around the brightly lit bandstand, where musicians are tuning up. A rare moment when you get to see some who never walk if they can drive. Mismatched pairs, Gramp, the horse-breeder, used to grumble as he sat on a folding chair watching Chris up there on the bandstand and Liz dancing around on the grass. Always worried that the Liz and Chris he had paired off might not stay together.

For Chris and Liz, the band concert had always been an escape from firework explosions and the huge bonfire on the beach. That secret terror had been a bond from the very first Fourth of July celebration. Gramp never gave it a thought, but Arthur knows. He is forever finding Liz out. At summer cocktail parties he will often stay near her, watching and listening and waiting. Protecting her, he makes her feel unprotected, neglected by her husband-brother. Trying to comfort, Arthur is never far removed from the stranger, surrounded by German-speaking students, whose scrutiny had hurled her into "Stolen Child." Hardly a day goes by that he doesn't inquire how her book is coming along. Each time he assures her that nothing is more important then using one's talent, he makes her feel she lacks all talent, while Chris is terrified she might have some.

Gramp would have been so pleased to see Chris, husband of Liz, up on the bandstand again among the local talent playing his recorder. The conductor, skinny Fred Timson, sways like a reed to an Irish medley; the fat lifeguard trumpet, Os Winet, a really good landscape artist, plays the violin. His adoring wife all in white, a picture, standing pretty, listens without hearing mistakes. Nino, the little old barber, is ready to sing his big aria from "Turandot."

The hundred percent white cotton shirt Liz ironed for Chris shows off his golden tan. His hair shines under the lights and his blue eyes sparkle while he pipes a little Irish jig everyone likes. "That boy was a born actor," Gramp would have said with regret. A musician. A natural diplomat. Never made anything of his talents. But didn't Chris, born actor, play his role of the wounded boy to the hilt? Chris the student was too hip to become a hippy. Chris the musician spent hours each day listening to the greatest recorded music in the world. Avoiding vulgar stress of performance. Chris born diplomat had used and always would use all his talents for his own enjoyment. Leaving strife of uncouth competition, to the likes of Dora, the singer, or other attention-getters who decide to write made up memoirs…

Dora can never get enough attention. Gramp used to say she deserves it. As long as Liz can remember she has been singing on the Fourth of July. And here she is again, walking up the steps into the bright light, turning the bandstand into her stage. She starts off by belting out her usual lusty, quavering "America the Beautiful." Firecrackers explode over there on the beach. The volunteer firemen's grinning faces glow in the light of the raging bonfire, while woods up on Witches Hill flare up in the glow of the sinking sun beaming down on the water tower, where names like Mike and Karin, Del and Jiggers, red hearts, as well as colorful obscenities, have been painted out and replaced with GOD IS LOVE.

The applause is for both the sunset tinting the sluggish sea orange-crimson as it sinks, and Dora in her glowing dress up there among the musicians. She grew up poor. No matter how many millions Len makes, she will always feel she deserves to get something free—even from a dead Gramp. When Elgar and Mike were in fourth grade she took the boys and Liz to see all the daffodils that have been planted in the field below the water tower in memory of those who had passed away. High up above, the perfect picture postcard view of Shoreland, Dora had sung "Jerusalem," because the dead might like a sacred song, but then she had rewarded herself, by picking all of Gramp's memorial daffodils

Now as she opens her arms her voice quavers while she gives it her all in her medley of waltz songs. The little ones dance around the bandstand. Mrs. Julett and old Fran, a couple of Garden Club ladies, waltz to Adolf Hitler's favorite tunes in the half dark behind Ellen and her single parents, who have gathered on blankets with baskets of food under an old twisted pear tree, where Jonathan and Billy perch, blowing big iridescent nonburst bubbles. Red gets up on his hind legs snapping and batting at them as they drift in the wind. Little ones—going around and around the bandstand skipping and dancing—reach up, jump to burst them, or bat them with little flags. Ellen and her singles club drink wine out of Coke bottles. One pudding-faced feminist has pulled out her big breast and is publicly suckling a big black infant, rocking him with the music. "Hey, Missie. No drinking in public. This is a dry town." The wind tugs on a "Save the Predators" tiger-balloon tied to the back of his stroller.

"Officer, officer!" Liz spots Denise and runs after her. "There was this ugly clown in the parade, dressed in a fur coat, handing out animal balloons."

"What?" Denise hitches her holster and cuts her off with a smirk. "You mean one of those Horribles wearing bras and wigs and lipstick? Always the same ordinary guys acting weird."

"No, I saw one in Boston with the same "Save the Predator" balloons. Slashed a woman's fake fur coat in a parking garage and is wanted by the Boston police."

"Why don't you report it?" She comes so close you can see that her little eyes have no lashes. She is famous for having cut them to make them grow longer, but they never came back. "Now I'm dealing with something serious right here."

The song ends and cars parked all around honk, applauding the music. Dogs bark. Popey, the shell-shocked veteran, passes out programs, shaking hands with little kids as usual and shaking the paws of dogs he befriends. The Legionnaires are selling popcorn kids have to have, and spill for a happy husky. One of them lets go of an alligator-shaped balloon and shrieks as it rises, gets caught in a tree before it drifts into the bonfire and pops.

During the short intermission, a sudden blast of rock music with falsetto howling broadcasts from an old convertible with huge fins parked on the dark side of the bandstand. Could it be Mike perching on the back of the driver's seat? He doesn't drive.

When Liz gets closer it's a man, not a boy. The forehead has deep frown lines. The mouth a slash, eyes deep-set, piercing blue, and red-rimmed. The mop of glossy curls is a wig. Not a Mike version of Robert Plant the wild-boy vocalist, but the old angry one he must have become. "Female wigs", Mike had said. The three boys in the back are wearing yellow wigs. Liz bites down on the inside of her cheek. Overcome by the sharp pain she leans against the drinking fountain, gulps water and splashes her face. The gang? Not after all that happened. The big vintage car could have been in the parade. How about the Maine license plate? "Are you from Portland?" she shouts to make herself heard. He averts his eyes not fast enough. She has read fear in the blank stare.

He turns the music up. "Sorry, can't hear you Miss."

It strikes her that the racket and the wigs are as frail a veneer as the gild paint on the rusted Cadillac. Boys putting on a show now and always, whether in armor or uniforms, white sheets or clown masks, trying to be scary when they are scared. Ready to hurt someone before they are hurt.

He slides down into his seat and grabs the steering wheel. "Fine tune, isn't it? Our own." Abused instruments blast in discord. "Wish you a pleasant evening."

"A pleasant fuck!" One of the youngsters makes himself heard as the car takes off and turns onto Hill street, swerving to hit a scampering black kitten. Liz runs uphill. The car reverses. She jumps behind a tree.

"Sorry, young lady. "

A kind voice and ugly laughter. Then they're gone. Liz drags herself uphill like a wounded creature, calling kitty, kitty, kitty.

She returns to the crowd as though she had been far away. A long time seems to have passed before she finds herself reporting to Denise that a kitten had been struck deliberately by a dangerous gang. Denise puts on tinted glasses that slide down her snub nose and gives Liz a hard look. "Unrestrained animals, unrestrained bad drivers in an unsafe vehicle, stripped to the waist. So what, what else is new? Wearing women's wigs. Arrest some of those Horribles? What's gotten into you today. Get real!" She swaggers after an unsuspecting, darkhaired young fellow, who is trying to go unnoticed with his run-of-the-mill aviator sun glasses, camera, and backpack.

Liz goes to look for the kitten. Rings a door bell at the nearest house. No one at home. Music starts to play "Yesterday." Angel Myrtle singing. Only yesterday, Liz and Chris had sat on a blanket with Bonnie. Elgar and Caleb would march around the bandstand. Liz leans against a parked car sick with a vision of the gilded car turning around and coming back. Misfits fitting in as part of a multitude of clowns, female wigs, noserings, torn jeans. They might find Mike, but this time Mike wouldn't be alone. When does clowning turn to killing? Disguise is harmless until something or someone turns carnival into combat.

There is Denise still following the unsuspecting stranger. She ducks down when he stops to take pictures of an old fish shack, with Doctor P Pet, his poodle, and Caleb Fairchild in the foreground. When he turns, Denise crouches behind the Stork Shop. Eve, the owner, comes out and asks her whether she needs to use her rest room. Always a line at the public facilities on the pier. You can't just talk to Eve. Denise is forced to visit, while tourists mill around from shop to shop, Caleb, under cover of little and big kids, wheelchairs and baby strollers, hands Dr. P the famous flea powder can. One moment Liz sees them standing near the Lobster Shack, the next they have vanished.

Denise, trying to catch up with her suspect in Harbor Square, ignores out-of-town teenagers at the public phone laughing beer foam into the receiver, doesn't even bother with a sweet-looking dark-skinned girl sitting on the curb by herself, her eyes rolling up until you see mostly the whites, which are pink. In front of the Icecream Patch a little one waves her arms and howls. "Give me back. Give me back my furry bear!"

"Officer, officer, a clown has stolen her fur toy," a small woman calls in a big mannish voice. "A twenty-five dollar bear."

The Cragley brothers in their old vehicle ride bumper to bumper and doff their leather hats. "Have you seen Mike?" Liz calls.

"Got off the float with Karin, but Em cut in."

"You haven't seen the Chief or Dutch?"

"Don't you worry. Not today. We'll be OK!" Caleb shouts back, as he and Dr. P. Pet and his poodle come out a narrow alley and get into the back seats. The twins grin and drive on. At the Pottery Shed Liz catches up with Denise. "You're kind of running scared, Liz. But guys in wigs, clowns and fur toys—clowns—this happens to be the day for it. Always has been. I called in about the cat. Keep it down. Cats have to wait. I'm dealing with something serious!"

The crowd in front of the candle shop is applauding the candle making demonstration, where slender Corella, thick brown hair tied back from wax and flames, presses glitter decorations onto one of her big green Christmas candles. The suspect pops up in her shop window, taking her by surprise with a kiss and a gift-wrapped package.

"Bravo!" shouts a fat man. The crowd claps and cheers and whistles.

Liz is standing beside Denise, who mutters: "Very clever. The package. This is it. I knew it. Make way!" Denise parts the crowd, takes the three steps into the candle shop in one leap and knocks over hot wax. The smell of spilled perfumed wax is sickening. "What are you accusing me of?" Plenty of witnesses hear that fellow cursing her, a female officer of the law.

Day trippers with ice cream cones, babies, grandmothers, mothers, uncles, lovers come pushing to the store. Denise reaches for her holster. "Step back!" The crowd retreats.

"Drug deal. I've been watching him. Don't make a move!"

"Hey, officer. How about his rights?" Mike makes himself heard. Skinny Emerald wearing her costume with wings is clinging to him. "How come this kid knows the law and you don't?" The young guy puts down his leather backpack and grins. "Let the police woman open your birthday present, Corella."

Denise grabs the package, rips it open, and out comes a Cabbage Patch baby doll with adoption papers. Denise holds it to her ear.

"No bomb. I just bought it. You can look at the receipt. If you cut the doll open you'll have to replace it." He flashes an ID.

Someone says: "FBI." The words pass through the crowd and turn into "CIA."

How many in the crowd really know what these letters stand for? Liz shudders at the suggestive power of abbreviations. How many Germans knew that RKFDV—consolidation of the German Race—was an agency for kidnapping? How about the VoMi, office for the repatriation of ethnic Germans? NSV Nazi welfare? Did I make it clear that these agencies had been set up to organize and document the most shameful cruelty with pride?

The town knows she has written a book. "What's it about?" the kindly librarian has asked. If she knew what it was about she wouldn't have written "Stolen Child." She marvels at writers who know what they are writing before it is written. This week she has been going over the galleys, to find out what she has written and also what she left out. Did she make it clear that Nazi Germany, the Thousand-Year Reich, was convinced it was doing everything just right, according to their laws? Does it show how this bygone era of "See no evil, hear no evil, speak no evil, and follow orders," is directly responsible for our time of fascination with disorder? Hearing and seeing and speaking more and more evil? Gobble up more and more of the whipped-up muck?

Soon everyone in Shoreland will say that the CIA agent was about to arrest the bank robber, who took $10,000 from the Elm Street Savings Bank last year; or the escaped rapist, Connecticut child murderer, who tortured preteen age girls to death; or the two escaped convicts carrying big knives who like to slice up old women.

It had all happened on TV, is happening in the streets. Denise Codget, officer of the law, descendant of Codgie the fanatical house-keeper, will increase her vigilance for murderers, for lunatics released from institutions, for addicts spreading AIDS on beaches, and escaped prisoners loose on Main Street. A female wearing a uniform has to prove that she's sharper than a man and faster on the draw.

The morning after the parade Liz wakes up shouting German words. Chris holds and kisses her but she is so scared that he gets scared too and loses his sex drive. "You don't know what that missing kitten is doing to me!" When he reports the facts that Liz had witnessed a killing, he has no inkling of what he is doing to vindicate officer Codget by sending her under the crawl space of 4 Hill Street. Finding Mrs. Peat's black kitten, Collette, murdered by the Portland gang who tried to willfully run down Liz Plant. Denise reports the driver a felon at large, wanted in the Grove Academy assault on Michael Plant.

Chapter 39

JIGGERS

The parade was the greatest ever. There are some who can't quite give up their costumes. Ellen keeps wearing the white doctor's coat for her consultations. Girls who decorated Queen Karin's float still run around looking like bridesmaids. The male ballerina, Speers, a cabinet maker much admired as one of the Horribles because of his fine legs, hasn't stopped wearing his wife Angela's little skirt and halter in his shop. Big joke, which shocks and entertains customers. "By golly," he says to Bonnie, who is getting a lot of feedback. "Men wearing little skirts, that's history. Anthony did when he started making out with Elizabeth Taylor in Cleopatra. Me and Angela, we saw the rerun."

Even Arthur's Doberman, Havelock had sorted out as useless at Grove Academy, keeps carrying the Tyrolean hat she wore in the parade. Known as the worst canine wimp in town. Then it happened he actually growled and snapped, when Billy tried to take the hat. It didn't hurt, but the brothers are having the best time making the champ look bad by smearing themselves with red and blue bomb victim makeup. Now the dog has been fenced in, but she still guards that hat. And in spite of the 100° weather Mike and the Suicide Four dress like winter vampires. No wonder this perpetual July costume party puts a damper on the return of prodigal Jiggers.

When Liz comes along with Saki, Jiggers is standing on a bench in Harbor Square wearing purple bloomers, red slippers curled up at the toes, and to top it off, two ratty braids tied with glitter-bands. A costume that brings to her mind both "Turandot" and "The Mikado," opera stories of a youth whose life depends on the answer to a riddle. "Jiggers. Is that really you?"

"Who knows? Who knows?" He talks about California, that magic land, as though it were Mars. "You want it, you get it. You want to do it, you do it." Good times while you're young, leap frogging a boring worka-day life by blowing your mind to work out the big riddle of whether Jiggers is Jiggers.

Windup boy, battery run down, his bloodshot eyes move slowly from side to side until they rest on the sewer pipe monument, encircled with Garden Club flowers as he is by the Harbor Square gang in tie-dyed T-shirts and thrift shop hats left over from the parade, plus a cluster of small brothers with skateboards one wearing a black beard, and small sisters in ballerina skirts with pink bows and scooters. His own little cousin, Gretchen, wearing a chef's hat and black lace gloves.

Jiggers holds up the front page of the "Shoreland Eagle" with the col-ored picture of Emmet Gray posing on his stationary bike in front of a map of France, wearing the white helmet and scarlet Spandex tights he got for the parade and holding a fitness expert Jack La Lanne sign, WHEN YOU QUIT EXERCISING, YOU LET GO, AND THE DEVIL WILL GET YOU. Emmet, had been pedaling his stationary bike while keeping an eye on both his odometer, and the old war map while following the road to Paris that the German army had taken. Emmet had already weighed well over two hundred pounds then. The army had found him unfit. He certainly changed that. Now that he almost has the mileage, Emmet gets carried away during the interview and brags about going into Boston for an evening in Paris with the alluring Thelma Nesbit in her pur-ple Cadillac.

"Just read this and read it good!" Jiggers expounds. "Here I'm back and looking at 'Help Wanted'. What do I see? an old body-builder freak— round belly, thin legs like a black spider—bragging about ridin' around like in that custom-colored purple Cadillac with the Nesbit woman. And I used to work for that bitch." He waves that memory away with both arms, and a bell on his pink psychedelic T-shirt jingles. Some of the little ones wave their arms too. "We have to work. Old guys have the money to do what they want," he concludes.

"They can't fuck!" says Svenson.

"Fuck. Can't fuck, fuck," the little ones say after him and clap their hands.

"My Granddad fornicates." Brian, the brain, pushes his dark-rimmed spectacles up his nose. "It keeps him young." The racket of the old Sunny Creek Milk truck cuts off details. But nothing wakes up big Caleb Fairfield, dressed in rags and snoring on the back bench, catching up on sleep since his father makes him get up at eight in the morning. Barney has stretched out in the shade under the bench. Elgar and Tom are trying to get Jiggers interested in driving them to the Grateful Dead show in his van. They are discussing jobs that would earn them enough money to pay for the tickets when Mike pops up from behind the sewer pipes.

"What are you doing here, Mom?"

She could ask the same question, since he usually sleeps until noon. "Looking at Jiggers."

Karin woke Mike up because she disapproves of his lifestyle. He is in a bad mood.

"Cool. Maybe I'll braid my hair too." No reaction from Mother.

"Mail order some bloomers. But what happened to the sound effects, man?"

"Dead. Dead."

"Going on the Dead Tour," Tick grins. "Cool, I'm with you, man!"

"Me! Me too! Me. I'll help pay for gas."

When Jiggers raises his arms he reeks as though he had been hung up and cured with incense. "Dead. My baby's dead. I'm through with women. All of them. Same in Cal. They don't want my kids. Del didn't even get rid of hers. It was born dead. All of them dead." He keeps staring at the sewer pipe, sniffing, breathing in the home smell of the Harbor Square sewer exhaust. "Day and night I see them little skeletons flying around. Indian man says to me, go meditate at the graves. Where are the graves?" He stops and stares. "That's what it's all about. Meditatin' at the sewer pipe."

Everyone closes in on Jiggers, waving arms in front of him, shooing dead infants like Hunter S. Thompson shooed away invisible bats. And Jiggers whimpers about losing his guitar, doesn't remember where. "Lost my music." Tunes of death in his head play out into nothingness, the nothingness of coming down.

Liz, the writer who isn't writing anymore, can feel tears run down her cheek.

"Mom, what's the matter? This is no place for you. She never cries. Why don't you go home." Mike turns on the skateboard and scooters gang, "Get lost. All of you, scat!" The younger brothers and sisters line up behind Liz. Jiggers is the one who starts walking away. Funny to see Jiggers move slow as a zombie-robot-windup toy, winding down towards his painted van which had stalled on Willow Road. A procession of the little brothers and sisters forms behind him. He turns around, growls, and barks as good as Eckert's Doberman tape. Kids bark back. So does Barney. They follow Jiggers, skipping and laughing. Tick, Elgar, Svenson and Mike fall in. Liz and Saki quietly tag along towards big houses that are set back on lawns above Meadow Beach. The Baker sisters come trotting along on horseback from Chestnut Lane and follow behind her.

Jiggers kicks a pink flower and breaks a blossom sprig, and the little followers start kicking blossoms too. Liz, tells them, "Stop hurting the pansies!"

Jiggers doesn't remember the names of flowers anymore or anything like that. Brian, who remembers everything, starts chanting the names of local flowers and blooming shrubs, as well as names of birds. When Jiggers takes the lane toward the headlands marked PRIVATE ONE WAY, Brian goes on to name the elderly people who live in the big old summer houses with big new cars in the garages. The last house, the Thelma Nesbit residence, is hidden behind blooming hedges that smell sweet. "Too much perfume," Jiggers says. The little ones hold their noses and shriek. He faces them like a tour guide and talks about the big house sitting above the ocean, the swimming pool where Thelma Nesbit floats around in heated sea water, red hair all piled up on top and wearing a purple bathing suit. How she would smoke a cigar while standing over him to make sure the hedges got a decent haircut. "Pull out the uglies, boy." For her flowers have to be purple or magenta; the others are uglies. Then there was Gloria, her pet pig. With a long snout and ears sticking straight up, an Amsworth sow. Wild old English forest pig. She'd tie purple ribbons around its neck. It bit, but it was smart, used its own toilet. Its own purple sofa, snored, rode around town in that purple Cadillac with her. Jiggers says he could see himself end up dressed in purple, leading the good life. She always made sure he had lots of good grub, and he ate like a pig in that house.

"I want to see the pig!" His little cousin makes herself heard." The pig toilet! Take me too. Me. Me!"

"The pig's dead. I had to dig this giant grave. Clymes, the artist, made her an eight hundred dollar sleeping pig headstone. No graves allowed in gardens, but that woman does what she wants to and you do as she says."

The big PRIVATE KEEP OUT sign at the driveway to the garage is new. The poisoned pig had made news and so had Jiggers, when he refreshed himself with her gin at the pig memorial service. Nesbit fired him. Nothing has changed. Purple rump of the purple Cadillac sticking out of the garage. He opens the door. Key in the ignition as usual. Low mileage. Pricey Cadillac just sits around waiting. "My old van won't even start."

"I'd rather have a Jaguar!" Brian, the seven-year-old genius speaks-up.

The weather changed and it was cold and windy. The day the mailman finally delivered the bound galleys of Liz's book. Reviewers all over the country are supposed to get one too. The sun comes out and fragrant steam rises from the road and gardens and the shore. She's proud, but also worried because the title has been changed to "Smiling Child", which Chris says makes it sound like a "how to" baby book.

At midmorning she allows herself to be consoled by Bonnie with iced tea and fruit tarts at the open bay window where the breeze fans you with the fragrance of lavender and the sea at high tide. "Now aren't we lucky," Bonnie says as they sit side by side looking out over the garden beyond marshland where shimmering deep blue water meets the sky. "Not a cloud. Perfect. Not too many calls this morning." Then one of the phones rings on the window shelf, which is full of notebooks, telephones, and geraniums. Liz can hear Thelma Nesbit clamoring, "Custom color, Bonnie. Purple, my Cadillac!"

All of Shoreland knew about Emmet's date with Thelma after the Emmet Gray interview appeared in the "Eagle." She was getting ready for their Boston evening in Paris, had an appointment at the Beauty Nook, her car was supposed to be washed this morning. Now it's missing.

Bonnie says: "Mustn't take it so personally, Thelma. Don't let that spoil your fun. Buddy Elberg often drives you into town. I'll call him and he can take you in his own limo. What difference does it make? No one can see whether the car is purple or not after dark. I'll call the police for you, but I bet you anything that the car will be back in the garage by the time you get back. The ten minute walk to the Beauty Nook will calm you down, Thelma. Have a good one now."

Another phone rings. Thelma again. Bonnie calls the police station and gets, "This call will be recorded." Then Denise gets on the line trying to sound friendly like Bonnie with a cheerful, "Can I help you? Stolen car? We're on alert for an escaped prisoner. Criminally insane. Must be looking for transportation."

"Denise, you always dream up the worst. Why should a mentally ill person come all the way out here to take Thelma's car?"

"Because he's crazy."

"Come off it, now!"

"You're right. Plenty of crazy kids right here. Emmet reported one speeding by yesterday. Long, curly hair. Mike Plant?"

"Mike doesn't have a license," Bonnie tells Denise.

"That never stops anyone from driving here. Why don't you ask Liz? She always knows what the kids are up to, but then she won't tell. Neither will Harriet. When I was taking riding lessons from her up at the pit with a bunch of girls, I'd be the one to report big cars in the quarry."

Liz slips away after Bonnie hangs up. Garfield stretches out in a sunny spot with geraniums, phones. He twitches and claws the air, dreaming of catching things, just like Denise. Bonnie has to laugh to herself. No one ever caught Jeff and his friends. They didn't mean any harm, those young guys taking a joy ride in any Cadillac they could get going. "Boys will be boys," she tells the sleeping cat. "Of course it's awful, but it used to happen all the time. Rare now."

They were usually dead drunk in the end when they'd send it down into a quarry. You just haven't lived if you haven't seen one rolling, rolling, and then smack- splash, and gurgling down to drown, Jeff would say to shock Bonnie. Something you never forget. "He was wild and wild about me too," she says to the cat. That was after Jeff's father lost his job in the

shoe factory and died. And walking through town he and his friends
never forgot to greet Cadillac owners. In fact, if those owners had had any
sense, they'd have known that those friendly kids had dumped their big
car into a quarry. That's the way it used to be done. Never really meant
any harm.

Bonnie calls her cousin, the riding teacher who continues to live in
the family house up at Tompkins Pit. After vandals had shut it down,
Harriet Tompkins Olifson took the law into her own hands, patrolling her
land with a posse of her regular horse-crazy schoolgirls.

"Glad to get you in. Thelma's Cadillac is missing. Is there a car in
your quarry?"

"Not my quarry anymore! You better call Len Myrtle. He took it away
from me."

"He doesn't live up there. You do. Best to put a stop to any of that old
car-dumping before they get started again. One thing always leads to
another. They mean no harm, but we can't just allow that to happen."

"Everything's allowed to happen, Bonnie." Harriet remembers how her
late husband Blakeley, a science teacher, used to carry on about the ocean
and even the sky being used as an open sewer. Ever since the days of the
first space travelers, mice. "Blakely laughed at me. Said I must be the only
person in the world who cried when they shot mice into outer space to
die."

"You're right, Harriet. I never gave it a second thought."

"One day there'll be a traffic problem up there in the heavens,"
Blakeley used to say, "with so much junk in orbit. Remember the days
when trucks dumped trash at the edge of the woods or, even better, sent it
down after the big cars that sat rusting in the cove quarries?"

Bonnie is thinking of astronauts landing on the clean, silent moon,
while hazardous waste on earth quietly piled up here, there and everywhere. Atomic tests blasted off. Nuclear energy plants threatened to poison
people and their food. No one worried about nothing. "Remember the
way ten year olds used to take shot-guns into our woods and aim at anything that moved? No more. You and Blakeley made the difference. You
got signatures and he wrote letters that helped pass a law to jail any Dad
who hands his rifle to a boy." Bonnie knows only too well that bombs,
guns, any kind of blasting or smashing or trashing comes naturally to boys.
By the time the law passed nothing much moved anymore in the woods.

The cousins had walked through the scorched parts that vandals had burned and left silent and dead as the moon. But that winter in the snow Harriet had seen the tracks of mice. The great survivors.

"You were the one who helped stop the car dumping years ago, Harriet, just by riding up there with all the horsey girls."

"Let Len Myrtle worry. Wicked, the way he bought the quarry out from under me."

"Len did have his men clean out the Little Cove Pit for the kids. I was there. You should have seen it. Trash, rusted cars, washing machines. Water covered with scum from all the garbage. What they didn't find! The New Testament in large print, hundreds of books rotting down there. Stolen bikes. The VW Beetle they hoisted on dry land hadn't had time to rust. Someone fixed it up. Put the hood of a drowned Cadillac on it."

Harriet laughs out loud, but she feels like crying. "Myrtle had himself written up as a conservationist one day. The next one, he shows up with a lawyer and chocolate covered ginger at Gold Meadow nursing home. That's Len Myrtle for you. Got my brother Flip to sign all those papers."

Bonnie does remember that Harriet's brother, Flip, old enough to be her father, had lost interest in everything except chocolate-covered ginger by the age of eighty nine.

"Flip would have sold his soul away for that two-pound box, and he refused to give even one piece to Len or the two lawyers. This proved he was of sound mind."

"All the same, Harriet, the moment cars are dumped in the pit, Len's lawyers will say undeveloped land is asking for trouble. Remember how they carried on about yuppies turning Tompkins Pit into a nudist quarry, inviting immorality, hints at the spread of drugs, disease and crime. Not to mention that murder in the woods?"

Bonnie is right. Myrtle company's big signs—PRIVATE PROPERTY; NO TRESPASSING—have been riddled with bullet holes. (Kids say by one of his own men.) So he can prove that the gun law no longer works. A picture in the "EAGLE" of cars being fished out of the pit could revive the good-old bad-old days, which might very well help Leonard to get his building permits for the condominiums, to make the wilderness area around the Tompkins safe by doing away with it.

"Leonard always thinks he's doing right. Crazy about Dora and Elgar. He means no harm," Bonnie says.

Harriet gets so mad she hangs up.

The phones in Bonnie's office are so quiet that she catches herself thinking of Jeff. How it had been easy to spot old Cadillac killers because, rich or poor, married, divorced, remarried once or thrice, they used to drive an old or new Cadillac. Jeff traded his in because Ellen made fun of it. Through the open window Bonnie listens to a mockingbird singing like a song sparrow. Beyond her garden monarch butterflies flicker among milkweed. "Garfield, I feel ashamed, but I don't really want Jeff back. Isn't that awful?" The cat has had enough sun and makes himself comfortable in the most uncomfortable spot between phone books and geraniums. One of the red cardinals likes to perch on the pink rose-geranium basket hanging under the crabapple tree. As Bonnie sits back in Aunt Codget's old wicker chair looking out towards the calm sky and calm water, basking in her moment of peace, she says a prayer for deliverance from all the terrible mischief in the world done by boys who mean no harm.

Chapter 40
NIGHT MUSIC

Harriet likes to do everything her own way, just right, always on time, and she is proud of it. Summer and winter she and her two dogs eat at 5:30. Then she checks up on Maggie. How many horses named Maggie has she had in her stable? She gives her a carrot and a hug for all the good horses. The August picture on her calendar is a white stallion. Harriet checks off Tuesday the sixth. Christ on the mountain. Feast of the Transfiguration. She goes out and sits on the highest rock with her rescued greyhounds to watch the sun go down.

Honeycomb sun patterns dance on granite slabs that could have been cut by Harriet's grandfather, a foreman at the quarry. Apartment houses in the big cities were built from Shoreland granite cut by him and all those hardy Scandinavians. He was 43 years old when he bought the quarry and surrounding land. The money, he said, came to him from Sweden. But he had been a dowser, well known for finding not only water but also lost objects. There were rumors that he had found gold up in the woods, buried under the cellar stones on the Common by the early settlers, who had lived in fear of war and pirates.

Greyhounds sit beside her, listening to changing sounds of the end of the day. Leonard did promise Harriet a new stable and the right to continue riding in Quarry Town after he put up his condos. There'd be no more bonfires and beer-guzzling teenagers. The nice people living in Quarry Town would enjoy tennis, cookouts, riding lessons, of course. But Leonard Myrtle can be forgetful, and he got so involved backing developers at Walden Pond that he never did get around to giving Harriet anything in writing.

At sundown she picks up her binoculars and trains them on the far end of Tompkins Pit, where the motor biker is taking off his pants and everything else, but he always wears a bathing cap. Real fussy about his hair which he has done at the Beauty Nook. She doesn't know his name, but she knows his ways, as she knows the ways of a gray fox who is a loner.

As vice president of the local Audubon Society, she likes to watch and protect all the different ways of wild life: birds, monarch butterflies, frogs. Early this summer, Jeff Martin did a land office business selling little nets to kids. They showed up at the quarries, caught frogs and tadpoles, stuffed them into buckets, and parents considered this a learning experience. The ones they let go were caught by a few out-of-town scrawny junior high boys, who showed off by torturing the creatures because girls didn't like to see them do it. They were ripping a bullfrog apart, stuffing another one with stones, squashing tadpoles, when the biker pounced on them, screamed all kinds of slogans about endangered species which they couldn't hear because he ducked their heads down in water they had polluted with bodies of tortured creatures.

Parents who consider hunting, catching, and killing part of the American way of life came after him. When he hopped onto his motorbike and rode away, they turned on Harriet. Mike Plant and his pals happened along in good time, and Mike delivered a lecture on how native Americans, like the bullfrogs, had been wiped out by trespassers. Once Mike gets started no one gets a word in edgewise, and when he is telling everyone what they should not do, you can be sure he is about to get himself into trouble. But his long sermon did wear the young parents down. They gathered up their kids, the nets, and coolers. "You're not welcome here anymore," Harriet told them.

The biker, a stranger, has become part of the natural order around her and is welcome. She likes the way he soaps himself and then hurls his fine white body into the pit. Red jumps after him and takes the lead, crossing the deep water. Something to behold. The little bit of soap will soon be washed away by underwater springs. On a hot day he and Red come once or twice a day, but they never stay long. She could hardly report the skinny dipper without letting everyone know she has been watching a naked man. Really no different to her from watching that kingfisher diving down on the west side of the pit, breaking the green reflection of boulders, darting down after a tadpole that will shoot into the deep darkness like a golden bullet.

Suddenly her dogs leap up, stand very still, and quiver. They hear something, expect something, before it even begins to happen. Then the natural way of everything is shattered. Someone laughs too loud. "Stay, wait," Harriet says to her dogs; they sit and tremble. Leaves flicker in the sun. She now trains her binoculars on a kid in some kind of theater costume running down a back trail. If this is that science fiction film, where is the crew?

"Crazy kids," she tells the dogs. "You should know that by now." Most of them have summer jobs, and on an evening like this they come up the trail at the north end of the huge pit with a keg. Then she will see the glow of their campfire and hear a guitar. Singing, laughter, and shouting of thirty or more boys. There is never more than a paper cup or two of beer for each at a big keg party, but police will come after them—trying to enforce the law as it had been enforced on them in their day.

Now the flaming sunset casts a crouching sphinx on the dark granite slab across the pit where shadows notch a cross which changes into a crooked cross as the light plays on rocks that preceded such symbols of recorded time. Her three dogs stand quivering, poised, ready to race, as the shrill voices echo; golden light trails over the deep water, and stoned boys tumble down into the pit, upside-down falling angels, both afterimage and foreshadowing.

❊ ❊ ❊

Kitchen windows are wide open. Mike, with Elgar, Tick, and Del's brother Sonny, enjoying a few beers behind the old brick grill, can hear every word without being seen. Mike, who already has a buzz on, stretches out on the warm grass watching buzzing loser bugs tap-tap bumble against the screen, trying to get into the lighted kitchen where they won't want to be.

Dad telling Mom that not even Bonnie believes that one of the movie guys stole Thelma's car. "But you think kids are victims of society and you're on their side. Isn't that what your book's all about? You have this illusion that Mike will straighten out at home with you and be just fine making up what he missed this year in Shoreland High."

"He was nearly killed at Grove, Chris."

"And he had difficulty breathing when he was born. He has no close relatives and is acting-out to get attention. You can blame Grimes, the Coach, all his teachers," Dad goes on. "Gang of juvenile criminals on campus who beat him up. And then the Nazis. Of course the Nazis! They changed the world. No moral values. Mike is a victim of his time, just like you."

Dad must be quoting one of his shrinks. "I hate to tell you, but Mike doesn't want you on his side anymore. You'll have to let go." He had heard Mike shout, "I hate you! Stay out of my life!" when she tore up Dad's check for the trail bike Mike wanted. Just because Fat Head, the last owner, is now in a wheel chair! Then she even questioned Mike about Caleb and the pet store manager and that flea powder. "Stay out of my life," he had told her again, this time without getting mad. More as an impersonal warning, like "Dangerous Curve," or "Don't Drink Tap Water."

"Your Dad sounds like a preacher," Sonny whispers. "He's born again. So is Ellen Burns. When I was working as a dishwasher at the Whale's Jaw last winter, there was a big prayer meeting or something. I saw them both there. Brother! That deliverance service with an exorcist was a real blast. Bonnie, the telephone lady, was there too."

Dad born again! It all makes sense. Just took a while before he stopped yelling and got that blank expression. Quite a shock. But Ellen? Mom clatters with dishes, public radio is playing a piece called "A Little Night Music", and Dad's after-dinner TV medical program on disgusting herpes wafts from the house with the good smell of beef stew and garlic toast. All the comfort and discomfort of home, interrupted by a special report: Federal agents have confiscated three tons of marijuana from a Bolivian vessel. The boys from the Suicide Four Band snicker. Tom the Tick says, "Lucky dogs, those agents."

"Hi! Any of you hungry?" Mom asks, when Mike leads the musicians, Tick and Sonny through the kitchen. "I'll leave some stew on the stove."

The self-closing cellar door slams behind Sonny, startling him. He let his bangs grow down to his nose since his last arrest, can't see too well and trips on the steps. His guitar clatters down.

"What's the matter—drunk again?" Tick says.

"Sure! His sister Del stumbles a lot too. That's how she had a dead baby. Me and Del got to be nervous from when Father got drunk. All those geeks make us nervous. All the picking up, cleaning, praying."

So different here. Sonny runs down through sticky cobwebs to the messy cellar, where Mike has set up his big drum set and amplifiers as well as the piano Elgar got at the dump. Mike used to get wine his father stored in the old root cellar. There is a new lock on the door, but Liz leaves ginger ale and home-made butter cookies in an antique ice-box.

The boys leave Liz feeling superfluous as they walk around and past her, like the old worn kitchen furniture, an obstacle. She can hear them belt out their songs, but the words are lost in a thunder of drums, thumping rhythm from the piano, and the waltz the kitchen radio plays each hour on the hour until midnight. Then, a poet starts reading "Shaft of terror, mindless cloud," while she is washing pots and Chris's television doctor holds forth in the parlor: "Incurable, contagious. You're on the air. Let's have your question." As she reaches for the hot water faucet, she knocks down a stack of store coupons and that booklet

AWAKE! ARE WE RUNNING OUT OF WATER? THE WATCH-TOWER ANNOUNCING JEHOVAH'S KINGDOM. THE HANDWWRITING ON THE WALL—DO YOU SEE IT? A LOOK AT DANIEL'S PROPHECY.

The picture on the cover shows a man's hand clutching a faucet. That Jehovah's Witness booklet has been around since the parade, warning her that the world is certainly coming to an end. Liz always believes everything missionaries say while they are talking to her. She's easily converted, but it doesn't last.

Children trained as disciples in Nazification School remained susceptible to all kinds of conversions. She wrote this long ago, when she was taking classes at the New School and was on her own in New York. Gramp had passed away, Chris had turned away from her when she met a bearded prophet on the subway who asked her to leave the sack of books and notebooks with her writing on her seat, leave the world behind, come away to a grand gathering on Staten Island with him, where she would enter the Bahai World of Faith. Vegetarian, non-violent, perfumed with sandalwood

incense, hair wispy as smoke, eyes soft as the night. What if she had gone
with him? Liz reads religious pamphlets the way her school friend Leona,
who never wore anything but jeans, reads fashion magazines.

The forlorn rhythms thunder up from the basement accompanied by
laughter. Then Mike starts pounding his drums again, while she finds herself drumming along with him on pots she has to dry and put away. When
the band stops, her own drumming has taken on the haunting rhythm of
Germanized children's marching feet. If any of them were ever returned to
their parents, how could this select and endangered species go back to the
loving imperfection of family life?

The cast iron lid to the garbage hole bangs in the garden. Then bangs
again. The big weightlifter, body-builder raccoon, must have moved the
brick and is holding the lid open for small ones who scoop garbage out of
the hole. A family troop of raccoons performing like circus acrobats. The
bathroom light falls on a fat young coon lying on its back, draining a beer
can the boys left out there. The trio down in the cellar starts up again,
with clanging and the thumping hard-rock clamor of abused instruments,
shout-singing and harsh laughter of teens abandoning parents, who want
them safe, for their conformist tribal life.

After Caleb lets himself in through the bulkhead, he makes himself useful
to his friends by picking the padlock on the old root cellar door, where the
Plants store liquor. Mike, who has been deprived of a trailbike, plays host
with vodka, which he pours into the half-empty ginger ale bottle.

Tick says there's a keg party at Tompkins Pit.

"Long hike." Elgar says. "Cops looking for Jiggers and the purple
Cadillac. Think nothing of locking us up."

"Your dad bought that pit. You own the land. They can't say we're trespassing," Mike speaks up and drains his glass.

"I can drive. I have my permit," Sonny says.

Mike could have been riding up to Tompkins Pit on that trail bike
right now, with Em, if it hadn't been for dumb Mother. She spoiled it all.
"We can borrow Mom's car."

They have a couple more drinks and listen to bootleg tapes from
Grateful Dead shows. Fair enough. Mike leaves the tape on, leads the way
soundlessly up the stairs and holds the door to keep it from banging shut.
The kitchen is empty, but Ringo squeaks and whistles, when he snatches

Mom's car key from the hook.

Her straw hat is in the back of the car. Sonny puts it on. Anyone would think she is driving them. The car weaves over to the left lane and wants to dance. A biker behind them honks his horn and tries to pass on the wrong side. Breaking the law! Caleb gives him the finger. "What's the matter with you? Are you drunk skunk?" he shouts out the window.

The biker roars by and turns onto the quarry road. "After him!" Tom squeals.

"He's getting away!" Elgar sounds relieved.

Sonny turns down the headlights and speeds uphill. The car swerves and bumps over a rock. They all laugh. No different from Saki chasing anything that moves faster, until Mike hears Elgar say, "I hate that guy." Del was OK until that creepy biker took over. "I bet he's been shooting holes into our NO TRESPASSING sign."

"Hold it. That's it." There in the undergrowth stands the deserted Nesbit Cadillac.

"Purple beast," Elgar is beside himself. "Lucky, lucky, lucky you. Dad just had the Pit chained off."

"Won't stop us, right?" Mike turns up the music. "Go, go for it Sonny." An echo of the voice ordering Big and the weasels to kill a boy dressed up in glossy leather. So, that's what it is like. Doing it unto others. Doing bad to feel good.

They get close enough to see the biker avoid the chain by riding around the post and through the bushes. "After him!" Sonny backs up the wagon, goes at it full speed, and the chain rattles to the ground. They all cheer. "Money your old man got for the grand piano we gave you should pay for a hundred chains or a thousand," Mike tells Elgar.

❀❀❀

Something made Harriet hang the lasso up on her bed post. Her bed full of dogs, she is watching the news about the MacArthur Foundation Genius Award going to a fifty-seven-year-old magician, who has used his skills to debunk self-styled psychics, seers, as well as promoters of miracle cures. Those women in the chicken farm better watch out. She dozed off and then wakes up with rhythmic pounding of the old granite days in her ears, echoed by the thumping of her heart from a worry-dream about the rooster she gave away. Homer, who has everyone all stirred up, walking back home to his hens and getting in front of a car. She didn't even pull down the blinds. That lopsided moon shining on her bed must have made her dream. On TV men and women are running and shouting, while a house is burning down. She turns it off. "Well, I never!"

She'd never forget the greyhounds standing at the open window side by side as though it were a starting line. "Shivering on a warm night like this?" A pair of self-styled psychics. Dorian, who has the eyes of an Egyptian prince is going "Mrrmmmam," his sound of serious warning sometimes half an hour ahead of time. She goes to the window and doesn't have to wait long before she can hear the sound of that bike. Followed by a car. Not like that one to bring company back up here. "How did a car get through the chain?"

None of her business. What if Leonard's boy Elgar rode up here? She catches a glimpse of her own ruddy old face in the mirror, transformed by the wicked smile of a chubby, horse-crazy school girl. Graham Plant had been the one who named her Harry, when she worked for him exercising horses. She was crazy about old Graham—started riding around dressed like a cowboy to make him laugh, and never ever changed her ways.

What would Bonnie say? She starts to shiver like the dogs and doesn't stop until she is in her saddle. And from the village, in the far distance, an unlikely rooster crows three times and then three times, again. Homer missing his hens.

Caleb is sharing his weed. "Riding high," Elgar chants, as the night turns into a video for their song. They scrape a tree stump at the turn-off to the water. "Where is he? Where?"

"Look out!"

The wagon hits something. Sonny brakes, jolting them, and they curse. "Did we hit him?" Elgar asks.

Mike leans over to turn on the high beam and Caleb staggers out. "Only his jacket and the helmet." He puts it on. Mike stays in the car and watches Sonny stumble through the headlights wearing Mom's straw hat, while Tick swings the empty vodka bottle and lets it fly against a slab of granite, to smash and splinter. Sonny trips, falls forward. "Hey, look. His gold chains and the big cross."

Caleb takes the chain from him and holds it in the beam of a head light. "Come and see, Mike."

The cross reminds Mike of Bonnie. "Put it back."

"Here are some clothes. He stripped!"

"But where's the bike?" Ticks high voice.

The racket of the engine starts up at the far end of the pit. Sputtering, racing, grinding, scraping. And then, "Splash down. Fucking splash down!"

"Why would he do that, now?"

"Shut up. Can you hear anyone swimming?"

Mike gets into the drivers seat and clutches the steering wheel. Here we go again! I come on the scene and someone OD's. He stares out at the dark quarry wall and feels sick. Dad will find the padlock to the root cellar has been sprung and will miss that bottle of vodka. Then the car. If I never come back would Dad be glad? Maybe Jesus Christ got the idea that his dad wanted him to be killed, because J. C. did too much good performing miracles? Bible stories Bonnie told come back and make sense. You turn the high beam off. Kill the engine and stare out into the dark until you see an invisible black cross appear on a slab of granite. THC becomes significantly more potent combined with alcohol, says Nancy Reagan.

"Hey, are you there, man? It's us!" boys call across the pit. Not a sound. Elgar says, "We shouldn't have chased him. Need a ride?" He shouts across the black pit. "A ride", the echo calls back.

An echo. That's the only answer ever, Mike is thinking. The distant, drumming, and clatter and barking. The grinding, harsh scraping, and the ultimate roar, the take off, an echo from the hell of Mom's fears. Splash down resounds in silence as the clouds drift and the moon drenches the boys in the icy light which ripples on stirred-up black water. They drown in silence.

"Shit. What was that?" The Tick breaks the spell. They take off and scamper leaving Mike behind.

In the bowling alley of his mind he's the kingpin, the last target for the last seconds of his world. You hear pounding hoofs gallop away your seconds. The polite voice of the executioner on an intercom broadcasts death from a gilded junkyard rocket where all that has gone before boomerangs from the descent, down, down. The car hits a tree stump, a door flings open smacking undergrowth as it rolls over bushes, bumping over rocks and down, down. Plunk, thump, faster. A young pine comes racing up hill to smack-bash the hood. It flips open. Only the good die young. Do you dream on when you die young? Hair keeps growing and fingernails. And after Christ was wasted, he made it back to his dad. Then all the Christian martyrs had themselves murdered too so they'd get up to heaven after him. Echo of death is always more death.

Mike listens intently to the sound of wind making music in a dead tree, last year's dry leaves clinging to brittle twigs. The tree creaks and snaps, crackling under the wheels. You cling with the dead leaves—hear one leaf drop, feel the world move on as water pours in. A captain does not leave a sinking craft. Mike tries to sing "Stairway to Heaven" as water rises to his knees, but a bitter taste comes up his throat; he starts to heave. Won't do. Won't do at all, a captain doesn't vomit in the cabin. Mike holds onto the wheel and retches, hanging out the door. Dogs bark, a horse gallops. A rodeo on Mars. All at once an invisible power encircles his left shoulder fastening tight under the armpit. "Get moving. Get out!"

The squeaky voice of fat Harriet Simons, the cowboy, wearing a coalminer's lantern, has him roped in. "You must be dead drunk or worse. Rolling down in that car. If it weren't for shrubs…" Her greyhounds whimper around him as he gasps for air to let out a scream when she yanks him away from the car over rocks, spikes and thorns.

He pukes, dogs sniff around him. She whistles, calling them off. "Look what you've done to that young pine! Get up on your feet." Mike struggles out of the rope. She pulls it in. "Out of here!" her voice booms. "Out of here. Vanish! Get off my land." Then she remembers it isn't her land. "Don't want to get mixed up with Myrtle." She sticks two fingers into her mouth and whistles. The white horse comes to her. "I know nothing. Haven't seen you. Get lost!"

Even the moon obeys and goes behind clouds. He lies in the dark unable to crawl out of his nightmares. Silence. Too much silence after she rides away. Followed by crackling and ripping. He stumbles as though he hadn't learned to walk when he tries to stand up. Falls to his knees and listens to the final splash, followed by sucking, bubbling, as the car that had carried him from school to school sinks down, taking the troublemaker he had been down with it. "It's over. I'm getting old!"

Chris should have walked out when Beatrice Strout came on. She has this trick of staring at you, or rather the camera when she says Americans are becoming hypochondriacs about cholesterol and worry about everything they do and eat. Half-starving themselves, or getting fat. Over-medication is drug addiction. Where are the smiling faces in America? On commercials.

"A reviewer who really loves that book let me have the bound galley of "Smiling Child." Story of one of those blonde children Nazis stole by the thousands. The author, Liz Plant, is a brilliant new woman writer. The book is a gem. You better believe it. Those Nazis were phobic. They did away with some of those children if hair turned dark. This is a wonderful story of a female child in a phobic male world."

Chris becomes phobic watching Strout plugging Liz's book. What if it becomes a bestseller? Chris imagines her in the orbit of the rich and famous with her dog and the computer, while Ellen the traitor is honeymooning in England with his psychiatrist. He can see himself left alone to fend for himself in the company of Mike, Saki, and the guinea pig.

His new, positive, vital self says, "Who's up watching talk shows in the middle of the night, anyway? Who'd pay any attention to Strout the femininist, that nut?" The new, strong, truth-loving Chris knows that every insomniac young woman in America is drinking her in and ready to buy "Smiling Child" and waiting to see Liz Plant the writer on TV.

And Liz is up there sleeping with Saki on the bed. She will get up at 5:30, put on her leotard, and work out in front of the set as usual. Then she will clean the kitchen, have breakfast with the animals, and run upstairs to her MATE II. Eckert was the one who asked her whether she is writing another book. "Just writing," she had said. "I'm used to it now."

Chris wanders upstairs and gingerly enters the room of the now famous writer. The computer is on. "Webster's Dictionary" and "Roget's Thesaurus" have been left on the floor. He pushes the books out of radiation range with his foot, kneels down, and looks for "phobia" in the thesaurus. Category 892. Starts with Phob(o) goes from mythical monsters, spookiness to (fear of people etc.) androphobia (men), gynephobia (women), parthenophobia (young girls), pedophobia (children); tyrannophobia.

No parent phobia! But the list goes on and on: fear of priests, the Pope, people, crowds, mobs, English and French, to Germanophobia. Japanese, Jews, Negroes, Russians, fear of all kinds of animals, things, natural phenomena. Disease! There is fear of situations, fear of places, fear of activities, like crossing the street. Ermitophobia, fear of being alone. Chris goes back to 14, fear of disease. Febrophobia, fear of fever. Quite a list. Fear of worms. But fear of radiation is missing. His jeans feel tight. He must be putting on weight from all the health foods. How about fear of dust and dirt? Lots of it around here. As he sits on the floor his eye wanders up to the computer desk. Something sticking out through the plastic bars on the side of DEC-MATE II: frail bent wire legs reaching out imploringly. Long antennae protrude trembling in the computer breeze. Radiation must have confused the praying mantis to crawl into the deadly prison.

Chris crawls along the dusty white rug like a cautious bug. It's really the protective duode, crystals, and bloodstones, moonstone—all kinds of junk he got at the Healing Center making his pocket bulge and jeans tight, pinching his balls without protecting him from teratophobia: fear of monsters. A natural male-eating female frozen in prayer position.

He stiffens and can't get up: stesophobia, fear of standing. Makes a mental list of all his phobias, starting with fire, water, (drowning), ergophobia (fear of work). On and on. And he has to add fear of radiation, which is not listed. No psychiatrist has ever helped him trace it all back to the phobophobia—fear of fear—of a brave little wounded boy. The ultimate.

The door opens to give Chris a start. "What you doing in Mom's funk hole? You going to write a book, Dad? Meditating on the rug?"

"Just studying the dictionary." Chris surprises himself. He is happy to see Mike, and happy to rule out pedophobia, fear of children. "You're wet. Did you go for a nighttime swim? Your mother used to jump into the water to scare me and swim around in her clothes when we were children. And I have a phobia about water. Quite natural." He picks up the thesaurus. "Funny. No water phobia."

"How about hydrophobia?" Mike speaks up.

"Not listed under phobias in Roget's. Just mophobia, fear of waves. And the sound of waves actually excites me."

"Phobias can turn you on. So can death, Dad. I almost drowned." Dad glares. "Not like you." He quickly lets Dad know he's not in in his league. "Mom's car rolled into Tompkins Pit. Didn't kill anyone. She's had it for five years. Must have it insured." Not a word. Too much silence. All Mike gets is a little smile. Must have driven Dad, who almost drowned as a boy, over the edge like that car. He watches him get up and turn to Mom's desk.

"Just as she is about to become famous," Dad says to the computer.

Chapter 41

IN LIMBO

"Do you think I was dead in this dream and the church thrift shop was heaven?" she whispers to Chris, the way she used to when newborn Mike slept in their bedroom. She had been afraid he might stop breathing after she brought him home from the hospital.

"More like Limbo."

"Funny, in this dream I was dancing through the air and I could also watch myself up there."

"That's what you're doing in your book. Haupter made me understand that."

She had dreamt she was driving her station wagon up a narrow ramp, and then it ended suddenly. No way of turning around. She was stuck in a huge, empty, crumbling parking garage, but down below a church sale was going on. Mothers and grandmothers all had white hair and wore white smocks. Clothing piled on long tables and hanging on racks was all white too. There Liz found a white tuxedo on a rack, a perfect fit, a top hat and white cane with a silver knob. She found herself tap dancing and rose up in the air. The women did not look up. She could see herself floating around while trying to get back to her car, dancing to "Heaven, I'm in heaven," on Gramp's Fred Astaire record. But she couldn't find the car anymore. Three tired people in dark overcoats came along walking slowly. When she asked for directions they sent her the wrong way. She was lost and alone in a white fog. "The car could have sunk all the way down with Mike."

"He didn't go down," Chris says without raising his voice. "Thugs didn't kill him. He didn't stop breathing as an infant. You weren't killed during the war, I didn't drown when the boat exploded." He is proud of his new, healthy equanimity. "The insurance company will give us some money for the car, and you will get a new one. No one was hurt. I did not overreact." He reaches out and holds her. "I don't know what doctors would say about your addiction to thrift shops." Chris turns over onto his back. "That Yesteryear woman sells dead people's clothes. You used to dress so well in New York. Why not go into town and buy something. My present."

Mike sleeps until noon. Eats one of his favorite spicy frozen pizzas. No one says anything or is mad at him. Dad hurries off to consult his nutritionist and then to a shrink called Haupter. His mother is making soup, a sure sign of stress. He is treated like an irresponsible two-year-old. This is driving him to drink. Saki follows him around, while he pours some of Dad's whiskey into the old MIKE milk mug that Bonnie gave him years ago. "Mind your own business. Scat." The pooch keeps glaring at him while he fills it up with orange juice and gulps most of it down. The click of the mail slot gets Saki to dash to the back door. They race to get to the mail. "No, you don't snitch letters, you untrained dog!"

But Mike snitches from Saki the letter Grove sent to Dad and reads it in the kitchen while he finishes his drink, then goes upstairs to speak to Mother, who is sitting at the computer.

"Would you believe it? Grove sent Dad forms to enroll me for their lousy Outward Bound summer session and forms for a re-admission interview. Must need the money and figure they can always throw me out again. Listen to this, 'developing self-esteem through acts of courage, discovering unique potential by overcoming obstacles. Seek-and-find missions. Rock-climbing, underwater survival'—wait till Dad sees this—I wouldn't go back if Grimes gets down on his knees. I have plans." No response. "Mom, you're not with it, are you? Naturally spaced out."

Mike would be disdainful of her natural, dream-induced flying. He, like a multitude of others, pay for dreammakers, sometimes with their life and always with their parents' money, as deadly dream merchants lure them from their families. Last night's dream—the sensation of dancing through the air, costumed as Fred Astaire, had been a powerful antidote to Liz's nightmare morning: bailing Sonny out of lockup, having her station wagon towed to a car graveyard, filling out forms and writing checks.

"You two don't have to worry. I'll be out of here by the fall." Mike sounds like an uncouth father, has shadows under his eyes, and needs a shave. "Anyway, here is a letter from your editor. Seems they have changed your title to dumb 'Smiling Child!'"

He hands over the brief note informing Liz that the new head of the sales department of Thompson & Perkins prefers a first novel on the fall list. The sales department thinks "Smiling Child" would be a better title for a novel. "You have no right to open our mail!"

"The Grove letter should have been addressed to me, anyway. I was just trying to give you some secretarial help." No reaction. "While I'm still around." He bites into a candy bar and lets the wrapper drop.

When Liz stoops to pick it up a Faser rage starts up inside her.

"You never listen, do you?" Mike goes on. "You'll soon be rid of me, Liz! Do you hear?"

A tornado starts up inside her, she bites her lip. Her face glows with seething fury; she grabs one of the clogs she keeps at the door, lets out a Faser scream "Mother" and hurls it smack onto his bottom. He laughs out loud. Puts his arm around her.

❋ ❋ ❋

The boy-sized statue of a Civil War hero on the porch of the Benton Community House has a Mike—I did it, and I'll do it again—expression. Inside the old building, doors to a big function hall are flung back. She is able to pass by ladies at card tables. Pale and white-haired under white fluorescent lights, busy with themselves, as the ladies in last night's dream. The kind of quiet mothers and grandmothers who would never hurl a clog at a son. She slinks off towards the left where an arrow points towards a closed door, PARENTAL SUPPORT GROUP.

"Come on in."

"Liz Plant!"

"Nice to see you."

"No, he's not going back to Grove either."

"Margo was thrown out too!"

She is welcomed into the smoky room by a chorus of Grove Academy parents. Jason, the father who married his son's high school girlfriend. Now Gloria looks older and pregnant. Ben the lawyer's face is sun-scorched from living on a boat to keep his boy out of trouble. "How about Mike?"

The leader of the group introduces himself as Peter, his wife is May. "We know what happened. Violet called to say you were coming. She must have told you all about Tough Love."

"We went to Pennsylvania, Liz, and trained with the founders," May speaks up. She is small, with short, dark hair. Eager as a little wren. "The idea is to seek cures, not causes."

"I teach Science. I have always found it hard to accept failure. He has gray hair, and a boyish smile. "Tough Love teaches us to stop blaming ourselves and each other for teenage problems." A duet. His wife May talks along with Peter softly. Her thin face shines with enthusiasm. She hands Liz a pamphlet with information: "The group meets every Wednesday, even on holidays. Names and phone numbers of members in case you need help during the week. (Keeping things private, we use first names only)."

"Talking about good things that happened during the week always comes first," Peter explains. "Newcomers get a chance to listen before they have their turn. Today Peter has some very good news indeed. He is a science teacher at the high school. He and May have four children. No trouble at all until the youngest, Jenny, started high school. She drank, used drugs, threw dishes at Mother, books at teachers. Stayed out of school and didn't come home for a day and night." Peter explains how they confronted Jenny with a Tough Love contract of written rules, but the girl tore it up and walked out. May remembers weeks of sleepless nights, anguish, waiting until the girl appeared at the door, ready to sign and agree to follow rules.

Veteran parents laugh, because they helped make this Tough Love kid go straight. They found jobs for her to work her way through college. "Next month she's getting married to a teacher. A lot like her dad," May concludes.

There is a round of applause. Peter laughs, but not for long. "Let's have more good news, Harry and Jill." He goes clockwise around the circle of parents just like Havelock Grimes. "We grounded Charlene for a week, didn't we?"

A stately couple, parents of Charlene, a thirteen-year-old alcoholic, report that she came straight home from school and stayed in all week. Charlene even cut and styled her mother's hair. A neighbor broke her arm and Charlene is now doing her hair too.

"You look so nice. Would she come over to my house and do mine too?" asks a young woman sitting next to her, whose bushy hair needs combing. She is newly divorced, has three children, and works as a clerk. Her thirteen-year-old George had vanished for a couple of days. Last week she took him to "The Chemist," a doctor, expert in medicating teenagers for chemical imbalance which can affect their behavior. George has been trouble-free for five days.

Everyone except Liz wants to have the doctor's phone number for a simple solution of needles and pills that produce trouble-free children. "Isn't that what the kids do for themselves?" Liz asks.

Peter looks over the rim of his glasses. "Kids can't treat themselves. They're not medically trained and use illegal, dangerous drugs." He turns a page in his notebook. "Here we have a typical case. Bill stopped talking to you, Bertha. Locked himself into his room, and talked to himself using foul language. We decided you should get rid of the key. You were going to take him to a psychologist. How did that work out, Bertha?"

"They get along well. Our boy talks to him on the phone almost every day." She has a habit of blinking while she hesitates. "Sounds strange, I know. His father is a little worried."

"Why? He took his gun. You were afraid he might kill you, and now he is talking to a doctor and doing better," observes an overweight mother.

Bertha smiles, showing crooked little front teeth. "Sounds silly, I know, but my husband wonders why this doctor charges so little. He's afraid George might be getting unnaturally fond of this man. Maybe The Chemist—."

"—Next," Peter says quite sternly. "Let's have more good news!"

Some kids have cleaned up their rooms. Others have helped in the house. Those who had to be locked out a couple of times to enforce a 10:30 curfew, are now home on time. But several single working mothers, who find it hard to remember good things, chain-smoke, waiting for their turn to talk about the terrible problem of pot smoking, pot growing in flower pots, the back yard, the woods, any old place. Kids on drugs stealing, cheating, threatening, getting disoriented.

By the time trouble-shooting begins, the room is hazy with smoke, helplessness, anger, and shame. Grove Academy parents Jason and girlish stepmother Gloria, who had to lock their bedroom door, had found themselves locked into Jason's study, while his son took over the house and liquor with his friends and partied. "Really mean," Gloria says. "Those kids were my school friends too. Locking me out. All this dancing. I'm pregnant and can't dance." Jason says he was forced to climb out of the window. This set off the burglar alarm. Not one passing car stopped.

"Who has an idea?" asks Peter.

"We have six children. If he's lonely he can come to our house, but he'll have to follow the rules like all the other kids." This father, a husky redhead, is a veteran of the group.

"What if he doesn't want to go to your house, what will happen?" Gloria asks.

"You have to get a restraining order and lock him out," answers the veteran father.

"You can't do that!" Gloria is in tears

"What if he runs away. Where will he go?" Liz asks.

"He's my friend. He's lonely since I married his dad; he might just vanish."

"Kids always find a way of moving in with friends," says Jason. It doesn't sound too convincing.

A group of parents, especially mothers, used to excite Liz and make her heart beat faster. Now it beats steady as a metronome. "Is it really a choice between being abused by your children or enforcing harsh rules and kicking them out, possibly losing them?"

"Just as likely to lose kids when you put up with their outrageous behavior, give in to their demands. Threats. That can become violent. And some of them simply abandon the family. Four boys went to a rock concert and haven't returned. Hortense, how are you doing?"

Hortense Johnson, who cultivated the look of the Queen of England in her exclusive White Rose Dress Shop, looks withered and shabby in sweat pants. "I hate rock musicians," she cries. "Drug addicts promoting drugs, violence and ugly sex. God only knows what they have done with my boys. I'm bringing charges!"

"I happen to know that the boys followed the band," Gloria says that she always wanted to go on the Grateful Dead tour. Kids follow them in painted vans. Everyone wearing old costumes and there's dancing in the aisles. Mellow music. Guys in top hats giving you fresh roses. "And that music is sweet. You can come and listen with me, Hortense, but it would be cool if you'd listen to tunes with those guys when they come back."

"They can't be allowed to just come back, Gloria," May quietly intervenes. "This is serious. Hortense hasn't heard a word from them for over a week."

The terror of losing children permeates the room like the cigarette smoke. Liz tries to open the one small window, but it is sealed shut. A table has been set up with instant coffee and a water urn, cookies, and plenty of ashtrays. There is a sudden need for the consolation of coffee and cookies.

"I always hide my welfare money from them in packages of frozen peas," says an unemployed actress, who wears her pink hair in pigtails and seems to be the clown in the group. They all laugh. Coffee does help. Peter refills his cup, stirring in plenty of non-dairy cream. Rich or poor, no matter how badly children have behaved, not one parent in this room seems to be capable of hitting a kid with a wooden clog.

"Stolen money. That's nothing," Ben the lawyer says. "I have a criminal on my hands."

"Have you ever spanked him?" Liz asks.

He squints. "He would complain to his mother and she would take him away."

"Do you ever want to smack him?"

"What I want doesn't matter. I have to do the right thing."

The door swings open and Violet Spiral is led into the room leaning on Dot Dewell's arm. They have been friends since grade school. Violet has given up on herself since she sold South Point and moved into the True Bible Community. You can see that, but she is most beautiful when she is desperate. Tears run down her china-doll cheeks. Those blue eyes and that red-gold hair have been passed on to Del and Sonny, but not her kindness. She goes and gives Liz a hug. "I am so sorry about your car. I feel really awful, but I don't have the means anymore. Thanks again for helping me out. You're so good to those boys."

"Always with them," says Dot who has a long chin, wears her gray hair in a bun and looks like an abbess in a long gray dress adorned with a large black crucifix.

Fathers get up and place chairs for the two women right next to Peter, who is reviewing his notes for the group: Violet has four children. Her husband, the dancing carpenter deserted. Teenager Del got pregnant and lost her baby, ran up a hospital bill.

"Stole all of Violet's furniture and sold it," Dot interrupts. "Bet she gave them the money." Round, wire-rimmed glasses enlarge Violet's stern gaze. "Things are bad. Real bad. Her big boy's becoming violent. Calls himself Scarpino."

Violet calls out. "He thinks of himself as Godfather."

"Beating up and punishing his brother," Dot goes on. "Scaring the baby sister. Violet gets home tonight, walks in. The boys are fighting. Sonny's face bleeding. She tries to stop them and Scarpino throws Sonny's knife at her and barely missed her head."

Violet wipes her face with the back of her hand. "He went through so much. When he was just a little fellow." She has to get up and get a napkin to wipe her tears. "He saw his father cut up the picture of Jesus I had above my bed."

Dot pats her head twice. "Violet had to come to our house in the middle of the night."

Violet sobs, "I don't want to talk about that."

"We had to call the police and they took Violet to the hospital. After that rape she had little Mary."

"That is all terrible, but we are looking for solutions, not causes," says Peter.

"I got fourteen nuns to pray for her," Dot says.

Violet wipes her face and blows her nose. "They're all praying for me at True Bible."

Dot sits up straight and sticks out her chin. "That boy takes after his godless father. Capable of anything."

"He isn't quite eighteen years old. Where would he go?" Impulsively Violet turns to Liz: "What would you do?"

"Don't stay, get out of the commune. The boys will stop fighting if you are gone. Leave with the young children. Run away! Hide!"

Peter thinks Liz has the right idea. "True Bible must have that house insured," says Ben, the lawyer.

The Carltons invite Violet to stay in their guest cottage. "Let a couple of days go by. Get Tough Love fathers to negotiate with the big boys. Make them sign a contract." Scarpino is working at the mall tonight, Sonny is weightlifting at the gym. Del is with her aunt. Violet will gather up her little Mary, a few essentials. Two young fathers get up at once to take her home.

There are more emergencies. An only daughter, involved with a twenty-two-year-old rich boy who keeps her enslaved and on drugs. And the brothers who had a gardening job on an estate arranged for them by a Tough Love father, have been growing opium poppies. The room smolders, the mothers and the few fathers are beginning to droop and cough. Then into the fog of smoke and emotions walks the white-haired Hollowells of the Grove Academy Parents' Association. The furrier and his wife, whose son vanished after they locked him out, have joined Tough Love to get support because they suspect that it was their son who torched the Hollowell Furs delivery van and keeps pasting SAVE THE ENDAN-GERED PREDATORS on their doors. Their boy used to go in for that kind of thing.

Liz raises her hand to have her say about the clown in Boston, town meeting, at the fox hunt, and at the shoreland parade. "Could be some kind of organization."

"One feels helpless," the actress laughs and a tiny golden butterfly pin dances on her great bosom. It's easy just to laugh with her when your mind is foggy with fatigue and charged with caffeine and worry. But her uneasy eye movements, the strange pleasure in her voice when she talks about her Ted, makes Liz wonder whether she isn't inventing this larger-than-life bad son, the way Liz had invented a mother during the years in boarding school.

"How about you, Liz?" Mr. Hollowell leans forward sympathetically.

"You didn't have your turn," Peter says. "And we're running late," adds May.

Liz smiles. "That's all right—"

"Next time. We'll talk about kids drinking and driving."
Peter smiles.

"You certainly had a good idea for us. And sometimes just listening helps," May says.

No one ever wants to listen when Liz mentions the clowns.

Chapter 42

INTO THE FUTURE

Liz turns MATE II off. The monitor is dark. No one is waiting for a page, a chapter. Galleys have been corrected and mailed back to the publishers, leaving her in a vast desert of uncertainty and dread. A small printing, just seven thousand, means that "Smiling Child" doesn't have a publicity budget. Only ten bound galleys have gone out to reviewers.

Little Plant Quarry has become a refuge for Liz during hot days that are stagnant and empty as the silence of not writing. She and Bonnie ride up on bikes for an early morning swim. "Take it easy, relax, Liz," Bonnie says when she has to hurry home to answer phones after an hour. But monarch butterflies don't relax, frogs squatting down near the water wait avidly for midges, mosquitoes.

Liz spreads a beachtowel over a granite slab and stretches out in her hide-away behind young pines and tall blueberry bushes. She has not been sleeping well. Pine branches fan her with glints of the blue sky. She dozes in the heat until the shrill voices of small boys wake her up.

"My turn now." "No it isn't." "You did that. You pushed me off." "Not fair!" The fight for a turn to walk on the floating log that has always been floating around the pit, remains an initiation ritual that has gone on generation after generation, sorting out those who can walk the full slippery length from the ones that can't or won't even try. The hero, this year, a small black mongrel with a bushy tail he moves to keep him steady is not around this morning.

Elgar and the Tick, two who never ever walk on the log, get off their bikes, take a dip and climb up on Cathedral Rock, the best place for seeing who is coming along the trail without being seen, while they drink breakfast beer. Liz remains invisible in her hideaway.

"Mike split," Tom the Tick reports.

Elgar Myrtle puts down his can of beer. "Where would he go?"

"Jamaica."

"Not without me," Elgar says without conviction.

"With that nut Emerald."

The $50 Liz gave Mike, when he told her he was going to visit his Grove Academy friend Bernie Chapman on the Cape would hardly get him and Emerald to Jamaica, but she should have called the boy's mother. She watches a skinny boy fall off the log and fail the test with a shriek.

"You O.K?" Elgar calls.

The skinny one responds by climbing back on again. In Hitler School, on a cold day, Liz, wet from a fall, had to cross a creek on a narrow wooden board. An obstacle course. Failure had been forbidden. *Fall runter Du bist tot*, you're dead.

"Same old log," Elgar says.

"Dumb kids!" Tom reaches for a beer.

"And just look at that dumb dog. Nothing bothers old Boots. There he is staring at fish," Tom says.

"Same old dog," Elgar says.

The brown Weimeraner stands in the water behind the islands, where shrubs are beginning to turn red. Little fellows visiting grandparents thrash past him, but he stays put, staring into the water watching the fish with those strange, brass-colored eyes.

"Boots used to be Spot. Until he rescued the Svenson boots," Tom says.

"When was that?"

"You weren't around, man. Anytime anything happens you have to go to Disneyland with your old Mom and Dad."

"Disneyland turns Leonard on."

"You know about Svenson and Nell. This cheerleader chick. Her dad hears something in the night. Tries her door. It's locked. Svenson jumps out the window from the first floor. Practically naked. Her dad finds a pair of strange boots in her room and calls the pigs. Breaking and entering, he says. Gives them the boots as evidence. Barefoot Svenson heads for the dump. Gets himself nerdy new shoes from the dump Major's boutique. Big shoes. Svenson misses his cool little boots. Ever seen such midget feet on such a tall guy? So cute. Nell paints his toenails gold.

"Svenson's attention span is down to about a second and he forgets all about gold toe nails. This social worker told him the army's as good as a mother and got him to register for the draft. Svenson forgets that too. A letter arrives from the army, calling him in for a physical. Mike says to go for it, stick it out for a few months and end up with a pension. But Svenson has to take his clothes off for those army doctors. Here is six-foot Svenson, all skin and bones. Those cute feet and gold toenails got to them."

"How about the boots?"

"Cops looking for the owner of the boots never bothered with Svenson, figuring he's too tall for such little boots. They make you try them on when you're in lock-up. Sort of like Cinderella. Except that those boots stink. Old Svenson got those boots at the Linden Tree mall a year ago during the winter sales, when he swapped his old parka with a display figure for a fur-lined suede number. Nell really went for him in that new outfit. He just had to have those lucky little boots back. He sleeps in a barn that belongs to the Cove Hill postmistress, his dead mom's cousin or aunt or something. She got this cool puppy, Spot. This Ethel, the dog-handler woman, rents the upstairs. And she got Spot to do tricks. Like staying off the road. Not get hit. Sniff something—go fetch. Spot drops in on cops, they feed him and he brings them newspapers and magazines he picks up on any damn porch. He's a natural-born retriever.

"Women always feel sorry for Svenson and he makes the most of it. And when they make him take a bath he isn't so bad. Ethel gets this cool idea that she can get his boots back. She lets Spot smell Svenson's socks, takes Spot to the station after dark, and tells him to go fetch. He comes back with a boot and Svenson feeds him pizza and blows pot in his face. Spot does it again. And that's how Svenson got his boots back. And that's how Boots got his new name and turned into a stoner and stares at fish."

"Same old nothing fish back again since Dad had me and some of his men clean out the trash," says Elgar.

One of the little guys, stretches arms into wings. "Take off. Operation

Glass Eye!" He leaps off the rock, comes up spitting water. "Operation Glass Eye was on the news. Secret jets. Can't be seen on radar. Hidden away in the desert. Fly at night." Known as Brian, the brain, is now eight years old with huge, deep-set gray eyes, sits around the library even during the summer.

"How come they talk about secret weapons?" Elgar asks.

"What's the good of having secret weapons if nobody knows about it and gets scared?" Tom tries to sound like Mike.

"Have you ever seen a real live dead man?" asks one of the freckled Bailey twins. "Me." He floats on his back, eyes closed, mouth open, freckled nose sticking up, stiff arms. Real dead. A dragonfly lands on his flat belly. The boy shivers and lets out a shriek, a few curses. Then the brothers chase each other up to the top of Cathedral Rock, pinch noses, and leap. All the others follow. Except for one summer kid, someone's baby brother wearing hand-me-down swim trunks that drop below his round belly and hang down to the ankles He is busy casting and reeling in without bait. A car stops. Elgar quickly brushes over his new growth of hair and picks up his empty beer can. Tom takes off his shades. "Here they come. Karin with all those creepy little girls. I told you it's too good to last."

She isn't skinny anymore and last year's two-piece black bathing suit looks like a bikini this year. She carries her worn rubber raft. Girls she babysits follow in a row like ducklings. "Are you big guys at Little Plant again, hiding out and littering?" she calls out.

Karin has this play group to help pay for college. The scholarship isn't enough. In the evening she has to work as a waitress at the Oyster Shell. The raft has been patched with big red hearts. When she tests it in the water, her smooth, straight-edged hair swings like a gold tassel. "Mike been around?"

"Left for Jamaica," Tom says.

"That so?" Karin says with a knowing smile. She lines her play group up to put on water wings, flippers, with kindness and knowhow.

Was Mike ready to be off? Chris, Ellen, even Bonnie, have all told Liz to let go, and she has let go of him and of everything else lately, as she removed her worn out self from everyone. She feels useless, sad, and uncertain without the certainty of writing every day.

"Me, don't push me.—Get off.—No, no.—" Girls shriek, whipping, gurgling, spouting water. They all try to get onto the raft. "It won't hold that many," Karin warns.

"We're sinking. Help, help, help!"

Karin stands by, but lets them fall off and learn their lesson. A couple of them thrash towards the island to display themselves on a block of granite shouting to the others as though they were miles apart. Boots, who doesn't like turmoil, gets out, climbs Cathedral Rock, and shakes himself, sprinkling Tom and Elgar. "What's the matter with that dumb hound?" Tom yells.

"Poor old guy," Elgar says. "No class."

Karin stretches out on the raft and two little girls tumble off. "What do you mean, no class? Boots belongs to the postmistress." Karin always gets Elgar wrong. Before he can think of something to say, a moped comes zooming along the path much too fast and jolts to a halt.

There is a chorus of, "Mike, Mike!"

Liz sinks down on her towel, and the hot sun suddenly feels luxuriantly Jamaican.

"You had it in pieces. Who put it together?" Elgar asks.

"Dad." Mike wears a rolled bandanna and a black Grateful Dead Garcia Magician T-shirt; sleeves look chewed off. His guitar is slung over one shoulder. When he lights a cigarette and offers it to Karin, she shakes her head.

"Give us a Bud." Brian makes himself heard.

"A Bud," echo the small girls. "A ride on your bike."

"Frogs, dogs, kids," Mike stomps out his cigarette.

"Hey. I thought you split," Tom calls down from the perch. "Where've you been?"

Karin comes ashore, takes Mike by the shoulders to study his face with a big smile. "You passed!"

"Passed what?" asks Elgar.

"G.E.D. Took me two days. I hitched down to Salem. Told my folks I was visiting this Grove dude. Did I ever score! Record-breaking verbal ability. I'm going on to college."

"You have another year of high school," Tom says.

"No way!" He doesn't just drop the moped. Not when Karin is watching, but carefully props it up. Some of her play-group ducklings hop around him. Then she dives into the water and crawls to the island. Mike jumps in after her in his clothes. The young children root for "doggy paddle world champion" and cheer when he pops up at the island before Karin does.

"What's it with you, Karin?" Tom shouts. "I thought you won all those races at the Y."

"She lets Mike win," Elgar says under his breath. Elgar likes to see Mike win. Everybody does. Especially when he beats the system. Tom wants to know all about the exam. And so does Brian, the little genius. "Why bother with boring school? I'll just go to Harvard."

"Because kids like you, Brian, who skip too much go nuts." Karin says.

Mike has his arm around her waist. They sit on a moss-covered rock. Even the island bullfrog seems to be listening to Mike's triumph. How he didn't tell anyone else where he went, in case he flunked. Only Karin. He really sweated. Karin whispers a question.

"Emerald? She goes in for these scumbags. Guys wearing female wigs, come like looking for her and almost killing me. Eckert keeps her grounded. She's earned money since she was born doing commercials, but they don't give her any." "Hey, Mike, how much does a moped cost?" Kids shout across to them.

"How much did your Mom's car cost?" "Your sneakers. How much did they cost?" "Holy Moses. And you go swimming in them!" "How about the designer jeans?" the girls twitter. "How much?"

Mike ignores them.

"How much does Mike cost? Add it all up, kids," Tom the Tick speaks up.

"I didn't even have enough for the exams. Had to borrow from Elgar for the trip."

"All that forced labor on minimum wage." Elgar reaches for another beer. "They don't even kick me out of the liquor store anymore. Used to just point at the door when I showed. Hard hat, cheap dark glasses make all the difference." He rubs his dark stubble. "Same old six-pack. Piece of cake, when you look old." Nothing will ever be the same now that he gets away with buying liquor. Karin toweling Mike's curls scolds because every-thing in his pocket is soaked, laughs and loves him. They kiss. Elgar takes up Mike's guitar playing tunes that tell how he feels about Karin, but also about Del. Nobody is listening, nobody cares.

A dragonfly, for a brief moment of its brief life, shimmers on the head of that small brother who keeps casting and reeling in, ever hopeful.

Fishing without bait, just like my writing, Liz is thinking, for the thrill of reeling in.

Mike shoulders his guitar, gets on the moped in his wet clothes, pedals it to a start, and spatters off onto Pond Lane. A car honks at him as he cuts in front of it. A limousine catches up with him. The driver rolls down the window.

"Drowning not work out? Trying to get yourself run over, Mike?"

Jiggers in a purple uniform driving Thelma Nesbit and Emmet Gray. A pigtail has slipped out from the oversized visor cap. Mike laughs. "This can't be for real, man!"

Miss Nesbit rolls down the window and leans out, dressed up in purple and reeking of violets. "I told the Chief that it was Jiggers who borrowed my car—not you." She is holding hands with old Mr. Gray, who sports a French beret. A tape is playing a French song. "Jiggers used to work for me and missed me. Now we're back together again. Drove all the way from California, you know. He's a fine driver. There's that French chef on the Cape..."

Jiggers has this strange way of moving his eyes slowly from side to side, but Thelma always liked to take a chance. Her father, Winston Nesbit, a judge, never did have any judgment when it came to his one and only Thelma, who collected odd pets and odd people. She had no children during her marrying days. Men never lasted, but she had cats and dogs, smoked cigars, and rode around town with her pig in one of those big purple cars. All that purple dates back to a purple ribbon that her pig won at the Topsfield Fair.

A whim of iron, somebody said, and it stuck. Even now, late in life, taking up with old Emmet. They are happy. Just as happy as I am just now Mike is thinking as they drive away. He has a glimpse of a backpack on the empty seat beside Jiggers and a road map.

No surprise later when it turns out that Emmet and Thelma ended up eating Parisian food in Quebec! Thelma has taken to Jiggers, as she took to the pig Cleo. A far out choice—if you can afford it—is the right one.

"Come on in, Mike." The automatic lights come on at the gate in bright sunlight. Then the nasty barking. "Sorry about that," says Eckert's voice over the speaker. The gate springs open. "I'm in my study."

Myrtle Turtle has turned the back of old South Cove into a Hollywood hacienda-type motel. Underwater lights, poison green tiles, creme de menthe pool. And man, can half a bottle of that stuff ever make you puke! Too much sweetness, too much of a muchness here. Bambi, Emerald's mom, the movie star sleeping in a huge hammock, has fat thighs. Everything else is OK and she is getting a nice tan. Better she doesn't see Emerald's black satin sheet, a Grove Academy trophy Mike used as a kind of gift wrapping. He hurries past her pulling his big bundle.

"Mike. What are you doing here?" Ellen, disguised as an Arab and lobster red, steps out of the poolside sauna.

"I could ask the same thing. Like is that Dora up there on the terrace. What is this, a harem or what?"

"I came for an informal session with Emerald, Mike."

Mike looks around, ready as any guy for an informal session with Emerald.

"She's gone to get into her bathing suit," Ellen, the mind reader, goes on. "Isn't this great? Sauna, whirlpool, the works. Len really did a good renovation job here."

Mike observes that the paint on the south side of the house is already flaking. "He does quite a job on anything."

The one tree he left is swaying. "Mike, Mike!" Ellen's two little apes are swinging and carrying on up there. If a limb breaks they'll bash their brains out on the tiles. "What's that you've got there Mike?"

"Atomic bomb."

Ellen has her wicked eyes on that big bundle and her hand is reaching out to touch it. "For Arthur," Mike says and moves on.

"He's in his office. Just off the gallery. Third door on the right."

The house smells of discounted hazardous building materials, but also the faint scent of a peppery fragrance Em brought back from Paris. Walls painted white are decorated with oversized messy kindergarten-type splash paintings that have probably cost a million. Thanks to Mike, the one Caleb and Tom made off with is back on the wall. If you look hard you can see a female scribbled with lots of slashed-in lines; a mean face, teeth crying out for an orthodontist, small breasts, target type nipples. Caleb was smart to give that one back. It is ugly even for Zip zippy art—that's for sure.

The runner patterned with a design of rushing rapids can make you feel wired when you're not. Mike knocks on the third door. "Come in!" Eckert's taste might be American sixties, but he sounds like a Prussian general. Doesn't bother to get up. Black turtleneck, black shades, he stays behind his glass desk, where the canoe trip runner ends in a whirlpool carpet. Mike salutes, puts his bundle down, unties the black sheet, and unveils the unharmed Marilyn doll. Then he takes Marilyn's glasses out of his pocket and puts them on her nose with a magician's bow.

Eckert applauds. "Well done!"

This sounds British like Dad.

"Sit down. Sit down. Wasn't that heavy?"

"A friend who drives the Nesbit Cadillac gave me a ride." The chair, that huge female hand with long red fingernails, is made of the same supple stuff as Marilyn's body. "I must say this seat is rather comfortable."

"You sound just like your father."

"So do you. It's catching." Mike leans back in the big hand and it even rocks a little.

"I understand you're going to college. I bet you'd like a beer?"

Caleb would get a kick out of the wall safe which is really a refrigerator full of liquor. But Mike is bothered by the half-naked child with a face quite like Mom's looking out of the three Catulle paintings hanging on each side of the desk.

Arthur pops open a bottle of German beer and hands it to Mike. "You like the paintings?"

"I'm not into art." Mike contemplating one bare red nipple which looks as though it had been chewed by a pervert, guzzles down the beer without tasting it.

"The artist died in a car crash on the French Riviera. His paintings are very valuable now." Eckert leans back, allowing the boring classical music to wipe him out, while he gives Mike a biography of the valuable Monroe. How she wanted to be a classical actress, an intellectual. That's why he had the artist add glasses. Her actual prescription. "You didn't break in here and take her, Mike. Why did you bring her back—is it a trade?"

Mike sinks back, rocking the big soft hand. "Sort of."

"What do you want for it, Mike?"

"Straight answers." A direct quote from Havelock Grimes.

Eckert laughs too much and takes off his shades exposing pale hypnotic eyes.

"These pictures and all that. What are you up to with Mom?"

Arthur Eckert stops smiling. "I bought the Catulles because the child reminded me of a schoolgirl I loved when I was not much older than you are. Devastating. I never got over her. All this longing. It's beyond your generation, I know. You expect instant and constant gratification."

The young having it too easy is an old parental subject Mike avoids by picking up his beer bottle and drinking his beer, slowly, the way you're supposed to make love. Arthur takes a clean handkerchief out of his pocket and wipes foam off his whiskers. "Bonnie once said it's better to have loved and lost than never to have loved at all. But we do try to replace what we have lost."

Seagulls are flapping around on the skylight which is speckled with their shit. One of them is tearing a fish apart and another one tries to pull it away. "Not with my Mom! You've got women in this house—you've got it made, man. And if you need to be reminded of some teenager, there's always Emerald."

"I came across your mother a few years ago by chance. We were having lunch at the same outdoor cafe. I remembered her in the leopard skin coat and ear muffs. I knew who she was, we had met years ago at a party. Catulle had talked about his model and her brother all the time. I became fascinated by the way my story and hers belong together. I've come to feel very close to her through the problems she has had writing her memoir."

Shadows of gull droppings on the skylight make the Marilyn mannequin doll look pockmarked and dirty. "That's finished now" Mike says.

"Not at all. It's not easy to have a best seller when you are a new writer. You need top promotion. No better promotion than the movies."

Eckert taking over Em and her career isn't the same as taking over Mom with his funky old romance. Mike gulps down the beer with a rush of distrust. "It won't do!" A Havelock Grimes slogan.

"Free country," Eckert retorts, with an expression Emerald and everyone at Grove picked up from Mike and passed on at home.

Mike puts the empty bottle down on the whirlpool rug. "Not for everyone."

"Touché, Mike. You're growing up. But it takes money to be free."

"Depends on how you use it. You spent yours on Havelock's reform school concept, to take freedom away from us," Mike says.

"And she used money her father sent her to buy a false ID."

Mike laughs. "Freedom!"

"To dance around half-naked in a dirty bar. Making herself a target. She's never learned that there are limits. By the way, you're her idol."

Mike doesn't want to give himself away. "It won't do," he repeats and tries to get up. The nasty giant hand won't let go. If this is a vulgar practical joke, no one's laughing. Mike tries to exit with a snappy salute, but he weaves as he turns around and escapes, closing the door behind him.

Tripping and drinking even one beer can suddenly turn the way he feels around. Mike suddenly admires his dad a lot. Out in the big bright glass cage, Mike stops and stares at this slash-line picture of a wicked female until she seems to stare back at him and wink. "You're Emerald." He backs off, but he can't get away from her. When he walks out the side door towards the pool, he finds her laid out on a white mat, hands folded. Candy-sweet in a black glitter Golden Oar go-go girl string bikini. "Hey, Mike."

He stares like a snake at a rat. She turns and stares back, like that slash painting. "If you hadn't done dirty dancing, or whatever, for creeps at the Golden Oar they wouldn't have come looking for you and found me." He scoops her up. She is tiny and light, and glows from the sun. When she puts her arms around his neck her eyes reflect the green water. He wants to keep holding her too much, so he just has to throw her into the creme de menthe pool. When she comes up for air with a wicked squint, spitting water and foul Golden Oar venom. Something happens. She goes down. Floats up, string bra around her neck. Down again.

He jumps in and scoops her up, letting the water carry her. Breasts are hardly there, but nipples glisten like beach glass. The mermaid he made in the sand. He kisses the breasts and tastes chlorine. She clings, to him and plastering her cold wet mouth against his. "Kiss me, Mike!" They sink down kissing, hair streaming up, rise kissing and it streams down they gasp and fasten in the shallow water, like they'd come together after being ripped apart.

"Mike. I love you Mike," she says mouth half open, lips rosy from kissing, turning herself into a girl selling bed sheets.

He pries himself away. "You're not on TV." she follows, wrapping herself and him into her perfumed towel. The sober Mike is ready to toss her again, but the other one—under the influence of German beer and

Eckert's German story—the Super Mike who saves people from themselves wants to keep uncontrollable Emerald just like this, but nothing ever stays the same.

"Let's take our wet clothes off in the sauna."

She's already naked. Nothing new for her. "That so. How about fucking those creeps from the Golden Oar?" A lecture Dad gave him about safe sex gets in the way. He dives to fish out her bra, ready to plunge into the sauna with her. Suddenly a few bars of music come on and Eckert's voice broadcasts, "Why don't you two come on up for some lunch."

"Go eat something before you starve your boobs away." And Mike brings about a miracle cure for anorexia. Ellen will declare it was her therapy session with Em and a Beatrice Strout subliminal tape. Havelock Grimes will insist it was his force-feeding technique and the Grove Academy Concept, but Arthur will somehow get the credit since he paid for it all.

Chapter 43

VOICES

Police Notices:
During the annual Blessing of the Animals at Mill
Pond Meadow in celebration of St. Francis of
Assisi, Emerald St. Claire asked Officer Codget for
help finding her new pet Max, a boa constrictor
that had escaped and was crawling around her car
somewhere. Police conducted some minor surgery on
the car before finding the snake, much to the
delight of Emerald, police reported.

The van radio plays a reggae version of "Beyond the Blue Horizon" as
Karin drives away with Mike from a gray horizon dull as an amateur painting with only one tall ship. Rain begins to fall. "They've gone. Thank
Heaven," Chris says, but Liz waves and runs out on the road. Bonnie
waves from her office window. The Professor stops his garbage truck to
wave. Red comes chasing after them. Back in the kitchen "Beyond The
Blue Horizon" playing on the kitchen radio brings tears to her eyes. Chris
turns it off and proceeds into the parlor to switch off the TV set. Then he
unplugs his hi-fi equipment in the music room, because radio magnetic
waves can damage nerve cells. Finally he posts a pamphlet on her bulletin
board.

MEET YOUR NEW NEIGHBOR THE SEABROOK NUKE.
WASTE PRODUCTS, OCEAN POLLUTION. RADIATION
MEGADEATHS. BLACKOUTS. NO MORE HOME RULE. IF THE
SEABROOK PLANT IS BUILT, IT WILL MARK THE END OF
LOCAL AUTONOMY.

"Looks as though someone broke in here," he says. Drawers have been
pulled out and closets left ajar after they had loaded the Dr. P pet van with
five trash bags full of college clothes, sheets and quilts, as well as Mike's
desk and chair. Finally Ringo in his aquarium. Liz wonders how they were
able to buy it.

There is Mike's trail of rainbow-colored T-shirts, tape boxes, pennies,
socks and old tattered jeans. Nathan had once helped her; now he is in jail
for selling cocaine in Harbor Square to the same boyish agent whom
Denise had stalked during the parade. Nathan had insisted that he made
no profit and dealt only to support his two horses and an addiction he got
fighting for his country in Vietnam.

After the bad publicity of that arrest in Harbor Square by an out- of-
town agent, the police considered it their duty to clear the benches of all
loitering kids. The day the Garden Club beautification ladies came to plant
their hardy mums around the sewer pipe art, lonely Svenson popped up
and was arrested for drinking in public. Harbor Square was deserted when
he got out of jail, so he went to the next corner and thumbed his way out
of Shoreland. The Eagle said he got into an argument in a Boston bar and
was stabbed to death. No one wants to believe it.

Last time they reported Svenson dead, he was in a coma for several
months. That was after he had briefly worked in the douche factory up the
line, crossed the highway without looking, and got hit by a truck. He lay
in the hospital—kids said—until one of them came and held a flask of
Bacardi under his nose. His lips moved, he opened his mouth. Turned out
that Svenson had been faking it for a while because he was crazy about one
of the nurses.

This time, the postmistress, his nearest relative, had to drive into town
to identify his body, but there had been been a lot of fatal accidents and a
few murders. She made herself quite ill, looking at unidentified bodies.
Came back and cancelled the memorial. "Svenson has more than nine

lives," she told Liz. "He'll show up for Thanksgiving, when Mike and Caleb and all the rest will be back." In the meantime she's leaving the big mess Svenson left in the barn for him to come home to.

Liz leaves the mess in Mike's room for him to come home to. She goes around wearing T-shirts Mike has outgrown and feels unusually tired during a week of storm and rain while she stays in every day, waiting for Mike's phone calls and the first copy of "The Smiling Child." On Sunday, when the sun comes out, she walks down to Harbor Square with Saki looking for company, but there is not one kid around.

A preacher dressed up in a white suit and pink tie has taken over a bench with a sample case of pamphlets and is reading out loud from the Bible in front of the gold and russet hardy mums. "I am the tree, ye are the branches." He stands up straight to support his barrel belly, has porcupine hair and a good, loud voice, but no one is listening. A woman whose right foot is in a cast decorated with names and phone numbers sits on a bench with her back to him, watching the Sunday pilgrimage of day trippers wandering in and out, shop after shop. He is only another pedlar selling something no one wants to buy. An old couple sitting on the nearby stone wall turn away to confer with each other.

A perfect Sunday, the ocean breeze blending sweetness of perfumes women wear for their outing with exhaust from the bumper-to-bumper cars that have no place to park. Daisy, the resident English poet, always dressed up in hat and gloves, follows the crowd as though she had no place to park.

"Liz, Liz!" Brian the brain runs across the street so fast he drops an astronomy book. "Go to the library and see. Your book has been written up big in the New York Sunday Times Book Review!"

Liz gives him a hug, which makes him blush.

"You're famous," he calls out. "She's famous!"

The preacher raises his voice. "Vanity. Success is a horrible disaster, worse than a fire in the home. Fame consumes the home of your soul."

"I bet whoever wrote that is famous," Brian responds in his high-pitched, clear voice. "And don't tell me you wouldn't want to be Billy Graham!"

The kind librarians have mounted "The New York Times" review on a big board which is soon covered with more rave reviews of this well-written first novel that makes such a timely statement about missing children.

"You must be so proud, Chris! What a thrill!" Bonnie says, when the book finally arrives. The cover looks like a rosy sunrise. "To think Mike took that lovely picture. Doesn't it make Liz look like a little girl?" While she holds it up for Chris, a note the publishers forwarded from a Chicago reader falls out.

Beatrice Strout is right. SMILING CHILD has much
substance and meaning in today's world. My mother
ran away and left me! Do you think the world as we
know it is coming to an end?

Respectfully yours,

Robert Wilder.

Only a thousand copies have been distributed across the nation. But at least one of them is already in the hands of someone named Robert Wilder in Chicago. Cause for new hope. Liz celebrates by answering his letter.

Dear Robert Wilder: The world as we know it is constantly coming to an end. Nothing is ever the way
it used to be...

Mike does not come home for Liz's autograph party at the Book Nook; Chris takes to bed with a bellyache because Ellen has invited Dr. Bigfield. Arthur calls from Vienna and sends flowers. Ellen's single parents all come. So do the Tough Love people, who take credit for helping Liz out. A crowd comes piling in to celebrate with wine and cheese and Bonnie's cakes and cookies. The Fairfields show up with champagne. Two hundred and thirty books are sold and quite a few are read right away. But some have been returned for an exchange the very next morning because a page is missing.

Now Bonnie has trained Del to answer phones and give Christian help where it is needed, while she gives help to Liz, going on the road with her when she does a local TV show. They both wear makeup for the first time. There are radio interviews and call-in shows too. Giving people a chance to be heard asking weird questions about sex under Hitler, or giving the author advice to stay at home and cook and be a wife and mother. Or, to give up slave labor as a house-wife. Then there are trips to the warehouse to pick up repaired books, also to buy some at a discount for promotion. Andy, the man in charge of the warehouse, who got interested in "Smiling Child" because of the missing page, is a Liz Plant and Bonnie fan. Now the women in the office are reading it, asking for an autograph and showing Bonnie pictures of their babies. Although Liz does not have an advertising budget for her book, Bonnie is learning a lot about publishing from Andy and has hopes that the enthusiasm at the warehouse might even pass on to the sales department.

There is reader response in the street and at the supermarket from those who watch novels on TV and don't usually read. A beautiful bouquet arrives from an old lady who used to be a war correspondent. Some of the mail the publishers forward, as well as letters sent directly to Liz Plant, Smiling Child, Shoreland, have to be cached in a shoe box.

Dear Liz Plant,

I waved. You didn't notice and went speeding right past my Corvette. I followed. You turned into the dump. I helped you unload three trash bags and you did thank me, but you won't remember. I have watched plenty of other men come running to unload your trash these days because you're famous and have this sexy smile.

I watched you vanish into that shack with the old guy. You didn't come out until the dump closed! From the Lord of the Dump you went straight to the bench in Harbor Square. Old men and young boys! It was worth paying a parking fine to learn the truth about Smiling Child. The likes of us, who leave home at an early age, are highly sexed.

I am rereading your book for the 8th time.

No signature. No return address. She has had enthusiasm from the "New York Times Book Review," "Kirkus" gave her the star, "Boston Globe" a rave review, but she is no bestseller. In fact her book isn't even in the Boston stores. But her picture in the local papers makes her a celebrity in Shoreland. Men like to help her unload trash at the dump now. She is not used to being singled out, but Walter says it's their pleasure. Everyone at the sanitary landfill is proud of her.

She was invited to speak to the Baptist Ladies Fellowship group. By the time her editor forwards the letter from the parents of a retarded New Jersey boy who collects autographs and the one from Cindy West, a Boston freelance reporter, she has to get another empty shoe box from Bonnie.

I am a free lance journalist and I admire your
writing and understand your book because I am sure
I was adopted. My parents are Irish. I am black.
That's why I married a "brother." But he is glad
that our three children are white. Then he insisted
on a pure-bred German Shepherd. Like the English
great grandmother in your book. Beatrice Strout
says that women novelists are psychic and she has
come out for you in a big way. My husband travels a
lot and he can pass for white. Do you think he is
playing around with white women?-Cindy West

A registered letter from New Jersey the same day:

I cried when Beatrice Strout reviewed your book
about that stolen child because Danny, my only
child, was stolen. We were happy together for
thirty-six years. I'm a wonderful cook. He would
never have left me of his free will. We were very
close. He was doing real well, going up in the
funeral insurance business, with Earthwhile and
Brooks, a big company. Buying up all the funeral
homes and offering special burial packages was his
idea. Then that woman, Andrea, that gravestone
salesman came after him. Andy, she calls herself.
Divorced with kids. Knew a good thing when she saw
it. Got a hold of my boy by giving him drugs and
whiskey. While I was in church she packed his
clothes and anything else she liked, and stole my
Danny. She has black hair on her arms, a big nose,
but no morals, so she might have AIDS. I am worried
sick. My only child has vanished! transferred.
Earthwhile & Brooks wont tell me where she keeps
him. Thought you might like this story for your
next book!
Yours, Mary Louise Winterbottom

When Mike took the picture for the book jacket, he kept telling Liz to try and look famous, eccentric and sexy. Liz became embarrassed, turned her head away, and he caught her in profile. There has been as lively a response to this picture as there had been to the Catulle paintings during her days as a model in Manhattan. Letters from men wanting to sleep with her, a couple from women who love her. A threatening letter from an American Nazi because she is making up lies about the Third Reich and its leaders. An angry letter asking what are a few thousand stolen children compared to the murder of all the Jews? Many of these letters are computer printouts. Could it be that the same people wait for book reviews and then send different versions of the same letter?

No publicity budget, small pre-publication sales. Her editor had tried to warn her. How could she ever have hoped that "Smiling Child" would be translated? She has little hope now of finding her lost mother. In the end she will have been rewarded with the joy of becoming a writer, speaking up, speaking out, much like the poet Rosalie Plant trying to perfect each sentence, each word, reveling in the luxury of owning herself for a few hours a day.

Chris doesn't see it that way. Letters keep coming, the phone keeps ringing. He had to answer calls from reporters, and he has to monitor calls from strange men and women. The same deep voice asking: "You know who this is, Liz?" several times a day and even during the night. He finally follows Ellen's advice to give Liz Bonnie's special answering and help service. Then he follows Dr. Haupter's advice to play golf and get rid of harmful anger with the combined therapy of smacking a ball and meditative walks when you are looking for a lost one.

"I couldn't put the book down. 'Smiling Child' made me cry so much," Bonnie tells him. "I always wanted a baby so much. Imagine losing your little one that way! I keep thinking of Mike being hurt. All you two went through. The way Liz kept at it. You must have been of great help to her, Chris. But now I'm told the book isn't in the Boston stores, but don't worry. I'll talk to them! And I'll check up on all the libraries."

Bonnie uses her maiden name—Codget Associates—when she calls book stores. She does direct promotion, too, when she takes calls: "This is Bonnie's Answering Service. Proud neighbor of Liz Plant, the author of 'Smiling Child'." The sun shines every day but it is suddenly cold as winter.

The town is packed with fall tourists, many of them well-to-do retirees who like to spend their money even on books. And this week Walter, the Major, is promoting. He bought a book and displays the big and little national reviews pinned up in the library section of the Dump Boutique.

Bonnie wanted to call more radio and TV stations, to get Liz onto shows, but she had a cold, developed laryngitis, and lost her voice. It even hurt to answer the phones. By Saturday she is getting better. Walter makes her hot tea when she drops in, and wraps her up in a vintage mink coat someone left in the Boutique. She is tall enough to carry it well and the wide sleeves make her laugh. Aside from a little rip under the arm, it is almost good as new—and heavy.

Walter has tickets for the matinee tomorrow, Sunday, their day off, and he is taking Bonnie to see "My Favorite Clowns." The production by the Shoreland Players has a cast of local talent. All the friends and relatives come piling in to see the show. Parents bring kids, even babies. It is supposed to be deep, but nobody cares. They come to see cute clowns pop out of big boxes and then call out their names and cheer. The director says audience participation gives the play an extra dimension. After each show there is a big cookie and cider and balloon benefit for the Shoreland Players. "My Favorite Clowns" is one big party.

Naturally Bonnie thinks the clown with all those animal-shaped balloons at the Linden Tree Mall is promoting the play. "Beautiful coat," says a gentleman as she passes in the vintage fur coat. He's one of the regulars on the bench under the man-made Linden Tree. Always dressed up in a gray suit, shirt and tie, always holding a handkerchief or something.

Bonnie's voice has come back. She is carrying a box of her butter cookies to the autograph party she set up for Liz at Walden Books. She's feeling better by the minute and goes right over to the clown. "Great promotion," she says. "I should have thought of something like that for promoting my friend's book. You're just great!" The clown keeps eating a hamburger out of a McDonald's bag. "I'll talk it up for you. I have been promoting 'Smiling Child'; mostly talking it up and— "

The clown grabs her arm and a hidden tape recorder blasts her with howling, roaring, screeching jungle sounds: "PUNISH THE MURDER OF ENDANGERED ANIMALS! SAVE THE PREDATORS." Bonnie lets out a better shriek than anything that box can produce. The clown drops his hamburger. "No more furs! No more murders!" he shouts.

Bonnie stands about a head taller than the clown. "This is no murdered animal. It's been dead a long time. This is an old, old coat. Older than I am—for sure. Let go of it!"

A few girls stop, laugh, then walk on. But Belinda Crabby, with her friends Doris and Bella, comes right over. Uniformed in pant suits. Hair all piled on top of their heads, carefully made up, sprayed with all kinds of perfumes they tried out at Jordan's. "What's going on here?"

"PUNISH THE MURDER OF ENDANGERED ANIMALS! SAVE THE PREDATORS." The racket starts all over again and the clown clings to Bonnie's wide sleeve.

"A friend gave me this beautiful old coat; it needs mending. You're going to tear it some more!"

"What are you, a Communist?" Belinda Crabby says to the clown. She puts her Secret Garden lingerie bag down on the tree bench beside the small, well-dressed gent. "Sir, don't you think a woman has the right to wear her mink?"

His eyes brim over. "My mother wore hers all the time. I had her buried in it!"

Doris, who is thin, bow-legged and sturdy, goes right up to the clown. "Let go of her coat at once!" She backs off and charges again like a terrier. "Pick up your hamburger, clown."

"You're littering," Bella makes herself heard from a safe distance.

The clown keeps holding Bonnie's sleeve while he reaches into his pocket for a rusty scissors. "Furs are forbidden! Torture and murder of animals forbidden!"

"Wait a minute," Bonnie says. "I never forget a voice. Do I know you?"

The clown lets go of her sleeve so suddenly, that she staggers back and ends up on the lap of the little gentleman. She's up again in a second. "I'm so sorry!"

He looks shocked, but pleased. "Any time!" Can't resist touching that silk and lace in the Secret Garden bag while the ladies take off after the clown. How he can run! Balloons bobbing and dancing. Two little kids bored with shopping and fed up with their Mom talking to other Moms run after him: "Gimme one! Gimme!"

Then other little ones follow, yelling: "We want one too, we want one!" The clown turns right, racing past Singer Sewing Machines, the Jog Shop.

The laughing and shrieking attracts more and more kids.

Belinda with her friends get caught up in following the excitement. "You better watch out for your youngsters. That clown is crazy," she calls to the young mothers. "He just tried to stab a woman with his scissors!"

"Did you hear that?" They race after the kids. "Come back here, Billy. Back at once, Mary! Toni! Al! Come back at once, Al!"

Al! The name rings a bell for Bonnie, but the cold has tired her out. The coat weighs a ton as she hurries to deliver her cookies at Walden Books.

There is a nice big table displaying reviews of "Smiling Child" and pyramids of the book in front of the store. Ms. Blossom, the retired librarian, is getting Liz to autograph three copies as Christmas presents, "To Meg Smith with best wishes," when the clown comes charging along, crashing into the table and books tumble down. He even knocks the money out of Ms. Blossom's hand, and steps on her foot. Little kids come screeching after him. "Balloons. Give me balloons!"

The two security men are on each side of the clown. Middle-aged—encumbered by protruding bellies, but costumed in tattered pants and garish T shirts like the boys they usually stalk—they are confronted by hysterical suspicious mothers. "What. You're still security?" One young mother who knows them from her shoplifting days, also knows how to bring charges against the clown who entices little kids.

"That's what he's paid for," one of the security men says. "McDonald's hires clowns."

The clown stands still and doesn't say a word. Liz doesn't say a word about the clown in Boston and at the town meeting, the parade and at the hunt, because the same security men had come after her with Mike and Caleb not long ago. She is playing it safe. No different from the women in Hitler School she described in her book.

It's Belinda who takes one of them by the arm. "My Secret Garden bag!" Her friends hang back, because they know she forgets where she puts things. "I want that clown to give me back my silk undies!"

"Underwear?"

"A rapist!" says a schoolgirl.

A little imp in pink-framed sunglasses keeps shrieking, "Sex offender!" Just like TV; kids love it. "Sex offender!" They shout at the two security men. One of the little ones jumps and snatches a balloon. The clown wards them off, waving his arms like a mime. The guards ask for his ID. He shrugs his shoulder, takes out the scissors, hands them to the guard and turns the pockets inside out. "Guess, we can get that later at McD's."

"I don't see that he has any of your underwear, lady," says his partner.

Belinda gets in front of the clown. "He does attack ladies in fur coats with those shears! And just look what he did here to this lovely author and her books. Did he bother you, honey?"

The clown stands still and doesn't say a word. More and more people gather around Liz. She can smell the sweet odor of the spray. A rollicking little tune starts up. Subliminal persuasion? They grab books. "Too bad, doing that to you. You're a local author. Saw your picture in the paper. Weren't you on cable TV?"

Bonnie starts passing around little cups of punch the bookstore put out for the autograph party and offers her cookies. "I saw it all," she says to the guards and hands them her business card. A tall businesswoman wearing a mink coat is treated with respect. "Little kids chased after him and they all wanted his balloons. Right!"

"Right!" says a serious girl.

"He didn't really touch any of you! He's calmed down now. Handed over the scissors." She even offers the clown a cookie and some punch, but he won't take any of it and mumbles something about going back to McDonald's. She peers into the painted face, and notes that dark hair protrudes from a mask that covers the chin. "It's you, Al. I know," she whispers. His painted lips press together drooping at the corners. "Why don't you go back with the ladies and see whether they left their shopping bag on the bench," she speaks up in her telephone voice. "There's that nice man. I bet he took it to the lost and found."

The second security guard walks right up to Liz. "Wait a minute! I never forget a face. I know you!" He turns to his partner. "She and two boys were shoplifting here this winter. Hand it over!"

Bonnie is right on the spot. "My friend, Liz Plant. The author of 'Smiling Child'. No way! She doesn't have a package, does she? This is slander—"

"—Sorry, Miss," says the partner. "I remember you and that nice smile and the boy with this ugly mask, but a girl had paid for it."

Commotion is the best promotion. "Book signing. Liz Plant?" Mrs. Wise makes herself heard. Making her way through the crowd with her white cane and tall Mr. Olson she feels her way towards Liz and gives her a hug. "Liz, Liz Plant. The mother of wonderful young Mike who was almost murdered at his school by a gang. We'll see that your book comes out in Braille." A line forms before Liz can explain that she has not written a book about her son. She has to sign books. Some come along and get in line to buy several copies of "Smiling Child" as Christmas presents. Because Liz smiles, they think it must be a happy story.

Liz has lost her chance to speak up about the sinister Boston clown. She is busy writing dedications to aunts, to mothers, to boyfriends. There is no time to think or worry.

A line always attracts more shoppers. The manager of the book store and one of the clerks are bringing out the last twenty books, but they'll take orders for "Smiling Child" written by Liz Plant, an accused thief. Mother of a victim. Crime pays.

A tall young woman pushes her way to the front of the line. "I'm a journalist. And I'm your witness. I saw it all. Cindy West. I wrote to you. Remember, about being black!"

She is white. Gramp would have called her "svelte."

"I'm adopted. My parents just won't admit it. They're Irish."

Without her Afro-wig, Cindy would have passed muster even at Hitler School. But she married an African-American, Liz remembers, and thinks he's fooling around with white women.

"I'm going to do a story about this woman-hater clown trying to hurt you. Nothing to do with furs. It's a conspiracy against women!"

Liz could have told her that self-haters in disguise will always find a cause, even a war, but she keeps her mouth shut like the clown who doesn't want to be discovered, because anything she says might be held against her by Cindy, who conspires against herself with all the bias of anorexic Emerald.

"What do you think?" Cindy asks.

Liz hands her a signed copy of "Smiling Child."

Chapter 44

LOVE AND LEARN

"You don't have to call me Beatrice Strout. Just call me Bea. Let's stay out here on the terrace and I'll take your picture. It's gorgeous here. Just like the descriptions in your book. I just love Shoreland. All those old houses with shutters, the blue water and the island. I take excellent photographs. Do you mind leaning over looking down over the water? The picture on the book jacket really doesn't do you justice. There, that's perfect; just lean over a little more. I think I got the reflection—'the mirage of a sunken vessel.' I could never write the way you do, Liz. Your book just blows my mind. I read it twice. I couldn't put it down. There, I like the smile. What is it you say about smiling? I'll always be a smiling child waving on the side of the road. Nazis stealing blonde children because of the shortage. I researched that. They were short of everything and stole. You made it all very real! I don't know how you did it. Just perfect for a movie.

"I couldn't write day after day, year after year on the same book. I'm working on two bestsellers at the same time, and you're the last interview for "New-Age Women Writers." You show how smiling beats griping to shrinks. A new self-concept, and the most fantastic self-defense. Sensational Femininism.

"You were a model in New York City, weren't you, before you married your brother? Nowadays the top models don't smile. They snarl and they strip. You didn't strip for the Russian, that male chauvinist artist. I really like the New York scenes. The sensuality. Men trying to exploit this model while she's trying to find out who she really is and find her mother. The truth is we are all stolen away from our mothers by men. Men are pirates. Except for my Max. And I suppose your brother. Max is a brother and everything else too.

"He watched your interview on 'Today's Woman'. You said you got up as early as four or five in the morning to write. I'm a night person myself. After Max heard you, he started getting up around eight and woke me up. This morning I already did some research at the local library. Never takes me long. I speed-read 'Historic Shoreland'. Love the way pirates buried their gold and forgot where they put it, the way dogs bury bones. Over there, under that old tree, that's the place where William Plant was supposed to have found the pirate's treasure. Then he built this house and—

"Who banged that door just now? Your husband? Late sleeper? I see...He should get up on a day like this. It's so gorgeous here. I bet some of the pirates must have dug up their loot and settled down. Yes, I'd love some coffee. Let's go in. I'm getting too high on this air. I can't really think out here, too much to see. Right!

"This is the most incredible house. What a gorgeous living room. I love a big fireplace. The ancestral woman. She had all those sons. No daughters. What a sad face! Your grandfather brought the carved table from Europe after the war? A collector. That how you got the idea of an American collecting a pretty child? Right?"

❀❀❀

The loud voice bothered Chris when he first woke up and he yelled, "Turn it down!" Now he tries to use relaxation techniques to get back to sleep by practicing meditation. "I'm breathing in, I'm breathing out." No use. That female gabble is back on. He jumps out of bed, ready to demolish the kitchen radio, but that voice comes live from the parlor. He has heard her before, but where? On the Carson show. Good grief! Beatrice Strout! One of the Carson show regulars has actually shown up here. Must be her MG parked in the driveway. He goes down to the kitchen using the back stairs, makes himself unhealthy instant coffee, and collapses. Gramp used to say loud women should be gagged. Strout isn't a bit funny, but Liz giggles and gurgles like a baby who hasn't learned to talk.

"I'm glad you showed me the old portrait of William Plant. Stunning man. You're right, the gravestone angel has the same sensuous mouth. I like men with long hair. How about your father-in-law, Michael Plant? He wrote to Amanda Garlic, the official Salem witch you know, asking her to help you find your mother. Amanda and I were on 'Women in Communications' together. She told me about this unusual man—if you know what I mean—But don't worry, I'm not going to mention Laurie and witchcraft.

"I'll take my coffee black, thanks, so that I can eat some of your cookies. How on earth do you have time to bake? It's amazing how much women can do and how well they do it. I did an excellent rubbing of the Plant angel on that old tombstone. It's in the car. I'll show it to you. Some old men sitting on the cemetery wall were watching me and said Mike Plant looks like the rubbing.

"Mike isn't your father-in-law? Your teenager! He faked the letter to the Official Witch of Salem. That's fantastic. Let me write all that down. And your husband is Chris Plant. I'm no good with names." No, no. Don't worry, I'll stick to you and your book; leave the Plant men to the local reporters. I work in depth on women and their self-concepts. The book will be about two hundred pages. I'm going to use a pen name when I write about my own work. I don't see anything wrong with reviewing oneself. After all, you really don't know what you have written until after the book is published. Yes, my first book 'Love and Learn' is still doing well; because of the 'how-to' new-age sex. Reaching a higher awareness through self-hypnosis and safe sex techniques. You have the book? Right!

"I didn't get reviews but had blurbs from the psychic Margo Woodstone, Dr. Borster, a sexologist, and a Hungarian hypnotist. We want to have even more sales next time. Response is always wild." Loud laughter. "You too! You're right. The same men must be sending letters to any woman who publishes a book. I got one really sweet fan letter. I knew it was from Max because his spelling is unique and he uses my computer. I'm making him read your book. You might get one of those sweet letters too.

"So you'd write during the night, or else get up at four in the morning and work for five hours. And then all the housework. No, I don't do any of that. I pay most of the rent and Max cleans and cooks beautifully. He's studying acupuncture in Boston. Thanks, yes, another half-cup. I know you have to go into Boston to the bookstores. Women helping women. Beautiful. The manager is right, posters and a window display will really help. You have to build interest.

"I know Boston would have been more convenient for both of us this morning, but I just had to see you in your typical environment. It's usually a mess? You actually picked up because I was coming? I wish you hadn't.— No, no, I wasn't just staring at a sock under the sofa, I am glad it was forgotten there. It's white, and I need a hypnotic light spot to focus on. I am more intense when I go into myself like this. You dance to Baroque music or rock while you pick up stuff your boy and husband throw around? Better than aerobics? Wouldn't it be more ethereal to dance without cleaning up after those two?

"Fascinating! Now, let's get to the book. Women have fantasies of being stolen, surprised in bed. Like the sleeping princess. Someone coming along and taking you away from it all. You do that so well in 'Smiling Child'. I love that innocent quality, especially in soft porn. When she finally grows up and goes out one night and finally has real sex with her brother.

"'They went to sleep together sharing a pillow, pale strands of her long hair tangled around both their heads and shoulders and they lay so still they might have been fastened together where they touched. Inseparable twins.'

"Luscious. Dreamy incest. I was fascinated by the legal aspect. And now you say he wasn't really her brother. She was adopted. Speed reading. I must have missed that. Thanks, Liz. These are very special cookies. I can't resist. Are you sure you didn't take Laurie's 'Witchcraft as a Science'? And here is the piece I am going to quote in my book:

" 'Skin so fair that their ear lobes, the inside of nostrils, and the peaked arch of upper lips shone transparent like a peeled nectarine. They even had the same discreet honey-colored tufts of hair at the pit of the flat, hard bellies.' You have a fabulous figure. Your big reviews are fabulous. One of the reviews says the past seems to be catching up with Liz Plant.—More like the future catching up with you!

"And you can't believe you actually ever wrote this sex scene? You must be writing in a state of higher awareness. Writers naturally use self-hypnotism. You sounded unreal, special, out of this world on the radio, very much "Smiling Child." Max said someone called in. A man or a woman— that kind of a voice—giving you a hard time, accusing you of trying to make the Nazis sound almost OK because the child isn't put to death in the gas oven. And she not only survives, she's the Nazi Camp director's pet. I myself see that camp director as a lesbian who has not come out of the closet. Is she?

"Who is that coughing? Mailman. You have so much mail he brings it into the house? Quaint. Where were we? You said you don't believe Frau Faser was gay. Of course you don't know. Women writers explore. Men come out with facts and think they know it all. We intuit! I see your writing as surreal. Very clear. You don't have to know whether that woman is gay or not. She doesn't know it either. That's why she's having sex with that brute of a doctor and the inspector. It's all sort of Salvador Dali. Who can ever forget those pancake watches in that landscape? Something from a dream. That's what your reality is like, Liz. Possibly a former life. I can tell by the way you write. You could have been a stolen child in a former life. In one of my last lives, I was married to an English parson. I had eight children and died in childbirth, that's why I don't want to get pregnant. Do you ever think of the way women used to be pregnant all the time? A sin. How they died giving birth and were instantly replaced. Survival of the fittest. And that's how we got to have generations of fantastic, powerful healthy women. Right!

"No, I'm not against premature babies, but saving a five inch fetus outside the womb can end up being a hobby for medical men, and they are not the ones that are going to raise brain-damaged crack babies. I know you love kids by the way you write. Of course it's not just a novel. You do describe your own face. You have amazing eyes. It's a great women's book. A many-layered experience. My review calls it an allegorical fantasy of overcoming a damaged self-concept in a male-dominated household—the struggle for your own identity…"

Chris finally flings the door open. It hits the wall and then self-closes with a bang. Beatrice Strout almost drops that old Plant eggshell china coffee cup. "You really startled me. But my fine intuition told me that there was someone outside that door. You're the husband of the author, right?"

Femininist Beatrice Strout. Long neck, small, pert cat face and the hat she wore on the Carson show: "Cat in the Hat."

"You should have joined us. I love your pajama pants, black silk! missing buttons…And don't look at me like that. You can sew on a button, right? There's nothing wrong with you sewing, Chris. A man is as good as woman and you can do anything a woman can do—and stop laughing, Liz—my Max has sewn a handsome patchwork bedspread. I could never do that!

"I know Liz has to go to Boston, you don't have to come busting in to remind me. And you were listening in on our conversation, Chris? You must be so proud of her. Now, what's the matter with you. You didn't have to bang the door again, Mr. Plant. But thanks for popping in. A half-naked man is always more exciting than a naked or fully-dressed one...I do hope he's still listening, Liz, he's gorgeous. And I can see where you got the idea of the twins. There really is a resemblance. The beautiful wavy blonde hair.

"You are fabulous! You do need the publicity. Chris Plant isn't going to help you? He's not doing anything right now? Well, if he doesn't want to be a broker or your publicist he can always be a male stripper. He has the figure. He doesn't even lift weights? He's a bit of a poker-faced comedian, I'd say. Better looking than Steve Martin, but that type. No wonder you describe men so well. Fascinating! Giving the two main characters your name and his. I like that. This is what I'm going to say: 'By using herself as a stand-in within surreal trappings, Liz Plant reaches a new dimension.'"

From his room Chris watches Liz carry rolled-up posters to her car. She looks unfamiliar in a buff-colored suit he hasn't seen before. Bea in purple pants and yellow jacket, follows behind her, wiggling an impressive bum. Good thing Liz took her around to the back or Strout would have noticed the cross on the rock. Newspaper reporters had used the cross in the back-ground as they swarmed around taking the picture of the brave four-year-old burned orphan boy.

When "Smiling Child" finally arrived and everyone made that big fuss, Liz put it onto his littered desk. She had explored what Bigfield calls "the one-upmanship of a survivor." The way she rewrote those lost chapters, full of never-ending, delayed reactions. Never getting over having to be brave. Had been enough to make him throw the book into the corner onto a pile of dirty sheets. When Liz had picked up the dirty linen, that first copy the editor had mailed to her ended up in a hot wash. What would femininist Beatrice Strout make of that?

She is holding up the gravestone rubbing for Liz to admire. Then she leaps over the door of the convertible MG, turns and waves to the house, and buzzes off. Liz follows in her second-hand station wagon, the replacement for the one Mike sank. The brakes are not too good. What if the worst happened? Huge red trucks, crushing the small white wagon, compacting posters, blown up reviews—everything. "Author Liz Plant, beloved wife of Chris and mother of Mike..." He sees a white wax Sis on a stretcher. The ultimate desertion. Negative emotions released after months of health treatment pour out like pus. He can feel tears run down his cheeks. (Brave little fellow. Never cries!) Legs turn to Play-Dough, gout biting his big toe, his throat closes in a paroxysm of both terror and relief. Then the phone rings.

Eckert back from Europe. "Liz at home?"

"She's gone." Chris catches a deep breath.

"Gone?" A pause. "She left you?"

"Driving into Boston with posters for a bookstore."

A pause. "Hold on a moment."

A woman is saying something Chris can't hear. A man that age. Always surrounded by good-looking women. Certainly improved his German accent in Europe.

"I need to see her."

Shoreland women are all smitten with him. Dora, Ellen. Why does he bother Liz?

"Chris, you still there? *Gut*, good. I have a surprise for her."

❀ ❀ ❀

The October sun is out in Boston; so are the early bird Christmas bargain hunters responding to an advertising campaign with pictures of Marilyn Monroe-type mannequin dolls modeling her old style—which is new this season. The pedestrian zone teems with street musicians, street people, shoppers, shoplifters, dealers, a carnival, a market place. And reindeers blink red noses and Christmas Santas shake jingle bells, collecting money for causes or for themselves. One is taking a nip from a bottle celebrating the earliest pre-Christmas season ever. A sudden rush of women sweeps Liz from the bright day into the night of the mall.

Posters are slipping, her eyes burn, but Liz doesn't mind. Her mood is festive. Bonnie was the one who spoke to Mabel, the Boston manager of Mutton Books. And Mabel had seen an article about Liz and asked Bonnie for posters of Bavaria or Vienna, and blown-up reviews for some of the other stores. If Mutton Books gives "Smiling Child" a prominent display, some of the other chains might order.

She passes a store window full of early Christmas cards, another one with discount stockings and see-through bikinis decorated with snowmen on special, then several dark, empty stores. Finally, at the end of the corridor, the bright light of Candy Land and Mutton Books! Liz has to edge around a big woman in a dark blue cloak who seems to be engrossed by the window display of "Coming", a slender volume with a decorous picture of a half-naked man lying on top of a woman.

Liz was glad when her editor decided against the book jacket of a silly-looking smiling child wearing a fur hat that looked like a hedge-hog. It was left plain. Perhaps too plain! No sign of it here. Mabel must be waiting for the posters and reviews. There is Marilyn Monroe wearing her big smile on the cover of yet another new biography. "Love and Learn," of course, and several horror books take up most of the window space. Which ones would the manager remove to make room for "Smiling Child?"

It is a warm day, but Liz shivers. The stout woman in front of the window display provides shelter. Light from the window shines on her smooth high cheeks, dark smooth hair, the long, dark-blue cloak hanging down over a big shopping bag on wheels.

Liz sees her as a reader, a woman with strong ideas and strong feelings, cultured, possibly European. "You must love books," she ventures to says. "I'm a writer. I wrote "Smiling Child." It is about a stolen child—"

The woman veers around as though she had been poked by a knife; something under her cloak jingles. "Stolen children, molested little gals, murder." A southern drawl. "That's all they write about. Ma own inspirational 'SIN' doesn't get a chance because foreign money people have taken over books in this country, getting rich promoting filth and murder. No end to it!"

Something heavy drops and Liz steps back. The woman in blue picks up a book and stomps into the store. Wheels of her cart squeak along with a piped-in boys choir singing "Holy Night" as Liz quietly follows behind her. Clerks are talking to each other at the cash register. The woman ducks down behind the window display and deftly replaces copies of "Coming" with "Sin." A white book with simple black lettering by Linette Weeks. Quite stark and startling among all the garish horror books.

"Do you work here?" Liz asks her.

The answer comes from faintly squeaking wheels. Liz goes to introduce herself to a bearded young clerk at the register. He consults his computer. "Liz Plant?" The young woman beside him is eating a doughnut and drinking coffee. "Have you seen Smiling Child?" he asks her.

The girl's mouth is full, so she shakes her head. "Let's try under the publisher." Girls on lunch break come wandering in talking to each other. Liz can still hear the faint squeak of wheels.

"I thought I saw "Smiling Child." Must still be in a box. We've been busy installing speakers for this new Christmas music. Supposed to stimulate customers to buy." She turns to unpack a box of the latest Marilyn Monroe biographies. "Mabel should be out soon. Can you wait?"

A line has formed at the cash register. The bearded fellow turns to his assistant. "Must be the subliminal music!"

What's this? 'SIN.' $5.95. A bargain." The young woman gulps down her doughnut. "Must have been put out before we came in."

Liz spots an empty tape-box on the counter with Arthur's picture. Eckert's "Subliminal Virtuality." The sweet sounds of harp, violin, and angel voices of young boys blend with the peep-peep-click of the cash register. She is suddenly overcome by a nostalgic longing for her unpublished self—alone with MATE II—as a one and only writer with something important and urgent to say.

She wanders off blindly among rows and rows of books, each with an urgent message, while piped-in angel voices now sing the subliminally persuasive "Oh Come All Ye Faithful." Her vacant gaze comes to rest on "Sin" turned around among romance novels, "Sin" among diet books, "Sin" in the mystery section, "Sin" among slender pastel-colored inspirational volumes and bibles.

There is no sign of the woman who had placed the book in every category. Right next to the "Joy of Cooking" among cook books, prominently displayed among bestselling novels. Girls are picking it up, looking at the blurbs at the back. "Hey. Sounds cool." Then they laugh and laugh. A good buy too. Nice jacket. Black and white is in." One pert young woman who wears her hair in girlish braids opens the book and laughs: "Crazy!" and puts it back. "It's a big joke. Something different. Love that title and that prize," says her friend, who picks it up again to be part of the rush on the bargain book "Sin."

No "Smiling Child" is on the shelf among new titles, but plenty of "Sin," even under autobiography and biography. The women come and pull them off the shelf, and there, at last, hidden away, is the nice little discreet blushing book jacket of the highly acclaimed $16.95 "Smiling Child." Liz takes her book and gets into line. The clerk is so busy he has forgotten her face. First she pays for a copy of "Sin," and then she holds up her own book. "Smiling Child. Remember? Your manager asked for reviews and posters."

"I'm sorry, but we are so busy... There is Mabel now. You can talk to her."

A plump, fuzzy-haired young woman has emerged from the back. Liz introduces herself, holds up her book and mentions the call from Cossets Associates.

There is a blank look in Mabel's eyes.

Liz digs around and pulls out a shrink-wrapped "New York Times" review. The posters slip down. "You asked for reviews and posters."

"That must have been last week. You're the model who wrote a book. The local sales manager for our chain has been replaced. We are not doing things that way any more."

"Mabel!" the clerk shouts. "We'll have to reorder 'Sin'."

"I'm a local author. This is not a novel. It's my own story. It's important." Liz holds up her "Kirkus Review." "I got the star!"

"Doesn't mean much. Lots of books get the star. You're not on any bestseller list, are you? They didn't give you a large printing. We're not interested in the product, we are interested in sales. I'm not allowed to display books that are not advertised anymore." Then she stops for a moment. "Music can really get to you. I'm busy. I must reorder a book, but I'll see what I can do. Just leave these at the office door. But I can't promise."

Liz takes shelter behind cookbooks. "Sin" has vanished. Mabel and the clerks are punching computer keys in a frenzy. Mabel is staring at the screen. "This system is fucked up.—So help me God. "Sin" isn't listed." No interest in looking at the product, the book, which is selling out fast.

Liz props her posters up against boxes outside Mabel's office. One of them has toppled and "Smiling Child" is printed on the side. The sales force clusters around the computer, no one looking, while Liz pries the box open; takes an armful of books, making her way around the store, replacing "Sin" with "Smiling Child" under Biography, Fiction, Non-Fiction. A wonderful title! Bless editor Robbie for changing it. "Smiling Child" fits in everywhere just like "Sin," among cook-books and diet and health books and inspirational fiction and nonfiction and it certainly looks good among baby books. Angel voices carol her back to the box and then to the front of the store. She builds a pyramid in the window.

"'Smiling Child.' Kidnapping. Beatrice Strout was talking about it on Channel Four," someone says behind her back. "She was kidnapped and then they tried to kill her son and he was saved by the blind." Women's voices. Manicured hands grabbing books she has just arranged. Liz hides behind health books, while the angel voices keep on soaring about baby Jesus. The register clicks and chimes. "'Smiling Child's' author has just been here. Used to be a model!" Mabel's voice. "Out of Sin, but we've got Smiling Child. Changed your mind about 'Sin?' OK 'Smiling Child' is on special; another ten will do it." Liz walks out breathless as though she had been to the peak of Witches Hill.

Years seem to have gone by since she walked through this mall. A single unaccompanied child voice is belting out "I Saw Mama Kissing Santa Claus." Outside, she sinks down on a bench in the warm sun. Two very young girls on a bench beside her are trying on makeup. "No, no. Not that pink, Laurie!"

Laurie. Laurie Clark? One of the many cards with pictures of missing children in her file. Liz looks at the face under the makeup. "Your name isn't Laurie Clark? You haven't run away from Mother?"

The girls pick up their bundles and run. "Go kiss Santa!" Laurie calls over her shoulder. Liz takes her copy of "Sin" out of the plastic bag. The back of "Sin" has blurbs by famous writers praising this book as a unique experiment, an experience, an event. Robbie had said he tried, even his own authors, but could not get a quote for "Smiling Child." Girls who had picked up "Sin" and opened it had all laughed, but Liz has to suppress a serious pang of envy. She opens "Sin" with glowing cheeks. No copyright. No publisher. "Sin" by Linette Weeks on the title page. "CONFESS NOW" on the first page. A 150 numbered pages—all blank. Laughter comes gurgling up her throat like vomit.

Chapter 45

THE RIDDLE OF THE ANSWER

Your painless spiritual and physical transformation. All in the privacy of your home. Not part of the crowd—above the crowds—for the perform-ance of a lifetime. Thousands of letters of testimony.

The promotion shows a new fitness evangelist in motion on a SANCTI FLEX FITNESS SYSTEM.

A healthy body is a gift from God. Keeping in top condition is your sacred duty. Why punish yourself, make yourself run, or work-out in a gym? The SANCTI FLEX muscle machine can do it all for you without effort, without pain. You will move to sacred music. Healthy mind in a healthy body. Pick up your phone right now.

The background music of warbling boys evokes for Chris an early memory of the choir in Norwich Cathedral. And this devout body builder on the screen is no hulk, but the Anglo-Saxon mature boyish Chris Plant type that Beatrice Strout admired, Ellen will pine for, and Bambi, the movie star, likes to play doubles with. "Chris, you are so wholesome," still in his ear, he rushes to the phone, calls the 800 number, and places a rush order.

Assembly jobs usually calm Chris down, but this one is the devil! SANCTI FLEX, he notes, had been pasted over SANI FLEX, and it should really be renamed INSANI FLEX. Keeping him busy all morning. He is bolting the system together in the upstairs bathroom which used to be a sitting room. It's more comfortable to work in pajama pants but he lit a fire.

Liz enters dressed like the TV weather woman in a skimpy suit that goes with predicting natural disasters. "Why aren't you dressed? We're going to South Cove."

"You're acting like a bride before the wedding."

"I wouldn't know," says Liz, sister, lover, wife.

"You were up half the night. Making yourself sick. I don't believe he found your mother. We don't have to go. Get Bonnie to call and make some kind of an excuse. He's the most manipulating chap I ever met. I know you're smitten, but he's worse than old Myrtle."

"Come on. I have to go. And it's really quite odd that you've never been to his house."

"Don't want to get in the way of this romance."

"He encouraged me in my writing. Especially after I lost my manuscript."

"I was a little drunk the night I read your piece about Gramp and me. Little Procurer. Really, now. Couldn't let that pass. But I didn't mean any harm."

Her formal clothes accentuate the childish horror on her face. She is speechless.

"I wish you hadn't told me!" Her heart begins to pound. Resentment, like an exotic disease wells up. "You actually read it and threw out those chapters?"

"I did you a favor. Look at your success."

"Everyone is always doing me such favors. First I'm stolen for my own good. Than I am sold for my own good, then I have to marry you for my own good. The one and only thing I've ever done for my own good is write this book. You throw my chapters out. Mike overwrites my diskettes."

"He was trying to be helpful—Brother's Keeper—he got that from school. These crazy letters certainly changed my life and—"

"—You would have changed your own life long ago, if I hadn't put up with everything—for my own good."

"You would have preferred being snatched away in Vienna by one of those odd types who made out you were their kid? Of course Gramp wanted to help me and himself out, but he did everything he could for you. He even gave you my house."

"His house. Not yours."

"You could actually kick me out."

"Why shouldn't I? "

"You know. Besides, you actually owe me. The Mutton Book people called and I told them what a great book it is." Mutton Books had to reorder "Smiling Child." Bookstores have window displays with posters of the Alps. Beatrice Strout has reviewed the book and raved about Liz and her book on TV. There will be a large printing and Liz is getting ready for a promotional tour.

Chris straightens up beside her in front of the mirror. Wearing jogging shorts that show off his long legs. The lotus blossom of his Health Center T-shirt opens below his bib of curly hair which women, who don't know that he does not have a hairy chest, like to pet. Bambi calls him darling, and much admires Chris for his healthy attitude towards a wife who has a career. Her ex-husband, the diplomat, had violently objected to hers. "You're not mad because of Ellen?"

"Ellen improved you, didn't she. Or was it Mike and the Healing Center?"

"Nothing wrong with the Healing Center. I'm not even involved with any of the women. Ellen is going to move to England thanks to Mike. So why are you so mad at me? It's that damned femininist Strout ruining what's left of marriage in this country. She should be arrested."

She doesn't trust herself to answer him, turns away to the alcove, and dusts Rosalie Plant's treadle sewing machine with a doily. The east windows frames the view of a motor sailor heading out of harbor in turbulent water. "Arthur didn't say anything specific?"

"He's never specific with me. I'm not going to his party. I'm allergic to Dora concerts."

"He's not having a party this afternoon. No house concert. Dora won't be there. Just us. And who knows—"

"I don't want to be part of this soap opera. The surprise is for you."

"Don't be silly!" Liz studies her own flushed face in the mirror. Chris seldom does anything he doesn't want to do. Is that silly?

"I do have to get going on my SANCTI FLEX and shape up, or best-selling author Liz Plant will replace me."

He is bolting a rail down and ruining the old hardwood floor. To calm herself she chooses to again notice how lean and strong he looks. This morning he had served her a great Healing Center breakfast of eggs, tofu, vegetables, English marmalade, coffee topped with whipped dried milk. Something he wanted to do. In grade school he had saved pocket money to buy an expensive toy mouse made in Germany for her, because he wanted to. Not because he felt he ought to. He might give presents to others as an obligation. He gave to his Sis, his Liz, because he wanted to. A lot like Gramp. Not at all like Arthur Eckert. "It's hot in here. The fire is smoking."

Exactly what she had said to him when she had come to his apartment that rainy night, practically naked under her raincoat. She is smiling again, when she props the door open with his tool box to let the smoke out and runs downstairs.

"You haven't even seen me work out." Her dress shoes make so much noise, she doesn't hear him. She could at least have given him credit for overcoming his fear of flames. Chris reaches up to adjust a tight strap, fastens himself in, limb by limb, and turns on the switch. His arms and legs begin to move automatically. A door bangs downstairs. Then the door bell rings and he can't get off. The switch doesn't work. Bang goes a door. He can hear voices downstairs. Mike home for the weekend. He always loses his key. They must have broken in.

Chris, locked in tight and forced to work out on the SANCTI FLEX MUSCLE MACHINE, composes letters to the Better Business Bureau, Ralph Nader, and Greenpeace while piratical kids plunder the refrigerator and his liquor cabinet. The radio starts blasting loud rock music. His heart rate goes up minutes before INSANI FLEX really goes insane, jerking his arms sideways and up. The flames shoot up, sparks fly, ready to set the chimney on fire. Chris is sweating. He calls "Mike. Mike. Mike!" A door slams shut. A vehicle takes off like a rocket. Kids leaving half-empty liquor bottles and a man screeching to bashing banging racket on the radio.

The cloudy mirror shows a man strapped onto a rack, his arms and legs tearing back and forth, back and forth. The head movement subsides and one leg is jerked up sideways like a dog's. "Saki! Saki!" Chris had befriended Saki, and then neglected him. "Saki! Saki!" The Tibetan dog takes his time. Enters brushing against the half-open door, and stares, wagging its tail.

When the Professor comes to collect garbage, his new, powerful hearing aid transmits a distant cry for help. Back door is unlatched. He follows the voice and comes upstairs, unplugs the machine. Chris and Saki stretch out on the floor panting side by side. The garbage man philosopher opens more windows and the sea air rushes in. "This is what life is all about. Opening up, letting in fresh air." Since he has joined the True Bible Community as a lay pastor, he recycles garbage for pigs (highly intelligent animals, agreeing with Miss Nesbit). He now shares his inspirations when he makes his rounds, "If you work you don't have to kill yourself working out."

No continental kiss on the cheek or hand kiss today, when Arthur comes to meet her at the gate. He's shed his Old World manner, his seductive self-esteem and designer wear, for faded jeans. Trying to make her more at ease? The wind whips the odor of seaweed into her face and roughs up his thick, graying hair around a well-matched hairpiece at the back of his head. A button missing on his denim shirt makes Liz inexplicably sad. He is conveying something that he can't put into words. Something has changed. Even the house with the million dollar view seems a mere gesture. He catches her looking at him with all the expectations he has stirred up and puts his arm around her shoulder.

"Yes. *Jawohl.* I met her again. I even handed her a rose. I carried a charming gold rose in my pocket, but she arrived wearing diamonds like a diva. She looks like one too. Slightly full blown. Expecting to be courted, loved, admired, although she is married to a high government official and has two sons. I should have talked about love. My old obsession with her."

"You told her all about me?"

"My admiration for you. The book. Everything." He starts to limp. Liz does not ask why, but falls in step with him. "There are days," he says, when his right leg feels wooden, and then he places his weight badly on the left foot. A mistake. Their hips touch as they make their way up the steps and into the house. Never closer and never further apart.

"I made a bad mistake of asking her whether she had perhaps had my child. She got into a rage. Threatened to have me arrested as a blackmailer, child molester and kidnapper if I went around with those stories and ruined her marriage… It hurts. Really hurts."

"Emerald," he calls the moment they walk through the open door. "Could you please bring my slippers." Liz chooses a straight-backed chair and Arthur sinks into the white sofa they once shared. Em appears hocus-pocus like a shoe commercial, cradling red slippers. "Hello," she sings out. Her white shorts and T fit like a pelt. Blond streaks in her hair catching the light, she kneels down in front of him and sits on her heels. "He was wounded and almost lost a leg, you know."

This seems to be the cue for him. To remember the field hospital, where he was looking out of the window from his bed and seeing orderlies carry arms and legs to big bins. "A foreign doctor was amputating German limbs. But there was a medical student from Vienna, about my own age, who got me out of bed and saved my leg."

Emerald unlaces his sneakers. He objects. She persists. Showing off—since she has an audience for her performance as a young slave easing his bad foot into the soft, gold-embossed leather from India, Turkey, or Morocco, where women spend their lives serving men.

What am I doing here? Liz asks herself, while he throws back his head and laughs, allowing the schoolgirl to indecently expose his need to be king and father, magician, Santa Claus. A string of geese are flying over the slate-blue autumn water. Neither the question-and-answer calls of departure nor the jubilance of their return each spring would be heard in this soundproof room, which Mike calls a glass cage. Kids will be home for the weekend.

Arthur pushes his sneakers under the sofa. "Well, I don't know how you are going to feel about it all."

Em stretches on the carpet like a cat. "Art bought the movie rights to 'Smiling Child'."

"Movie rights?" Liz turns to face him, knocking over a table lamp. He picks it up. "You mean you are going to make the film?"

"I'm going to be in it." Emerald answers for him. "My first real acting part. But I've done lots of commercials."

On the other side of the harbor, Liz can see Bonnie, off-duty from the telephone-mothering of Shoreland and raking leaves under gaudy autumn trees while Emerald goes on raking through her short life and long career as an actress, which started off before she had learned to talk and walk.

"They'd tell me about the baby bear losing her porridge, pull the cereal away and I'd burst into tears. When I was ten, I had a big part in an Italian

film. Playing a deaf-and-dumb girl who has a vision of the Madonna. I
could always cry on command. But my father didn't want me to be an
actress. So I cried." Her piercings and tattoos that had been forbidden at
Grove Academy and admired by Mike are concealed. Today there is no visible mutilation.

Arthur leans over and passes his hand over her head. More of a bene-
diction and absolution than a caress, while he assures Liz that the film
would definitely help to keep her book in print. "Well, we must celebrate.
A little Campari, Liz?" He exits cured of the limp. "Emerald can't wait to
fill you in."

Em titters like an indulgent parent at "the mess": autumn flowers, candles burned down, a few glasses and a bowl of grapes. Arthur and her
mother Bambi partying the way they always do when her mother has to go
away. "So I go off to his office with a pizza and a couple of drinks and
'Smiling Child'. Whoa—those paintings of your face in his office! Artist
having this super weird time painting your kinda face all the time. The big
one—special order or something—the kid with a rose and a drop of blood
on the finger. Awesome, like the kid Artie slept with a hundred years ago
and always talks about."

Teen language void of the litany of obscenities is as effective as Arthur's
perfect diction with a foreign accent. Em says she didn't have a clue, but
her mother, Bambi, thinks it was Catulle who turned Arthur on by telling
him the story of Liz, the model. Liz had not found her mother in Europe,
but she had found both little Roger and Ken, while she had played the role
of the seductive child Catulle had imposed on her. "Once your face
becomes famous, you turn into a commodity."

"Like me at the Golden Oar. Havelock had me grounded and now
Artie has me grounded. I know what it's like." Emerald leaps and lands
beside Liz. Her legs alone could make her famous, but close up now,
drained of color in the glare, a scar, piercings, and tattoos, show through
the make-up.

"That pregnant kid on the farm with that mean aunt. Sick the way
they let her suffer giving birth." She folds her arms around her flat belly
the way Del often did to protect herself by showing off. "The way they
gave her something for the pain and poisoned her milk. Poor baby crying
and crying, handed over to some women. Just like me when Bambi was
filming, or going out. Scary." Her face turns into a mask of maternal grief.

Tears run down her cheeks. On command? "Do you think I'll be good?"

"I do." Pleasure boats sail out of the harbor and flit out of view swift as thoughts.

"I made that up just now. To get real with his old paintings and his old story. He wants to have the high school kid with the rose and everything up front. That means I'll be in the first scene."

Liz, jumps up. "What do you mean? That has nothing to do with my book!"

"An awesome script. How these Germans are on the road in this black car and he helps steal his own kid, but doesn't know it."

"That's not in my book!"

"Bambi says it makes it like Doctor Zhivago. Several stories. She'll get to play me—I mean the girl as a grown up, meeting her German in the end."

Liz gets up slowly as though she had suddenly grown old and weak. She steadies herself holding onto the glass wall with the million-dollar view of sandpipers and toddlers running on the autumn beach, the way Mike did, back and forth from waves that crash over sandcastles decorated with seashells and dead crabs. She stifles a sob. "My book has nothing to do with Arthur. The German army must have left behind hundreds and thousands of pregnant girls."

"But the movie makes it into this big true story."

"What if she takes him to court?"

"Let her husband think that she had a German baby? She might. To get money. Scummy. It really got to him. But a lawsuit is wicked cool promotion for the movie." Emerald closes her eyes and lifts her head like the dream girl from the bedding commercial. "I'll learn to play the accordion for that kitchen scene. I am a good artist. In the garden scene I'll paint at an easel."

"The mother doesn't paint. She embroiders. A musician plays the accordion." Arthur has taken over her story, now Em has his updated version. The young mother sitting in the rose garden embroidering dresses with cross-stitch roses, playing games of make-believe with happy endings, waiting, hoping, and demanding happiness forever after from Fifinella is left behind in the book. The strange, sweet scent in this room reminds Liz of the mall, the odor in the bookstore. Cloying scent, and cloying stories, to make you buy something, anything. "Did Arthur ask you to tell me all this?"

"He said it would be easier for me," Emerald starts to giggle as he comes back into the room carrying a tray. Rose-colored bittersweet aperitifs glow in the sun.

"Remember how I recognized you at the café? We had you cornered and I behaved very badly."

He's behaving worse now, since he has gambled away his dream. "You are changing my book and combining it with another story?" He sips his drink.

"My story."

Once more he has her cornered and laughs, pleased with himself. Unable to tear himself away from impossible possibilities, trying to hold Liz prisoner sealed in his glassed-in room, his insulated past. "Does my editor, Robbie, know?"

"Come. Let's sit down. Since we are friends he felt I should talk to you about it." He passes to her a drink she doesn't want and juice for Emerald who would like a Campari. Passes nuts, olives, cheese and sits down in the same sofa with his back to the window. "Film makers have to make changes to get more drama."

"I read the end first," Emerald says. "Girls supposed to talk about their mother in social study class, all bragging about how they drink, sleep around, divorce, raise dogs, horses and pigs. Then the stolen child gets her turn and talks about this awesome mother in England. So the teacher asks her to write about the good times when they dance, sing and paint pictures of flowers in an English garden."

Liz gets up ready to just walk out. "She doesn't paint, she embroiders!"

Arthur says: "Liz, *Liese*, please sit down. A film has to be dramatic. Natasha in 'War and Peace' is a singer. Remember charming Audrey Hepburn in the movie? She paints."

Liz doesn't sit down. She can feel her face flush pink as the Campari.

He ignores this. "No matter what we do with the script, you'll sell a 100,000 books."

"Everyone in Shoreland will think you're my father."

This makes him smile. "I like daughters." Emerald sidles up to him and steals a sip from his drink. "This gifted child is getting her big chance. A lucky girl," he says looking at Liz, who is used to being told that she is lucky.

On auntie's farm, then as Faser's pet, as Jan's courier. In the Catholic shelter, at the Manor, and finally as Chris's new Sis and wife, Mike's mom—very very lucky—finally, to have her first book adapted and herself adopted by this seductive father disguised as a sloppy kid.

His dramatic timing is perfect. He knows when to change the subject. Grove Academy is quite different this year. There was another unfortunate incident during the summer session.

"Outward Bound endurance training," Emerald says. "A boy almost drowned."

"Mr. True is back in office. Following some of the guidelines. Havelock is taking the Concept to other parts of the country. Possibly even to Europe."

"What happened to the boy?"

"He is just fine."

"But he ran away."

Liz wants to run away through a field of wildflowers, escape from caring, interference, that sweet odor of persuasion, hopeless obsessions brought about by what Mike calls a "fucked-up environment." But she has been adopted once again and she adapts. Sips her drink, eats the little good things Arthur offers. Aware of his thieving generosity, she finds herself turning the surprise he had staged for her into a cocktail party. She finds herself telling the story of the moose in love with a cow named Jessica.

"Do you know what happened to that moose?" Arthur asks.

"No. I don't."

He hands her a globe. "Open it up and you find a cordless phone: "Call Vermont and find out. I give you the world, call anywhere!"

She calls information, the number of the library in Shrewsbury, Vermont. Always the best place for information. "Whatever happened to the moose that fell in love with a cow named Jessica?"

A cheerful motherly voice. "Almost an endangered species. No one messed with him." From the corner of her eye Liz can see a van come along the road fast, as though she had willed it to brake at Arthur's gate.

"You're smiling. What happened?" he asks when she hangs up and is looking out of the window.

"The moose shed its antlers, and then just walked away." Liz repeats.

Arthur throws back his head and laughs. "A happy ending."

"No it isn't," Emerald says.

"A good ending then. How pretty Liz is and how happy. All because of the moose?"

Liz is gulping her drink. "Or are you secretly pleased about our movie?" Arthur smiles with Emerald by his side. Happy with himself now in his scenario of subliminal bonding, he seems to have forgotten Em's escapades. The Golden Oar, the gang who came looking for her and found Mike.

The electronic Doberman bitch goes into action. Tom the Tick jumps out of the Dr. P van wearing a top hat, followed by Karin, Dell and Elgar. Mike's at the gate.

"*Ach so*, company has arrived for Liz." Arthur says, "Some of them may already have been here. Uninvited. Ask them all in. Maybe we can use them as extras when we start shooting."

Mike would no doubt have some input about turning "Smiling Child" into an alien, who inhabits Himmler's room decorated with furniture made from the bones of his victims. Caught between the new version of her past and a science-fiction future. "I promised to drive them to a Grateful Dead concert."

Emerald wants to come along. "No," Arthur says with a smile. The girl says she'll be going anyway. Springs up so light she seems to levitate and float like a trapped butterfly around the glass in an expanse that had once been several private rooms with private windows framing a private view; window seats for reading, daydreaming, confiding, or flirting and being secretly in love. Old Shoreland houses had rooms with ornate keys. There's nothing left to say but a quick adieu.

Liz allows the carpet rivulet to float her through the gallery. Famous paintings flit by. Jagged lines slashing a female onto a white canvas. This had to be the one Caleb and Tick took without giving it a thought. A green one, splattered with yellow, red and blue looks like wild flowers in an unmown field, where a thoughtless boy had once stopped to pick a child. His own? Perfect ending for Arthur's script by making his story hers, and her story his.

Chapter 46.

OUTWARD BOUND

Grateful Dead show. A youth rally. "How many? Ten—thirty thousand. All those skulls—like SS badges—And roses, Mom," says Mike. "I knew you'd like it. No guns, no daggers. Thousands of fresh roses." Lights shine down onto the balcony drenching kids red as roses or blood. "Garcia, Garcia, Garciaaaa! ahhhhhrrr—"

A shout, hoot, roaring battle cry, hands shoot up in the victory sign, saluting peace, to amplified torrents of electronic sounds awash with colors. Mike and the others are off, down below, milling around turning green in green lights, pushing through packed passages to emerge in the blue ripple below the podium. And skunk-flavored smoke rises up to the balcony, fogging the mind. Homey, honeyed country rhythms, nursery-rhyming singsong and bedevilment, as the white-bearded Garcia strums a twang-along, stepping it out in tight black pants: a barefoot go-go Santa. After each song a roar goes up and dies to an African drum sad as a bony ghost banging on iced windows.

She is out of it, then back into the beat of the dance, thousands reaching out hand in hand, arm around arm, stomping in place. Big, shy, Vermont boys, their first concert. Stoned for the first time. Moose, cow? Never heard of moose in love with a cow named Jessica. Never seen so many people. Whipping around, bobbing, hopping up and down, on and on, dancing the time away, fast and faster towards the stampede and turmoil of intermission.

A top hat dives up from the teaming aisle. "Liz! Awesome lady!" Caleb, tall and baby-faced strongman. "It's me, Caleb Gray. Oddball Emmet's nephew. Fugitive from Grove Academy." Red roses decorate the T-shirt, a white skull shines and grins on a tattered black top hat. "Like the hat, Liz?"

"The SS had skulls on their uniforms."

"See it glow? I painted mine. That's art. Awesome hat. Vintage from uncle Emmet. Dad says I look a mess. In rags. Let him try to go around like this for a day. Then he'd know what it's really like to be different—like a black, or a Jew, homeless—whatever. Here, here." He holds a small crystal flask to her mouth. "Go on, go on!"

"The crystal flask. There is a Fifinella in there ready to follow your command!"

"Fifinella. That's a new one. Go ahead. Drink. Drink up."

The surge of kids in costumes talking, waving hands, kissing, or collapsing, recedes as twin Pillsbury Doughboys chuckle themselves into one half-forgotten Caleb Gray. "What did you give me to drink?"

"The best, the best." He is hiding something behind his back; a bomb, a gun. Chris warned her what can happen—drug addicts, sex fiends. Stampede of Hells Angels. She ducks. Caleb is quick on the draw. Pointing a red rose at her. Perfect, fresh as the one that had bloomed on in Arthur's mind. Roses, roses, Mike, Elgar, Tom, and Joe kept in a bucket at the back of the Dr. P Pet van, fragrance of roses while she had transported the troop mile after mile, tune after tune—a blast.

Caleb doffs his hat and performs a Dead Head bow. "I took the thorns off for you." He puts the rose into her limp hand and closes it. Emily Dickinson makes her say "I'm nobody. Who are you?"

"A good question. Somebody all right. 'Caleb the Killer' at Grove. And then they almost killed me, Liz. Dad sent me to summer session to have Havelock build my character while he and Mom were in Europe. Havelock calls it Outward Bound. Tie up feet and hands, then throw you into icewater that freezes your—you know. You're supposed to get the rope off underwater, come up like fucking Houdini, and be reformed. Only I stayed down. The coach says I'm a sinker. He's a fucking drowner. Later on

I get drunk, beat them all up, and escape. My uncle believes traveling is educational. Now I'm on the Dead tour. Gave me his hat, plenty of money. Wanta come? I have enough money. Where is Mike and everyone? Go on. Drink. Fly. Like it's never going to happen again. Wicked good to blow away all that eating, sleeping, everyday shit."

Long-stemmed bridal girls in long pale dresses, each carrying a long-stemmed rose come drifting around him swaying lank hair. "You all look the same. Sisters? All go to the same school, awesome, which one? That's where I wanta go." And they drift on with him. Lights pick them up down below in smog and dust, dancing to thunder and clang-twanging tune-up. Girls screech, thousands of hands rise up in testimony.

A conveyer belt starts up carrying Liz from a happy, soft, slow song into dream gliding. "Dance and fly. I was dancing in the air in a top hat." Nobody hears her. Twinkling stars of Bics, balloons floating over bobbing heads, bubbles drifting over and out in blue moonbeams. Gossamer ghosts, smiles of unborn infants, slow drifting on a cloud carpet of smoke, billy-goats bleating, drumming and flaying arms, steady rotating slash rhythm: subliminal persuasions and illusions, children dream-dancing—marching, carrying swastika flags or roses—to the tunes of old men.

Outward bound. All of life—or all of death. Two girls holding up a slumping one. Roses droop and the heads of small girls, giving forth loveliness lovelessly as flowers, monstrous underwater roses below waterfalls of fire and exploding stars. Angels devil worshipping in a bedeviled world.

"Ants. There are all those ants." A tall girl screeches and jumps up on a seat. Billions of ants crawl on waves, and your soul has wings, rising in a pink balloon among stars, many-colored beams, crystal suns. Bubbles, new iridescent worlds blooming in the universe until they burst: three big exit signs twist and fuse.

Exit motherless mother of ants, crawling into soft rain. A small girl holds up crayon pictures of roses she has drawn, trading them for food, or another trip, money to buy tickets for the next Dead concert in Philly. Threats and peril to some, promises and profit to others. Business as usual. You get what you pay for. A wall to lean against when you slide down to the sidewalk and talk to Arthur. Father?

"Hey, Mom. There you are. What you saying? I don't understand German. Try French. Are you all right?"

Mike's shirt is covered with revolving stars. "Ellen's hamster ate his young. Caged father. Ready to devour a daughter to keep her, save her."

"Awesome. What love," Mike laughs. "What lust."

"King Lear, Prospero. Shakespeare. Caged fathers...*Gott in Himmel!* Invisible father." Nonsense makes sense and sense is nonsense.

"Far out," says Elgar.

"Did she take anything?" asks the Tick.

"Shut up. Mom's not used to anything. She get's stoned just breathing. Give me a hand."

"A poncho. Yeah." Kids bed her below the overhang on the sidewalk.

"Bright world where sinister clowns lure children. *Weine nicht.* Don't weep. *Himmel Mutter*, Holy Mary don't pray, fight!"

"Shit," Tom squeals. "She's talking in tongues."

"Bonnie's fault," Mike says.

Elgar puts his arm on Mike's shoulder. "Call your dad, Mike. He's her brother."

"He'll kill me." A light rain is falling and the kids huddle around Liz, sheltering under the overhang. "Did anyone give you a pill, Mom?"

"She looks so pale. Even the lips. And those eyes!"

"Karin. Karin! Get Karin and Del away from the endangered clown weirdo."

"Did you feel something like a thorn, Mom?" Boys in top hats, barefoot girls in long dresses gather in a circle.

"My rose has no thorns!"

"What's up?" Karin's babysitter voice. Murmurs of accusations and regrets. "She needs a coke, ginger ale. Something to drink."

Someone is holding her tight and giving her a bottle. "We should find a doctor."

"No. No doctor. No branding iron!"

"They could arrest her, you know."

"Bloody awful!"

"Drink more. Come on now."

"Kids are cooking. I can smell a stir fry. She needs food," Karin says.

"Can you hear us, Liz?" asks Elgar.

"I can hear. Everything, from way back and way ahead." Boys confer in low voices. Sparse traffic hisses on the wet throughway interrupted by a rattle-bash of an incident or accident. While the troop argues, sparrows twitter under the overhang around empty nests. Squabbles no matter what goes on, today, tomorrow, and the next day, generation after generation. The same nesting, the same twitter. Rain drips.

"Just swallow it down. There you go." Intoxicating odor of unwashed children in a war zone, a hungry troop holding Liese to feed her. Girls dry her face and run a comb through her hair. "Pretty curls. Pink coming back in her cheeks. She sees us." They prop her up against the damp wall. Getting her ready, as generations of females now and always make something happen by preparing for it.

"Try to walk. Easy. Easy."

You can hear a pennywhistle piping the same tune over and over. "Look who's here," Mike says, as the barefoot dancer comes around the corner, rose in one hand, hem of her wilted dress in the other.

"All right," Tom says. "Dress she wore on TV." Karin takes Mike by the hand. "Wasted!" No better word to describe Emerald in the wilted dress performing feeble leaps. Ankle bracelets gleaming, she stumbles, wiggles along in the middle of the road. The gilded junk-yard convertible screeching around the corner and stopping behind her, all part of the scene.

"Come on. Get out, darling Hank. Come on out and dance with me." The driver's hand reaches over the door and catches her wrist. The engine races. He holds on.

Liz pushes the kids aside. "*Los lassen*! Let go," she wavers as she runs. A boy in a yellow mermaid wig stands up on the back seat, swings a bottle above his head and lets go. It grazes Liz on the right shoulder, then shatters on the ground.

"What are we waiting for?" Mike's roars. Three sharp whistles. Grove Academy leadership training. No sweat, no sweat at all turning a crowd into a pack. A leader has to instigate. Where do they all come from so fast with so much yelping and hooting?

The car shoots forward, dragging Em over the broken bottle glass. She cries out. "I wanta fly. Go on, faster!" She swings out. Her foot is bleeding.

Liz flies to her; bells on her costume jingle. "Let go. *Los lassen*! With all the brute punishment she once received and witnessed, she slaps that hand and scratches from elbow to wrist. The response is harsh laughter. She sees a face ravaged by the self-punishment of rage. Old as the Hitler war, old as the modern world of killers without cause. A doomed executioner.

"That's him!" Mike leaps up and grabs that wig exposing a face scarred with lines.

"Let go, for God's sake!" Karin calls out.

He lets go of Emerald with malice. She falls into the gentle pose. "Whoa, bravo!" Girls in granny wedding gowns clap their hands and waltz around her. "Atta gal. All right!" Kids hop up and down, surrounding the hate-mobile, shrieking, flicking Bics. Boys let loose a ballpark roar. A bearded marathon runner wearing a long embroidered peasant shirt leads a squad of tall guys in funereal wedding attire, trailing animal-shaped balloons (nitrous oxide doesn't float balloons, it floats you, kills brain cells). Then prodigal Jiggers in his California harem glitter.

"Del, beautiful mother of my dead son!"

Del ducks, pushing her way through the crowd, and flees to a clown, who has lost his balloons. The sign he carries on a pole has been tattered down to SAVE THE ENDANGERED. They run hand in hand after the gilded car and leap into the back. Kids follow. A gust of wind lifts Del's hair, and carries off Caleb's top hat. She starts clapping and singing, "What a friend we have in Jesus." The cargo of kids sing the hymn in a medley of words as the junk-yard chariot carries them off....

"Sure to attract attention. Cops will pick them up," Tom says.

"How about me? Me?" Emerald makes herself heard. "My rose. Where is my rose?" She crawls around on the grimey road. "Oh no! Now look what you've done. You stepped on my rose !" She holds it up, accusing Liz.

"Car ran over it." Mike, the hero, is ready to defend his exclusive right of putting the blame on Mother, which keeps a boy a boy while he declares himself a man.

The Harbor Square troop gathers for Em's big scene of bawling for roses and tunes, endless floating in an ocean of kids, nameless as a drop of water in the bliss of belonging and obscurity.

Liz places Caleb's rose in her hand. "Thorns have been cut off."

Emerald's lips tremble, tears flow. (On command?) There is not a sound from the spectators, as she kneels, holding the rose to her face. "But that's like taking claws off a cat." The tremor takes hold of her, transmitting onto others pain she has never felt, passion she may not live to know. "Hey, Mother. What do you think—does a rose know it's going to wilt?"

Liz kneels down, takes Em into her arms, and holds her as she had been held and warmed by kids. She finds comfort in comforting, finds Mother in mothering, finds herself as a writer spellbound like a Fifinella in a crystal flask.

Printed in the United States
49917LVS00003B/21

9 780977 064007